Soulstealer

Book I of The Unraveling

El McInerney

May Chel be with you,

Book Cover by 100 Covers

Map by Stardust Book Services

ISBN 978-1-7384305-1-2

To Pouf,

You were there for my first breath, and I was there for your last. Your love, curiosity and spirit infuse every part of this story, which would never have been born without you.

Icelands
Crendar
Endless Sea
Western Sea
Great Maelstrom
Chelak Islands
N
Vycenia
Northland
Neopoli
Deepwood
Wren
River Arin
Glade
Arindel
Snowhorn Mtns.
Sorin
Ferin
Yaro
Tarsis
Straits of Ruin
Kharas
Middle Passage
Greatport
The Federation
Tine
Skywarden Mtns.
Riftlands
The Blade
Nazare
The Federation
Nazarene River

Contents

Prologue

The man called Ilis stared down into the pit. They were all laid out in neat little rows, gathered by the scavengers from the battlefields.

Bones.

Leg bones. Arm bones. Hand bones. Foot bones. Skulls, rib cages, and backbones. The bones of men, the bones of women, the bones of dogs and wolves. And sinew, tendon, and half-rotted muscle. Guts and slime and blood. Talons of bears and birds, wicked and sharp.

Burning sun blazing down on it all, raising a putrid stink. Maggots worming and feeding, crows circling and screeching, 'Death, death, here is death.'

But it was he who was the lord of death, death his dominion and his domain, the army that marched at his command. Through death, he would conquer life. And in conquering life, he would be master of all.

He opened his mind to the Tapestry, to the myriad glimmering threads that bound all creation together. Then he made a hole, a careful splice in the fabric. On the other side lay Chaos, that vast primordial power, the source and end of all things. He reached through with invisible fingers and made himself the channel. Chaos poured into him, a raging torrent, a singular searing agony. He screamed. He screamed and he screamed. His heart stopped. His bones bent and broke. His blood became fire.

Weeping, he took hold of the threads, wove them with the flood of Chaos, spun out a thousand filaments of life-giving power. Shimmering strands found gory remains of things once alive, curled and wrapped around them, attached gut and sinew to bone, put light into empty eye sockets. Gave an instinct to kill and wound and maim.

The Ilk rose together. A thousand strong they climbed out of their pit, the stench of death around them. Each one connected to the Tapestry and to his will. His enemies would crumble before his army. Tremble and fall to their knees as the dread took them. And when they died they would rise again and be his.

Chapter 1

Ina

Those cursed with Sīut's power may not remain in this world, for they are a danger to all creatures who live in it, and indeed to the Cloth itself.

—Teachings of Old Tsu

Ina[1] stared up at the jagged, knife-edged slopes of the mountain that contained her destiny. Collared in green at the base, it rose steeply to pierce the mists far above, its bare crown lost in swirling white. Long ago, the elders said, fire had belched out of its insides, but now it was still and quiet. If the mountain itself was silent, though, its slopes were not. All manner of creatures lived among the rocks and trees, and one in particular that she would soon seek.

---

1. The "I" in the Chelaki language is usually pronounced long, as in "ee" in English. Ina's name is therefore pronounced "Eena".

An elbow in her ribs, jolting her out of her reverie—Oyu, her hunting partner. Then she realized why. The two elders were speaking, giving their blessing to the four assembled hunters.

"Chel, weaver of this world, creator of all creatures great and small, walk with these, your people," they intoned, hands outstretched toward them, feathered headdresses shivering in the morning breeze. "They seek to join themselves with the rulers of the sky, as we have ever done and as you have always willed it."

The drakiri, Ina thought. It was the drakiri they had joined with in the past, and on whose backs they had flown. But the drakiri had been lost in the Exile. So now they must make do with lesser birds.

The elders continued, "Steer them to their prize, and shield them from Sīut and his wiles, that they may return to us whole and hearty, strengthened by their new bond."

As always, Ina shivered to hear Sīut's name, was reminded that the chaos god never strayed far from her, that he had claimed her as his own, even if she sought to reject him.

The elders lowered their hands. Then Elder Naomi spoke. "You know the rules of the trial, but I will say them again as is customary. You have two nights and three days to climb Ilij'ai and retrieve a hunting bird. Those of you who succeed will become yakiri."

Skyhunters. Only the best of the best achieved the title. But it wouldn't be enough for her.

"Ina'Ya, Mūak'Ya, it is your responsibility to lead your partners, and if you return successful, you will also become hunt leaders for the village."

As he spoke, Ina glanced at Mūak, who towered above everyone else, and a full head above his hunting partner. His broad face was set with resolve. *I'll show them I'm greater than you. In this, you will not win.*

Her eyes moved to Suni, her beloved and Mūak's bondmate, standing a few paces away. She was striking as always, her fine, black hair sparkling in the early morning light, her eyes shining palest honey. Strung around her neck and over the swell of her breasts was her thick healer's garland of green grasses, a reminder that she was there not just to wish them well but to tend to anyone who might be injured in the trial. Clinging to the long, yellow barkcloth wrapped around her hips was her daughter, Tani. She looked much more like Suni than Mūak, a fact that greatly pleased Ina.

The elders stepped away, allowing others to come and wish them well. Of course, Suni went first to Mūak, Tani close beside her. Ina tried to look like she didn't care. *I'm going to win, I'm going to show them who's best.* Suni said a few words to Mūak, low and close to his ear so that Ina couldn't hear, while Tani threw her arms around his thighs, too small to reach any higher.

But Ina's mother, Mia, was on her then, drawing her attention away. "Through your skill, you will prevail, but be mindful of Sīut, who can lead even the best of us astray," she said.

Ina heard the warning in her words, in the formality with which they were spoken. Mia still didn't trust Ina to resist the temptation of her cursed gift, didn't believe she had become such a good hunter without its aid. Ina tried to stamp on her anger, but her answer was stiff. "Chel will guide me."

Her mother attempted a smile, but it didn't hide the concern marked in her amber eyes and the lines of her brow. "I pray they will." She pressed Ina's hand, then stepped away to allow Suni to approach her.

"You know I must wish you both success," Suni said, her smile a true one, raising an ache in Ina's chest. "Whichever of you succeeds in this contest, our people will have gained a valuable hunt leader, maybe two, and that's what truly matters."

No, it's not.

Suni kissed her cheek and then returned to Tani, who was still talking to her father. When she had steered the child away, the elders signaled for them to begin.

The hunters didn't hesitate. Mūak and Renki chose the winding route that went around the eastern side of the mountains, where many cresthawks were known to nest. But she and Oyu made for the narrow track that led directly up to the mountain's misty heights. Dense ferns crowded on either side, some reaching as high as their heads. But it hadn't rained for weeks, so the earth was dry, and they were able to cover the ground at a jog.

"Are you sure this is a good idea?" Oyu said. "It will be so much easier to get a cresthawk. We can beat Mūak and Renki by getting back with it first."

"We're going to catch a mist eagle." There would be no turning aside from this goal. Either she succeeded or she failed utterly. Nothing in between would do.

"But no one has ever managed to capture one," Oyu complained. "We'll be humiliated. It's going to take most of the day just to get up to that nest."

"I heard you the last twenty times."

"Maybe if I say it often enough, you'll finally listen to reason."

"You agreed to be my second. Are you changing your mind?"

Oyu let out a grunt. "No. I swore to you."

"Then stop talking and save your energy for the climb."

He was quiet after that, but she could sense his frustration, see it in the bunching of his shoulders and the set of his jaw. *We'll get the mist eagle. I'll show him that I'm the best. I'll show them all.* She pictured the birds in her mind, with their white plumage and dark blue breasts. She had seen them many times, swooping down to pluck a fish from the sea or circling high up in the mists. They might not be as large or as powerful as the drakiri, but on these islands they were the undisputed rulers of the skies, twice as large as a cresthawk, infinitely more difficult to capture. Yet Ina had found a nest they could reach, and she was going to get one.

They continued jogging until they were almost a quarter of the way up the mountain. Then, the path became steeper and more difficult, and it wasn't worth the risk of a twisted ankle. They entered the cloud layer close to midday, where many trees thrived alongside the ferns. The dominant sound here was a constant dripping, interspersed with the croaking calls of achaks and the distant howls of trapper monkeys. It was much cooler, but their exertion kept them warm, and Ina drank deeply of the scents of wet earth and moldering leaves.

When they broke out of the fog, the sun had well passed its midpoint in the sky. It quickly burnt off the droplets of moisture that clung to their skin and hair, but it wasn't as hot as it had been at the base.

It was impossible not to stop a moment and look around. From here, it was like they were floating on top of the world. All around them spread the mists, blanketing much of the island, except for the edges, where they became tattered, displaying flashes of coastline. Her eyes turned northward, to the other islands. The two smallest, Yon'il and Uruk'il, were invisible, but Olon'il's highest peak poked sharply through clouds. The tips of the mountain ridge that formed the spine of Kan'il were also visible, rising even higher than Ilij'ai. Her father would be there somewhere, on the western coast, with his new family. She'd sent word about her trial, but he'd not deigned to come and see her off. The old pain writhed in her. *I was never good enough for you, was I?*

"So, where to next, hunt leader?" Oyu said, squinting up at the mountain.

Ina decided to ignore his teasing tone and turned her attention back to the mountainside. "The nest is at the top of that ridge." She pointed. The ridge ran parallel to the path they were on, but crossing over to it required a sheer descent and an even sheerer climb.

"Could you have found a more awkward spot?" he groaned.

"A hundred more," she replied. "This one we can actually get to."

"If we don't kill ourselves."

"If all you're going to do is complain, I can do without you," Ina snapped. Couldn't he see that this was her destiny? *Their* destiny?

"Let's just get on with it," he muttered.

"We can tie a rope there and slide down." She pointed to an outcrop of rock.

Oyu uncoiled the rope he was wearing around his neck and did as she suggested, then tossed it down the mountainside. "I'll go first," he said, already turning himself around and taking a grip on the rope.

He descended swiftly, arm under arm, legs coiled around the rope. As soon as he hit the ground, she was over the side to follow him. To reach the other ridge, they had to scramble over rock and scree, sometimes using their hands to stop themselves from falling. But they were both fit and agile, and while it slowed them, it was no great obstacle.

"This is going to be fun," Oyu said drily when they finally got to the bottom of the second ridge.

She stared up at the pocked seams of grey and black rock. Yes, it would be dangerous. But there were plenty of hand- and toeholds, and the challenge of it made her pulse run faster. Oyu should have felt the same, and she didn't understand he was so negative. It made her harsh toward him. "Then just stay here. I don't need you."

"You might need help if the parents are there," he said grudgingly.

He was right. She wouldn't be able to take a fledgling from such an awkward spot while also fending off an angry mother. "Fine, but I'll go first." She opened a pouch at her waist and tipped out powdered chalk onto her palm, rubbing her hands together until they were caked in it. Oyu silently did the same. Then she unhooked her water skin and set it down on the ground along with her night pack. The only things she would take with her were her belt knife and a sack slung over her shoulder in which she could carry the bird.

This done, she returned her attention to the rock face, craning her neck to find the first toe- and handholds, the most efficient route to her destination. When she was satisfied, she wedged her right foot into the first crack and pushed herself up. She moved quickly, strength and experience lending her speed. At the same time, it was hard not to feel the yawning gap that was growing between her and the ground. Soon she was high enough that any fall would kill her. She knew better than to look down, though, keeping her attention on the rock wall, on tracing the path ahead. Sweat stung her eyes, threatening to blind her, and she rubbed her forehead against the back of her arm. But the chalk was working well, keeping her palms from becoming slippery.

The top was in sight, and her elation grew the closer she got to it. A whole lifetime waiting for this moment—soon, so soon, she would have her prize! She swung her right hand up to the next hold, a crooked finger of black rock. But as she transferred her weight onto it to seek a higher position for her right foot, it snapped off. *Chel!* Her chest contracted in fear, sending blood rushing about her body, lending her strength while she sought a toehold for her foot. But while it soon found a home, she could find no new grip for her hand. She leaned back as far as she dared, looking left and right for other options.

"Stuck?" Oyu called.

She didn't answer. It was obvious.

"Can you jump down to that ledge just to the right of you and below? From there, I think I see a way."

Ina glanced down. The ground seemed very far away, their packs tiny specks, and dizziness swept over her. She swallowed drily, focusing on her breathing to quell the rising tide of fear. *I've climbed this high before. And I don't fall. Ever.*

"Do you see it?"

She could, a tiny shelf of rock. If she misjudged the jump, she was almost certain to tumble to her death. She looked up and around again. The only other option she could see was another jump, but upwards, an even riskier prospect. "Are you sure there's a way from there?" she said, turning to face him again.

"Yes." There was a trace of impatience in his voice.

This is the part I hate. But she reminded herself of the prize, visualized the look on Mūak's face, on everyone's face, when she returned with a mist eagle. *Dear Chel, guide me.* She tried to banish all thoughts of Sīut, to hide herself from him. Then she counted herself down. *Three, two, one. Go!* Out into the open air she sprung. Her right foot landed on the ledge, but her left missed, her toes scraping painfully down, dragging the rest of her with them. She scrabbled wildly, caught the fingers of her right hand on a tiny wedge of rock. Just enough to stop the fall, to get her second foot onto the ledge. The shock hit her when she was standing safe, leaving her shaking and fragile. *I made it. It's all right. Not far now. Chel is with me. Chel is with me.* She breathed as she'd been taught, expanding her belly to fill her lungs with air before slowly expelling it. Her heart slowed in response but was still beating hard when Oyu joined her on the ledge. There was barely space for them both, his shoulder pressing tightly against hers.

"That was a close one," he said. "Reminds me of that time we climbed the Spine of Kan'il."

"If your belt hadn't snagged on that bush ... You looked so ridiculous." She forced a laugh.

"What was that, four cycles ago?" he said, head up to the blue sky, eyes focused inwards.

"Five," she said. "You were still a skinny boy."

"Which was why I missed and you didn't."

"We'll say that was the reason." She was teasing him, but it was the truth. Oyu had been late to come into his growth, and she'd been taller than him for many years. Now, though, he had several fingers' height on her.

"Do you see the way?" He pointed at the rock face.

She followed the line of his finger. Yes, it was doable. Easy, even. "Let's go."

It took her only four movements to reach the top, and very soon she was curling her fingers around the edge of the ridge and pulling her body up and over. The ridge was extremely narrow, its sides sweeping down vertiginously on either side of her. One misstep and she was done for. At least there was little wind, and she had often tested her balance on narrow branches. This was nothing new to her, other than the drop. *Don't think about that.* She stepped along the ridge, foot before foot, arms out. Behind her, she heard Oyu join, but she didn't look back. There was only forward now. And she was so close to the prize!

Finally, she estimated she'd reached the point above the nest and hunkered down, putting her hands onto the rock and sliding her knees around each side of the ridge to grip it between them. Then she lowered her torso and leaned out to find the nest. She'd been so intent on maneuvering into position that she hadn't noticed the unusual silence—a silence that revealed itself as emptiness when she looked for the nest. It wasn't there. There were no birds.

At first, she thought she was looking in the wrong spot and cast her eyes up and down, seeking the nest. But no, there was the ledge, covered in scattered twigs and broken blue eggshells. The babies had once been here but were here no more. Something had destroyed the nest. A storm, perhaps. But it was a devastating blow. Her chance was gone. She would come back with no mist eagle. She would come back with nothing at all, and Mūak would win again. She suddenly felt so heavy and weak she almost tumbled off the ridge. Her head fell against the rock, tears prickling her eyes. *This can't be. This can't be.*

"Are you alright?" Oyu called.

She didn't have the strength to answer him.

"There's no nest, is there?" It was more statement than question.

She forced her head up and shook it, unable to speak or look him in the eye. *This can't be.*

He paused. "We can still get a cresthawk."

But Ina didn't want a cresthawk, and even if they did catch one, they would surely return later than Mūak, which meant he'd win. No, it couldn't be. She wouldn't *let* it be. Her fingers dug tightly into the rock, turning white at the tips. She needed a mist eagle fledgling. There had to be another nest. She just had to find it. But already the sun was near the horizon, the sky streaked with whorls of amber and honey. "Let's go back to the path and find a place to camp," she said wearily.

They used rope for most of the descent, so it was a lot faster than the way up. But it seemed to take twice as long to cross back to the other ridge and then climb up to the path, their energy lost in defeat. The moon had risen by the time they reached their destination, the first stars twinkling far above. They found a boulder against which they could rest their backs and sank to the ground.

"We'll get a cresthawk tomorrow," Oyu said again.

Ina said nothing. She wasn't ready to give up yet. There had to be another way.

"Here, you need to eat." Oyu handed her a strip of dried noukmeat.

Absently, she took it from him and began to chew, staring over at the ridge where they'd met their failure. A dangerous notion was starting to form in her mind. She shouldn't even be thinking it. But now that it had occurred to her, she couldn't shake it loose, like a tick that had burrowed into her skin.

It was forbidden. Dangerous. Wrong. She'd be calling on Sīut, turning her face away from Chel. If Oyu realized what she was doing, he was sure report her to the elders, and that would be the end of her life in this world. He was her closest and only true friend, but the laws were the laws. And her mother—oh, she'd prove her mother right.

On the other hand, if she succeeded, she'd have her mist eagle. She'd save herself from eternal humiliation. A hunter only had one chance at the sky trial. She wouldn't get another. Neither would Oyu. Her stubbornness would mean that he too lost a cherished dream. They'd planned this since they were old enough to use a bow. And he'd trusted her, agreed to follow her because of his belief in her abilities.

"Let's try to get some sleep," he said. "We'll be up with the dawn tomorrow." He unrolled his mat and got into his sleep sack.

Ina did the same, but she didn't sleep. Even as Oyu's breathing deepened, she was battling with her temptation, trying to suffocate her dangerous idea. If she let Sīut get a foothold in her, who could tell what would happen? She might cause grave harm not just to herself, but to Oyu, to the world around her. And yet the idea of Mūak winning this challenge was unbearable. She couldn't allow him to have everything—to be a man, to have Suni for bondmate and Tani for daughter, *and* to be recognized as hunt leader. The thought of his face when she returned empty-handed made her sick with rage. And anyway, it wasn't as if she was going to actively use her powers to do anything. She wouldn't be making any of those dangerous holes in the Cloth that led into Sīut's Realm. This would be more of a release, a loosening of control.

So as the moon crested the cloud layer, with its faint blue sheen, she dared to lower the barriers she erected around her mind. The threads of Chel's Cloth appeared in all their startling, multitudinous glory. They formed a glimmering overlay of the world, twined and knotted, patterned in infinite variety, flowing through rock and sea and sky, through every living thing—plant, insect, or animal. Other threads she sensed only as vibrations or hums, her body responding like the skin of a drum being beaten by a thousand hands. The storm of sensation tossed and buffeted her awareness, threatening to overwhelm and drown her. But she'd been here before, and bit by bit, she switched off the inputs, homing in on the threads and pulses that signaled bird life, and then more specifically, the mist eagle. She should be able to identify it. She had learned its pattern as a child, before her mother had discovered her cursed gift and banned her from using it.

But it was one thing to identify the pulse of a creature near her that she could see with her regular vision. It was another entirely to cast out her awareness and seek it amidst the chaotic soup, and a sharp pain began to develop behind her left eye. She ignored it, focusing her awareness along the cliffs and ridges of the mountainside. The pain grew, threatening to shut down her senses entirely. But she didn't stop. There had to be more eagle nests somewhere. There had to be.

And then she finally found them. Tiny, clustered pulses of eagle life, not too far from where she was. She rose and peered into the darkness.

The moon was only half full, but she thought she could see where the nest was. The location seemed virtually inaccessible, but maybe a route would show itself in daylight. She just needed to find a way to tell Oyu how she'd discovered the nest. Bubbling with excitement, she withdrew and reinstated the controls over her mind. The world grew blessedly quiet, and she let out a relieved sigh.

Moments later, though, her excitement gave way to profound exhaustion. She had barely crawled into her sack before she fell into a deep sleep, her dreams all of birds.

Oyu woke her at dawn. "We need to get moving," he said, shaking her arm.

Blearily, she opened her eyes. Then remembered her discovery of the night before and sat up. "I want to go up further," she said. "I'm sure there's another nest around here somewhere."

"I really don't think this is a good idea," Oyu said. "We're going to lose spectacularly if we don't go for a cresthawk now."

"The mist eagles be up with the dawn too, looking for food," she said. "Let's at least look while we eat."

She angled herself so that she was looking in the direction of the nest, chewing on her dried noukmeat and praying to Chel that a mist eagle would appear in the sky above it. It remained stubbornly empty, and Ina was tempted to cast out with her awareness again. But she was scared that Oyu would somehow know what she was doing, and held herself back. The parents must surely need to hunt soon. It was an endless task for the birds, to feed themselves and their young. A sick knot formed in her belly. What would she do if the eagle didn't appear? How would she persuade Oyu to go there anyway? She knew she'd tested him to the end of his loyalty already. She couldn't ask much more of him. His annoyance was palpable. He was already giving her more than she deserved. Her fingers curled into her palm. Damn that storm, which had robbed her of her prize!

"Look!" Oyu exclaimed, pointing.

A bird, soaring into the air from behind the ridge that housed the nest. She squinted. It was the right color and size.

"I think it's an eagle," Oyu said. "In fact, I'm sure of it!"

Ina smiled to herself. He sounded just as excited as she was. He wanted this prize too, even if he hadn't been willing to admit it. "You know, I think you're right."

"Come on, let's go quickly!"

They scurried to pack away their things and then peered to find a way over to the ridge.

"This path eventually swings around in the direction of the nest," she said. "I say we follow it until it gets us a close as possible?"

"Can't think of a better idea."

So they kept walking up and around. While they were still a distance away, they saw the mist eagle return, a dead creature hanging limply between its talons. They trained their eyes on it, watching as it descended to its nest.

"I think this path will take us quite close," Oyu said. "See?"

She did see, and elation ran through her. Surely, this was a sign that she was blessed by Chel! They picked up the pace, moving as fast as they dared, buoyed by hope. But when they reached the heights above the nest, they were faced with a sheer cliff and no easy way down.

"I can lower you on the rope," Oyu said. "That way, you can have your hands free."

"That'll work." Ina was trying not to get too excited, but tremors ran through her anyway. Destiny within her grasp!

Oyu wrapped one end of the rope crossways around his chest, and the other she wrapped around the tops of her thighs and waist. Then they sat and waited for the parents to leave the nest.

The sun was high above them when their moment finally came. Oyu found himself a spot on the ground where he could dig his heels in, while she went to the edge of the cliff. Once he gave her the nod, she stepped off it backward and walked down the cliff face. Her life was in his hands, but she trusted him completely. They'd done this many times.

She could already hear the twittering cries of the young eagles, and her blood surged. The nest came into view, a huge construction of intertwined twigs and vines that could have contained the largest of the village cookpots. To her joy, she could see two fledglings still in their coat of brown, picking on meat their parents had left them. Flinging open the covering of her satchel, she retrieved a piece of heavy nouk leather and threw it over the fledglings. They squeaked and squawked in indignation, trying vainly to shake it off. Ina reached under the leather to lift the first eagle chick out of the nest. She gasped when it delivered a vicious bite to her hand, but she was proud of the little creature's fire. It was heavier than she'd expected, and bigger too, and she needed to use a second hand to maneuver it into the satchel. Once she'd got it safely in, she plucked up the second one and then folded the satchel cover over them both.

"I've got them!" she shouted. They chirped and wriggled indignantly, and Ina tried to soothe them by placing a hand over the satchel. It did nothing to calm them. If anything, they became even more vocal.

But as Oyu began to draw her up, a furious screech pierced the air. Ina turned her head to see a mist eagle descending on her—the mother, judging by its immense size. It was at least half as big as she was, with talons long and sharp as knives. She barely managed to throw her free arm over her face before they raked her, drawing long gouges in her flesh. The eagle spun and flapped its wings to gain height once more. Ina drew her knife, but it seemed tiny and puny in the face of those great talons. A stone sailed through the air, narrowly missing the bird—Oyu, trying to help. The second stone went wide, though, and the bird swooped down on her with impossible speed. Covering her eyes with one arm, she stabbed out blindly with her knife. Pain billowed again as the claws tore into her chest. But her knife found a home in some part of the eagle's flesh, and it screamed before disengaging.

"Just pull as fast as you can!" she shouted at Oyu.

He picked up the pace, but only fractionally. She put her knife between her teeth and started to haul herself up the rope.

Another shriek of rage, and a second adult eagle swooping toward her. *Dear Chel!* The first was also spinning around for a fresh attack, clearly undeterred by the threat of the knife. The father landed on her head, a crushing weight that bowed her neck. His talons dug into her head while it bent forward to peck at her eyes, and she swung wildly at it with her knife. It drew back but didn't get off her head. Now the mother was on her, talons forward to rake her again. Between them, they could kill her, or at least severely maim her. She couldn't fight them both off. Not hanging like this. Panic overwhelmed her, but amid that panic, she did something instinctual, something she'd never done before. She threw open her senses and *pushed* at the birds.

They spun away from her, apparently dazed, and plummeted down the mountainside. Pain lanced through her head, and she lost her grip on the rope, falling to its full extension. Oyu had been pulling steadily, but the sudden weight obviously caught him by surprise, the rope sliding until she was level with the nest before he got control over it again.

She looked around. No sign of the mist eagles. With a stab of fear, she realized she'd done what poor little Rāou had when he was only six years old. The elders had made him drink the starweed poison immediately. Would Sīut seek her now that she'd called on him?

Her next fear was for the fledglings. If she'd killed them, it would all have been for nothing. She lifted the flap a fraction and found them completely still. Her breath catching, she reached out with gentle fingers to touch them. They were breathing, their tiny hearts still beating. She breathed thanks to Chel.

But then a third fear struck her. Could Oyu have seen what had happened? He was still out of sight, still pulling her up. *Oh, dear Chel, I'm sorry. Please don't turn away from me. I won't do this again.* She repeated these words as a litany as Oyu continued to pull her up, while keeping an eye out for the mist eagles. They didn't return, but she hoped they'd recovered before reaching the ground. They were too magnificent to lose their lives like that, to Sīut's power.

At last, she was heaving herself over the cliff edge and onto solid ground. Still kneeling, she removed the satchel and set it carefully down.

"You got them?" Oyu asked, eyes bright, sweat beading his entire body.

"In here." She lifted open the satchel cover a fraction.

He hunkered down to peek at the prize, delight crinkling his eyes. "Two of them! We'll have one each."

She grinned through her pain and worry. "Twice the work but twice the gain."

He was about to hug her, but then stopped with his arms outstretched. "Dear Chel, you're covered in blood!"

Ina looked down at herself, discovering she was slick and red all over. "And you only noticed now?" she said drily.

"I'm sorry," he said with chagrin. "I was so focused on the birds. Let me tend to you." He helped her into the shade, then poured seawater from a flask over the wounds, raising a sharp sting. After that, he made a paste of mud and anan leaves and pressed them over the gashes, which continued to leak blood at a frightening rate. This done, he wrapped barkcloth tightly around her arms and chest.

Ina sat quietly as he worked. She was feeling increasingly sick, the pain in the left side of her head so sharp she could think of nothing else. This was her punishment, she reflected. Although if it was the only punishment that came to her, she'd be beyond grateful.

"We'd better get moving if we're going to make it back by midday tomorrow," Oyu said when he finished. He helped her to stand.

The world spun wildly around her. She squeezed her eyes shut, trying to steady it, and took a few paces forward.

"Are you alright?"

"Fine," she managed. Her skin was raging with heat while inside she felt deadly cold. She wanted nothing more than to rest, but there wasn't time. She managed a few more stumbling steps, black spots prickling her vision. Then it was like her legs turned to water, for suddenly her knees were crumbling. She lurched forward, her foot expecting the ground and not finding it. Her ankle doubled over as the ground came up to meet her.

"Ina, Ina. Can you hear me?"

Water on her face. She opened her eyes. Her head hurt, inside and out. Her arms too, with a fierce burning pain. "What happened?"

"Drink." Oyu pushed the waterskin against her lips and she took a few sips, fighting the nausea in her belly.

"What happened?" she croaked again.

"You fell and hit your head."

She noticed there was little light left in the sky. Her spirits flagged. "We're not going to make it."

"I've been carrying you all afternoon," he replied with a small smile. "I had to leave our mats and sacks behind, though."

She sat up, the world spinning crazily again. But she could see they were in the cloud forest.

"We're about half the way down," he said. "We can do the rest in the morning."

"You must have been pushing a hard pace. I owe you."

"You got the eagles, it's the least I could do." He grinned.

She perked at the reminder of her victory. "How are they doing?"

"Awake and lively, eating."

"Can I see?"

He carefully lifted the satchel and flipped back the cover. The two little birds fluttered their half-grown wings. Ina smiled at them, warm pride rushing through her.

Oyu tied the sack again. "I've been worried about you. You don't seem to have a fever. But how do you feel?"

This is my punishment, she thought again. *Sīut's doing, or perhaps Chel's.* "I've been better," she said. "My ankle hurts," she added, only now becoming aware of it.

"Let me take a look." He moved so that he was sitting by her foot. "Which one?"

"Left."

He carefully picked it up and placed it on his knees. "It's swollen." He tried to turn it, and she cried out in pain. Then he poked and prodded with his fingers, asking her where it hurt. "I think it's just a sprain," he said at last. "But Suni will know better."

"Let me try walking on it." She got slowly to her feet, leaning on Oyu to do so. But sharp pain shot through her ankle when she tried to put pressure on it.

"Put your arm around me."

She did as he suggested and managed a few limping steps. "I can walk, but too slowly." She tried not to despair. They couldn't have got this far only to fail because of a bad ankle. Sīut's work indeed.

"Let's go as far as we can now. If I need to carry you again tomorrow, I will."

But while she wasn't feeling as terrible as she had before her fall, she was still weak and nauseous, the pain from her various wounds adding to the stabbing pain in her head, and they were soon forced to give up. It was getting dark anyway, but Ina couldn't shake her worry that Sīut was doing everything he could to prevent her victory. That would be typical of the chaos god, to lend her his power so she could capture the birds only to hamper her progress after.

Despite her worry, she soon fell asleep, her body demanding its rest to heal. She woke with the first rays of light to find Oyu feeding worms to the fledglings. His eyes glowed with tender love, warming her.

He looked over at her when she sat up, a smile breaking on his long face. "How do you feel?"

She did a quick check over. The pain in her head had mercifully eased, and she was no longer feeling sick. Her arms and chest were fire, though, and she worried that her wounds had become infected. The pain in her ankle also seemed less severe, but when she tried to stand, she found she still couldn't put all her weight on it.

So, once they'd broken fast, they began a slow and awkward walk with Oyu supporting her. Ina soon tired, weakened by her wounds and the aftermath of whatever it was she'd done to the eagles the day before. She turned that over and over in her mind, shame and fear squeezing her. She had given into weakness, and surely further punishment would come.

"I have to carry you," Oyu said at last. "We won't make it otherwise."

"Are you sure?"

"It's not that much farther," he said gamely.

But she could see he was tired too. He had carried her for a long time yesterday.

He hunkered down so she could climb onto his back. It was broad and well-muscled, as were his stout legs. Once she was in place, he moved at a lumbering jog, his breath coming hard. The friction aggravated her chest wounds, but she clamped her teeth down on the pain, willing strength to Oyu.

Even so, it felt like they were going too slowly, that they would never make it to the camp by midday. How awful it would be to fail after coming so close to total success! Yet somehow Oyu kept going, even though she could sense the crippling exhaustion building in him. And she loved him all the more for it. "I'm going to give you the best bits of my meat for the next moon," she told him through gritted teeth.

"You'll owe me far more than that," he grunted, not quite managing a laugh.

"Anything you want," Ina said. "I'll do anything you want if you just get us down to that camp on time."

"We'll get there."

That was the last of their conversation, each of them fixated on finishing their journey, on enduring the pain until then.

When they finally heard voices drifting up the path toward them, Oyu had slowed to a walk. But hearing them reanimated him, and he broke into a run again, grunting with each step. When they emerged from the woods and into the clearing where the elders had made camp to wait for them, the sun was burning down brightly from above. Mūak was sitting next to Suni and Tani, talking and laughing. In a cage next to him was a small bird.

Ina looked up at the sky then down at their shadows, a barely visible outline around their feet. It was midday. They'd made it. They'd made it! "Let me down."

Oyu didn't hesitate, bending his knees and releasing her legs. She saw his back was stained red and looked down at the bandage to see it soaked with blood.

Suni was already on her feet, hurrying over to them. "Are you badly injured?" she asked Ina, eyes wide with concern.

"I had some angry eagles to deal with," Ina said. She was feeling a bit woozy again.

Oyu, meanwhile, stood with his hands on his thighs, breathing heavily.

"Come to my mat, and I'll take a proper look at you," Suni said to Ina.

Ina took a limping step. Seeing her trouble, Suni put an arm around her. Despite her pain and exhaustion, Ina felt a bolstering thrill at the contact.

"Did you say eagles?" said Alik'Ri, getting to his feet.

"Shall I?" Oyu asked Ina with a grin, holding out the satchel with the birds.

She wanted to be the one to show their prize, but he deserved the moment for all he'd done to get them down here. So she nodded for him to go ahead.

Oyu went to the elders, who were both standing expectantly. "Two mist eagle chicks," he said, pulling back the flap.

They exclaimed in amazement.

Ina shot a look at Mūak. The smile had fallen off his face. His first expression was one of surprise, and then dismay. Ina tried to keep herself from looking smug, knowing it wasn't becoming. But it was hard to keep her triumph from showing. She had the mist eagles, and stories would be told about her and Oyu for decades to come.

The two elders conversed quietly for a few moments while Suni tended to Ina's wounds and Oyu cleaned her blood off him.

The elders ended their conversation and regarded the hunters. "You have all hunted well," Naomi'Ri said. "And it is with great pride that I name you skyhunters. But for the exceptional skill Ina has shown in taking home a mist eagle, we must name her hunt leader for the village. From now on, she is to be known as Ina'Yakir'Suk."

Ina glowed, her worry over Sīut's punishment melting away. She had finally claimed her destiny, and Mūak would never be able to match her.

Chapter 2

Ina

Sīut has only one purpose where Chel's Cloth is concerned—to tear it to pieces and undo Chel's creation.

—Teachings of Old Tsu

Through the glossy green, crescent leaves of the koua tree in which she was perched, Ina spied the black snout of a nouk snuffling low to the ground. Long, curving white tusks thrust out proudly on either side, promising certain death if she were to mistime her jump. Next in view were the small, pebble eyes and the domed head with its black crest, and then the round body, thick with muscle and fat. A shiver of excitement ran through her. What a fine kill for the feast tonight.

Her eyes went to another large koua tree on the opposite side of the trail, seeking Oyu. His red-brown skin closely matched the color of the bark, making him almost invisible. He'd clearly seen the nouk and was poised to leap. She pointed at herself with two fingers, then at the nouk, to signal she would initiate the attack, and he made a circle of his thumb and forefinger to show he'd understood.

Then, giving into a temptation that seemed to grow ever stronger, she opened her mind to Chel's Cloth. The sounds and sensations of the forest flooded through her, chaotic and overwhelming, but she fought to master herself and narrow her focus to the nouk. Her heightened senses told her its next move and her best path of attack, and she raised her long-bladed spear above her shoulder, tensing for the strike. Above her, a honeybird trilled a call and was answered from farther away. The nouk paused, pressing its snout lower to the ground, then took another step forward.

Now.

She leaped to the ground next to the nouk and thrust her spear through the thick hide into the flesh above the shoulder. At the same time, she raised the barriers around her mind—but too slowly to block out the animal's terror and pain. She grimaced as it loosed a piercing shriek and bunched its short hind legs to leap forward and away. But its life was already rushing out of it, and its knees continued to fold until it sank back into a half-sitting position before toppling over. It kicked and twitched several times, then stilled.

Ina withdrew the spear, and a jet of hot heart's blood spurted out, splashing her legs and soaking into the nouk's stiff, grey bristles. She fixed on the nouk's glassy black eye, still reeling from the shock of sharing its death. *I shouldn't have given in, this is how I'm punished.* Struggling to hide her emotion, she knelt beside the nouk to murmur a quick prayer. "Chel, we thank you for the flesh you have given us. Please take the soul of this creature to live in peace with you." The words settled her, reminding her of her place, the necessity of death to bring life, ordained by Chel themself.

Oyu dropped noiselessly out of his tree and hunkered beside her. "A good kill, hunt leader."

There was a teasing twist to his pronunciation of her new title, and she punched him lightly in the arm. At the same time, though, she did her usual mental check—had she been too fast, too accurate? Could he guess her secret? She resisted a fresh temptation to open herself to the Cloth and use her powers to delve into his emotions. That was too wrong. Instead, she looked at his bright green eyes and broad smile. There was no suspicion or jealousy in them, just warm admiration. "Let's fix it up quickly. I want to get back to the village."

"Suni was due back this afternoon, wasn't she?" Oyu said, his tone even more playful.

"I want to hear what news she has of my father," Ina replied, which was true, but only a little.

"Of course."

Oyu was smirking, and Ina couldn't help but smile herself. She indulged in a moment of fantasy, imagining Suni's expression when they met, then shook herself free and began to search for a fallen branch to carry the dead nouk back to the village.

"This will do," Oyu said, and she turned to see that he'd already found a good stout branch. Before long they'd tied the creature's legs to its length and hoisted it onto their shoulders to begin the short walk back to the village.

The animal was large and weighed on her despite the strength she'd gained through years of hunting and grappling. She hated being a woman at times like this, when she was reminded of the lesser strength Chel had inexplicably given them. Other times, she was glad. Men smelled strange, and they had too much hair. A vivid memory of Suni's soft skin pressed itself onto her mind and urged her on. The moon had gone through a full cycle since they'd last seen each other.

Each day had seemed longer than the one before, with only the joy of training the baby mist eagles to break it up. Then she remembered that Mūak would be there, and her joy dimmed, but only a little. Suni might still love her bondmate, but Ina could give her things he couldn't. And it wasn't as if he'd stand in their way.

The walking became easier when they reached the main trail back to the village. Ina could smell it long before she saw it. Most powerful was the scent of the wood smoke that fired their earth ovens, interlaced with the aroma of roasting fish and baked ananfruit. Her stomach stirred hungrily. It was almost highsun.

They rounded a dense clump of ferns, and the village came into sight, the circular wooden buildings with their grass roofs blending seamlessly into the forest. Some dwellings were built around the trees themselves, with covered platforms constructed on the lower branches in homage to their ancestors, who had made their homes high in the great silverfoil trees on Chelakan, their lost home. As she often did, Ina tried to picture what those homes would have looked like, with the drakiri nesting side by side.

They veered left toward the butcher's tent, which was little more than four poles with heavy green fibercloth stretched over them to keep out the sun. Han was sitting on a log stool, marking the intakes on a stone tablet. Despite his stockiness, he rose with easy grace and looked over the nouk appraisingly. "We'll eat well tonight."

"Ina brought it down alone."

"I knew you'd make a fine hunt leader," Han said to Ina, his smile taking up his entire face. It was a smile that made many a heart sing, but the song was always sung to deaf ears, as Han had eyes only for his bondmate, Ria.

Ina forced herself to remain grave. "Thank Chel for the blessing."

Han scratched his charcoal stick on the tablet. "I suppose you'll be wanting some morsels for Laiki and Faiki."

"We're going to start lure training them later," Oyu said.

"Does that mean you aren't free to practice for the Games today?" Han said.

"We can manage both," Oyu said with a glance at Ina. "Can't break with tradition and let ourselves lose this year, can we?"

"Mark four in the training grounds?" Oyu said.

"I'll tell Ria."

But Ina was thinking only of Suni. "Have the healers returned yet?" she asked Han.

"They're with them now," Han said. "Two new apprentices with them."

Ina was unable to suppress a grin as she and Oyu picked up the nouk to bring it to the back of the tent. Two butchers were chopping an earlier kill, large knives rising and falling rhythmically to cleave meat and bone, and the air prickled with the smell of blood and flesh. They left the nouk on the skinning table, but Oyu took some choice pieces of rabbit for the birds. "I'll meet you in the aviary," he said.

"I won't be long. I just want to say hello to her," she said, turning already toward the House of the Elders. It was a round building like the rest, marking out the very center of the village. Long miala creepers spilled down the sides from the roof, their white, bell-like flowers luminescent in the morning sunshine. The fibercloth door shutter was still down, and Ria, tall and lithe, was standing guard next to it. Her black hair had been freshly cut around her ears, and Ina instinctively ran a hand through her own dark crop, which was getting too long.

"Chel be with you, Ina," Ria said.

"Are the returned inside?"

"They've been there for at least a mark."

Just then, the door shutter rolled upwards, and Ina found herself face-to-face with Suni. As her eyes lit on Ina, they widened with surprise, then crinkled briefly in pleasure before regaining a poised serenity. With somewhat less serenity, Ina stepped away from the doorway and allowed Suni to exit, closely followed by two unfamiliar boys aged around ten. The apprentice healers Suni had brought from the other island, no doubt.

Then Nāin, the head healer, appeared, his headdress of green and white feathers thrusting up from his shining, bald head. Suni greeted him and introduced the two apprentices. They exchanged words about Suni's journey, then Nāin told his new charges to follow him away.

As soon as they'd left, Suni's hands went to Ina's, gentle and warm. "How have you been?"

Ina kissed her on the mouth, briefly, wishing it could be longer. "I've missed you."

Suni smiled. "And I you."

When she smiled like that, Ina felt as if her soul became visible. It was hard not to reach out with her mind and seek a deeper connection. *It must have been so pure and wonderful in the old days.*

"Mami!"

Ina stepped away from Suni, whose face had brightened with a more intense joy.

"My little berry! Come here." She stooped and opened her arms to her daughter, Tani, who ran into them screaming with joy, dark tresses flailing behind her.

Mūak was close behind, his tall frame blocking the sun. Although Ina was as tall as some men, he stood two hands higher, and she had to crane her head up to greet him.

But he gave her only the briefest of nods before addressing Suni and Tani. "Come, now. We've prepared a surprise for you." The words were said lightly, but there was something forced to his smile, and his right hand was balled into a fist by his side.

"How exciting!" Suni exclaimed to her daughter, who giggled in delight. Suni hugged her again, then straightened up, her eyes flickering with concern toward Mūak.

"Come on, Mami!" Tani took Suni's hand to lead her forward. Mūak turned toward their hut and started to walk even before his bondmate and daughter reached him.

"See you tonight," Suni said.

Ina watched as the family disappeared among the huts. Seven years it would be, before Tani was of age and Suni was free of her bond to Mūak—as long as they had no more children, of course. She vowed to herself again that she would not take a mate. She would not lie with men to spawn children, tradition or not. Her place was among the trees, not the women's circles, and they wouldn't take it from her.

Oh drakiri
Rise, rise, into the sky
Sing your song and awake the dawn
Cross the rivers and the great wide sea
Pass over the hills and the whispering trees
Oh drakiri, rise, rise,
Sing your song, awake the dawn

Oh drakiri, rise,
Rise, drakiri, rise

As the voices sang, the flute trilled and swooped, weaving in its melody to recreate the flight of the drakiri. But the sounds washed meaninglessly around Ina as she watched Suni through the fire, an ache in the pit of her stomach. She was sitting with Mūak and Tani, her slim legs visible beneath the hem of a dress that was the color of koua leaves in high summer. A long necklace of red and brown seeds hung between the swell of her breasts. Ina closed her eyes and imagined running her fingertips over her bare flesh.

When she opened them again, she saw Suni's smiling face and the gleaming firelight in her eyes. The longing grew in her, carried and intensified by the drums, which pounded out the ecstatic culmination of the birds' flight. Too late, she remembered to add her own steady beat on the bass. Suni met her eyes but quickly looked back to Tani and then up at Mūak, who was sitting still and silent, seemingly looking at nothing at all. *If I were him, I'd be happy. I'd have her in my arms, like Han has Ria now, and Tani would be ours.*

"Ina, are you alright?" Oyu said when the song ended. "I don't think you've kept time once tonight."

"I'm bored of these songs." She unslung the large drum from her shoulders and rested it on the ground.

"It's her, isn't it?" Oyu squinted through the fire at Suni.

Ina said nothing, silenced by her jealousy and the shame of it. To desire another for oneself alone was wrong, to claim another's mate for oneself utterly forbidden. But Ina didn't want to share Suni, not with Mūak, not with anyone.

"Forget her for now. You'll have your time together." He slung an arm around her and squeezed her shoulder.

Ina sighed, allowing herself to be pulled against his warm bulk.

"Smoke?" The offer came from Han, who was holding out a long, intricately carved koua-wood pipe that gave off a sharply pungent smell of arrowleaf.

Without releasing Ina, Oyu took the pipe and put it to his mouth. The red in the bowl blazed more brightly as he inhaled.

"Can I have some?" Ina said on impulse.

"Really, are you sure? It's not like you." Smoke streamed out of Oyu's mouth as he spoke.

"Just a little, why not?" Although she knew very well why not and could hear her mother's voice warning her against it as clearly as if she were standing next to her. It wasn't something she could share with Oyu, though, or anyone else, not even Suni, whom she loved more than her own self. But she was suddenly fed up with control, fed up with having to watch herself day and night. She wanted to experience the dreamy pleasure that was already causing Oyu's pupils to expand and his face to grow slack.

"One puff only," he said, passing her the pipe. "You're not used to it."

She filled her lungs with the pungent smoke. It scratched her throat and made her cough. Oyu handed her a water skin, and as she drank, her mind began to stretch out to the stars, light, airy, and free. She was about to inhale more smoke, but Oyu took the pipe from her.

Closing her eyes, she let herself enjoy the light breeze as it caressed her face, glancing first across her left cheek and temple to cool the humid heat of the night. *It would be nice to swim now, yes, that's what I should do, she loves swimming too.*

"We'll win the relay this cycle," Oyu said, his voice close to her ear. "You were so fast the last day. We're going to win everything."

"Hmm?"

He repeated his words and they drifted to her one by one. She snatched at them and strung them together, and when she grasped their meaning, her lips curved into a half smile. "We were all fast." Her voice was barely a whisper, floating on the breeze.

"Some more?"

Her eyes opened to glowing embers hovering in the air above her, sending up thin streams of grey smoke. She took the pipe, enjoying the feeling of the warm wood between her fingers as she inhaled again. Then she looked for Suni and saw her through a fog, her features blurring with the flames of the fire. The pipe was taken from her hands. *If only I could sit with her. Why is Mūak so stern tonight? She seems uneasy too.*

Someone said something to Ina, and she turned her head in the direction of the voice. "What did you say?" Her own voice seemed to come from very far away, as if it didn't belong to her.

There was an answer, but it was lost in the haze. The fire seemed to have grown, to fill all her vision. Old Tsu had started a tale and the fire dancers had sprung up around the flames. She broke free of Oyu and lay on her back. The stars were dancing across the sky, shooting out bright tails as they swirled to the music. She closed her eyes. *Everything will be fine.*

"Ina?" Oyu, leaning over her, but now the different parts of his face were melting into one another, eyes into nose, ears into cheeks, mouth into chin.

She opened her mouth to speak but a sickening faintness swept over her, making her feel as if she were standing over a great cavern.

"Ina, are you well?"

A rush of noise and chatter, the boundaries of her mind shifting and porous.

"What's wrong?"

Howls and screeches echoed in her ears and bounced off the sides of her skull. She tried to pull herself in, to build a dam against the clamoring cacophony, but she might as well have tried to stop the sea.

"Someone, give me water!"

Wave after wave of sound and feeling crashed into her, buffeting her consciousness with snatches and fragments of half-formed thoughts and intentions. *Ani's over kreeeek kreeeek must do better next how do what the fire dancers wuff wuff wuff he's so ouuuuuuuu annoying should have crik crik now wrong with Ina kreeeeek wuff wuff wuff.*

The threads of Chel's Cloth filled her vision and the world exploded with dazzling light. Wheezing for breath, she tried to claw free but was drawn in ever deeper, until her entire being fragmented and dissolved.

Oyu said something again, but she couldn't understand him. Shards of brilliance danced across her vision, sharp and cutting. She half-struggled to her feet, fell again, put her hands to her ears, but it was no use because the noise wasn't coming from outside.

A skin pressed to her mouth, water trickling across her tongue and down her chin. She choked and coughed. More water, and this time she swallowed. Hands under her armpits, pulling her upright. They were taking her away, into the darkness of the forest. She stumbled, but they held her tightly between them.

As they drew away from the fire, the babble began to lessen, and the pieces of her started to come back together. The threads of the Cloth, though, still blinded her.

Who was there? Oyu on one side, and she could read him clearly. *He loves me. No, he desires me.* The realization was like a spear through the gut. She wanted to break free, but Ria was holding on too. Her feelings were equally plain—worry, surprise.

They stopped and she vaguely made out the open doorway to the hunters' lodge through the shining threads. They brought her to the room she shared with three other hunters and sat her down on her pallet.

"What happened?" Oyu asked.

She tried to answer, but her words were a mumble.

"Too much smoke," said Ria. "The best she can do is sleep it off."

Ina lay down and closed her eyes.

Someone took her boots off and pulled a blanket over her.

"Rest, Ina," Oyu said softly.

A form of sleep came upon her, but the noise followed her there, allowing her no real rest, yet no escape into wakefulness either. And Mūak stalked the pathways of her dreams, looking hard and angry, while Suni, following him, was afraid.

Ina's first thought upon waking was of Suni. The second was how she'd shamed herself and she groaned. But there was worse. Oyu. He desired her. How would she face him? She closed her eyes again, putting an arm across her face to block out the light.

Her mother's voice came through the shutter. "Ina, child, are you awake?"

Ina groaned a second time. She would be unforgiving of this.

The shutter rustled and Ina opened her eyes to see her mother slipping into the room. "I've brought you some honeyed white tea."

Ina watched silently as her mother deposited a steaming cup on the low table beside her sleeping pallet. She was wearing the red-beaded necklace of the crafters over her sleeveless dress, and her thick, deep brown hair was twisted into a knot at the back of her head.

"Sit up, child."

Ina didn't move. "I'm a hunt leader, Mami."

"It didn't seem that way last night." Her mother's voice was stern, her expression sterner.

"Please, not now." But she wriggled into an upright position. The world swung wildly, then settled back into its normal state.

Her mother rearranged the pillow to support her back. "How could you have been so stupid? You know the dangers arrowleaf brings."

Ina picked up the tea and brought it close to her face. Its vapors soothed her aching head, and she sipped from it.

Sitting cross-legged on the grey fur next to her bed, her mother regarded her as she drank, hands clasped between her knees. Her amber eyes, the best feature that Ina had inherited from her, were now filled with admonishment and concern. "You were shouting and screaming for quiet as if there were voices in your head. Some thought you'd gone mad."

Ina didn't remember this, only the hideous noise. "I smoked too much."

"I'm not a fool, child. What made you so careless?"

Ina sipped from her tea, knowing her mother was right and hating that fact. She knew what would come next.

"I haven't spent twenty-one years protecting you so that you could announce it to the entire village."

"It just happened," Ina muttered, staring into the tea.

"The worry I've endured on your behalf, Ina. To put ourselves against the village, our traditions ..."

"Well then you should have given me up, let the elders send me back to Chel like the rest of them, even if the Godstone didn't reject me!"

As soon as the words had left her mouth, Ina regretted them, along with the sharpness of her tone.

Her mother pressed her lips together, her gaze reducing Ina from hunt leader to spoilt child. "It would do you good to find a mate. You're of age. The duties of motherhood will be good for you."

"I'm a hunt leader. I have plenty of duties already."

"Even a hunt leader must bear children. If there's no man here who'll serve, why not go and spend some time on one of the other islands?"

"I'm not looking for a mate or children," Ina said. "Stop going on about it." *Oyu. You fool.*

The door shutter rattled and then Suni's face poked through. "Chel be with you, Mia'Nui."

At the sound of her voice, Ina jerked forward. Hot tea splashed onto her chest, running between her breasts and down to her belly. She paid it little mind, calling for Suni to come in and gazing at her greedily when she did.

Her mother unfolded and rose in a single motion. "I'll leave, but I'll return to see how you are later."

Ina shouted a distracted goodbye as she left, then turned to Suni. "I so longed to be with you last night."

Suni looked grave. "What happened to you? You frightened us." She took her mother's place on the fur, her bare legs tantalizingly close. She smelled of herbs, of the forest.

"Too much arrowleaf." *She hasn't guessed anything, has she?*

Suni took hold of her hand, stroked the back of it. "I'll never understand why people like fogging their minds with that herb. I thought you knew better."

"You sound like my mother."

"I'm sorry, I don't mean to," she said. "But what made you smoke?"

Ina shrugged. “I just wanted to relax, laugh with the others.”

“You can laugh without it.”

“Yes, I laugh with you,” Ina said, tightening her fingers around Suni’s.

“You know what I mean.” Nevertheless, she smiled.

“I promise that tomorrow I’ll laugh all day like crazy Luk.”

“No! That would be far worse!” Suni said, laughing herself. Then she sobered. “I can’t stay. I only came to check on you.”

Suni started to get to her feet, but Ina grabbed her wrist. “No, a moment longer. I haven’t angered you, have I?”

Suni swooped down to land a light kiss on her forehead. “Of course not. You just gave me a fright, like the rest of us. But I do have to go. Tani and Mūak are waiting.”

When she said the names of her daughter and mate, Ina thought she caught an edge of something. What was wrong? “I want us to be together tonight.”

Suni’s forehead crinkled with reproach. “Not tonight. Mūak and I, we have to … But tomorrow, one mark after highsun, in the forest, our place?”

There was definitely something up. Mūak hadn’t guessed anything, had he? Told her about it? No, how could he know? If she’d been able to hide it from Oyu, who’d been with her, then there was no way Mūak could guess her secret.

She watched as Suni left, frustrated desire sharpening the pain in her head. Then she became aware of another sensation, dulling and blanketing. It was an all too familiar one. She stared down at the nearly empty teacup. “To Sīut with you, Mami!” she cried aloud when she realized what had happened. But she couldn’t muster any real fury because the poison that her mother had put into the tea was already acting on her senses, shutting her down and closing her off. It was stronger than any dose she ever administered to herself. As strong, she realized, as those daily doses Mami made her endure as a child, confining her to bed for days and weeks on end. A poison designed to block her cursed gifts, but which also blocked every other feeling and sucked the very life from her bones. She set the cup aside, her eyes growing heavy.

There came yet another knock at the door, this one louder, more forceful. It was Oyu, his face showing the effects of the feasting. "I'm glad to see our village madwoman is alive," he said with a teasing smile.

It was obvious now, how he felt about her. *Look at his eyes. How could I have missed it before?*

"Has the arrowleaf taken your tongue too?" He squatted next to her pallet, elbows resting on his knees.

"I don't feel very well."

"I don't think I've ever seen anyone react so badly to the smoke," he said. "I see why you never take it." He paused. "Some of us are going for a swim. Will you come?"

"I need to rest some more." *You fool, you fool.*

"It's the best cure."

She couldn't bear to see the disappointment in his face and closed her eyes. "I need to sleep." The words came out thick and slurred.

To her relief, he didn't push any further, and as the door closed behind him, she sank down onto her pallet and gave herself up to the clawtongue.

Suni was late for their meeting the next day, and Ina peered into the trees, mistaking every shadow, every passage of animal or bird for the arrival of her beloved. Would she come at all? Perhaps there had been a problem with Tani, or she'd been called at the last minute to tend to an injury. She began to pace, kicking at the mossy ground to create little dents in its soft carpet.

Then, at last, a slight rustle in trees, and there she was, stepping carefully through the undergrowth, her hair shining whenever it was struck by a sunbeam.

Ina made herself hold back and savor the last anticipatory moments, waiting until Suni was but a few paces away before moving forward to meet her. Without giving her a chance to speak, Ina pulled her into her arms and found her lips with her own. Suni stiffened at first with surprise, then her body relaxed against Ina's, her arms slipping around Ina's back to pull them more tightly together. Then, without ending their kiss, Ina pushed Suni's hips away, and they began to fumble with clothes and fastenings, laying out a bed for themselves to lie upon.

"I love you," Ina whispered as they lay down together, skin against skin.

"And I you." Suni kissed her again, and Ina gave herself completely to the embrace, her lean hunter's form melding into Suni's more voluptuous curves. Gradually, a tension began to build in both their bodies, and with it a rhythm, at first regular and then more disjointed as they strained against one another, breaths coming faster, fingers digging into flesh, pressing hard against muscle and bone as if trying to penetrate right through, hearts thudding in tune to a rising crescendo, until finally they fell away from one another, panting and spent.

They lay side by side on their backs, holding hands and staring at the shifting canopy of the trees. Other than their labored breathing, the only sounds were the whispering of the breeze and the squawk of the yellow-feathered achaks perched nearby. Ina pulled Suni toward her so that she came to rest her head against Ina's shoulder, draping an arm loosely across her waist. Ina liked this position. It made her feel protective and strong. But soon she began to sense a restlessness in the other woman. She remembered how Suni had been the day before. Something was wrong. "What's bothering you?"

"You can always tell, can't you?" Suni said, lifting her head and propping herself up on one elbow. Her long hair spilled forward across her face and tickled Ina's stomach.

"Tell what?"

Suni pushed her hair back over shoulder and fixed her with a knowing look. "You have it too."

Ina stiffened, guessing but pretending not to. "What do you mean?"

Suni hesitated. "The curse."

Ina couldn't stop her eyes from flickering away as cold fear woke in her belly. So Mūak *had* guessed something? "Why would you think that?"

Suni's eyes seemed to bore a hole through her. "Maybe it isn't strong in you. Maybe that's why you passed the Test, but you have it. I can tell. I can feel you sometimes, on the edges of my mind. And the other night, it was as if you were possessed."

"You're imagining it. That's just ... love ... I suppose. And I'd had too much arrowleaf."

"You're too fast. You're too good at the hunt."

This had always been the most difficult to hide. Even without her senses fully open, she had an intuition that told her exactly when and where to strike, that steadied her aim so that she never missed. There were other hunters who could match her, though. None from their island, but a few from the others had provided a genuine challenge at the annual Games. She said as much to Suni.

Suni looked as if her next words had stuck in her throat, then she spilled them out in a rush. "If your parents found some way for you to pass the Test, I want you to tell me."

Suni's eyes were bright with tears, and Ina forced her voice to become steady and firm as she met her lover's gaze. "Suni, I don't have the curse."

The tears began to roll down Suni's face, and her hands moved to cover it.

Ina pushed herself upright and prized Suni's hands away. "What's wrong? What's this about?"

"Tani has it," she said hoarsely. "Don't tell anyone. Please."

Ina swallowed, her mouth dry. "Are you sure?"

"Mūak saw the signs when I was away. He's furious. He blames me."

So he didn't know what she'd done. Relief washed over her. But then she felt ashamed of it. "Why does he do that?"

"Because there have been two purges in my family in the past sixty years."

"That's ridiculous."

"I know, I said that to him. But I think he just needs to blame someone."

"It might be nothing. All parents are nervous before the Test."

Suni shook her head. "I saw it too, last night."

Ina waited.

"She threw a ball and it hit the opposite wall quicker than it takes to blink your eye."

"Are you sure it wasn't a trick of the mind?"

"No. It wasn't normal. And she's always had an uncanny ability to sense our intentions."

Ina couldn't think of anything to say that wouldn't betray her.

"They'll send her back to Chel. I can't let her go. I can't let her die." The tears glimmering in Suni's eyes became choking sobs that contorted her whole body.

Ina took her in her arms, whispering words of comfort as Suni's tears wetted her collarbone. But she wanted to cry herself, because she'd lied and now something was broken between them. And Tani, poor, sweet little Tani. "We'll find a way to save her."

Suni pulled her head away to look at Ina, grasping her arms fiercely. "So you do know? You did find a way to pass the Test?"

"I passed the Test like anyone else does," she said. Though, of course, the Godstone hadn't lit up to her touch because her mother had dosed her with so much clawtongue she could barely see or stand. One thing she'd never told anyone, not even her parents, was that the Godstone sometimes seemed to call to her, whispering at the edges of her mind, as if it were alive.

Despair had whitened Suni's features, and Ina realized the full extent of the terror her own mother must have felt. For the first time, she understood why her mother had been so fierce with her, never leaving her alone, keeping her from the other children, claiming that she was ill. But she couldn't inflict the same on Tani. And she couldn't share her secret with Suni. Or could she? If Suni would save Tani ... Ina opened her mouth to unleash the words, but her gut and throat tightened, making it impossible to speak. No. Suni might tell Mūak, and who knew what Mūak would do? She might also push Ina away, just like her father had.

There had to be some other way, one that didn't risk Ina's secret or force Tani to endure the clawtongue. It came to her, absurd but wonderful. "We could leave." No one ever left. No one could leave. But Suni went still, and Ina realized she was giving the idea serious thought.

"How would we do it?" she said eventually.

Ina wiped her tears away with her fingertips. "I don't know yet, but we'll find a way. We have almost a moon. Just keep her out of sight for now."

"Do you promise?"

She knew that Suni was aware of the impossibility of the task. But as long as they did something, as long as they tried, then perhaps the flood could be contained.

Chapter 3

Mūak

We must remember that the Cursed Ones did not ask to be cursed. They were born that way; pawns of Sīut. So we should show them empathy and return them to Chel with love.

—Teachings of Old Tsu

Mūak's teeth clamped tightly together as he watched his daughter pick up a fragment of pale grey rock by the pool and turn it over in her hands, examining it carefully. She was biting her bottom lip in concentration, a mannerism she'd inherited from Suni. He glanced over at his bondmate, sitting on a fallen tree not far from Tani. She was also watching their child, her mouth a tight press, her shoulders stiff and raised.

"Ashstone!" Tani exclaimed, holding the fragment in the air, glancing between him and Suni.

Suni forced a smile. "That's right!"

He schooled his own features into a semblance of fatherly pride. "And what can you do with ashstone?"

"It's good for making a pit to cook food in," she said confidently.

For a moment, his pride was genuine. But despair quickly returned to crush the feeling. He forced himself to speak past the lump that had lodged itself in his throat. "And why is that?"

She lowered the stone. "What's wrong, Papi?"

"I asked you a question." The words came out stiff and harsh, and she flinched as they landed.

"Because it won't explode in the heat," she said in a small voice, glancing briefly at Suni, who was flushed with anger, eyes boring into him in accusation.

Shame twisted through him. He took a deep breath, tried to inject warmth into his next words. "That's right. You've learned your lessons well."

But she seemed to barely register the praise, looking again at her mother, who forced another smile and told her to look for another type of stone. Tani opened her mouth as if to speak, perhaps to ask again what was wrong, and he braced himself. But she seemed to think better of it, put the rock down next to the three others she had collected, and then cast around the clearing for another specimen.

He remembered doing the same project at her age, set by Old Tsu when his hair was still more black than white. Remembered too that Ina had found rock types no one else had, roaming farther and wider than she should have—and without her parents, who had come, taut with worry, to his family's hut to see if she was with them. As always when he thought of Ina, a ball of irritation knotted his belly. He didn't understand what Suni saw in her, or Oyu, for that matter, who had been besotted with her since he could walk. She was cold and proud, thought herself better than all of them.

Tani picked up a flat pebble and turned toward the pool. Then with a swift, practiced motion, she launched it at the water. But it didn't skip across the surface as it should have. No, instead it quite clearly vanished and then reappeared above the water before sinking with a splosh, sending glimmering ripples out to the edge.

"No!" Suni cried out, leaping up and running to her daughter. "You mustn't do that! What did I tell you?"

"I only wanted to make it dance on the water," Tani said, eyes filling with tears. "Why do you keep shouting at me?"

Mūak found himself rigid. He was always hoping, but then she'd do this again and the hope proved itself the delusion it was. His daughter had Sīut's Curse, and for that, she must return to Chel. *She must die.* He let the words circle in his brain and shape the movements of his tongue. *She must die to protect our people.* But how could a child so sweet and innocent be Sīut's pawn?

Suni was hugging Tani, looking over the child's shoulder at him, her eyes liquid with pain. Rage boiled deep in his belly then spewed up to consume all of him, causing his head to spin. The idea that Tani might be made to drink the starweed, that he would see the life fade from her, her soul leave her tiny body, made him want to retch. It couldn't be. It wasn't possible. What had he done that this horror had been visited on him? He clenched his fists so tightly that his nails dug into his palm.

There had to be some way to save her, some way to fool the Godstone. Then he flung the thought away like the trash it was, fresh shame grinding through his fear. To do that would be to break their most sacred law, to put his own selfish desires above the greater good of his people.

Suni released Tani. "No more throwing stones," she said. "Promise me you won't throw anything anymore."

"But why?" Tani's voice was so quiet he could barely hear her, her bottom lip quivering, although she was bravely holding the tears in.

"Because you're too old now, like I said," Suni replied, her voice dead, as if she had no air to breathe life into it.

"But the older children make the stones dance on the water."

Tani looked at him for confirmation, and he thought of his friend Rāou, who at the age of six had uttered a scream that had left everyone around him insensible for several marks. The elders hadn't waited until he was nine years old to give him the Test. They didn't give him the test at all. Instead, they awarded his family a single day to say goodbye before forcing the starweed potion down his throat. They'd do the same to Tani. His heart splintered and words burst out from him. "You're using the cursed powers when you throw stones. It's forbidden."

Suni stared at him in horror.

Tani's brow wrinkled, fear and surprise and ... knowledge? "I don't mean to. The holes just happen and the stone goes through them." Tears sprang into her eyes.

But he carried on, born on a desperate wave. "If you want to pass the Test, you *must* learn to stop the holes," he said. Such a terrible lie. If it were that easy to switch off the powers, no one would ever be betrayed by the Godstone. But he needed her to believe him so that she might spend a few more days in the sun, at least until the Test was nigh.

"Mami, is that true? If I can make the holes go away, I'll pass?"

Suni shot him a look filled with grief and anger. But then she looked straight at Tani and choked out the lie. "Papi's right. So promise us you'll stop?"

"I'll try really hard," she replied. "I'll stop throwing stones too."

Mūak suddenly found he could move. He rose smoothly to his feet and then fell to his knees next to Suni and Tani, enveloping them both in his arms. They sank against him, and for the briefest moment, he felt strong again, able to protect them. "Let's go back to the village," he said. "It's nearly highsun, and I'm starving." He released them and scooped up the stones Tani had gathered, putting them into his belt pouch.

They walked back toward the village and the family fire, each taking one of Tani's tiny hands. Would this have been easier to bear if they'd had other children? Tani had been something of a miracle. In the back of his mouth, he tasted again the bitterness of the potion he'd diligently consumed for two years before she was born, and then for three more after, until they'd given up, deciding it was not Chel's will they be granted a second child. A darker thought struck him. Had Chel stopped them from having another because Tani had been claimed by Sīut? He shouldn't have taken Suni for a mate, knowing one of her ancestors had been cursed. But that thought shamed him, and his shame deepened when he recalled how he'd said it to her in a rage.

They reached the fire to find other parents there already with their children, removing small green packages from the glowing embers.

"Can I go get Puki?" Tani asked.

Mūak's instinct was to say no, that she had to wait until they'd eaten. But instead, he waved her on. If she needed her doll for comfort, let her have it. It was more comfort than he'd have.

As Suni went to the fire to retrieve their food, he saw Ina coming over. His belly tightened. Why was she here again instead of with the hunters at their fire? As Suni's lover, she had reason enough to join them here, but she came all the time now. Too often.

Suni handed him his meal and sat next to him, then waved at Ina, who changed her course to join them, a wary smile on her face.

Then it hit him, why Ina came so often now. "You told her, didn't you?" he said to Suni, who was unwrapping the thick green anan leaves to reveal the stewed white fruit inside her meal.

She paused a moment, her gaze still fixed on the ananfruit, uttered a low "Yes."

"You should have said nothing," he said. The rage swirled in him again. How could Suni betray them like this?

Now Suni deigned to look at him. "She's my amiki. I can't hide such things from her."

"That is *precisely* the kind of thing you must hide," he spat. He wanted to shake her. How could she be so stupid?

"It won't matter in the end, will it?" Suni said dully. "Everyone will know once the Test happens."

He had no answer to that.

Ina reached them. "Chel be with you."

Her presence made him even angrier. He tossed his wrapped ananfruit to the side, his appetite gone.

Tani returned, straw doll clutched under her arm. "Ina'Yakir'Suk! Did Papi show you my rocks yet?"

"No, my sweet," Ina replied, looking at him.

Hands shaking, he roughly untied his pouch and emptied the stones onto the ground. He couldn't play this game a moment longer. He would explode. "I've remembered I have to talk to Han. I'll eat with the hunters."

"Oh, you never ..." Suni stopped when she saw his expression.

"See you tonight," he said. "I'll be hunting all afternoon." He forced himself to kiss his bondmate and daughter, then rose and marched toward the village. But as soon as he was out of sight, he made for the forest. He needed to hit something. He found a stick and crashed his way through the undergrowth, assaulting ferns with heavy strikes, forcing the jungle to provide a path. Soon he was sweating and panting, his rage barely cooled.

Eventually, he found himself on Crescent Beach, a tiny cove too rocky for the canoes or for swimming. But it was a place he'd loved as a child for its clear turquoise waters and the fascinating lifeforms that clung to the black rocks and wallowed in the shallow pools.

He dropped his stick onto the soft, black sand and went out onto the slick rocks, enjoying their coolness beneath his toes. The tide was out, exposing long fronds of dark green seaweed and knobbly clusters of limpets and clams. He climbed to a rock shelf that jutted out above the shifting waters and sat with his legs dangling over the edge, staring out to sea, to the hump of the Godstone island on the horizon, where his daughter's fate would be sealed.

Then he thought of Ina again. Would she betray Tani? No, he had to admit that it was unlikely. Whatever her faults, she clearly loved Suni. And she was no rule follower. She'd questioned the elders much as a child, before the long illness that had made her silent and sullen. But he still sensed a skepticism in her when she listened to a sermon or moral tale. Perhaps that was why she annoyed him so. It was like she was silently mocking them all.

He let his mind drift to the day of Tani's birth, the joy he'd shared with Suni, and the tears gathered and trickled down his face, their salt mixing with the salt of the sea.

Chapter 4

Fay

A priest must attend all the required prayers and services every day unless undertaking another errand or duty in Lumia's name, such as tending to the sick or travelling as an envoy.

—The Lumin Priest's Handbook

The voices of over a hundred priests dedicated to the worship of Lumia, daughter of Lunari and Solari, Lady of the Flame and Banisher of the Gloom, rose together to recite the evening prayer.

Lady of flame and fire, this
we pray to you:
Shine a beacon in the dark-
ness
And guard us from the
Gloom
Shield us from all evildoers

And ward off demon spawn
Lady of flame and fire, this we pray to you

The words tasted sour on Fay's tongue. Once, the prayer had seemed so powerfully protective. She would whisper it to herself at night as a child, to conquer her fear of the dark and of the men who caused her mother to cry out in the room next door. Now, the lie of it gnawed at her, whispered to her of her naivety. The goddess might be watching, but even her most holy were tainted with corruption. Even her temple was not safe.

As the High Luminate began to utter the last words of the ceremony, Fay blinked through smoke-seared eyes at the forest of slender white candles that ringed the circular worship room, thinking yet again how much more effective a few well-placed glowglobes would be. No weaverwork for the followers of Lumia, though, even if the candles left shadowy pockets in defiance of Lumia's promise to drive all darkness away. Magic was dangerous, forbidden. Yet she couldn't help but find it ironic that Lumia, the vaunted Lady of the Flame, provided poorer illumination to her temple than Madam Sisi had to her brothel.

Her gaze drifted back to the High Luminate, resplendent in robes spun of gold and silk, the red of Lumia's flame glittering on his breast. *A hundred rubies, they say. Those robes would feed Arindel's poor for a decade. But we fill them with prayers and platitudes instead.*

Fay regarded the crescent rows of white-robed men and women standing with their hands clasped before them as they gazed reverently at the statue of the goddess on its dais. Lumia smiled back down at them, holding her burning torch high to illuminate the sunburst ceiling. A virginal girl at the height of beauty and youth, carved out of the whitest marble.

Bet it was men who made her, Fay thought, *made her like someone they wanted to fuck so that they could adore her.*

"Go forth in the light of the Lady." The High Luminate's words cut through her thoughts, and along with the other priests, she made the Sign of Light, placing her hands first against her breastbone, right over left, then raising her arms straight up in the air before fanning them out to imitate a sunburst. Finally, she pressed her palms together and bowed.

The priests silently filed out through the double doors, but a hubbub of chatter arose as soon as they reached the corridors. Fay didn't want to speak to anyone, so she pressed against the wall and turned right to leave the main flow of bodies, seeking the stairs by the novice mess hall.

She climbed up to the first floor then hurried across to the other side of the building to reach her room. The sun hadn't yet risen high enough to enter through the narrow rectangle of glass above her writing desk, but the sky was a clear, pastel blue, giving her more than enough light to see by. She went to the small oak wardrobe and removed a light green cloak, which she flung over her white Lumin robes. Then she reached for the worn leather satchel hanging from the back of her door and slung it over her shoulder.

This done, she went back down the stairs and left the temple by a side exit. Outside, amidst the graceful buildings and wide avenues of the Lady's Quarter, she breathed deeply of the morning air, her nostrils filling with the scent of roses from the gardens of the rich. It was already warm, too warm for a cloak, but needs must.

Walking west, she soon came in sight of the arcing Temple Bridge, her way across the River Arin's broad expanse. Its white stone blazed in the morning sun, causing her to squint as she approached. A stream of merchants' wagons trundled over it, nearly all going in the opposite direction—toward the upper-class homes and establishments of East Arindel. On the other side of the bridge, she turned off the main boulevard and down the road that would take her to the Rainbow Quarter, wedged between the docklands and the southern wall.

The area got its name from the tiny, multi-colored glowglobes strung across its narrow streets. As always when she caught sight of them, she was hit by a flurry of excitement and shame. Here was Arindel at its gayest and most decadent. Here she had plied her trade as a whore in Madam Sisi's. And here she still came to escape her priestly prison and lose herself in hedonism and delight. Already its main thoroughfare teemed with a mass of humanity, and she kept a careful hand on her satchel as she ran the gauntlet of hawkers and peddlers.

"Flower for your 'air, priestess?" A black-toothed woman with a basket of red poppies.

"Cake or honey?" Hissed by a hunched man at a street corner. No cake or honey in sight, but that wasn't what he was really selling.

"Candles, ten a vic!" These no more than rushlights, sputtering, stinking, and smoking. Fay was well rid of those.

"Meat pasties, fill your belly with meat pasties!" This time she was tempted, as she'd had no breakfast, but one look at the pasties told her they were probably mixed with sawdust.

As she passed through the uneven streets with their hodgepodge buildings, she remembered the book she'd read about the destruction wreaked during the Great Siege. The Rainbow Quarter had been one of the worst hit, and two hundred years later, it still showed. Some of the original buildings were intact, uniform in style, constructed of large blocks of white stone and rising to three or four stories. But many of the newer ones were small and narrow, with two sometimes wedged together where one would previously have stood. They were more often made of wood or plastered brick, and in some cases were painted in bright colors. Oddest of all were the buildings that had been only half destroyed and then patched up, giving them a disorganized appearance that echoed the general chaos of the quarter. Fay never tired of looking at them, always finding some new detail, some quirk she'd previously overlooked.

She turned off onto a quiet street, then onto another slightly busier one. This brought her to her first destination of the morning, a ramshackle alehouse called The Goat. Its splintered window shutters were thrown open to allow the morning air in—and the fumes of sweating bodies and stale beer out. Before entering, she wrapped her cloak more tightly around her, ensuring she covered any shred of cloth that might reveal her identity as a Lumin.

The common room was rough, loud, and dirty, a place where money was made and lost in a breath. A quick scan took in card and dice tables heaped with coin, men crowding round, cursing or cheering as their luck went. Pinboard too, with more watchers than players, everyone staking something on the outcome. In the back rooms were other kinds of dealings, few of them legal, and it was to one of these that she went.

She rapped out a pattern of knocks, and the door opened, revealing Chop, a heavyset bruiser with a missing eye. She nodded to him as she walked in, then trained her gaze on the center of the room, where Hook was hunched over a table, counting silver.

He didn't pause in the counting until she was standing right in front of him, his thin lips moving as he stacked coin on top of coin. While she waited, she studied the puckered red scar that circled around from the edge of his left eye to the corner of his mouth, screwing both sideways. It made him seem like he was always scowling, and he certainly knew how to use it to intimidate. Still, he wasn't the worst of Moth's scorps. Some of them would freeze the blood in your veins with a look.

Finally, Hook pushed a stack of silver to one side and gave her his attention. "So, is it the sick or the starvin' this morning?" he said with a skew-mouthed grin that only made him look more menacing.

She returned it with a smile of her own. "The starving are always sick, and the sick starve themselves. But I'm doing rounds today." She patted her satchel. "What word from Moth?"

"Lumia's tits, you even sound like a priest," Hook said, scratching his scar.

Fay realized she hadn't reverted to street speech as she usually would. *Used to be hard to talk properly. Now if I don't pay attention, it's the other way.* "Too many years wigging."

"S'pose it's a good thing, but don't you go thinkin' you're better than us." Hook showed more of his broken teeth to indicate he was joking.

"I've always been better than you, Hook, I don't need priest's robes to prove that." She winked and thrust out her hip.

Hook gave her a good look up and down, then mock-growled, "And don't be remindin' me o' what you ain't sellin' no more."

She allowed her smile to broaden a fraction. "Speaking of which ..."

Hook grabbed a long scroll from the side of the table and jerked his chin toward the door to the small side room.

Surprised, Fay followed him in. Hook rarely set her tasks so sensitive that not even Chop could hear.

The room had no window, but there was a glowglobe attached to the wall, which Hook rubbed to activate. It began to emit a dull, flickering light. One of Moth's cheap knock-offs, no doubt.

Hook rolled the scroll out on the tiny table in the middle of the room, and she stepped closer to look. It showed the plans for a building. Moments later, she realized what that building was—the Temple of Lumia. "What's this about?"

Hook stabbed a large finger at the very center of the map, to a square behind the main worship room. "Moth wants to know what's there."

Fay shrugged. "Storage rooms, as it says."

"He wants to know what's *in* there."

"That area is off limits to me," Fay said. "It's archpriests only."

"Well now we know why Moth wants you to scope it out."

Of course he bloody does. Moth doesn't like unanswered questions. "But I've no way of getting in," she said, unable to stop a whining note from creeping in and berating herself for it. That wasn't going to help.

"You'll find a way," Hook said. His tone was mild, but Fay heard the underlying threat all the same.

She pressed her lips together, staring at the map. There was only one entrance that she could see, and that was through the vestry behind the main worship room. Only archpriests had access to it. *It* is *a bit strange, I suppose, that it's so sealed off. What* do *they keep in there?* The storage rooms ran to two floors, she knew. Directly above them on the third floor was a roof garden, a very pleasant one, from whose center rose a vast torch that was lit day and night.

"Oh, and you got a week."

"A *week*! What's the big rush?"

Hook gave her a look that said, don't ask stupid questions.

"Can I take the map?"

Hook shook his head. "It's Moth's. Don't you know your way around?"

Fay heaved a sigh. "I suppose I can get another one."

"And no talking to anyone about this, not even Tom," Hook warned. "Moth says he'll have your hide and mine if he learns someone else has got wind."

"Understood." Her mood soured, she left The Goat and went to a neighboring street to make her first sick visit of the day. The door to the building she sought was half hanging off its hinges, the wood blackened and rotting away. She carefully pulled it open, entering a dark, narrow corridor that stank of mold and damp. There were creaky stairs at the end of it, and she climbed up four floors until she reached a landing at the top of the building. She knocked on the nearest of the three doors that confronted her.

"Who's that?" The woman's words dissolved into a long, hacking cough that ended in spits and curses.

Fay waited until the sounds had subsided before answering. "Hi, Marge. It's Fay."

"Door's open, Your Light," came the rasping answer.

Fay turned the knob and stepped into a sparse room with a single window that let in a thin streamer of daylight. It illuminated a boy of five and a girl of seven playing on the ground with sticks and a piece of string. They didn't pause their game to look at her when she entered, although she knew them and they her. Beyond them was a large, sagging bed on which Marge lay, as always. Her black hair clung greasily to her too-white face, and sweat glistened on her fevered brow.

"Children, don't be rude," Marge said feebly, trying to push herself upright.

In response, the pair finally looked at Fay.

"Hello," said Jinnie, pushing a strand of dark hair behind her ear.

"Your Light," added Cabe, pinching his sister on the arm.

"Ow! What was that for?" She slapped his shoulder in return.

"You gotta say 'Your Light'," Cabe said, pinching her again.

She screeched.

“Children!” called Marge in a voice drained of hope.

Fay crouched down beside the two. “I’ve got a surprise for you, but you have to stop fighting.”

That stilled them, and they cast their eyes on her expectantly.

Fay reached into the pocket of her robe and plucked out a handful of raisins.

The children held out their hands, expressions lighting as she dropped the raisins onto each little palm. *Have they even eaten today?* she wondered, as they popped the first raisin into their mouths, sucking on it joyfully.

Fay went on to Marge and sat by her bed. “How are you?” she said, filling her voice with priestly concern. It wasn’t all faked. Fay pitied her and her children, was glad she’d escaped a similar fate. But there was only so much misery you could see before the feeling dried up in you, and Fay had seen enough for ten lifetimes.

“I don’t think I’ve long before I greet the Lady,” Marge said, coughing again.

Fay opened her satchel and took out a pouch full of herbs. Their pungency was just enough to counteract the smell of sickness and death that hung in the room. “This is enough for two doses,” she said. “Take one this morning and later tonight.”

“I’m worried about my young ’uns, Your Light,” she whispered. “When I’m gone.”

“Is there other family they can go to?”

“My sister’s a whore,” she said. “I’m not having my little ones around that.”

No, best not, or we know where Jinnie will end up. Cabe too if he’s unlucky enough. “If you have no family, there is the orphanage we run,” Fay said.

"It won't be the same, though, will it?" the woman said. "They won't have a mother."

"Lady Lumia will be their mother," Fay said, feeling sick as she uttered the empty words.

"Bless her name." Marge burst into another wracking cough that ended with gobbets of blood on a stained handkerchief.

Panic burst in Fay's chest. She needed to get out of here, away from this depressing gloom. The world tilted and swayed. She blinked rapidly, trying to set it straight.

"You alright, Your Light?" Marge said.

Fay looked at her and saw her own mother, pocked with sores. She squeezed her eyes shut, clutched her satchel hard. "I'm fine," she managed. She took a steadying breath. "I'm fine," she said again, relieved to hear her voice strengthening. "But I must go now." She raised her hands over Marge and uttered a blessing. "Lady, shine your light, hold Marge in your warm embrace until her time comes."

Marge closed her eyes. "Thank you," she breathed.

"I'll be back in a few days to see how you are." Shakily, she said goodbye to the children, who were still sucking on their raisins, and then left for the next sick house. It was going to be a long day.

Her final visit ended in the late afternoon, and with weary steps and a wearier heart, she returned to the temple. Although she wanted nothing more than to rest, she went straight to the library to get a plan of the temple before finally going up to her room.

She spread it out on her desk, hoping it would reveal something that Hook's plans hadn't. But they were virtually identical. *I wonder what they've got in those rooms. And why only that one door through the vestry?* It was most likely locked, the entrance to the vestry no doubt the same. She wasn't the best lockpicker going, but she wasn't totally useless. She'd have to give it a go and hope she got lucky.

The bell rang out for evening prayers, so she rolled the map up and shoved it into the chest by her bed before going down to join the other priests. She would make her attempt at midnight, the hour of deepest darkness, when most priests were asleep, dreaming of their goddess.

Her friend Maev found her on the way, and they entered the worship room together. "How was your day?" she asked cheerfully. As always, her tawny hair was wild and unruly, giving her a mischievous air that was reflected in her dimpled smile.

"The usual." She liked Maev, hated how she lied to her.

"How's Marge?"

A stab of panic as she recalled the scene. "Worse."

Maev squeezed her shoulder sympathetically.

Little did she know that it wasn't really Marge that bothered her. It was knowing that any failure, any slip, would send her to a fate as bad—or worse.

The archpriests began to file in, and they fell into silence as they waited for prayers to begin. Fay paid little attention, instead picturing how she would sneak back in later that night, a knot of anxiety growing ever larger in her belly.

Afterward, Maev suggested they walk the rose gardens, but Fay was in no mood for talk, and said she would go to her room to read. It wasn't her books she took out when she got there, though—it was her picks, along with a pair of locks she'd been given for training long ago. But she knew the locks too well, and they gave without trouble. She doubted she'd be so lucky later. Still, she kept fiddling with them, using them as a sort of meditation to keep the worry at bay.

Finally, it was time. She took an oil lamp to light her way, one that could be quickly covered with a cloth if someone came across her in a place where she shouldn't be. A couple of insomniac priests crossed her path in the corridors, but the worship room itself was empty of people—if not of light. There was only a handful of torches lit around the perimeter, and all the candles had been quenched, but even so, the smell of smoke and wax hung heavy in the air.

She went around the back of the silver and gold filigree screen that stood behind the marble altar. After five years of spying in the temple for Moth, she was well used to doing things she shouldn't. But this felt sacrilegious, and her heart thundered in her ears.

There was little to see behind the screen other than the door to the vestry. As she expected, it was locked. Crouching down, she shone her oil lamp at the keyhole. It seemed straightforward enough. She inserted the first pick and began to wiggle it about, seeking the mechanisms inside. But the lock turned out not to be so simple, refusing to give in to her attempts. She loosed several highly unpriestly curses, some aimed at the lock, most at Moth, and a final few at herself. Then, deliberately, she closed her eyes and focused inward. *Patience, patience, that's what Digger always said.* When she had calmed down, she got back to her task, working methodically, trying not to think about the time ticking by.

A noise, footsteps. Someone had come in. Fay froze, hand shaking as she tried to hold the pick still in the lock. They were kneeling, probably praying. *Dammit!* Very slowly, she withdrew the pick. It clicked off the keyhole, making her freeze again, but there was no movement from beyond the screen. The pick free, she remained sitting as still as possible, trying to make her breath noiseless despite the surging panic. Sweat gathered on her brow and under her armpits. Five years of wigging for Moth, she thought bitterly, and she was still as frightened as the first time. But it was better than the whorehouse. Better to serve a goddess whose priesthood at least pretended to care than a man who thought of her as nothing but a hole to fill.

A rustling of clothing, a creak from a bench and the person was on the move, but not toward her. Toward the exit. They were gone. Fay heaved a sigh and dried the palms of her hands off her robes. Then she got to work again. This time, she was rewarded, and the mechanism tripped. Feeling giddy with triumph, she pocketed her picks and pushed the door open.

The room beyond was dark, and she shone her lamp to illuminate a scattered handful of padded chairs. Wardrobes lined the walls, no doubt containing archpriests' robes. Fay didn't pause to explore but instead crossed over to the single other door.

This too was locked, but the lock was like the one she'd just picked, so it took her considerably less time. To her surprise, this door opened not into a room but into a dark and narrow passageway. She stepped through, and her lamplight gleamed against a shiny metallic surface on the inner wall, bluish in color. *What is that?* She pressed her hand against the metal. Smooth and cool.

The passageway stretched left and right for as far as she could see. Fay decided to go left and found that it curved right about twenty paces along, then right and right again until she was back where she started. She didn't come across a single door, a single change in the uniformity of the passageway. *What in dear Lumia's name are they storing in there to make it so hard to get to? And why the metal?* It was no metal she had seen before, although she did have a suspicion of what it might be—nicoleum, mage-metal, which stopped weavers from doing their magic. She'd heard it had this color.

Could there be magical objects on the other side of that wall? Was that why only archpriests had access? *Oh Moth would be soooo pleased if that were the case.* He was obsessed with magical artifacts of all kinds, and not just to buy and sell. Fay did a round again, pressing her palms against the wall that surrounded what she presumed to be a room, but found no mechanism or trip. *How do I get in there? Is there even a room?* Finally, she decided to go and investigate the first floor, to see if there was a way in through there.

So she left, careful to lock the doors after her again, and trooped up the stairs. However, as she'd suspected, there were no doors to the storage room on the first floor either. The passageway that circled it was freely accessible but lined with the same stone as the rest of the temple. If there was another inner passageway, she could see no way to get to it. *The entrance is hardly through the roof garden?* But as she recalled, the giant torch to Lumia was directly above the storage rooms. All the same, she climbed up to the third floor and went out onto the roof garden to confirm that she was correct.

The huge, oil-fed torch was lit, billowing red-orange flame that could be seen across the entire city. Around it was a mosaic of tiny white and gold tiles. If there was an entrance, it was under the mosaic, and there was no way that Fay could dig it up without everyone knowing about it. Heaving a sigh, she sat on a bench surrounded by a purple clematis and stared at the torch. *So I tell Moth there's no way in.* Maybe, if she was lucky, he'd let it drop. There wasn't much more she could do. But she knew Moth. He was like a leech. Once he'd dug into something, he was almost impossible to prize off. And he had no tolerance for failure.

The knowledge pushed her to sit for a while longer, contemplating her problem. But no solution came to her, no idea of how to get into the mysterious room without calling for a destruction crew. So with heavy heart and heavier steps, she took herself off to bed for the few remaining hours of the night.

When she went to The Goat the next morning to relay her findings, or rather lack of them, Hook gave her a pitying look.

"*Don't* say anything," she muttered, feeling her exhaustion in every bone. "I did all I could."

"Come back this evening to see what the boss says," he replied.

She went off on her round of sick visits, plagued by worry over her failure, but also wondering what in Lumia's name the archpriests might be hiding behind a wall of nicoleum. The message from Moth when she returned to The Goat was entirely predictable.

"He says there is a way in and you're to keep trying," Hook said.

"He wouldn't happen to have mentioned *where* that way in is?" she asked irritably.

Hook shrugged.

"Has he given me more time at least?" she said, trying to stem a rising teariness. *I'm so bloody tired.*

"No. He says don't let him down, or he'll replace you with someone who's up to the job."

How real a threat was that? It had taken years to implant Fay fully in the temple. Four years as a novice, one and a half as a confirmed priest. Unless he already had someone else in the novitiate, waiting for her to mess up. Yes, Moth would do that. She was unlikely to be his first earwig in the temple. And if he pulled her out, her new job would hardly be a promotion. No, it would be the whorehouse. *I'm not going back to that. I'll die first.*

"I'll figure it out," she muttered. She left Hook and went straight to the bar. All she wanted to do was get drunk, forget the miserable world for a while. *Ilk take Moth. Why won't he give me a break?* She ordered an ale and knocked it back in one. It made her feel a bit better, so she ordered another and brought it to a dark corner, staring moodily out at The Goat's raucous denizens. *If there's a secret way in, the archpriests must know about it. But how would I get that information out of one?*

Nothing occurred to her, and for lack of anything better to do, she rolled out her plan of the temple on the battered table. She stared at the layout of the temple's three floors. *Please, tell me something. Show me a way.* Everything was so symmetrical, so perfectly laid out. Then her eyes fell on a room on the third floor. The Archpriests' Library! She almost jumped out of her seat with excitement. If there was an answer, surely it would be in there? It was totally out of bounds to the likes of her, which meant they must be hiding secrets in it. To celebrate her discovery, she ordered a third ale, and when that was finished, returned to the temple. But back in her room, her doubts and fears began to creep in again. What if she couldn't get into the library, what if someone saw her?

But there was nothing for it, and when midnight struck, she set off with her picks once more, anxiety gnawing at her belly. She encountered no one on her own floor, which was dimly lit with the odd torch. The third floor, however, was in almost total darkness, and she had to light her oil lamp to navigate its corridors. As she neared her destination, her tension rose, stiffening her shoulders and neck. If anyone were to stumble across her now, there would be questions asked, questions not easily answered.

But she reached the Archpriests' Library without incident and put her lamp to the lock, set directly into the heavy, ironbound door. She immediately realized it was beyond her lockpicking skills. She'd never seen one so complex, with spaces for narrow teeth jutting out in every direction. She gave it a go anyway, but even after a solid hour, she'd got no closer to figuring out the mechanism. She cursed and stamped her foot. *I doubt even Moth's best beetles could get this lock open. There must be some good stuff in there, though. Books I'd be able to sweeten Moth with, even if I can't get into that storage room.* She just needed to figure out how to get a key.

She returned to her room, mulling over the problem. The only solution she could think of was to steal a key from one of the archpriests. And that meant getting close enough to one to figure out where they kept their key. But who to choose and how to go about it? Fay was only a lowly priest, beneath the attention of archpriests. Then she remembered that in two days they were announcing the new candidates for High Luminate. All the archpriests would be there, even those who lived outside Arindel. And candidates for High Luminate needed priests to vote for them. Not just that, they needed allies, campaigners. People seeking power were always vulnerable, eager to be sold something. Fay smiled. *I'm not done for yet.*

Chapter 5

Fay

To serve Lumia well, all priests must be pure of heart, body, and mind. For this reason, a novice can only be accepted with a letter of recommendation from their local priest.

—The Lumin Priest's Handbook

The air in the worship room was more stifling than ever, with virtually every priest in Arindel, plus many from outside the city, wedged inside to learn which archpriests would put themselves forward for the Lumin order's highest position. They hadn't lit all the candles—there was simply no space—but even so, there was enough flickering flame to choke the air with smoke.

"Who do you think will go for it?" Maev said to Fay as they took their seats toward the back of the room.

"Everyone's saying that Lothar's a certain," Fay said. She glanced at her petite friend, who had started fanning herself with a sheaf of paper.

Maev's freckled nose wrinkled. "Do you think he's got a chance?"

"Depends on who he's up against, I suppose. He has a strong following with the older priests."

"I don't like him. There's something creepy about him."

Fay opened her mouth to agree, but then the great bell rang above, five long clangs, and the room silenced. The sound of the last strike was still resonating when the High Luminate, Erik Neilson, and the seven archpriests filed out from behind the screen.

They came to a halt in a row in front of the altar, the High Luminate at the center. The archpriests wore high-collared robes of white silk, trimmed with sinuous lines of gold thread. Gleaming orange opals clustered into the shape of a flame on their breasts.

"As you all know, we're gathered here today to announce the candidates for High Luminate," Neilson said. "There will be a period of three months during which the candidates will make their case for taking the hallowed chair." He continued, but Fay lost track of what he was saying, her attention instead going to the archpriests.

Her favorite was Nuria. Dark-haired and olive-skinned, Nuria was forty, one of the youngest archpriests ever, in her position a bare year and member of the Vycenian Consulate only a year longer. As always when she saw the archpriest, Fay's old crush reignited. It wasn't sexual—she didn't like women that way, didn't like anyone that way. But from the first day Fay had experienced Nuria's teachings, she'd felt an almost magnetic pull toward her. It had helped that Nuria's classes were all history—the history of the Lumin order, of Vycenia before, during, and after the Ruin, of the weaver mages and the great weaver families—how it had all shaped the republic they lived in today. The archpriest stood still, her face impassive, her hands clasped together in front of her, only a single golden ring adorning her long fingers. The ring of an archpriest, crowned with a dazzling fire opal.

Standing next to her was Archpriest Celeen, a rare convert from the Federation state of Tunia. She was stern-faced, with skin so deep and rich a black it shone. Stationed as she was in Rastia, northernmost province of the Federation, Fay barely knew her. Celeen was tall, but the woman beside her was even taller, with the slanting blue eyes and white-blonde hair typical of Northlanders. Fay guessed she was Aniya. She spent all her time in the provincial capital, Isgod, and it was the first time Fay had ever laid eyes on her. The last of the women was Marcie, with the wispy white hair and soft, rosy cheeks of a cheery grandma. But Fay knew not to be fooled by this appearance. Marcie was sharp, a skilled diplomat who now lived in Arindel after a long stint as ambassador to Yaro.

Then there were the men—Rogierro, Davvid, and Lothar. Rogierro, broad and hearty, olive-skinned like Nuria, was stationed in West Vycenia. Pale, slender Davvid lived in the southeast, near the Iron Mountains that divided Vycenia from Federation lands. Both were grey-haired, but while Rogierro always looked like he was about to break into a guffaw, Davvid was serious, almost morose.

And finally, there was Lothar, a man whose rolls of flesh strained against the silk of his robes and spilled over his jewel-studded belt, whose chin and neck were buried in hanging jowls that jiggled with every movement. Fay had had few dealings with him and even less desire to have any. She'd noticed how his gaze often lingered on the female priests when he thought they weren't looking, and sometimes even when they were.

"... candidates, please come to the fore."

Nuria and Lothar took two steps toward the front of the dais. Immediate murmurs broke out. Nuria was a surprise, no, a shock. No one had ever sought the position of High Luminate at such a young age, with such little experience behind her. *But she's already on the*

Consulate, political to the bone. Can High Luminates be consuls too, or would she have to give that up?

Both candidates were smiling, catching the eyes of those in the room, the maneuvering already begun. Nuria's charisma and beauty were magnified by her smile, and under its effect, it was hard not to feel that the Lady's warmth shone through her. Lothar's own smile was that of the benign father, promising comfort, certainty, and security. But Fay knew too many men like him and could see the scum beneath the shimmering surface.

"Wouldn't it be great if Nuria won?" Maev said excitedly.

The expressions of some of the younger priests showed that they shared her sentiment. But the older ones were regarding Nuria with skepticism if not outright disdain. Lothar's followers.

"I was sure Marcie would go for it," Maev continued. "I thought Nuria would wait—a decade at least."

"Marcie's getting old."

"Exactly. The High Luminates are rarely more than a breath away from their deathbeds."

Looking at Neilson, with his silver crop and watery eyes, Fay couldn't disagree. Lothar was certainly over sixty, which made it all the more striking to regard Nuria's smooth face and near-black hair.

So, one of those two. How susceptible would Nuria be to Fay's machinations? The thought of trying to manipulate her made Fay feel an unusual level of guilt—guilt and intimidation. No, she couldn't use Nuria. *It must be Lothar, then. And I already have something he wants.* She instinctively crossed her arms over her chest. *I only need one opportunity. It will be easy.*

It was customary for candidates for High Luminate to hold stumps in the main worship room the day after their announcement to declare their plans and policies. Fay, like many priests, planned to go to both, although she, of course, had her own motives.

Nuria spoke first, straight after morning prayers. The room was as packed as the day before. Most in attendance were young, under the age of forty, but there were plenty of conservative old-timers too, who regarded her with varying degrees of skepticism.

Nuria appeared on the dais to applause, waiting for it to die down before beaming down at the priests, her large, near-black eyes meeting those of her audience.

"I know that many of you will have been surprised to see me announce," she began. "It's true that I'm young—although when I was a novice, forty would have seemed impossibly old."

Chuckles at that, especially from the older priests.

"But Caris the Restorer hadn't even reached her thirtieth year when Lumia descended and spoke to her. The outcome of that meeting was change—a new order of faith that would restore light and life to the world after its destruction by magic. The Lumin order. *Our* order."

A bold move to liken herself to the founder of the order, but no one seemed to have taken affront. Indeed, from what Fay could tell, Nuria's little rhetorical trick had worked nicely, certainly among the most youthful. They were all nodding, some of them smiling, eyes lit.

"Isn't she wonderful?" Maev said. "I bet you she could have been another Caris if she'd been born then."

Fay was about to murmur her agreement, but Nuria began to speak again.

"For two hundred years, we've shone the Lady's light into the darkest parts of our republic and beyond," the archpriest said. "Recently, though, we've stagnated. Crime is rife, especially in the slums. We have many believers among the poor, but it weakens in the most desperate, who need more than prayers and a bowl of watery soup." Nuria paused for effect, her expression all solicitude and concern, and it was mirrored around the room. But when she spoke again, her voice rose and her eyes shone with passion. "This must change. It is time we became a beacon once more, a light that shines the path to a better, more prosperous future for *all* people."

Many approving nods to that. *Does she really care or is it just politics?* Fay sensed that Nuria was being sincere. *Or am I letting myself be taken in?* It would be nice to think that someone did actually want to do something, but Fay was used to empty promises.

"We need change—a new direction and new allies," Nuria continued, her tone and expression growing even more fervent. "Together, we can create that change. I already sit on the Consulate of Eleven, and I have worked with the other consuls to spread Lumia's influence, not just in Arindel but in *all* of Vycenia. The consuls have just passed a law ordering that all children receive instruction in Lumia's teachings, even if their parents hold a different religion. That was due to my influence.

"If you elect me High Luminate, I can use my connections to expand the number of schools we have and bring literacy to everyone—to the slum dwellers, to the shepherds and the miners, even to the prisoners. With literacy will come faith and morality, a deeper appreciation of Lumia's teachings and laws, but most of all, opportunity, an alternative to violence and crime."

Is she really that naive? Literacy certainly wasn't going to stop Moth running his rackets. The man was more literate than all the archpriests put together if his interest in books was anything to go by. A scan of the faces in the crowd confirmed that Fay wasn't alone in these thoughts. But others seemed inspired, excited even, at the picture Nuria painted.

"I'd love to teach," Maev declared. "It would be wonderful if they opened more schools, especially in New Arindel."

"You could apply now," Fay said.

Maev's expression soured. "I did, but they said they don't need anyone, not in Arindel, and I don't want to leave the city."

Nuria was speaking again, and they fell silent to listen to her. "I will also expand the House of Succor in Arindel and build new places of healing in all our cities and towns so that everyone can avail themselves of medicines and counsel when they need it," she said. "We must bring not only Lumia's light but also her care."

It was all very noble, but where would the money come from? And indeed, when Nuria opened to questions, money was at the forefront of most minds.

She had her counterarguments, though. "The weaver families are wealthy far beyond their needs and can contribute to the cost."

"They're weavers! They care only about their own!"

Nuria smiled patiently. "*Some* of their members are weavers, but only a minority, and of course, none of the consuls."

Weavers couldn't be consuls, weren't allowed to have any direct political power at all since the Ruin. But weaver blood ran strong in all the families. That was why they were so wealthy in the first place, and everyone knew it. As Fay expected, a number of objectors pointed the fact out.

"I hear your concerns," Nuria said, remaining calm. "And I don't claim that it will be easy to persuade the families or the consuls to back my plans. But it *is* possible. All we need is a simple majority, either on the Consulate or in the House of Delegates, and I know many members of both.

"If we can gain control of the education system of this country, we'll raise the entire population in Lumia's light. Think of the future influence it will bring to us, when all those little children grow up, thankful and recognizant of what Lumia has done for them."

That one worked a charm. Even those Fay expected to fall in with Lothar seemed to agree.

After the questions were over, many people lined up to speak to Nuria and pledge their support. Maev joined the line, but Fay wasn't ready to declare yet, not until she'd spoken to Lothar. "I can't hang around. I need to meet someone," she said to her friend. "But let me know how it goes."

There were just as many people present at Lothar's stump that afternoon, but the age profiles were reversed. Fay needed to make herself noticed by him, so she arrived early and sat up the front. Maev didn't join her, saying she had no interest in listening to what he had to say. Fay didn't encourage her. It made her task easier.

Lothar waddled in exactly on time, bald head shining, moist lips parted in a benevolent smile. As soon as he started talking, she knew he had prepared to counter many of Nuria's claims. But it was clear also that he knew what his followers wanted, and he gave it to them.

"We must stamp out immorality. As this city grows, so does its degeneracy. The so-called Rainbow Quarter is a pit of debauchery. One needs only pass through there once to see the depths to which it has sunk. Whorehouses multiply, drug dens abound, and buggery rules."

Banning whoring, I could get behind that. But then what would the whores do?

Lothar's voice rose a notch, gathering intensity. "And let's not even speak of New Arindel, where every vice and crime is multiplied tenfold. The only realistic and workable solution is to clear the slum. The degenerates who live there can be put to work in camps or on sailing ships, or recruited into the army."

Fay stifled a snort. There were tens of thousands living in the slum. There weren't enough sailing ships to hold them, even if they were all rammed in like stuffing in a carcass. And she doubted the Consulate wanted to expensively swell the ranks of the army when Vycenia wasn't at war. Still, many around her murmured and nodded in response to his words.

"Those who have come from outside must be sent back to where they came from," Lothar continued, his tone hardening. "We simply cannot hold more outsiders, and paganism is rife among the Tarsan refugees, many of whom now preach about the Zenian war god Farax. He has gained a grip in Tarsis—and who is surprised by that?"

Farax—the name wasn't familiar to her. But then she knew little of the Federation and even less of the Zenians who ruled it.

Lothar modulated back to warmth and concern. "At the same time, there are Tarsan nobles who are sympathetic to our religion and who would listen to us if we were to grant them military aid. If I were made High Luminate, I would urge our glorious republic to intervene and bring Lumia's light and peace to the Tarsans. Only then can we stop the scourge of war and stem the influx of foreigners."

A clearly popular idea that had nearly everyone bobbing their heads. The Tarsan civil war had been going on for ten years. Vycenia had always refused to intervene despite being requested to by one or other of the nobles vying to take control of the kingdom. Fay suspected that the Consulate preferred the war to continue. It ensured that Vycenian arms flowed out steadily and that Tarsan gems poured in cheaply. But could Lothar really convince the Consuls to do something?

"And finally, we must make our friends among the great merchants of our realm, who seek to break the power of the weaver families. We must fight to further restrict their power and ensure that it resides where it belongs—among those who love Lumia and her blessed parents."

That really was playing to the crowd, and sporadic clapping and cheering broke out. But Lothar didn't proceed with any concrete suggestions on how he was going to attain this lofty aim.

Many of the questions afterward focused on how the slum would be cleared, with several Nuria supporters arguing that Lothar's plans were impracticable and inhumane. But Lothar repeated that the slum-dwellers would be gainfully employed, kept too busy to indulge in crime and degeneracy—and that was certainly enough to satisfy his own followers. For her part, Fay doubted the consulate would intervene, whether it was to implement either Nuria or Lothar's plans. Its members had never shown much interest in New Arindel, seemingly content to let it sprout like a cankerous boil on the edges of the city. And no one from New Arindel was eligible to vote in delegate elections, which meant the House had no stake either.

When the questions were finished, people lined up to speak to Lothar as they had to Nuria. His numbers were slightly higher, but Fay reckoned it was because he had spoken second, and more had now made up their minds. To avoid being seen openly speaking to him, she waited until everyone else was done and followed him as he was leaving.

"Your Radiance," she called as he reached the door.

He turned back, frowning quizzically.

"I'd like to support you to become High Luminate," she said. She put on her best smile, a professional, well-practiced, and oft-used smile, precisely calculated for the fooling of men. "I spend a lot of time in the Rainbow Quarter and the slums, and I agree that something drastic needs to be done. Your ideas sound far more workable than those of Archpriest Nuria."

His return smile was all fatherly benevolence but, she was sure, equally practiced. "What's your name, daughter?"

"Fay." She fluttered her lashes, pushed her chest out ever so slightly.

A very unfatherly hunger lit in his pale blue eyes. "Well, as I mentioned, I'll be organizing a campaign meeting next Lumiasday. I hope you'll come?"

"Well, I've been thinking—wouldn't it be useful for you to have someone in Archpriest Nuria's camp? Officially, I could back her. It won't look suspicious as many of the younger priests are behind her. I can get close to her, let you know what she's planning—and, I already have some information that you might find useful for your campaign." She didn't, not really, but she'd find something.

"Is that so?" he said, a different hunger now igniting in his eyes.

"Perhaps we could meet somewhere private?" she said, shooting him another of her special smiles, one that promised everything and nothing.

Speculation, a hint of greed. "Come to my chambers tomorrow," he said. "At one after midnight. I often work late."

Fay smiled again. "I'll be there, Your Radiance."

Afterward, she wasn't sure whether to be frightened or relieved. There was something about Lothar that left her deeply uneasy. Something rotten. But she only needed to visit him once, just long enough to drug him and then steal his key. Then, she could quietly shift her support away, back to Nuria, and that would be the end of it.

Chapter 6

Alexios

I know precious little about the Keeper's traditional role. No Keeper trained me, as would have been normal before the Ruin. All I know, I learned from Epiktet and Cassander, the one a bricklayer, the other a diplomat. It's laughable. But I will note all my thoughts and discoveries in these pages in case something befalls me before I am able to train a successor.

—The Keeper's Role, Alexios Arathraxis

Alexios's heart lurched as the four men bore his aged daughter toward him. She lay quietly on the litter, her face alone visible above the soft grey blankets, the skin deeply rucked and wrinkled, the white hair arranged in a corona around her head. The two rulers walked behind, halting midway while the litter-bearers continued their solemn approach.

Next to him, his daughter Demeia coughed, the sound swiftly choked. Alexios spared her a glance. Only twenty-two, taking part in her first binding, perfectly composed until now. She pushed back a wisp of fair hair that had escaped the knot at the back of her head, caught him looking at her and shifted from foot to foot.

He didn't acknowledge her, instead eyeing the small, square room. As always, he was caught between two scenes: the real one, which only he and Demeia could perceive, of a simple chamber built from red brick, and the illusory one, with walls of white marble, a floor mosaic of a golden spinning wheel, and a dome-shaped roof like a morning sky. An illusion he had designed himself, inspired by descriptions of the Keeper's Sanctum in Eios, capital of drowned Eleusia.

The litter-bearers stopped at the bier in front of him. It too was made of common red brick, but they saw the traditional, red-veined marble. As the men carefully lowered the litter onto the bier, his daughter's eyes flickered open. Brilliant sapphire blue, flecked with silver like his, startlingly youthful in contrast to her shriveled frame. Unbidden came a memory of her birth ninety years earlier, and of her mother, Dione, long gone. Dione, beautiful, wildly intelligent, like their daughter. And now he was to see their child pass on, like all the rest.

Gripped by deep weariness, he rose from his throne—golden to them, a wooden chair to him. His robes of purple velvet were real and fell heavily around him, the cuffs and hem weighted with precious stones—diamonds, rubies, onyx—for true sight, for life and death. He approached his daughter. "Dear daughter. Eliana ..." Words failed him. *Again, again, again.*

"Father," Eliana whispered, her voice as papery as her skin. "My time ..."

Alexios swallowed back sudden revulsion. *I don't want to do this.* He looked at the pair of illusory statues flanking the bier—male and female, in whitest marble, silver thread strung between their hands.

The Makers, their command. He closed his eyes briefly, gathering his strength.

Meanwhile, the litter bearers positioned themselves in a line along the bier, facing him. Men of middle years with greying hair, none of whom had attended a binding before. Looking at him with frightened awe. An honor for them to have been chosen, but to Alexios it was a curse. They would never unsee this.

He fell into the ritual words, raising his hands toward the statues on either side of him as he spoke. "As is ordained, we are gathered here under the watch of the Makers to preserve the sacred chain of memory." He stretched his arms out toward his daughter, seeing her again as a bouncing child bubbling with laughter. "Magos Eliana Arathraxis, here before us, has agreed to be forged as a link of her own free will and volition. May she one day rest in peace with the Makers above."

Everyone joined him for the next part, even Eliana, although her words were too faint to hear. "For all that is past must be remembered, all that is given must be repaid, and all that is broken must be remade."

When they'd finished speaking, the litter bearers divided into two pairs, walking around each side of the bier to stand next to his throne. Alexios stepped closer to Eliana, close enough to touch. Loneliness welled in him as he spoke to her, his voice soft and tender. "Are you ready to bear this burden with me?" The souls he carried began to stir, making him feel their desire for release, though they tried to hide it.

Eliana's shrunken lips tugged into a faint smile as she uttered the expected response. "I am ready to join my soul with yours."

Alexios nodded, swallowing to hold back tears. He enveloped her two hands in his own. Dry and hot. Then he opened his mind to the Makers' Lace, to the intricate pattern of shimmering threads that bound all creation together. He found the threads that connected him to Eliana and her to the Lace, threads only a Keeper could see. Then he nodded to Demeia. Blue eyes solemn, she stepped around the bier until she was standing opposite him. In her hand was a small bottle of red-brown liquid which she now unstoppered. She held it out to Eliana and the elderly woman parted her lips obediently. Three drops of liquid fell onto her tongue. Demeia re-stoppered the bottle but stayed where she was.

After that, he neither moved nor spoke, all his attention on the Lace. Soon, the threads connecting Eliana to it began to thrum ever so slightly, then with increasing intensity until they started to detach. Her soul was casting free its earthly chains to leave the world.

But Alexios would not let it go. Instead, he swooped in to gather the threads and spin them toward him, knitting them to his own pattern, weaving them in with the threads of the others who had joined him over two centuries. This was the most difficult part, and in earlier days he'd sometimes fail—he'd miss a crucial thread, not make the binding quickly enough. But he was practiced now, and none escaped him. As he finished, her soul joined his, and with it the vibrant force that had sustained her life.

The shock of the binding was brutal, slamming into him with such power that he roared. He was barely aware as hands grabbed him, pushed him into the throne, wrapped rope around his torso and legs, pinning him down. His bones seemed to expand, to swell beyond the confines of his flesh. He hurled himself against the bonds, unable to bear the dreadful pressure. His ears whined, ready to burst. His head snapped back, landed against a hastily placed cushion. The breath heaved out of him and then back in. A rod was shoved between his teeth, and he clamped down hard, pain shooting through his jaw.

A life of memory and experience seared his mind, too quick to grasp. He wept and cried and begged to be freed.

No one answered.

Time stretched on, each second an hour, a lifetime to be endured. He continued to struggle, to plead for release, the souls pleading with him. But eventually, the pain started to lose its force, to come in gentler waves, until at last it died entirely.

In its place came heady joy, sweeping through him to repair his ancient body, to restore him to false vigor and youth. His teeth ground into the rod, the euphoria agonizing in its own way.

After that came the vision. His consciousness trembled and then shook itself free from his body, rose up and away. He flew through the Lace, across space and time, borne by the hands of the Makers, until he came to a vast rift in the land guarded by mountains of belching fire. Spinning down into the earth he went, down through a warren of warm tunnels and into a yawning cavern. It contained a giant pit, dug into the very rock, filled with rows of corpses. But the corpses were not those of ordinary creatures, nor of anything that walked the earth. It was like someone had chopped the heads from animals and attached them to human forms. Their flesh was scaly and grey, neither dead nor alive.

Much more shocking was the jagged tear in the Lace above the pit, primordial power seeping through into the blazing body of a young man standing at the pit edge. From him the force streamed into the corpses, feeding them with unnatural life.

Alexios stared at the things, wondering if they were what he thought them to be. Then he looked at the man, wondering if he too was whom he thought him to be. But he was little more than a boy—handsome, with copper skin, golden eyes, and black hair that fell to his shoulders, fine and straight. His face was a rictus of pain, as if the magic he wielded were torturous to him.

And so it should be, for what he did was terribly, terribly wrong.

Abruptly, the tear in the Lace knitted itself, and the power ebbed from the youth, his posture and expression losing their rigid tension. He turned toward Alexios, and their eyes met. A mocking smile.

A jolt to his senses, trying to call him back. No! He had to see what was happening here. "Who are you?" he demanded.

He was being pulled. He resisted. He had to know. Past, present, or future?

A wrenching force, dragging him away. No, no! He stretched out, tried to get closer to the pit, but he was speeding backward, back to his flesh.

His eyes opened to the Sanctum, to the two rulers watching him, the flaring of their eyes their only sign of discomfort at seeing him so undone. He blinked. The vision, what was it he had seen? The creatures in the pits. He could think of only one name—Ilk. But the Ilk were gone, long gone, the man who had spawned them defeated, killed, two hundred years ago. The past, surely the vision had been of the past? He blinked again, tried to speak, but his jaw was locked.

The litter-bearers, seeing that he was awake, moved into action. One prized his mouth open and removed the rod from between his teeth, while another sawed off the ropes that bound him to his throne. Then they arranged themselves in pairs on either side of the bier, looking at him with nervous expectation.

Now it was time for the proof. Demeia came to him, bearing a slender dagger on a red cushion. The steel was keen but the hilt plain, wrapped with old leather. In the past, the dagger would have been ornate, crusted with jewels, but this was all they'd had to hand when Alexios performed his first soulbinding. And then the tradition was established, and Alexios would hear no talk of procuring another.

Still unsteady, he rolled up the sleeve of his left arm. Demeia gave him the dagger and stepped aside. Then, holding his forearm out for the witnesses to see, he slashed it along the length, ensuring it bit deep. Pain washed over him, and he welcomed it, feeling it ground him. A red line bloomed in the wake of the dagger's path, but it had barely finished its journey before the skin was knitting itself back together, hiding all traces of the injury. In seconds, the healing was complete.

Demeia took the dagger from him and cleaned it with a red cloth before replacing it on the cushion and setting it aside on a low table.

"It is done," Alexios said, still reeling from the after-effects of the binding. "The chain of memory is preserved."

"Praise and glory to the Makers," intoned the litter bearers and witnesses.

Then the former turned to face him and bowed with hands crossed over chest before picking up the litter and carrying Eliana out. She would be cremated on the morrow. Alexios watched them leave, taking deep breaths to stem the energy still rushing through his body, trying to master his sorrow at the loss of yet another of his children. *She's not entirely gone,* he told himself. *Not like most of them.* He reached out to her. "*Eliana?*"

"I'm here, father."

The other souls welcomed her with joy, although to him it felt muted, forced. Who could be happy to endure for so long in this world when the Makers offered so much in the next? Guiltily, he shook the thought away. *We do what we must.*

The litter-bearers were passing through the door that would bring them out of the building, he realized. He placed two hands on the armrests of his throne and pushed himself to his feet.

Seeing him move, the rulers—Theophila and Castes—walked to a lectern to his left, grey heads bowed, hands clasped in front of them, wine-colored ceremonial robes swishing about their feet. Alexios drew in another great lungful of air, then nodded at Demeia, whose shock showed itself in the rapid blinking of her eyes. She returned his nod coolly, and pride swelled in him. So calm and strong, worthy to replace him, although he was determined she'd never have to. He walked on trembling legs toward the lectern, and she followed.

Waiting on it was a large leatherbound book, next to the book fresh ink and a quill. Theophila picked up the quill and dipped it in the inkwell while Castes opened the book. The first quarter was already filled with entries, all written in a different hand. Castes continued to flick through them until he reached an empty page, and then stepped aside to allow Theophila to write.

Alexios began to describe the vision, while Theophila recorded his words in the book. She paused when he recounted what he had seen in the cavern, her shocked expression mirrored by the others.

"You're certain you have no way of telling when this took place?" she said.

"I never do," Alexios replied. "Not unless I already know the event has happened."

"It must be the past," Theophila said. "The Ilk Lord is long gone, the way of making Ilk gone with him." But there was doubt in her eyes, and she looked to Alexios as if seeking confirmation.

"We destroyed him," Epiktet's soul whispered.

"Lost everyone to do it," murmured Cassander.

"Perhaps it wasn't Ilk you saw," Castes said, "but some other monstrous creation?"

"I'm quite sure it was Ilk," Alexios said. Why were the visions always so unclear? Why couldn't they show a path of action?

"Even if it is a warning, what can we do?" Theophila asked. "It's not going to change anything, is it?"

Alexios nodded. "The illusions will keep us safe."

"This blind confidence will be our ruin someday," Castes said, flushing. "The Makers have granted us this vision for a reason."

"I agree with the honored ruler," Demeia said, sounding unusually meek. "We shouldn't just ignore it."

A looming dark shape. Rotting stink. Teeth long and jagged, and red, red eyes. He curled his fingers inwards. The souls cried out in fear.

"Keeper, are you well?" Castes said.

Alexios blinked away the memory. His own or one of the souls'?

"Let's discuss the implications of the vision later," Theophila said. "The citizens are waiting."

Castes opened his mouth, then shut it again, jaw bulging. He gave a short, sharp nod. "Very well, we'll take it up at the next council meeting."

Demeia also looked dissatisfied but said nothing more. For all her talent and resolve, she had no rank here, and had the sense to know it.

So Alexios finished his account, and they all signed their names to it. This done, Theophila closed the book, and Alexios took it back into the vestry behind the throne, along with the dagger.

Other than the oak wardrobe in which he hung his clothes, the vestry contained a chair and a small iron safe, one of the few metal objects they had in their town. He stowed the book in the safe but paused in the action of replacing the dagger. *If I stabbed myself in the heart, would I die? Or would Eliana's soul seal the wound too quickly?* From his tests, he knew that the fast healing lasted for several months after the soulbinding, becoming slower and slower until it returned to normal. But he'd never tested it on a wound more severe than the one he'd inflicted on his arm. *It probably wouldn't work. I'm not allowed to die.* An overpowering desire to scream seized him. Suddenly, he was reversing his grip on the dagger, pointing the blade at his chest. His knuckles turned white, and his arms shook, caught between the desire to end it all and the obligation to keep going. The familiar hollowness expanded inside him, eating away until he felt as unreal as one of his illusions. He was so lonely, so very, very lonely.

"You are not alone, son," Epiktet said gently.

No, and perhaps that was the worst. There was no escaping the souls, except for brief periods when he could push them out of his consciousness. He might never be alone, but the older he got, the more distant he felt from everyone around him. It might have been easier if he had other Keepers to talk to, as he would have had in the past. But he was the only Keeper in Neopoli, and the other Keepers, children of his, were in distant enclaves.

He stared at the gleaming blade, imagined how it would feel if it were to penetrate his heart. But there would be no place for him at the Makers' table if he abandoned his duty. Tears welled in his eyes as he slowly lowered the dagger and placed it on top of the book. He slumped onto the chair, suddenly unable to stand.

"You have the strength to carry this burden," Cassander said, stiff as always when it came to emotion.

"Leave me, all of you, a few moments," Alexios said.

"Alexios—" Epiktet began.

"Leave!"

The souls obeyed, retreating so that he was barely aware of their existence. He sighed, then stood and locked the safe. His robes had never felt heavier, and he was too hot, but he couldn't remove them yet. There was another ceremony to preside over. *Why must we have these sacred dramas directly after a soulbinding? I need to rest, to be alone.* But tradition was a powerful dictator.

Still on loose legs, he returned to the Sanctum, where Demeia and the rulers were waiting for him. Together, they exited into a passageway that linked the Sanctum with the outside world and the Temple of the Makers.

"I look forward to seeing this new interpretation of the Fall of Mataios," Theophila said.

"We trust you won't be disappointed," Alexios replied. He glanced at Demeia, saw her try to hide nervousness behind a cool demeanor. It was she who had led the reworking of the drama. She was skilled, and he'd wanted to give her the opportunity to do one of the important tales. But she knew as well as he that people didn't always take kindly to change, particularly when it came to a drama as old as this one.

"No doubt you will be regaled as you always are," Castes said.

There was a bite to the words, and Alexios knew he meant something deeper. It triggered his dislike of the man. He was always sniping, never content with how things were.

"Makers be with you," Castes added with a thin smile, and Theophila echoed him, but more warmly.

Then the rulers turned left, toward a door that opened into the worship room. Alexios and Demeia, however, took stairs that led them up to the small gallery overlooking the hall. Already there was Nixos, whose job it was to maintain the background illusions for each scene.

"Did all go well?" Nixos asked them.

"Things went as they always do," Alexios said, thinking again of the vision. The past, it must have been the past.

"Don't be so sure of that," Cassander said.

"I agree with Cassander," Epiktet said. *"We need to consider this more."*

"It's just a warning," Doris said dismissively. *"A reminder from the Makers of what can go wrong if we let the world find us."*

That brought immediate objections, but Alexios had no time to indulge the souls and went to the small window in the screen that hid the gallery from the worship room. Directly below him was the dais on which he conducted the holy ceremonies, now transformed into a palace throne room through Nixos's work. The rows of benches that stretched out beyond it, along with those in the surrounding galleries, were packed full. Half of the town was in attendance, and the other half would see the drama the next day, as tradition decreed.

"You haven't had any problems?" he asked Nixos, turning away from the window.

"Will you ever have faith in me, father?" Nixos said, with a small smile to show he was joking.

But Nixos wasn't far off the mark. Alexios had produced the dramas alone for half a century until he'd allowed his children and grandchildren to join in. He still wrote them and performed the songs, but his instinct was to be here, making sure everything ran smoothly.

"I'm ready," Nixos added, more serious. "I can start when you are." He wiped a handkerchief across his forehead, which was beaded with sweat, causing his dark curls to stick to it.

"In that case, we'll go down," Alexios said. "May the Makers be with you."

"Good luck, brother," Demeia added.

"Try not to forget your lines," Nixos said to her, teasing.

She reddened but made no retort. Alexios shot Nixos a warning look. He liked to joke about Demeia's failure during her first sung performance, when she was only twelve, and knew she hated the reminder. Why was it that no matter how old they were, siblings never grew out of their childish rivalries?

"I believe in you," Nixos added with a wink.

Demeia rolled her eyes and then turned to Alexios. "Shall we go?"

He motioned for her to walk ahead of him, and they descended into the hall. The air was thick with incense and the breath of a thousand lungs, and Alexios felt suffocated in his robes. There was a low hum of voices, people at the front elbowing each other in excitement when they caught sight of him. The dais was ahead of him and to his right, but he and Demeia slipped behind the screen that had been erected at the back of it to hide the waiting performers.

Most were huddled in small groups, talking too fast and laughing too loudly. A couple of singers sat on their own, eyes closed, lips moving. Alexios went to each group and person in turn to check they were ready and give them his blessing.

When he was done, he left Demeia and stepped out onto the dais to address the crowd. As soon as they saw him, a hush descended. Alexios waited until he was sure that every eye was on him. Then he spoke, his voice steady and strong. "We are gathered today, on this sacred Day of Memory, to commemorate our great past. The chain of memory has been preserved, and our beloved Eliana Arathraxis now bears the burden with me."

A stamping of feet, six times, to acknowledge and celebrate this fact.

Alexios waited until the sound began to die, then raised his hands to ask for their attention. Into the rustling quiet that followed, he proclaimed, "This year, we present to you a retelling of the Fall of Mataios, a cautionary tale."

King Mataios, Eleusia's last king, who had thought to become immortal, to be as one of the gods themselves. King Mataios, who believed his voice more golden than that of the gods, his hand more sure, his wisdom more certain. King Mataios, who in his vanity and pride had pitched brother against father and mother against daughter, reaping nothing but terror and death. A worthy story for the sacred day.

Alexios returned backstage, where the musicians—a flutist, a drummer, and a trumpeter—had taken up their instruments for the opening song. Demeia handed him his lyre and then lifted her tambourine. At Alexios's signal, they went to the dais, where they were greeted with stamping feet.

The musicians sat on stools, Alexios to the very right. He began the song, a new one, strumming the opening chords on his lyre, using the threads of the Lace to ensure the sounds carried across the crowd, amplifying the notes to make them fuller and more beautiful. Then he added his voice.

Oh, hark ye children of Eleus
Heed this mournful tale
That tells of proud king Mataios
Who was doomed to fail

As always when he sang, Alexios found himself transported, carried to another plane, one holier and more sacred. He gave himself wholly to the song, no longer conscious of himself or of the people around him, forgetting the pain that had almost driven a dagger into his heart. Music was the language of the gods, his privilege to speak, and he reveled in its glory.

When the song ended, he returned to himself, scanned the audience to see what they thought of the new rendition. They mostly seemed pleased, stamping their feet enthusiastically, although a few were whispering with discontented expressions. But that was inevitable.

The musicians left the stage and were replaced by the actors playing King Mataios and his advisor Senes. Mataios proclaimed his intention to ask the Keeper of Eios to share the secrets of the soulbindings with him, that he might live a long life and rule for two thousand years. But when summoned, the Keeper denied him his presumptuous request and Mataios decided to climb Mount Deimos to make his demand of the Makers themselves. His words fell on deaf ears, and so he cursed the gods and returned to Eios. There, he began to gather up an army of those loyal to him, who hoped also to receive long life. Once his army numbered ten times a thousand, he made the same request of all the Keepers of Eleusia: grant us our desire or be slaughtered.

Of course, the Keepers were not easily cowed, and the third act portrayed the civil war, which ended with the defeat of Mataios and his horde.

The war was reported rather than shown, as was traditional. But as Alexios listened to Demeia's reworked recitation of the last great battle, he remembered how she'd argued in favor of a more direct portrayal. "We shouldn't shy away from depicting the violence," she'd said. "It's better for people to see for themselves the cost of war."

"That can never be truly represented," Alexios said, who'd lived through the Ilk War, who'd lost everything to it. "Be glad you've never known it."

"War is horror and pain," Epiktet agreed. *"Death and blood and fear."*

Nixos had backed him. "Father's right. We don't need to represent something so abhorrent. And violence just excites base emotions. It isn't art."

Demeia's response was a glare. "*Must* you agree with *everything* he says?" Ever fiery, like her mother, Melissa.

The play wrapped up with one final song, this also new and led by Alexios.

Ne'er again shall reign
Kings, proud and vain
Nor queens who by their birth might claim

A right to earthly rule
Instead, one woman, one man shall be
Chosen by the citizenry,
To hold sway for ten full years
Aided by an assembly
Under the watch of the Makers above
And of the Keepers, in their great love
These glad tidings we now sing of
And peace forever more

After, the audience clapped and stamped their feet, and the actors and musicians filled the dais to accept the applause. When the noise began to die, they left the stage, and the people rose and began to file out, murmuring in low voices. Exhaustion hit Alexios like a stone, spiritual rather than physical. The soulbindings always left him thus. His tenth now, and it never got easier.

But the evening was far from done, and he squashed the feeling, thanking the performers for their work before sending them to the feast outside in the square. Demeia, he called to him. "Later, we'll discuss the soulbinding. I hope you didn't find it too trying."

"It wasn't me who did the binding," she said. "I should be asking *you* that question."

She sounded cool, almost flippant, but he could tell from the flicker in her eyes that it had discomfited her. "I'm well used to it," was all he said, smiling to hide his despondency.

Demeia cocked her head and narrowed her eyes, weighing him.

"Congratulations on not messing up, sister!" Nixos's voice, carrying from the opposite end of the dais. He came to them with long, energetic strides.

"Would you ever just let that go!" Demeia snapped.

Nixos raised his hands. "Fine, fine. I suppose I should tell you instead that you sang so beautifully the Makers themselves wept to hear it."

"It's such a shame your voice will only ever cause the Makers to weep in pain," she retorted.

He smiled. "But my artistry brings joy, does it not?"

"You did very well, both of you," Alexios said. "The gods will be pleased."

The rulers, who'd hung back to talk to some members of the Congress, now approached them.

"Wonderful," Theophila said. "I particularly liked the final song. A work of genius."

"That was Demeia," Alexios said with pride.

Demeia inclined her head, acknowledging the compliment.

"Indeed, I was rather surprised by the change," Castes said. "You have always been so wedded to tradition."

It was a dig, and a poorly disguised one, but Alexios swallowed his annoyance and smiled. "It's good to surprise now and again."

"Indeed, and surprises make me hungry. Shall we join the feast?" Castes said.

"It's beer that I most want," Nixos said. "It's been thirsty work." As if to emphasize the point, he dabbed once more at his forehead with his handkerchief.

"Let me take these robes off first," Alexios said. "I'll follow."

As he went to the Sanctum, though, his thoughts returned to the vision. Who was it he had seen? The Ilk Lord in the past, growing his horrific creations, or someone making them anew today? But Neopoli was safe, hidden from the outside world by his illusions. No one could find them, no one had done so in two hundred years. Even so, he couldn't shake off his unease. The Makers had shown him the vision for a purpose, and he knew not what.

Chapter 7

Alexios

Fifty years after Neopoli was founded, we outgrew our ability to sustain our population without expanding farther into the woods. This would have made it difficult for me to hide the town from outsiders with my illusions. So we sent my son Cereus to found an enclave in the high mountains of Northland. I had already trained him as Keeper, but it was a blow to let him go. I lose so many. My one comfort is that he hasn't left this world but is merely absent.

—Eleusia After the Ruin, Alexios Arathraxis

Alexios stepped onto the raised plaza outside the temple and into a roar of song and celebration. As always on the sacred day, dense crowds thronged the square below him, spilling out into the surrounding streets. On the eastern side sat tables laden with food and drink, and the musicians were playing drinking songs on the temporary stage erected in the center.

He went to the long table that segmented the plaza in front of him. Already there were Nixos, Demeia, and the rulers, along with High Illusionist Hereia, High Artefactor Oxil, and the master of the guard, Periklis. Plates of chicken, fish, venison, and pheasant were spread out before them, along with a dozen varieties of fruit and vegetables—dried, fresh, and cooked. Alexios took his place at the center, Theophila and Castes flanking him.

He looked across the square to the matching table set up outside the Hall of Congress, at which sat the twenty-three illusionists and artefactors. His dark-haired granddaughter Thais caught his eye and waved across at him. He forced his mouth into a return smile, the muscles of his cheeks still stiff and aching—all his muscles aching.

"Beer, Keeper?" said a serving man.

"Please."

"I miss wine," Epiktet said. *"We Eleusians are not beer drinkers."*

"An Eiosian red," Cassander said. *"There is surely no finer in all the world."*

"I've never had the luxury," Epiktet replied pointedly. Unlike Cassander, he was of common descent and liked to remind him of it.

Alexios had tasted wine once, several decades ago, on a trip to a Vycenian village. He'd liked it well enough, even brought some back to Neopoli. But they didn't trade regularly with the Vycenians. There was too much danger of discovery.

"Need to preserve our ways," Cassander said, and the other souls agreed, save Lycurgus, as always.

Alexios put some roast pheasant and vegetables onto his plate, but picked at the food with little appetite, his eyes roving the square. If he switched off his magesight, it was almost possible to imagine they were in Eios or one of Eleusia's other great cities. All the surrounding buildings were cloaked in illusions of white, red, or green marble, maintained by Nixos, Demeia, and Alexios's grandson, Miro. Graceful columns supporting square arches, glittering, multi-colored mosaics, domes of gleaming copper and gold.

"Eios was the most beautiful city in the world," Cassander said wistfully.

Alexios's own memory of Eleusia's capital was fuzzy. But Epiktet and Cassander were able to grant him clear visions, which he had used to design the illusions in the first place. In the early days, they had tried to put the whole of Neopoli under illusion. But as it had grown from village to town, this plan had been abandoned. It was too much work and made repairs tricky. So instead, people could come here, to the inner ring, to pretend they were still in their homeland and contemplate the greatness of their lost civilization.

As Alexios ate, he watched. A man with his arm around another, swaying drunkenly. Two young women sharing a lover's kiss. Children chasing one another in a side street, followed by a barking dog. A husband and wife cooing over a baby. All gay and carefree, enjoying the special day. *And it's up to me to ensure things stay this way. We've made life work for us here. Our ways have been preserved, our blood kept undiluted. No enemies can find us, no outsiders can see us.* But the memory of the vision niggled at him.

As he finished the food on his plate, the musicians started to play dancing music, and people formed in two lines before the stage.

"Father, will you dance with me?" called Demeia.

"The next one," he said. He didn't feel much like dancing, but it was expected of him. Dance was a sacred celebration, a way of worshipping the gods, just like the music he played and the dramas he wrought.

"You taught me to dance, father, remember?" said Doris.

"He taught us all," said Eliana. The voice of her soul was faint. It was still adapting to its new state.

"I taught you all, but you were all better than me," he said, smiling despite himself at the memories.

"Nonsense, and you know it!" cried Eliana. *"We got our skill from you."*

"It's well accepted that women are far more graceful than men," he said.

"We won't argue with that. Achaikos had two left feet for sure," Doris said, giggling girlishly.

Achaikos stirred but said nothing. Doris's brother, he was usually quiet, a restful soul both in life and in death.

Demeia rose to her feet and called him to join her. He nodded in acquiescence, and together they descended into the square. People saw them coming and opened a passageway for them, crossing hands over heart as they passed.

They reached the dancing area as the musicians finished the last song. The next one they struck up called for individual pairs, and Alexios took Demeia's hand in his own, holding it at shoulder height.

"I've been thinking about that vision," Demeia said as they took the first steps forward, side by side.

He glanced at her. "As have I."

"We need to prepare ourselves." They stepped backward.

"For what?"

"An attack, of course."

"The illusions will protect us," he replied. "No one can find us here." He let go of her hand, and they each did a single spin on the spot. Then he took her hand again, interlacing his fingers with hers.

"I think we're putting too much trust into them. We've let ourselves grow soft," Demeia said.

Her words stoked the embers of a long-quenched fire inside him. But he would give it no fuel. "We're artists and creators," he said. "Not warriors." They stepped forward together again, then backward.

"We were warriors when we needed to be."

Alexios said nothing. Demeia was as stubborn as her mother had been, and he didn't feel like having an argument, didn't trust himself to keep those embers from sparking.

"You're infuriating," she said to him as they parted once more.

"Let's just enjoy the dance for now," he said when he had her again. "We can talk about this tomorrow."

Her lips tightened, but she allowed him his temporary victory.

When the dance was over, they returned to the high table, still tense toward one another. Alexios was thirsty from the dancing and the evening heat, and filled a cup with water, staying on his feet to drink it.

"Have a beer, relax for once," Epiktet said.

"I—can't." He'd made that mistake in the past, had almost lost control of himself in front of everyone. Tomorrow he might drink, but today no. Today, he was fragile.

He put the cup to his lips, looking out at the square as he drank. The sun had fallen behind the buildings, and the glowlamps had sprung to life, casting pools of white and golden light. They were on illusory poles of spiraling silver, as they would have been in Eios, but the reality, of course, was plain wood.

"Keeper, will you play us a song later?" called Theophila from the table.

He turned to her. She looked tipsy, her soft cheeks flushed beneath her white braids. "The musicians are doing a fine job," he said, not wanting to play again. He loved his lyre, and he loved to sing. But less so on a day like this, when he'd just lost a daughter.

"I'm still here," Eliana reminded him.

"I know, and I'm glad of it," he said. The problem was that most of them didn't stay. They grew old and returned to the Makers—his sons, his daughters, his wives, his grandchildren, his great-grandchildren. His friends. And on this day of memory, he couldn't help but wallow in the fact.

He sighed, started walking around the table to take his place at it. But as he did so, he was hit by a strange wrenching feeling. He paused. The feeling came again.

"What's wrong?" Theophila asked.

Another shock rattled him. What was going on? It was ... No, it couldn't be.

But it was.

It *was.*

"What's going on?" Castes demanded.

Another wrench and then a kind of snap. He reeled, put a hand to the table to steady himself.

Nixos and Demeia jumped to their feet, looking wild-eyed, and Nixos's chair crashed to the ground.

"Speak, what's wrong with you all?" Theophila said, her voice rising in alarm.

"The illusions that hide the town—someone's trying to destroy them," Alexios gasped, trying to pull his spinnings back together. Who could be behind this? Who would even know the illusions were there, other than his own mages?

"Not just those, my illusions too," Nixos said, his voice tight and pained.

Indeed, Nixos's illusions of the Hall and temple had begun to fray, blinking in and out of sight.

"And mine," breathed Demeia.

Moments later, the illusions of the square unraveled entirely. A chorus of gasps as the revelers saw the buildings in their full reality—not marble but bare red brick, squat and ugly. Some cried out to the Makers in terror.

Alexios tried to reform his own illusions, but he was being battered from too many angles. It was like trying to fill a sieve with water.

Then, a more disturbing presence forced itself on him, a terrible sense of wrongness distorting the Lace. He tried to focus in on it. There was something almost familiar ... "We must go to the wall!" he shouted.

"Raise my voice first so I can talk to the crowd," Theophila said. "We need to calm them."

Alexios wanted to go directly, find out what was going on, but she was right. People were panicking. There were shouts and screams, pushing and shoving, children crying. Nobody had ever seen what the buildings in the inner ring really looked like. They knew that something had gone badly wrong.

As Theophila began to speak, he searched for the tiny, invisible threads that carried the sound of her voice, using ear rather than eye. Once he had isolated them, he plucked them lightly so that the vibrations increased. Immediately, the volume of her voice tripled, causing her words to carry easily across the square.

"My people," she cried. "Stay where you are. Please do not be afraid. The magic has failed, and we're looking for the reason."

"Periklis, stay here," Castes was saying to the master of the city guard, who had also risen from the table and was frowning out at the square. "Keep a check on the crowd."

Periklis started calling people to him, shouting orders, sending runners to the guardsmen on duty below.

Theophila finished speaking and suggested they go around the back of the temple to avoid the crush. With a nod of agreement, Alexios set off at a half-walk, half-run, Nixos, Demeia, and the rulers following him. As soon as they were out of sight of the crowd, he broke into a full sprint along the cobbled streets, all pretense at decorum abandoned. Demeia and Nixos kept pace with him, but Castes and Theophila soon fell behind.

His legs and lungs were burning by the time he reached the wall, and he was forced to slow as he ran up the steps onto the wooden ramparts. It was almost sundown, but there was still light enough in the eastern sky to illuminate the acres of patchworked fields that spread out below to end in a black line of dense forest. Streaming out of the forest in uneven columns were two-legged abominations with shining, blood-red eyes.

"What are they?" Nixos said, squinting.

"Ilk. What else?" said Demeia, leaning out so far she would fall if pushed.

Alexios used the Lace to extend his vision, bringing the monsters into close view. At the vanguard came large, shambling creatures taller than any man, covered in green-black scaly hide. They had claws for fingers and wolf-like jaws powerful enough to crunch through bone.

"They are *Ilk,"* Cassander said. *"Rippers, we called them. Oh, dear Makers, bless us and save us."*

The souls echoed his words, but Alexios forced them out of his consciousness. He needed clarity and calm, not the frightened wailing of ten dead men and women.

"Makers, there are people out there!" Nixos cried, pointing.

He was right, a small group who had for some reason decided not to join the town in the celebrations. They were running for the town gates, which were still open. But even as he watched, a monster reached one of the stragglers and swept out a clawed hand. The man pitched to the ground, but the creature picked him up easily and closed its jaws around his throat. Alexios looked away, unable to bear the sight.

When he looked again, he saw lines of smaller creatures emerging from the trees. They were humanlike, both in stature and appearance, but their hide was scaly. Unlike the rippers, they carried weapons—spears for the most part, but also swords and long knives.

A dreadful scream shattered the air, and Alexios clamped his hands over his ears. He cast his eyes up and saw a huge bat-like creature circling above, leathery wings black against the purpling sky.

"Skreek!" Epiktet exclaimed. *"They say you only hear its cry once. Stuff your ears!"*

Alexios shouted the warning to the others, and Nixos began to slice strips from his sleeves with his knife, cutting himself in his frenzy. He gave two wads to Alexios, who shoved them into his ears. The skreek cried out again, bringing one man wailing to his knees.

Theophila and Castes reached the wall, joined by others bearing what poor weapons they had—wooden pitchforks, flint axes, knives, slings. A laughable sight. What good were they against these creatures of corrupt magic?

Still the abominations continued to stream out of the forest, trampling across farmland, grinding crops into dirt, filling the air with their poisonous reek. A creeping dread possessed Alexios, leaching the strength from his bones.

Theophila grabbed two nearby men. "Go around the wall and see if they've come from any other direction. Count them as well as you can." The men nodded and hurried off, one left, one right.

Alexios forced himself to watch as the monsters continued their rampage across the farmland, tearing apart anyone they caught with claws and teeth. The screams carried clearly, each one a barb that wounded him to the core. He looked toward the gate. Still open, people staggering through, falling to their knees on the streets. The monsters were less than a hundred paces away. The gate would have to close soon, dooming those still left on the outside. What a horror, to be the one to make that decision.

But then the monsters suddenly stopped, letting the remaining farmers reach the safety of the walls. The gate slammed shut behind them, and Alexios heard the heavy bolt being dropped into place, surely the first time it had ever been used. The Ilk began to fan out into a single line, staring up at them with their glowing red eyes.

A man came to the fore. Lean, not very tall, wearing black silk robes and a bone mask with curling ram's horns. An Ilk mage? The same man he'd seen in the vision?

He realized that everyone was looking at him. He was the Keeper. He had to do something. Say something. He leaned out over the parapet. "Who are you?" he shouted.

The man walked up to the wall, stopping just outside of bowshot. "Hello, Keeper." His voice reached them with ease, powered by magic. The Eleusian was accented but clear, the tone light, almost cheerful.

"Why are you here?" Alexios cried. Although he knew. Oh, yes, he *knew.*

"The slaves of Antiphos returned," Cassander said, and the other souls echoed him, frightened.

"I must say, I'm quite excited," the man said, his voice hollow through his ghastly mask. "So much planning, and at last it's all happening."

A mature voice. The vision had shown him a youth, but it could have been of the past. This could be the same man, his army of Ilk now spawned, now standing at their gates. Why hadn't the Makers shown him this vision earlier? *Would it have made a difference?*

"Try to take him down," Castes hissed to nearby bowmen.

Several bows twanged. The arrows flew true and straight, but they bounced off the Ilk leader. And now Alexios could see it, a blurring around his body. When Alexios activated his magesight, he could see the threads had been rewoven to create a barrier. It wasn't any magic he could do. It must be Chelaki magic—the magic of the dark god Antiphos—returned after two hundred years.

"How did you find us?" Alexios asked. How had the illusions been so thoroughly and so swiftly broken?

The mage straightened. "Rumors!" he said brightly. Then he dipped into sarcasm. "Of an impenetrable forest that swallowed the unwary traveler."

So, their very means of concealment had announced their presence to their deadliest and oldest enemy. Alexios remembered years of bitter argument. Open ourselves to the world. Create a truly great city rather than skulking in the woods like filthy Chelaki. No, we'll lose our identity, our ways. And he'd always called for hiding, for preservation. Guiltiest of them all.

"Your illusions were ... not bad ... but feeble compared to those of your dead ancestors."

Alexios felt himself blush. Those illusions had been his proudest work, the result of years of experimentation. *I've failed to protect my people. My greatest duty, and I've failed. I've failed, I've failed.* The souls wept.

"They were certainly not enough to withstand my power," the mage continued.

Alexios forced himself out of his self-pity, tried to focus on the enemy's words. Where had they come from? How had the Ilk reached them?

"The war against the Unraveller never ends," Cassander said. *"He will always seek to tear apart the Makers' creation."*

"I am a ruler of this town," Theophila called. "What do you want?"

"I want you to die!" the mage said mirthfully.

"It is your abominations that will die on these walls," Castes said with far more conviction than Alexios felt.

The mage laughed. "I'd rather watch you starve."

Did that mean he planned not to attack? Or was it a ruse, to make them lower their guard?

"Anyway, very nice to meet you," the mage said. "I'll come back tomorrow to say hello." He raised a hand, as if he were waving goodbye, and then walked off into the ranks of the Ilk before disappearing. The disappearance was too sudden. An invisibility illusion? Was he one of those who had Eleusian blood mixed with Chelaki? Alexios couldn't use the Lace to detect him. The Ilk warped it too badly; it was painful to touch the threads that surrounded them.

"What now?" Nixos said, still gazing at the Ilk.

The monsters weren't moving, simply staring at the walls with their brutish red eyes, their very presence seeming to suck the last of the light out of the day. Looking more closely, Alexios realized that the smaller, armed creatures outnumbered the wolf-like ones by around two to one.

"It was always like that," Epiktet said. *"Or so I heard. Golls, they're called, those little ones, on account of the noise they make."*

"The skreek is flying west," Demeia said, pointing.

"Makers, it might attack!" Theophila exclaimed.

But the skreek continued its flight over the town until it reached the western end, where it began to circle. Guarding the way out.

"We must summon Periklis," Castes said. He grabbed the nearest man and sent him off in search of the master of the city guard.

The runners Alexios had sent returned, confirming what he'd suspected. The army was small, perhaps six hundred. The bulk of it was concentrated here, on the eastern side, and the rest by the south gate. There were no Ilk north of the town, unsurprising given that it was banded by a steep ravine.

"Is there any hope of taking the battle to them?" Nixos said.

Everyone turned to Alexios. But he wasn't a true Keeper. His souls and memories spanned only the two hundred years of his own life, not the millennia of the great Keepers of yore. And neither Cassander nor Epiktet had been on the front lines in the last Ilk war, both too old, using their skills in other ways.

"I mightn't have fought, but I know this," Epiktet said. *"We can't hope to sally out against them. An Ilk army is worth at least three times any normal army. They don't feel pain or fear. The dread you experience now, that sense of hopelessness, that is their deadliest weapon. The closer you get to them, the more you'll feel it, until it completely overwhelms your senses."*

"He's right," Cassander said. *"The Gloom, that's the worst thing about them."*

Alexios related what the souls had said. He could see the terror in the eyes of each listener, saw some of them try to firm themselves—clutching weapons, curling hands into fists, grinding teeth until jaws popped.

"And we aren't warriors," Theophila murmured.

That they were not, and even less so than in the past. Their bows were used for killing deer, not monsters. And only a small number of city guards had ever wielded a spear. Swords, they didn't have.

"We can defeat them on the wall," Demeia said, eyes blazing, fist clenched. "The mage has given us the gift of time. Let's make him regret it."

Her fire sparked those embers deep inside him, and a flame sprang up. Would his people never be free of the plague of Antiphos? Well, they would fight, they would have to.

"And we must win!" Epiktet hissed, echoed by the others.

Why was the mage delaying? The Ilk could surely take the wall, even with a force of that size. Was it to humiliate them? To show them just how easily he could destroy them? Or was it simply a game to him? He sounded half mad, that laughter ...

"We need to send messengers to Vonopoli and Potas, find out if they've been attacked too. Warn them," Castes said.

Theophila looked dubious "Through the Ilk lines? How?"

"We could send illusionists," Castes said.

"Let's meet in private and decide on a plan," Theophila replied.

Alexios turned to Nixos and Demeia. "Go, summon all mages who are of age to the temple. Tell them what's happened. I'll come and speak to them later. In the meantime, consider what can be done."

Periklis came running around the wall. Tall, with bulging arms and a wide chest, he cut an imposing figure. He saluted Alexios and the rulers with a short bow. "How may I serve?"

Theophila gestured for Castes to speak, and he obliged. "Gather all your captains and arrange a watch on the wall through the night. If the abominations attack, send word to the Hall of Congress. When you've done that, join us in the Chamber. We'll have need of your insights to organize the defense."

Periklis bowed again. "As you command."

They left him then, the sound of his voice following them as he barked out his instructions.

Chapter 8

Ina

The Godstone was a miracle provided by Chel so we could ensure no Cursed One would ever tear apart her world again.

—Teachings of Old Tsu

Despite her promise to Suni, Ina couldn't think of a realistic way of escaping the islands. She could take a canoe, but where would she go with it? The barbarian lands lay to the east, where it was rumored some of her people had fled at the time of the genocide, led by Lin'Elkir, the last Skyrider. But the Great Maelstrom blocked their way. Even if they tried to go around by the north or south, the currents would pull the canoe into its seething waters. No one knew what lay west. It was called the Endless Sea for good reason.

Seven futile days passed and Suni began to wear a permanently drawn look. Her wondrous eyes lost their glow, and her love began to increasingly turn away from Ina and toward her child. Every effort at lightening her spirits failed, and sometimes led her to snap bitterly, as if she blamed Ina for what had come to pass. But even then, Ina found it impossible to share the truth with her. More than once, she tried to tell her about the clawtongue tea that had dampened her powers and fooled the Godstone, but each time it was as if a ball had got stuck in her throat, choking her into silence. Revealing her secret could mean her death, and she didn't want Tani to suffer its poisonous effects as she had.

So instead, she began to toy with another possibility—go to the Godstone by herself and try to destroy it. But fear of what might happen if she went made her painfully indecisive, and at last she decided to confide in the only person she could confide in, her mother.

She went to her mother's hut after breakfast time, when she was likely to be alone. Sure enough, Mia was sitting cross-legged outside the doorway, stringing a necklace. A small, koua-wood bowl full of multi-colored beads was between her legs.

"Mami."

A warm smile spread across her mother's face when she saw Ina. "Chel be with you, my darling. Isn't it a fine morning?"

"Yes, it is." Ina stood in front of her, shifting from foot to foot, suddenly unsure of what to do.

"Come, child, sit." Mia patted the grass next to her.

Ina did as she was bid, trying to suppress her irritation at being called a child. She gazed out toward the Elder's Tree, rising high above the other huts, its great branches spreading out over the center of the village like a watchful protector.

"What's bothering you?"

The words clogged in her suddenly dry throat. She cleared it, then swallowed before speaking. "Suni's child, Tani ... she ..." Ina stopped, lowered her voice to little more than a whisper. "She has the Curse. She's distraught."

A rattling as Mia dropped beads and necklace into the bowl. "I hope you didn't say anything about yourself!"

"Great Chel, Mami, is that all you can think of?"

But Mia gripped her elbow, fingers digging clawlike into her flesh. "You didn't tell her, did you?"

Her terror washed over Ina, breaking through the barricades of her mind. It was burning, raw, and Ina scrambled to block it out. "I didn't say anything to her, I didn't tell her about the tea. But I can't bear to see Suni so miserable."

Mia loosened her grip but didn't release her. "We can't help, if anyone found out what we did, they'd send you back to Chel and it would all have been for nothing."

But Ina had reached her tipping point. Her fear for Tani, her agony over Suni, the years she'd spent hiding and ashamed. It was too much. "Don't you think it's terrible, what we do to the children?"

Mia reared back, eyes wide. "Never speak of that, to me or to anyone," she said in a taut voice. "Never question. Our laws are our laws. They've helped us survive."

But Ina's mouth continued to spit out words. "What thought did you give for the laws when you fed me the clawtongue? Isn't it just selfishness not to help Tani and Suni?"

"Don't be a fool!"

Ina was starting to feel light and free, as if the voicing of the heresy had released her of a burden. "I don't see why it's a curse. I don't see how we can justify the deaths. And I want to know what that Godstone is. Why was it put there?"

"So that we could fulfil Chel's purpose." Mia flushed as soon as she spoke the words, intoned by the elders before every Test.

"But have we understood Chel's purpose correctly? I'm not sure we have."

Mia put a gentle hand to Ina's cheek. "Please, speak no more of this. Go on with your life."

Ina shied away from her mother's touch. "They say that the old powers are a curse of Sīut, but tell me honestly, is that how you think of me? Am I a daughter of Sīut or a daughter of Chel?"

Mia winced. "Ina, stop this. It does no good."

Ina's mind lit with memories of nights spent in terror of the Chaos Maker, when she was still convinced he would come and take her away to his dark realm. "In your eyes, do I belong to Sīut or Chel?"

"Aren't we past this yet?"

Ina punched out the words again. "In your eyes, do I belong to Sīut or Chel?"

Mia sighed. "As long as you don't use your powers, you can't do Sīut's work."

And how often have I given into the temptation, even if just a little bit? "Have you ever thought that the Godstone might have been put there by Sīut?"

Mia stiffened. "What makes you say such a thing?"

"The Godstone calls me, in my mind, it wants me to go to it. It's done that since I was a child."

"What do you mean? What words does it speak?" Her mother's voice was high, almost shrill. It attracted the attention of two passing gatherers, who turned to her with a quizzical expression, but Mia frowned at them, and they looked away.

Ina waited until they were well out of earshot before speaking again. "It doesn't say any words, I can just tell it wants me to go to it."

"Why have you never told me this before?"

"Sometimes, I think I'm imagining it. I can only really feel it if I'm on the beach or out at sea." And mostly Ina tried to block it out, to tell herself it was only her imagination.

Mia grabbed hold of Ina's wrists and pulled her toward her. "You must forget all this," she hissed. "If the Godstone calls you, it's because it wants to betray you. Stay away from it, and don't speak of it to Suni. She'll have trouble keeping the secret from Mūak, and there's no telling what he'll do. Men are different about such things—harder."

Ina remembered the bitter arguments between her parents about the clawtongue, but her father had relented eventually. Relented, but he'd left them as soon as he could. Ina had seen him only a handful of times since she'd turned sixteen. "I won't speak of it. But think about it, maybe Chel wants us to do something. Maybe that's why they led you to the clawtongue. Maybe she wants us to change our ways."

But her mother was shaking her head. "We can't know Chel's will. I tried every root, flower, and herb on the five islands to discover one that would smother your powers. Perhaps Chel led me to it, perhaps not."

Ina pulled her arms out of her mother's grasp. "I don't want to continue as before. I want to understand what the Godstone is, why it calls to me."

"And what if the Godstone *was* put there by Sīut?"

"There's only one way to find out." Ina got to her feet.

"Ina, wait!"

She paused, hopeful. "Will you help me?"

"Don't go to the Godstone, don't tell anyone. I couldn't bear to lose you."

Her mother was so obviously riven with fear that Ina almost relented. But then she thought about Suni's fear, and about Tani dancing among the butterflies by Chel's shrine, and she knew she had to do something. "I'll try not to get caught."

Mia's pleas followed her as she walked away, but Ina deafened herself to them. She would do something, she would—the only question was what. Old Tsu, he might have some answers about the Godstone. She would go and ask him.

As she expected, he was under the horizontal, shade-spreading branches of the Learning Tree, seated in his high-backed chair. It had been molded long ago from koua wood to fit around his portly body, wood and man blending together to fulfill a single purpose. That purpose was to pass on the stories of their ancestors and teach the ways of their people to their children. Five of those young ones were sitting on the nearest of the benches that radiated out in semi-circular formation from the Chair. Tsu was reciting a poem, his resonant voice carrying easily across to her from her position at the back.

The lonely exiles, three hundred few
Piled into boats and journeyed forth
Across the great expanse of blue
Twelve days and nights they rowed before
They found the promised isle of Lun

With such a great and glad relief
They walked across the golden sands
And set up camp amidst the trees
Clear waters, how they did abound
And many fruits for them to eat

The twelve tribes pledged to live as one
They swore the binding Oath of Peace
And in the days and weeks to come
Found three more isles across the sea
That they named Olon, Kan, and Yon

On the barren rock of Uruk'il
Takan'Ri did find a stone
'Twas put in place by mighty Chel
So that her few remaining folk
Could cleanse themselves of Sīut's spell

Each year we go to that small isle
And climb its high and rocky peak
To undergo great test and trial
And ward ourselves eternally
From Sīut—and his dark guile

Ina listened intently to the poem, although she knew it word for word. Everyone over the age of nine did, for their knowledge of the ancient lore was tested again and again to be sure that no Chelak would forget his or her ancestry. She knew she would find Tani among the children—this poem was taught to those who were preparing for the Test.

Suni's child was sitting in the very middle of the row, her hands clasped on her lap. She had her mother's eyes, and they were wide and solemn as she listened to Tsu's words. Did she know what awaited her? Ina had. She was eight when she started making holes in the Cloth, holes that opened into ol'sīut, Sīut's Realm. The Cursed Ones used to travel great distances through the chaos god's domain, but Ina didn't know this at the time. All she knew was that things could fall into them, and that while they sometimes reappeared in another room, they often didn't reappear at all. She had been terrified that she would fall into one of the holes herself. At last, she'd told her mother about it and knew from her reaction that she had Sīut's Curse. The clawtongue put a stop to the holes, and now she didn't know if she could make them even if she tried.

Tsu stopped chanting but waited a moment before he spoke. "And that is the *Story of Exile*."

A round-faced boy stuck up his hand and waved it to catch Tsu's attention.

"Yes, Umi?"

"Why didn't Chel protect us? Why did they let all our people get killed by the Eleusians?"

"It was Sīut's doing," Tsu said. "He gave great power to the Eleusians, and to the barbarian magic users from across the Wide Sea. They have a terrible, destructive magic."

"I don't understand—if the Cursed Ones get their power from Sīut and the Eleusians and the barbarians do too, doesn't that mean that Sīut's people were fighting each other?" Umi said.

"Sīut doesn't care who wins, silly. He gives them his curse so they can cause chaos for him," said a moon-faced girl sitting next to Tani.

"That's right, Kana," Tsu said.

I don't belong to Sīut, Ina told herself. *I serve Chel and only Chel.* No child had prayed more to Chel than she had, no child had made more sacrifices in their honor. And didn't her powers bring her closer to Chel's world, closer than any of the rest of them? Even so, the fear wormed inside her.

Tsu looked at the sundial carved into a stone plinth next to the chair. "This lesson is over. Go on to your duties."

There was an immediate outburst of noise as the children's repressed energy was finally released. Ina watched them run off, envying their innocence. For a moment, she allowed herself to wander through the gloomy pathways of her own childhood, but then shook herself free and stole around the benches to Tsu. "Chel be with you," she said. "Would you have some time to speak with me?"

His smile caused a web of wrinkles to spread across his weathered face. "Chel be with you, Ina'Yakir'Suk. My next lesson doesn't begin until one mark before highsun. I'm going to drink some teeka. Why don't you join me?"

As they walked to the teeka tent, they spoke of small things—Tsu of the children he'd been teaching, Ina of her preparation for the Games.

The teeka tent wasn't far and was empty inside apart from the old server in charge, Numin. "Freshly made with sweetmint," he said as he passed them a small, blue glazed pot and two clay cups. "The gatherers brought some earlier."

They took the teeka outside and sat on a long koua log. Tsu waited for her to speak, but Ina found herself silenced again by fear, and simply sat sipping her tea, gazing into the forest. Her cup was half empty by the time she finally got her words out. "I was passing by and stopped when I heard you telling the story of the Exile." She paused, thinking how to frame her words. "A question came to me." Once more she was silent. She couldn't ask the question she really wanted to ask, but would her other questions be treated with suspicion?

"All questions are welcome," Tsu said in his gentle voice.

Ina found her voice again. "How did the Godstone actually get to where it is? Did Takan'Ri just find it there?"

To her relief, Tsu smiled. "Takan'Ri found it as it is now. Chel had placed it in advance so that we could protect ourselves from Sīut's Curse and preserve the little that was left of our people."

"And, well, I was wondering ... what is it made of? It's not like other rock. It isn't worn by wind or rain. Nothing grows on it."

Tsu raised his shoulders in a shrug. "It's not a normal stone. That's all we really know. It's been infused with Chel's power, and Chel clearly intended it to remain there forever."

Why does it call me? Does it call all Cursed Ones or just me? But Ina couldn't say these questions aloud. "The stories say Takan'Ri had a vision from Chel that told him the Godstone's purpose. But I was wondering ... have you ... have you ever heard of the Godstone acting strangely? Has it ever made a mistake, reacted to the wrong person, or let someone pass when they shouldn't have?" Tsu gave her a penetrating look, and Ina began to regret the question. Could he see it in her?

"I've never heard of such a thing," he said. "Have you seen or heard something that has disturbed you?"

Ina shook her head. "No. I suppose with the Test coming soon, it was on my mind."

Tsu sighed. "It's always a trying time for us all. But Chel's will be done."

"Chel's will be done." The ritual words had never felt hollower to her. Were they really doing Chel's will? If Chel had put the Godstone there, why did it call her? *Maybe because I escaped when I shouldn't have.* Ina felt a chill despite the heat of the morning sun. Of course, that was the most likely explanation, wasn't it? The Godstone wanted to repeat the Test.

Tsu interrupted her musings by saying he needed to answer nature's call and then return to the Learning Tree. Ina bid him goodbye but remained where she was, thinking about what to do. One part of her was tempted to go to the Godstone and find out what it wanted, if only to confirm that it *was* indeed calling her to repeat the Test. And then she could try to destroy it, ensure that Tani would be saved, that all the children yet to come would be saved. *Or is that Sīut whispering to me?*

It came to her that she should go to Chel's shrine, seek guidance directly. She leaped to her feet and went at a jog, pausing only to drop the teeka cups back into the tent.

"Ina!"

She was so lost in thought that she didn't hear the voice at first, not until the call was repeated and a hand landed on her shoulder.

"Ina, where have you been? We're supposed to be practicing the relay for the Games!" It was Oyu, his features tight with irritation. "I came back to look for you."

She cursed inwardly. She had completely forgotten about the practice session. "I thought it was starting now."

"Well, we started half an hour ago. Let's go quickly."

They ran to the Practice Ground, a large grassy clearing behind the village, where Han and Ria were playing a game of touch. They were laughing, and it was making them less skillful as they tried to escape each other's reaching fingers. As they arrived, Han scored a touch on Ria's shoulder and raised his arms triumphantly into the air. Ria slapped him on the behind.

"Found her!" Oyu cried.

They abandoned their game and turned toward them. Han's face broke into its usual radiant smile, as if their arrival were the best thing that had happened to him all day. "Where were you?" he asked her.

"I forgot. Sorry."

"Well, let's get started, I don't have much time left before I go fishing," he said.

The target had already been set up at the other end of the clearing, a thick tree trunk that had been roughly carved into the same size and shape as a man. A piece of white cloth had been fastened to the center of its chest.

They took their positions. As the best spear thrower, Ina would go second last, with Oyu, who was the fastest runner, following her. Ria started, sprinting up to the pre-determined mark, then launching her spear from the spear thrower the moment she reached it. It landed at the very top of the white target, barely close enough to pass. She continued running until she reached the target, then pulled the spear out.

Han crouched in a ready position a few paces before the change-over line. He burst forward at exactly the right moment, but Ria presented the spear and thrower at an awkward angle, forcing him to slow as he took it. He continued toward the target, stopping several paces before Ria had, at the throwing point for men. His spear landed slightly to the right of the white cloth. With a cry of disappointment, he ran up, yanked the spear out, and sprinted back to the throwing point. Then he turned and threw again, and this time his spear landed true.

Now it was Ina's turn. She prepared herself, trying to slip into that mental place where her senses were heightened, where she could feel more than see the world around her. But her argument with her mother kept returning to her, and she couldn't find her focus. Han was coming. He was too close. She sprinted forward, but he was over the line before she caught the spear thrower, losing precious moments. The spear, when she threw it, landed a fingerswidth outside the target. She stood and stared, disbelieving.

"Come on, Ina, go again!" Oyu shouted.

Still bewildered, she ran up to get the spear and made a greater effort to enter her special zone. But full immersion again escaped her, and she was forced to make the shot without her usual certainty. At least it hit the white cloth this time, and she was able to go and get it back to Oyu. She ran to him at full speed. He was coiled and ready, his face a mask of concentration.

As she neared, he exploded forward with a roar, cleanly snatching the spear thrower from her before powering on to the throwing point. He always claimed that the shout helped him to run faster, though Ina thought it wasted energy better spent in his legs. Still, he was one of the fastest runners in the village. His spear hit the mark, and then he was back again.

"What's wrong with you?" he said to her, still breathing hard.

"I didn't sleep well last night."

"I don't think I've ever seen you miss a target, ever." He looked at her as if trying to read something inside her.

"And you've seen me do it too many times, eh," Han said, jostling him lightly.

"Well, we certainly won't win any prizes like this," Oyu said. "Ria, you were late off the mark."

Ria flushed but said nothing.

"Let's see if we can all do better this time," Oyu said, but he sounded irritable, not his usual encouraging self.

Their performance when they tried again was even worse.

"Let's do this another day," Han said.

"There are only four weeks left before the Games," Oyu said. "We should be practicing harder."

"Tomorrow will be better. Ina's obviously not herself," Han said, peering at her with concern.

Oyu shook his head in frustration and opened his mouth, but Ria spoke first, saying she agreed with Han. Oyu threw his hands up in defeat. "Fine, tomorrow, highsun?"

They agreed to the time, and Oyu said he was going to stay in the field to do some exercises by himself. Ina started to follow Han and Ria to the village, but Oyu called her back. She stopped reluctantly, knowing what was coming and not wanting to face it.

"Are you well?" he said, still terse.

"I'm fine." She looked at Han and Ria walking off arm in arm, so comfortable with each other.

"I don't mean today, or at least I mean more than that. You've become secretive. You don't speak to me."

"I'm speaking to you now."

"I mean from here." He punched his chest. "Have I offended you?"

"No." Ina picked at a broken thumb nail, wishing she could be anywhere else.

"Every time I ask you to do something you have an excuse. We used to spend nearly all our time together."

With an effort, she fixed her eyes on him. "What do you want from me?"

Oyu seemed to crumble a little, but then he straightened himself, gathered his pride. "I'm your closest friend. Or I was. But now you treat me like all the rest." His words tumbled out all together, as if he'd planned them and couldn't say them quickly enough. "I defend you to the others, tell them you're not proud, that you don't look down on them. But maybe I was wrong. Maybe you do think you're better than everyone else."

The words stung. If only he *knew*. But she'd made a mistake, letting him get so close. "You don't want to be my friend. You want more than that." Her own words dismayed her. She wished it would all go away somehow, that things could be normal between them again.

"I've never asked anything of you other than friendship." His cheeks and ears glowed with emotion.

"You should find someone else to love, Oyu." He looked like he was going to cry, and Ina wanted to run away and not see his sadness. Hated herself more for what she was.

"I have other friends. But without me, who do you have?" he said, bitterness creeping into his tone.

Ina steeled herself, said what she had to say, to protect them both. "I care for you, Oyu, but maybe we shouldn't spend so much time together."

Oyu's face hardened, his next words harsh, spitting. "If you think me so unworthy of your friendship, I won't force it on you."

"No, that's not what I meant ..." But he had already turned away, was striding off, back rigid. Ina watched him leave, swallowed back a rising sense of loss and despair. She was alone, had always been alone.

But out of that despair, she formed a resolution. She wouldn't let Tani share her fate. She would find out Chel's purpose. She would learn what the Godstone was and what it really wanted.

Chapter 9

Fay

Lumin priests must be chaste. This means they may not give their body to another outside of marriage. The sanctions are as follows:
First incident – a verbal warning and ten-day fast of penance.
Second incident – a written warning and twenty lashes before your fellow priests.
Third incident – expulsion from the priesthood.

—The Lumin Priest's Handbook

Fay finished her last round of the day and gladly went to The Hungry Maiden to meet her friend Tom. As always, the popular eating house was full, but they had reserved a table, and Fay wound her way through the press of bodies to find Tom sitting at it already.

He was as handsome as ever, strawberry-blond curls framing high cheekbones, large dimples appearing in each smooth cheek when he smiled. “Hello, darling,” he said, standing and giving her a light kiss before enveloping her in a hug. “How have you been?”

Fay sat down, tempted to tell him about her orders. She nearly always shared things with Tom, even when she shouldn’t. But he was her best friend, and he worked for Moth too. The serving woman came to take their orders. “Two glasses and a jug of your house white,” Fay said. “And the pork stew for me.”

Tom ordered the same, then, when the serving woman was gone, fixed her with a penetrating look. “I can tell something’s up.”

Fay decided she could share at least some of it. “I need to break into the Archpriests' Library to get something for Moth. But it’s not going to be easy.”

“What is it he wants?”

“That I can’t tell you,” she said.

Tom knew better than to press her. “Have you figured out how you’re going to do it?”

She told him about her plan to get into Lothar’s chambers and steal his key.

“Sounds solid. And you’ve got the sleepfast?”

“I’ll get some later this evening.”

“Well, while we’re on the subject of archpriests, I’ve got something you’ll be *very* interested in.”

Fay raised her eyebrows. “I’m listening.”

But the server came with their wine, so they waited while she poured it into long-stemmed glasses.

Tom raised his glass to Fay’s, and they drank. “Go on then, tell me,” she said, setting her glass on the table and leaning toward him.

He took another sip of his wine, before slowly putting his glass down, eyes crinkling with mischief. He liked to tease her like this, draw it out.

She planted her elbows on the table. "Tell me!"

"Your crush, Nuria, visited Danial Thane in the Spire last night."

Fay jerked, elbow knocking against her glass and spilling some of the wine onto the table. "What?" Archpriests did not consort with weavers, especially when those weavers were ranking. Thane was third in the Spire hierarchy, behind only Elwin Morgan, the First Weaver, and Arianna Velden, the Guardian. Although Thane was the official ambassador of the Spire to the nations of the world, there had never been an ambassador between weavers and Lumins. Too many years of mutual hatred and suspicion.

"I saw her sneaking in at night," Tom said. "Pure chance, really. I was on my way to Papa Julia's. She was all covered up, but I know her face."

"She's just announced for High Luminate," Fay said. "There *must* be some connection. Although I'm struggling to see what it is."

"She's on the Consulate," Tom reminded her. "And it's no secret Thane wants the weavers to be granted a chair again."

She could use this to get in with Lothar. No, no, she couldn't. She wanted Nuria to *win.* But she hadn't yet come up with anything particularly juicy to share with him that night. And this was perfect. "Can you keep tabs on her, let me know if she visits again?"

Tom nodded. "Anything for you, my love." He winked.

Their food arrived then, and they tucked in. While she ate, Fay pondered what Tom had told her. *What the pits is Nuria playing at? What does she hope to get from Thane? He's not even a member of a great family.* But oh, she wanted to know, she wanted to know badly. *Moth would want this information too. Well, Tom will give it to him, I suppose. I can probably expect an order to investigate. Unless I can keep a step ahead, give Moth something before he's even asked for it. That will get me some favor.*

She didn't stay much longer after finishing her meal, her mind all on her upcoming meeting with Lothar.

"See you soon at Papa Julia's?" Tom said as they parted. "Been a while since we've had a wild one."

"I'm going to need it," Fay replied, thinking of Lothar. "I'll send a message."

They exchanged a final hug, and Fay returned to the temple, glad of the wine's softening effects. The closer the time came to the meeting, the more her anxiety was rising. *It will be fine,* she told herself. *It will be fine.*

Back in her room, she opened the bottom drawer of her desk to take out a fresh candle clock. She counted the marks, each one representing an hour, before scratching a larger one for the meeting time. Then she lit the candle and placed it inside its protective glass box on top of the desk.

This done, she went down a flight of stone stairs to the ground floor to take a bath. She knew the novice on duty, a girl called Ish, only twelve years old, with long fair hair and calf-like eyes. When Fay arrived, she was prodding at one of the crackling fires with a long black stick, sweat forming a sheen on her soft features. Over the fire was a large cauldron of water, prepared at the same time every day so that priests might cleanse themselves before bed. There were five cauldrons in total in the women's bathing area, with five fires to heat them, and the air was thick with steam.

"Would you like me to draw a bath, Your Light?" Ish said.

"Please, child. But you do the cold water, I'll get the hot." Some priests let the novices do all the work, but Fay would never feel comfortable watching while others waited on her. Too many years in a different life.

She fetched a bucket and filled it with boiling water, then brought it through a pointed arch into the adjoining bathing room. No one else was there yet, so she had her choice of the ten wooden tubs, set out in a row along the white-painted wall. She chose the one in the furthest corner, half shrouded in darkness. It was lined with undyed linen to protect the body from splinters, and the water soaked quickly through the cloth, tautening it and pressing it flat against the curving wood. In the weaver's Spire and in the houses of the well-off, they had no need of fires and cauldrons to heat their baths. No need to haul boiling water in buckets, risking burns and scalds. Their bathtubs were lined with heatstones that needed no more than a touch to activate, and their water came straight to the tubs through pipes and taps. So Fay had heard, anyway, for Lumia would never allow her priests to use such comforting magic. No, they must make do with flames and torches and smoke and oil. Not that she disagreed entirely. Magic had destroyed half the world. Still, the comforts it brought ...

She returned to the fire to fill her bucket again, hearing behind her a gurgling and splashing as Ish added the cold. It took four rounds before her bath was ready. She took off her robes and hung them on a hook in the wall by the tub while the novice brought her a bar of plain soap and a towel. Other priests came, but she was already cocooned in her bath, facing two walls, and none came to greet her.

She had hoped that the bath would soothe her nerves, but her heart only increased its rapid patter while her mind leaped from one worry to another. What if Lothar realized she was playing him? What if she couldn't put him to sleep? Worse, what if he caught her stealing the key? The hot water turned stifling, suffocating. It was too much, she had to get out. Better to be doing something, distracting herself.

She stepped out of the bath and dried herself quickly before putting on her clothes. Then she tipped the bath water into the gutter that ran along the wall and returned to her room. Here, she put on fresh robes and applied a touch of floral scent to her neck and wrists—nothing too strong, nothing too alarming for a chaste priest. This done, she removed the glass vial of sleepfast from the little chest at the end of the bed. Three drops into his drink and he would sleep for the night, the apothecary had said. She tucked the small vial into the pocket of her robe. Next, she removed a rectangular wooden box. Inside it was soft clay for taking a mold of the key. After slipping the box into another pocket, she checked the candle clock. It had burned two-thirds of the way to the one o'clock mark. She took a steadying breath, then sat down at the desk to think about what she would say to Lothar. Again and again, she imagined their conversation, what channels it might take, what escape routes she might need. She muttered words to herself like a charm, pictured herself dosing his wine, getting his key. Giving Moth everything he asked for.

Finally, it was time, and she rose from her desk and blew the candle out, then went down the stairs to the archpriests' quarters. As she'd expected, there was no one in the corridors, no one who saw her knocking softly on Lothar's door. He opened it immediately and ushered her in with a soft, many-ringed hand.

His room was at least three or four times the size of hers. Damask curtains, black with gold leaf, were drawn across a window that she knew looked out over the internal garden. To the left of the window stood a four-poster bed and to the right, against the adjoining wall, a large bureau of polished redwood. Nearer the door was an oblong table and a set of four chairs, the legs of each carved with ornate, gilt leafwork. The top of the table was black marble, with a sunburst of gold in the center.

Lothar sat her down on one of the chairs and filled two bowl-shaped glasses with red wine from a crystal decanter. "To our new alliance," he said in his light tenor, jowls wobbling with every movement of his mouth. He raised his glass to hers, and as before, she caught a flash of unbridled hunger in his eyes, swiftly hidden behind his benign smile.

A fresh tremor of fear ran through her, and she brought her glass to her lips to hide it. The wine was rich and full-bodied. Expensive. "Thank you for putting your faith in me," she said. "I know I'm only a lowly priestess, but I hope I can help you."

"It is I who should be thanking you," he said with his fatherly smile. "Your backing is valuable." He took another sip from his wine. "I'm afraid I can't spend too long with pleasantries, however. I have much work to do. What was it you wanted to share?"

Oh, you're *eager.* "I've learned that Archpriest Nuria met secretly with the weaver Danial Thane two nights ago."

Lothar raised his eyebrows, fat fingers clenching around his glass. "And do you have any idea why?" His voice thrummed with barely repressed excitement.

"I'm not sure what she's getting out of it. But it's no secret *he's* been trying to get a seat on the Consulate for the weavers. He has most of the consuls in his pocket, but of course, Nuria has the veto."

Lothar's eyes tightened. "Even Nuria wouldn't let that happen." But there was a flicker of doubt.

Fay didn't think Nuria would allow a weaver onto the Consulate either. It went against everything the order stood for. And while she claimed to stand for change, surely that was too much, even for her.

"She must be dangling a consulship as a carrot." Lothar tapped a finger against his wine glass, looking thoughtful.

Fay used his silence to think of a way to get the sleepfast into his wine. Perhaps if she offered to refill it? His glass was half empty already.

Lothar's finger stilled. "I want to know exactly what she's plotting. If we find evidence that she's helping the weaver gain a consulship ..." He smiled, and again, naked greed crossed his face.

Fay mirrored the smile. "I'll find the evidence, and then her quest to be made High Luminate will surely be at an end. And you will be without a real rival ... Your Radiance."

He heaved himself to his feet and moved toward the bureau. "Come."

Fay paused. His wine glass was sitting alone and undefended on the table. She reached into her pocket for the vial and tried to unstopper it one-handed, but it was too tight. *I'm an Ilk-damned idiot. Should have loosened it before.* With slippery, shaking hands, she removed the vial from the pocket, keeping her hand hidden under the table. Lothar looked back, frowning when he saw that she wasn't following. She got to her feet to join him, slipping the vial back into her pocket and cursing herself again for her idiocy.

The archpriest opened a drawer and took out some paper. Then he took up a goose quill, dipped it in ink, and began to write. Fay looked curiously at the long, sloping words as they emerged on the page. A letter, addressed to the High Priest of Glade, instructing him to meet with a ... pepper merchant. She frowned. Why would an archpriest meet a pepper merchant? Lothar rolled the scroll and then tied and sealed it with wax. "I need to have this delivered to High Priest Gillin. I don't want it to go out in ordinary temple post. Could you see to it?"

"Of course, Your Radiance, anything to help."

"Take it to a mail station in the city. And don't speak of its contents to anyone."

"Yes, Your Radiance." Fay pocketed the scroll. She glanced toward the wine glasses, abandoned on the table. "Is there anything else I can do for you, Your Radiance?" She stepped toward the table, hoping to interest him in the wine again.

He smiled, and this time, it was the smile of a predator. "There is *one* more thing." A fat arm lunged around her waist, dragging her toward him.

She screamed instinctively, tried to pull away, but he grabbed the front of her robe with his other hand. The smell of wine was strong on him, and under that, cloves and the rank pungency of a man who sweated too much. "Please ... Your Radiance."

The greed was now plain, twisting his fleshy lips into a leer. "The High Luminate need not hear of your errant past." His hand dropped to squeeze her buttocks. "Because you'll serve me well, won't you?"

He knew. But how? "Please—let me go," she whispered. Did he know she was spying too?

"Not until you've given me what I want, my sweet whore."

"Why are you saying these things?" Tears flooded her eyes, only half a pretense. She couldn't breathe. *This is all my fault. I've brought this on myself.*

"You know perfectly well why." He grabbed a fistful of her hair and then pressed his mouth roughly against hers. Her spirit fled, leaving her flesh limp and lifeless, but it only made him hold her even more tightly. His teeth broke the skin of her lip, and she tasted blood.

He withdrew his mouth but kept his grip. "Do you think I was stupid enough to accept your offers of help without learning why you'd made them?" He yanked her hair up, forcing her onto her tiptoes. "I thought it was Nuria who sent you at first, but even she doesn't know about your filthy origins, does she?" Winey breath, hot on her face. "*Does* she?"

So, he doesn't know everything. Think, think. "It wasn't Nuria who sent me."

He pulled harder on her hair, and she bit back a cry of pain. "Who, then?"

"A weaver." A lie, but a believable one, surely.

He laughed and, to her relief, released her, stepped away. "So, I've uncovered one of their whisperers. I hadn't doubted they had at least one or two among us. Tell me, what secrets have you shared with them?" He went to the decanter and refilled both their glasses, then thrust hers back at her.

She sipped at her wine before answering him, glad to have a moment to think. But it turned her stomach, and she wanted to retch. "I keep them abreast of any doings in the temple. I've told them about the two factions for High Luminate—yours and Archpriest Nuria's, about what you think of the Spire." This was all true. Moth hadn't asked her to steal or sabotage anything.

"And who is this weaver you report to?"

She chose the first name she could think of. "He calls himself Peyter, but I never see his face. He hides it."

"Peyter," Lothar said quietly, his eyes going distant. "Let's see if we can play a little game with them," he said. He reached out, stroking her cheek with sausage-like fingers and she flinched. This made him smile. "You'll continue your spying, little whore. But I expect you to deliver your report to me before you meet him. And next time you see your handler, you will tell him that Nuria plans to betray the weavers. I'm sure you can spin a convincing story."

Fay had no need to ask what would happen if she refused. But at least Lothar seemed to have forgotten about his other desires. Maybe it had been a ploy to get her to talk. He'd worry that it would give her too much power over him. A man who had forced himself on a priestess, former whore or not, could not be made High Luminate.

But then his eyes changed focus, began to look over her body with want—that and another, crueler desire. She had seen this expression in men's faces before and dreaded it.

"Take your clothes off."

Breath-clogging fear squeezed her tightly. "I could tell the other priests. You'd never be made High Luminate." *Not again, not again.*

He slapped her across the face, leaving a stinging burn. "You will tell them nothing." He slapped her across the other cheek, this time with the back of his hand, his archpriest's ring striking her cheekbone.

Tears of pain sprang to her eyes, and her hand leaped to cover her cheek. Instinct screamed at her to run. But she had to follow through, get the key.

"Who would believe the word of a whore over that of a respected archpriest?"

He was right, of course.

"Take your clothes off."

Her fingers went to her girdle, trembling and clumsy. *I was done with this. I was* done *with this.* Fresh tears came to her eyes, but she blinked them back. He'd enjoy that and she wasn't going to give him the pleasure.

"When you're done, go lie on the bed and wait for me." Lothar abruptly turned away from her, began to walk to the far end of the room.

She paused, watching, wondering. Maybe she could hit him over the head. That Lumia figurine on the sideboard would do the job. But if she didn't get Moth what he wanted, what would *he* do to her? The archpriest opened a door on the far side of the room, went through it. She heard him fumbling with his clothes, then came a thundering stream of piss. The privy.

She ran to the door, thinking to leave, but it was locked. Of course he'd locked it. The key was in the door. *No, hang on. The sleeping draught.* Ruination, why was she being so stupid? The piss stream started to lose power. Where was his glass? Not with him? *Please, not with him. No, there it is.*

She scurried over to the side table, put her hand into her pocket. The vial wasn't there. It had fallen out. No, yes, it was there, down in the corner. *Breathe, breathe.* She plucked it out, tried to unstopper it, but it slipped out of her shaking hands and fell to the ground with a little clack. A moment of terror while she waited to hear it shatter, but Lumia, dear goddess, was watching over her. The vial didn't break but instead rolled under the table, out of sight.

She fell to her hands and knees, feeling blindly in the semi-gloom. This was taking too long. The piss stream quietened, dribbled into silence. *Where is it? Come on, come* on. Her hand brushed against smooth glass. She grabbed the vial and jumped to her feet. From behind the privy door came the sound of his huffing as he rearranged himself. She used her teeth to remove the stopper, then tipped a few drops of sleepfast into his glass, hardly daring to breathe. After hastily pocketing the vial again, she ran on tiptoes with the glass and the rest of the wine to the bedside. The privy door swung open, and she began to work again at her girdle.

She had expected anger, but he chuckled when he saw she was still wearing her clothes. "A modest whore, I didn't think they existed."

He waddled toward her. His robes were half open, and curling grey chest hair poked out over the fold of them.

"Some more wine, Your Radiance? I brought it here for you."

"How thoughtful," he said sardonically. He took his cup, drank a little from it, then set it back down. He hadn't drunk enough. She was sure it wasn't enough. He looked at her, and she saw uncertainty, embarrassment almost. Not used to whores, she realized. He desired her and wanted to be the master of her. But he wasn't quite sure how to do it. She almost laughed at him. Instead, she said, "Forgive me, Your Radiance, but I also need to use the privy. When I come back, I'll show you I can be just as ... thoughtful ... under the sheets."

"Go, and quickly." He picked up the wine cup again.

Calling on her old training, she walked to the privy with slow grace, feeling his eyes on her. Once inside, she took as long as possible to relieve herself, give the draft time to work through his system.

"I said quickly!"

Steeling herself, she went back out to face him. He was sitting on the bed, the wine cup still in his hand, now almost empty. His pale eyes were half-hooded. "Come, my little whore, the night is getting on and this wine hasn't satisfied me." The words were slurred, and he seemed to be swaying slightly. It was working already. Or was it just drunkenness?

She took the cup out of his hands and knelt before him. "Allow me to help you with your boots, Your Radiance."

"Yes," he sighed.

She began to undo the laces. The leather of his boots was soft, light tan in color and well polished, but with a scuff on the big toe. She finished one boot, grabbed it by the heel, and pulled it off, along with his sock, to reveal a gnarled, misshapen foot. No wonder he didn't wear sandals like the rest. A pungent smell drifted up, but she called again on her training and didn't wrinkle her nose, refused to let the disgust touch her.

Lothar swayed backward. "Careful, little whore," he mumbled.

It was working. It had to be working. And as swiftly as promised. She undid the other boot, taking her time, hoping he would fall asleep before she'd finished undressing him. Off went the second boot, and this time, the motion caused him to fall back onto the bed. But he wasn't done yet. "Come atop me and send me to sleep sweetly."

She slowly climbed onto the bed. His eyes fluttered, then closed. She paused, holding her breath in anticipation. They didn't open again. Soon his breathing deepened and slowed. Relief made her weak, and she stumbled as she slipped off the bed. Or was it the wine? She tried to clear her head. Where might he keep his key to the Archpriests' Library? She cast around the room, her gaze falling first on the bureau and its twin drawers. The nearest drawer, from what she had seen, was filled only with writing things. She rummaged through it just to be sure, but there was nothing. Behind her, Lothar groaned. Her heart leaped, and she whipped her head around, but he was still asleep. She took a breath, continued.

The second drawer didn't move in response to her tugging. Ruination, locked. She had brought some picks, just in case, but she couldn't afford to fiddle endlessly with a lock. There must be a key in here somewhere. Where might it be? Her eyes lit on Lothar's bulky form. In his pockets, probably. So she went back to the bed, carefully searching one pocket of his robe, then the other. Nothing in them but some balled pieces of paper.

Where, where, where would this second key be? She edged around the room, looking carefully, trying to put herself in his mind. In the plant pots, no. On the bookshelves, no. Under the bed? No. The wardrobe? The paintings! She lifted the first one away from the wall, a gilt-framed portrait of Lothar himself, looking slimmer than he did in real life. But the painting revealed nothing but a pale patch where it had protected the wall from smoke. The second painting was of Lumia appearing to Caris the Restorer in the wreckage of the Ruin. And yes, there it was! A little tiny bronze key resting on the bottom of the canvas frame. *Not so clever after all, Lothar.* She took the key and returned to the bureau, her heart finally slowing a little.

The key worked and she pulled the drawer open. A stack of papers, curling slightly at the top and bottom to show they had once been letters. Sensitive, no doubt, maybe useful to Moth. But she couldn't waste time going through them, so she just took them out and set them on top of the bureau to see if there was anything else in the drawer. She struck lucky. There was a key right at the back, large and heavy, embossed with the Lady's torch. Teeth jutting out at odd angles. This had to be it. She plucked it out, returned the papers, then closed and locked the drawer once more. Putting both keys in her pockets, she let herself out of Lothar's room and hurried to the Archpriests' Library, which was on the other side of the building.

As before, most of the corridors were in darkness at this hour, but she lit neither candle nor lamp, not wanting to risk being seen. She walked as quickly as she dared, almost tripping over a couple of novices, who, when they saw her, scuttled down a side corridor, no doubt afraid of being punished for being up after hours.

After what felt like an age, she finally reached the door to the library. Still, she dared not light a lamp, instead feeling for the keyhole with her hand before trying to fit the key in. It took a few attempts, but when she succeeded, she opened the door only a little before shutting it again. She could return another time, when she didn't have to worry about Lothar. So she closed and relocked the door, then opened her little box of clay and pressed the key into it. Once the clay had taken the shape, she wiped the key clean with a handkerchief and fumbled her way back to Lothar's room.

Outside his door, she was hit by a fresh wave of fear that momentarily paralyzed her. What if he'd woken up again? What would she say to him? How would she escape? But with a deep breath, she gathered her courage and opened the door a crack. There was no sound other than light snoring, so she opened it wider and stuck her head around to find that he was indeed still asleep, lying in the same position in which she had left him, his mouth slightly open. The sleepfast worked as well as she'd been promised. She tip-toed into the room and replaced both keys. Before she left, she looked at him one more time, tempted to kill him. It wouldn't be the first time she'd disposed of a trick who'd got troublesome. But that had nearly ended both her livelihood and her freedom. And there was Moth. So she slipped back out again and returned to her own room.

It was only once she got there and had turned the key in the lock that it all hit her. Lothar knew her secret and he was going to make her pay for it. A violent shaking spread through her. She had to leave the temple. But would Moth let her go? She needed to get him his wretched answers first. Well, she could have the key made in the morning and search the library that same night. With any luck, she'd find what she was looking for, please Moth so he'd get her out. Until then, she'd have to be careful to stay clear of Lothar.

But none of this stilled her quaking, so she went again to the little chest at the end of her bed and removed a small leather flask. She unstoppered it and took three mouthfuls of the apricot brandy inside. The sweet liquor set a soothing fire to her stomach. Much tastier than the cheap, bliss-laced jun she had drunk daily at Madam Sisi's, which had left her with blanks where memory should have been. *I won't be a whore again, though, not for brandy, not for Moth, and certainly not for Lothar.*

She had planned to put the flask away again but took it to her narrow bed instead. Sitting with her back against the headboard and her legs drawn up to her chest, she drank until it was empty, trying not to think.

Chapter 10

Alexios

I conducted my first binding at the age of 15. Traditionally, Keepers bound only members of their blood family. Epiktet may not have been my father by blood, but he was a father in every other way that counted, and he requested the honor. I would have died without his sacrifice. I was extremely ill, barely able to perform the ritual. But his life force helped me defeat the disease that afflicted me. Of course, that's not why a binding should be conducted. Epiktet had more years of life in him. But they were more afraid to lose me than him, and so the rules were bent.

—The Role of the Keeper, Alexios Arathraxis

Alexios mounted the steps to the plaza in front of the Hall of Congress, Theophila and Castes on either side.

A frightened and curious crowd had followed them as they marched from the walls to the Hall but milled around at the bottom of the steps. "We should say something to them," Alexios said. But what could they say? How was he going to save his people from *this?*

"I'll speak," Theophila replied.

"Tell them we'll announce a plan in two hours," Castes said. "They'll need something to hold on to."

Two hours. Two hours to think of a way to defeat the Ilk when they had all but wrought the destruction of his homeland two hundred years earlier. And his illusions had failed. All the illusions had failed.

They turned to face the milling crowd in the square, the Temple of the Makers rising at the opposite end, also now showing its red bricks.

"Alexios, could you raise my voice?" Theophila said.

"Of course." He called up the Lace and began to work it, nodding at her when he was ready.

"My people," she began. "As you know, we've been besieged by an army of abominations led by a Chelak corruptor. For the moment, we are safe, and a guard has been set. I urge you to remain within your homes and avoid the walls. Please, look to the children especially." She continued in the same vein while the crowd anxiously shifted and muttered. None called out, though. That would have been inappropriate.

As she spoke, Alexios tried to think of what they might do, how they might survive. But his mind kept filling with images of the wolf-Ilk, the rippers, tearing limbs from farmers.

Theophila's words pierced through the scramble of his thoughts. "While you wait, pray to the Makers above. Go to the temples. Ask them for the strength to withstand this new trial."

Alexios noticed then that the High Artefactor, Oxil, and the High Illusionist, Hereia, had arrived and were standing to the side. Oxil, grey-haired and straight-backed as always, looked out over the crowd with a furrowed brow, considering. Hereia, the lines on her face deepened by worry, kept her eyes on Theophila, who was now finishing her speech, telling the people to regather in the square when they heard the gong again.

With that, Castes and Theophila made their way into the Hall, followed by Alexios, Hereia, and Oxil. They first passed through a reception room lined with wooden benches for supplicants and visitors, and then into the Hall itself. At the far end was a pair of oak chairs for the rulers to sit on. Facing the chairs were four rows of pews, for the members of Congress.

Theophila and Castes tried to hide their discomfort at seeing it all as it truly was. But while their expressions were serene, their eyes darted about, taking it all in. He'd shown them the reality once, when they'd been made rulers, but that was almost a decade ago. Easy to forget you live in an illusion when that's all you ever see.

"Will you call Congress?" Oxil called from behind as they walked between the pews toward the other end of the room.

Theophila half turned. "Yes, but tomorrow, I think," she said. "We can't form a plan with a roomful of bickering representatives."

They circled around the rulers' chairs to access another door that led to the Ruling Chamber. This was a small room with only ten seats, organized around a large oval table. Only the rulers and members of the High Council sat here, making decisions on the daily running of the town and formulating policies to bring before Congress. Alexios sat at one end. Theophila and Castes sat to his immediate left and right, and Oxil and Hereia next to them.

"Suggestions?" Theophila said, planting her elbows on the table and spreading her hands wide.

"How many men of fighting age would you say we have?" Oxil said.

Alexios did a quick mental count. "Perhaps four or five hundred?"

"Pathetically few," Castes spat. "In days of old, all men would have been trained to give service. We would not have been so dependent on illusions." He shot a meaningful glance at Alexios.

Oh, you're happy now, aren't you, to be proved right? Is the death of our city worth the price of your victory, though? But he couldn't deny the sickening truth. His strategy had failed, and now they reaped the consequences.

"Dangerous to take the attack to them, then," Oxil said. "Even if we armed every grown man, our fighting force is tiny." It was rare for him to be downbeat, and now he looked lost.

"The women can fight too," Theophila said, her eyes and tone daring them to disagree.

"Against those wolf beasts?" Castes scoffed.

"Only the strongest warriors would be able to stand against those," Alexios said. "Even our men would be like babies against them." *Our people were never warriors. It was only those wretched Chelaki who made us so.*

"What do you know about the Ilk?" Hereia asked Alexios. "How can they be defeated?"

Alexios called on Epiktet and Cassander's memories of the Ilk War, but they were fragmented and uncertain. Neither had fought on the front lines.

"The Ilk were always led by mages," Cassander said. *"They're little more than animals and can't think independently."*

"So if we can kill the Ilk mage, they'll abandon the siege, or at least become disorganized," Alexios said.

"Easier said than done. Ilk mages are hard to kill," Epiktet replied.

Alexios relayed what Cassander had said, finishing by saying, "If we can't destroy the Ilk, then let's destroy their leader."

"It's the best plan *I* can think of," Theophila said.

"I'll go," Alexios said, though he dreaded the thought of killing. "I'm our strongest illusionist." *This is all my fault, those were my illusions out there. But* can *I kill?* He nursed the flame, but it was still small and weak.

"Absolutely not!" Theophila exclaimed. "You're the Keeper. You're too important to risk."

"Aren't we forgetting that this Ilk mage has already broken all of our illusions?" said Hereia, arms folded across her ample chest.

Alexios flinched.

"I think this plan is mad," she continued. "We don't even know if killing the Ilk mage will help. We should try to get help from Vonopoli and Potas."

Theophila shook her head. "Even if we can get a messenger through to the other enclaves, it would take weeks. And we don't know that they haven't also been attacked."

"We should seek help from the Vycenian weavers," Castes said, his expression challenging. "Their magic was always strong against Ilk, was it not?"

"I agree with the honored ruler," Oxil said. "We've isolated ourselves for too long, and look where it's taken us."

"I always said we should open ourselves to the world," Lycurgus said.

Disagreement from the other souls, although a couple now doubted. But Alexios wasn't prepared to concede that point yet. They could still fight and win. He had to believe it.

"No," Theophila said firmly. "We've had this debate many times already."

Hereia echoed her.

A flare of frustration in Oxil's eyes, normally so placid. Castes was obviously angry, shaking with the effort to contain himself. He opened his mouth to speak, but Alexios jumped in first, wanting to head off an argument. Wanting not to call on the weavers and lose all hope of hiding from their former allies. "The illusions weren't closely guarded. We didn't think someone would actively try to break them, the weavers don't have that magic. Obviously, this Ilk mage does. There are ways to build them stronger." That was true, it had to be. *Otherwise, I'm an utter failure.*

"*Get help from the weavers,*" Lycurgus said, sounding more animated than Alexios had heard him since death. "*We can't win alone. We never could. None of us ever could.*"

"He's right," said Cassander. "*Our mistake was not to join the Vycenians when the Ilk Lord first struck. By dividing us he destroyed us.*"

"No! No, we can deal with this ourselves," Alexios said. Two hundred years they had kept themselves apart, kept their traditions safe and sacred. He wouldn't bow before the first challenge.

"Very well, if we are set on this path, then who do we send to kill the mage?" Castes said.

"Nixos?" Theophila ventured. "He's strong, one of our best illusionists."

"No, we can't order someone to go on such a mission," Alexios said. *I won't be the one to speak the name.* "Let's ask for a volunteer." *It should be me.* But he said nothing. *They're right,* he told himself. *I'm the Keeper, I have the memories, and I must preserve them. Demeia isn't ready.*

"The volunteer must come from our strongest to have the best chance of succeeding," Castes said. "If you won't name someone, then decide first on a shortlist of candidates, ask each one in turn if they're willing to take the risk."

"Four to start with, I think," Theophila said. "Ask them if they're willing, then test them and choose the best."

"I still think this is madness," Hereia said, shaking her head.

"For once, I agree with her," Oxil said, and Hereia shot him an irritated look. "We can't hope to do this alone. We need allies. The Vycenian weavers have powerful magic. The time for hiding is over."

Yes, it's madness, but what else can we do? If we call on the Vycenians, our ways will be lost. We'll disperse, fragment, become no more than a footnote of history. The souls, with the exception of Lycurgus and Cassander, agreed with him.

"We'll send out an illusionist to kill the mage," Theophila said firmly, and Castes nodded in agreement.

"But let's keep it to ourselves rather than raise hopes," she added. "We should continue to make plans to withstand an attack. The Ilk mage may be trying to fool us with his talk of waiting."

"How will you test them?" Castes asked Alexios.

"I have an idea." It would be simple enough, test their illusions, test if they could kill. He knew the names on his list, too.

"Who will you choose?" Theophila asked.

"Nixos for certain, but also Youno." He glanced at Hereia. Youno was her grandson, as powerful an illusionist as she was, if not more so.

Hereia shook her head, an angry, frustrated movement, but said nothing.

"I think Epi and Miro also," Alexios added. Those names pained him. They were his grandchildren. But his bloodline was the strongest.

Theophila sent runners out with instructions for the four to gather in the Sanctum immediately.

Periklis arrived then, face flushed, and they began to make plans for the distribution of food and the management of the defense, agreeing to call a meeting that night of artisans and artefactors to discuss weapons design.

They were still wrapped up in these discussions when Alexios received word that the illusionists were waiting for him. He took a back door out of the Hall of Congress to avoid the crowd in the main square and then cast illusions so they could slip down the street and into the side entrance of the temple.

Standing in the Sanctum were the four illusionists, talking quietly among themselves. They stopped their talking as soon as he entered and turned to him expectantly.

"You have been summoned here because you're among our best illusionists and known for your courage and discipline," he began.

Flickers of pride in their expressions, but by and large they hid it well.

"You no doubt know there is an Ilk mage leading the abominations. I believe that if we can kill the mage, the monsters will lose their organization. It's our best hope of defeating their army. We need a single volunteer to go out under illusion and carry out the task."

They all clamored to put themselves forward, as he'd guessed they would. He'd picked them for their strength of mind as well as their magical skill.

He put up a hand to silence them. "Your courage isn't in doubt. However, none of you has killed before."

"I can do it!" Nixos shouted amidst the voices of the others.

Again, he raised a hand. "I'll set a test," he said when they'd quieted. Then he explained it to them—one at a time, they would have to make themselves invisible and stab an illusory man while Alexios attacked their castings.

There were no questions, only quiet resolution, and his blood warmed with pride before cooling again with fear. *They're so strong and brave, but what if I lose them?* But he couldn't let himself be distracted by these thoughts. They all had a duty.

He sent them all into the vestry to wait. Once they'd left, he created a full illusion of the Ilk mage, incorporating all the senses so that the man would seem to be truly living and breathing. When it was ready, he sent for Miro. Then he made himself invisible.

The door to the Sanctum opened, but Alexios saw no one come out and no tell-tale twisting of the Lace. A perfect illusion. He launched attacks, pulling on the Lace, trying to make Miro's casting become obvious. But his illusion held.

He waited for the knife to collide with the illusion of the mage. He'd know it only through a whispering, a tug on the Lace. But while he was still waiting, Miro became visible again. He was holding his knife, point down, to stab into the mage's heart, shaking violently.

"There's no shame in it," Alexios said. "We aren't killers." *Could* I *do it? I'm not sure. And yet I ask it of them. I'm a coward.* "Return to your tasks." He stepped over to the young man and placed a comforting hand on his shoulder.

"I'm sorry, I'm sorry," he said, again and again, until Alexios gently pushed him out.

Epi was next, his grandson, named for Epiktet, who had been like a father to him. But when it came to killing the mage, Epi's grasp over his illusion loosened, and Alexios was able to break it.

"I'm sorry, grandfather," he said, his expression all shame.

"Please, no apologies," Alexios said. "None of you has prepared for this."

He was about to call for Hereia's grandson Youno when the door to the Sanctum flew open. Demeia strode in, eyes flashing, green dress sweeping about her legs.

"Daughter, you shouldn't be here."

"Why not?" she demanded, coming to a halt before him. "I'm as strong an illusionist as the others, if not stronger."

Indeed, she was the best other than Nixos. "How did you know to come here?"

"Did you leave me out because I'm a woman and you think women aren't capable of defending our town?" she cried, hands on her hips.

That had been part of the reason, of course. He'd wanted to spare them the violence. "Well—"

"I've been training for this my whole life," she said. "If anyone should go it should be me."

"Listen, you really shouldn't ..." Then her words penetrated the fog of his confusion. "What do you mean you've been training?"

"I'm a Blade," she said, chin lifting.

He was so shocked that he did nothing but blink at her. A Blade? One of his own, a Blade?

"I joined not long after I came into my gifts," she said. "Are you really so surprised, father?"

"You've been training to fight, all these years, and I never knew," he said. He felt betrayed, and it cut him.

"You'd have forbidden it, been angry."

"I'm not angry, I'm ..." *I* am *angry, but maybe she was the wisest of us all, in the end.*

"Test me," Demeia said. "You'll find I'm the one to send."

"We can't lose you, you're the next Keeper in training," he said. *She's so like her mother, so full of fire.* A pang of longing for Melissa. Her loss he had never recovered from.

"There's little Hestiles," Demeia said, naming his great-grandson, only ten years old. "And others will be born. We both know I'll never be Keeper, you have too long left to live."

"I—"

"Demeia, why are you here?" Nixos, emerging from the vestry.

"Come here, brother," she said. "I have something to show you both."

Puzzled, Nixos approached them while Youno watched from the doorway. Alexios, still nonplussed at his daughter's revelations, remained silent.

When Nixos was but a few paces away from her, Demeia stepped toward him rapidly, one arm reaching out across his chest while a foot clipped him at the back of the knee. He tumbled to the ground, arms pinwheeling. A second later she was sitting astride him, holding a knife to his throat. She looked back up at Alexios. "You see, father."

Nixos turned red. "Get off me!" he said, pushing at her. "You could have warned me."

Alexios remembered Melissa again, and realized he was beaten. "Fine, you've proved your point."

Demeia smiled triumphantly and got to her feet in a single, graceful movement.

Nixos clambered upright, dusting himself off and glowering at his sister.

"Both of you, go to the vestry. Demeia, you can try next."

Alexios waited until the door to the vestry closed behind them and then prepared his illusion of the mage. When it was ready, he called for Demeia to enter.

She came out, and as he'd expected, created a flawless illusion. When Alexios felt her knife go through his Ilk mage, he made the man scream, made blood spurt out, thick and red. The knife stabbed into the illusion again, and then again, and the Ilk mage fell to the ground, crying for mercy. The knife went through his throat. Trying to quell his own horror at the sight, Alexios made the mage die.

Demeia reappeared, her expression fierce. "You know I can do this."

"Yes, so I see," he said. His voice came out a little ragged, and he coughed to cover it. "But please, go back to the vestry and wait. Send out Youno."

Youno was able to strike the first blow, but when the Ilk mage began to scream and bleed, he lost his invisibility. His face white, his eyes wide with shock and dismay. Him, too, Alexios sent away with reassuring platitudes.

Then came Nixos. He killed the mage with quiet efficiency, his illusion never faltering. Alexios wasn't surprised at Nixos's command over his illusions. But he was a little surprised at how coolly he had killed. "Are you one of them too?" he asked. "Like your sister?"

"A Blade? No."

"So you knew."

Nixos smiled sheepishly and shrugged. "I'm her brother."

And I'm her father. Do we ever truly know our children?

"I know she'll insist on being the one to go," Nixos said. "But see, I can do it too. You should send me. I'm the elder." Nixos would never let his sister outdo him, even if that meant killing when he was no killer.

"A moment," Alexios said, then called Demeia back into the room. She joined her brother, eyes still full of fire. Nixos shot her a brief smile, but she just looked at Alexios expectantly.

"It must be one of you," he said. He paused, unwilling to make the choice, wishing they would both refuse.

"It must be me," Demeia said. "He hasn't prepared for this like I have."

"No, send me," Nixos said. Alexios recognized the stubborn set of his mouth. It was very hard to convince him to act otherwise when he wore that look. Like his sister and mother. "You can afford to lose me. If this fails, she can help train other illusionists to fight."

"There's no point in sending him," Demeia said. "It's one thing to kill a man who isn't real. It's another entirely to kill one who is, and to do so under illusion. The Ilk mage won't be standing there quietly waiting." Her eyes blazed with determination, challenging him to deny her.

Another time, Alexios might have been annoyed by the defiance in her gaze. But instead, he was moved to tears by her bravery. The souls echoed his feeling, and he blinked rapidly and dug his fingernails into his palm to master himself.

Alexios didn't want to choose between them. Both their arguments made sense. What would give his people the best chance of success?

"We could both go," Nixos said. "The illusions will be more powerful, and one of us can maintain them while the other attacks."

"Actually, he's right," Demeia said. "Two is better than one. We usually train in pairs."

And like that, the alliance between the siblings was sealed against him once more.

Alexios sucked his teeth and considered what to do. They were probably right, but it seemed a terrible risk. Still, he didn't want to choose, didn't want to be the one to say a name. And did he want to send one out all alone? Maybe to die alone? "Very well, you both go," he said at last, the words half-strangled. "We'll wait until the darkest part of the night. It will be easier for you to hide." *At least Melissa is dead. She would have raged at me for doing this to them. Although she would have volunteered to go herself.*

"What if the Ilk spawner isn't there anymore?" Nixos said.

"He must be. To control the monsters," Alexios replied. "But he may be hiding in the forest, so be sure to look widely."

"We'll find him," Demeia said determinedly. "We'll end this before it's begun."

"Come, let's go to the Hall so we can talk to the rulers and establish a strategy," Alexios said. They slipped outside and spun illusions of invisibility to hide themselves from the people still standing anxiously in the square, waiting for news despite Theophila's exhortations that they should visit the temple and go to their homes.

Only the rulers and Periklis were still in the Chamber when they returned. Alexios supposed that Hereia and Oxil had been sent to speak to the mages. He told them of the decision to send Nixos and Demeia together, and the rulers approved.

"We've finished here," Castes said. "It's time to go and present our plan to the people." He stood.

Alexios spoke to Periklis. "They'll need weapons." He jerked his head in the direction of Nixos and Demeia.

"I have my own," Demeia said.

Periklis smiled at her, a knowing smile. He was the head of the Blades, that much Alexios knew. He felt a stirring of anger against the man and repressed it. After all, Periklis had been right to train them, right to prepare. It was he who had failed.

"We should practice together first," Demeia said to Nixos. "Telos is also a Blade, he can act as the Ilk mage for us," she added. Telos was another young illusionist, her third cousin. "We can go to the Blades' training room." She looked at Alexios questioningly.

"Yes, do that," he said. "I'll go with the rulers to speak to the people and then to the wall to find the best place for you to go over when the time comes. I don't think we should use the gates. They may be watched."

It was fully dark outside, but the air was warm and close, with not even the slightest of breezes to freshen it.

Castes went to the great gong outside the Hall and beat it himself, three times to signal an official announcement. The crowd was already thick, reaching into the streets beyond the square, so they didn't wait before speaking. Castes went first, and Alexios raised his voice so he could be heard clearly.

"My people, the enemy is at the gates, but with fortitude and the grace of the Makers, we'll survive this great trial, as we've survived before." He paused a moment to let the words sink in, then began the instructions. "Every able-bodied man between the ages of 16 and 45 is to go to the guardhouse in the morning to sign up for defensive duties. Older men may also choose to do so, as may women of any adult age, but not if they have children under 12."

So Theophila had won that argument, at least in part.

"In the morning, you are also to count the food you have stored or can produce. You are then to send a written accounting to the Provisioning Office, which will be set up in the Hall of Congress. Food will be gathered over the coming days and then centrally distributed to ensure we can last as long as possible. Checks of homes will be conducted periodically, and anyone found hoarding food will be shamed and pilloried on this very plaza."

Alexios hoped none of it would be necessary, that Nixos and Demeia would succeed in their mission. That they wouldn't die in the attempt.

Castes finished his speech by exhorting the people again to pray and to stay away from the walls unless engaged in defensive duty. He also promised a daily briefing at midday and again in the evening to keep them apprised of developments. With that, he sent them home. But the crowd dispersed only slowly, many staying to discuss what had been said. The rulers turned back toward the Hall, but Alexios bid them goodbye and went to the wall.

"Find us in the Chamber and tell us what you decide," Theophila said. "We won't be leaving this night."

Alexios nodded and then spun invisibility to get him through the crowd unseen. It didn't take him long to reach the wall once he'd got past the immediate press of people. Dim glowlamps now lit the ramparts, silhouetting the city guard while they watched over the besieging abominations. When he climbed up, he saw that the Ilk had gathered around fires, and the smell of roasting meat wafted toward him. It sparked a sharp memory of farmers who'd run too slowly to the gate. His stomach roiled, and a few minutes passed before he'd recovered enough to continue his walk around the wall.

The light from the Ilk fires made it easier to see their lines—they were still concentrated at the eastern and southern gates, and the skreek continued to circle above the western one. He did a full round and finally decided on a spot midway between the south and east gates, which was out of view of the bulk of the Ilk. Then, judging he still had time, he went to the Keeper's Sanctum to seek the wisdom of the Makers. The streets were nearly empty, and criers were running around, imposing a new curfew. One reached out an arm to stop him, but then realized who he was and backed away with a bow and hasty apologies.

Nixos and Demeia met him later in the Sanctum, their faces red and shining. In their belts were a pair of knives. Demeia also wore a short sword. How strange, to see weapons on them. A memory popped into his mind, of marching Eleusian soldiers in nicoleum mail and grey livery. One of Epiktet's. Or perhaps Cassander's? "Let's pray together," he said. "And then go eat."

When they'd finished their prayers, they went to his house for a simple meal of nutbread and goat's cheese.

"I keep wondering, has the Ilk Lord returned?" Nixos said. He only picked at his food, which was unlike him.

"Impossible. He was destroyed in the Ruin with his armies. But clearly, the secret of Ilk-making wasn't buried with him as we'd thought," Alexios replied. He thought again of the vision. It *had* been a warning, but one that had come far too late.

Demeia swallowed a mouthful of bread and cheese. "But if this Ilk spawner is someone new, why has he come against us now? What relation does he bear to the old Ilk Lord?"

"Antiphos will always lead his slaves against us," Alexios said. "It is our doom to fight him throughout time."

"Well, we'll end it quickly this time," Demeia said determinedly, hands curling into fists on either side of her plate.

"I hope she's right," Epiktet said, and the souls chimed their agreement.

They spoke little after that, each occupied with their own thoughts. Once they had finished their meal, they went to the wall. Castes and Hereia were waiting for them, and for a few minutes, they stared down at the shadowy forms of the monsters. Some of their fires had gone out, and many of them appeared to be sleeping. But Alexios could make out sentries moving in the darkness.

He wove the initial illusion, to hide the rope ladder that Castes threw out over the side of the wall. Nixos went first, and then Demeia. Alexios covered their descent with fresh illusions. Once they were on the ground, they took over with their own casting, vanishing even from his sight.

"Makers be with them," murmured Castes.

The wait was agonizing. Alexios stayed on the wall, but Castes and Hereia returned to the Chamber, where plans for the defense were still ongoing. He didn't try to sleep, felt no need for it, the energy of Eliana's soul sustaining him easily. But he doubted he could have slept anyway, not with the knowledge that Nixos and Demeia were among those monsters.

While he waited, he scoured his memories and those of the souls for anything he could remember reading or hearing about Ilk and Ilk mages, but nothing new came to him. The vision had given him an insight into how they were made, using the elemental power, the power of Antiphos. But what happened once they'd spawned? And how many Ilk mages were there? Were there more armies, attacking the other enclaves?

His thoughts drifted to Nixos and Demeia. Where were they now? Had they found the Ilk mage yet? He wished he were with them. It felt wrong, to send them out while he stayed safely on the wall. *What kind of father am I? I should be protecting them, shielding them from this.* Melissa would have been so angry. She'd had so much fire in her. But her fire hadn't been enough against the fever that had taken her, too young, at the age of forty-one. He hadn't been able to love since. All the women seemed too young, and he had lost too many. *No one should live this long.*

His eyes lifted toward the heavens, to the stars twinkling above. *Great Makers, why do you make me carry this burden?* Then he felt guilty and small. Who was he to question the gods? He had a duty to his people, and that duty was greater than he was.

He began to walk along the wall, peering out into the darkness after every few steps, hoping for a sign that his children had succeeded. But nothing changed. The Ilk remained mostly still and silent, the watchers on the wall equally so.

Chapter 11

Ina

The Great Slaughter may have been carried out by the Eleusians and the sorcerers from across the sea, but it was Sīut who drove them. And the Cursed Ones were his pawns.

—Teachings of Old Tsu

Chel's shrine was inside a grassy hollow, surrounded on three sides by tall rainbow trees whose roots made great humps in the mossy undergrowth. The elders said that these trees had also grown on old Chelakan, and they were long favorites of their people because of the brightly colored bark. Ina loved them as much as anyone else and paused to place her free hand against the trunk of one of the trees. It was cool to the touch, and she pinched a piece of peeling red-orange bark between her thumb and forefinger, pulling it off to reveal a vertical strip of new green growth beneath. As it matured, it would pass through the full spectrum of colors before coming away like the piece she held in her hand. By the time it turned red, how much would things have changed for her?

She let the peel fall onto the forest floor to feed the teeming life that she could sense more than see. Something would change soon, of that she was certain. What was uncertain was whether the change would be for the better or worse. For now, she needed guidance, and she hoped that Chel would provide it. So, on she went into the hollow, following a worn path that wound between outcrops of grey-black rock.

The shrine was at the north end of the hollow, tucked into a natural grotto backed by a sheer escarpment. Clear water tumbled down the rock face to the right of the grotto, then disappeared underground. Beyond the escarpment rose steep slopes covered in a dense canopy of trees. The higher ones were shrouded in mist, hiding the huge conical mountain, Ilij'ai, that occupied the very center of the island.

Relieved to see that no one else was there, Ina approached the towering statue of Chel, shaped many years ago from the warm red-brown wood of the koua tree and now glowing in the early afternoon sunlight. She dropped onto her knees to place an offering of spiky purple and yellow ooja flowers. Other flowers and small objects lay on the ground already—colored stones collected from the sea, necklaces made of beads or feathers, little handmade carvings of Chel's creatures.

Having laid the bouquet, she moved back a few paces and sat on the grass in a cross-legged position, facing the statue. It had a beaked face and partially outstretched wings, said to be like those of a drakir. Its legs were those of a cat, though, and were carved with a scale-like pattern to resemble the skin of a fish or reptile. But it was the pendulous breasts, the round belly and the erect penis that caught and held Ina's attention. These were a reminder that Chel was both mother and father to the world, the source of all life. Rebelling against their father, Sīut, they had shaped the world from his primordial Chaos. Sīut had taken a sneaky revenge, though, and given a portion of his power to some of Chel's creations so that they could do his work, and one day destroy Chel's world. Chel had discovered the flaw in their creation too late and was forced to rely on the pure-born to keep their world safe. In exchange for fighting Sīut, all people born in their world would have a place in eternity at their side. Even the souls of the Cursed Ones could return to them, but to protect the world they had to be purged young, before they came into the fullness of their power.

At least, that was how the story went. But despite this, despite what the elders said, Ina couldn't feel that her powers had been granted by Sīut. She identified with Chel, had always felt half man, half woman, embodying more than most Chel's androgynous nature. And when she opened her mind, as she did now, she was even closer to the world Chel had created. She could not only hear the birds with her ears but also sense where they were, what branch they perched on, which current of air they rode as they traveled across the skies.

How could this power harm Chel's world? Did Ina really belong to Sīut, and if she did, did this really mean she was a danger to the Cloth? Did it mean she was doomed to cause chaos and war? She had sworn the Oath of Peace like the rest, and had never broken it, nor wanted to. *Why does the Godstone call me? What is it really? Chel, please, show me a sign. What am I to do?*

For a long time, she sat there, as the shadows lengthened and the sky darkened. The only solution that came to her was to go to the Godstone, and with each passing mark, she became more convinced that this was what she had to do. She would go alone that very night to find out why it called her. And she would destroy it if she must.

Getting to the island would be far from easy, though. The currents around Uruk'il, the island of the Godstone, were strong. Her people usually crossed on a large canoe, rowed by a team of their strongest men, but she would have to cross alone in one of the small, one-person dugouts. However, if she plotted the course carefully, and picked the right moment with the tides, she might be able to land on the western side of the island. Here, the waters were calmer, even if rocks lurked close to the surface.

As she was on her way back to the village, though, she was struck by a sudden strong sense of being watched from above. She peered up at the green canopy of the trees and the indigo sky but saw nothing. A heartbeat later, the feeling was gone, and she dismissed it as a quirk of her senses.

She waited until after the fire had been put out and the last stragglers had gone to bed before slipping out to South Beach, where the canoes were kept. Most of them were inside the long, rectangular canoe hut, made of sturdy wood that could withstand the storms when they came. A couple of one-man canoes had been left on the shore, though, and she decided to use one of these. They were relatively light crafts, made from dug-out koua wood, and she dragged one into the shallows with ease. It would be at least another month before the summer storms arrived, so the breeze was only slight and the waves were gentle, offering her little resistance as she waded out into the warm ocean.

Before she got into the canoe, she paused to look out toward Uruk'il. The moon was full and the stars bright in the sky, making it possible to see its hunched outline against the horizon. She closed her eyes and opened her mind, and sure enough, she could feel the Godstone's pull, an insistent, wordless whispering that goaded her on. Opening her eyes again, she got into the canoe. Then, taking up the paddle, she began to push out into the ocean, using the stars, the swell, and the shape of the land to plot her course. Soon she was sweating freely, her arms and chest humming from exertion.

She was about halfway to the island when the breeze unexpectedly picked up and shifted direction from southerly to north-easterly. The waves rose with it and became flecked with white. The Storm Wind? It couldn't be. It was too early in the season—far too early. There hadn't been a hint of it in the air. This must be just a squall, albeit one that was coming from the wrong direction. Nevertheless, the outcome was that it now took much more effort to try and keep the canoe moving in the right direction.

She rowed for perhaps half a mark before she realized that she was not only no closer to her destination but also drifting eastward. Gritting her teeth, she redoubled her efforts, a sharper burn building in her muscles. It still wasn't enough. She decided to try and point the canoe straight west, hoping that this would counter the eastward drift. But it was as if the waters had turned against her, resisting her efforts and spinning the canoe back around between each stroke. If she continued in her current course for much longer, she would be pulled to the east side of the island, and potentially into the powerful currents that swirled toward the Great Maelstrom. Fear knotted her belly, but she swallowed it down, refused to let it cloud her mind.

It was obvious that she had to go back home. There was no hope of landing on the westward side of the island, not that night. But as she turned the canoe around, it got caught up in another current that dragged it even farther to the east. She strained to keep the turn going, but no amount of effort would take her where she willed. The breeze became a whipping wind, and heavy clouds rushed in from the northeast, blanketing the moon and stars, leaving her in complete darkness. She could see neither the island ahead of her nor the island behind her, but she knew she was being pulled directly toward the Maelstrom. Terror took full grip of her.

"Chel, please help me!" she cried.

The waves were growing, coming chaotically from two directions and causing the water to roil around her. Her canoe rocked ever more wildly in the rising swell and began to fill with water. Rain poured down, driven by the wind to sting her exposed flesh. The paddle was ripped out of her grasp, quickly spinning away into the darkness. She cried out in despair, but the wind stole her breath. Water lashed her face until she was nearly blind.

A towering wave advanced toward her, high as a cliff. It caught the canoe and lifted her up into the air, and as she rose under it, she experienced a moment of such intense fear that it became something like joy, as if she had come into possession of a deep, fundamental secret about life itself. But then the moment was gone, and she was upended violently into the turbulent waters. Her hands instinctively rose to protect her head, and the weight of the canoe slammed against them. Yet she barely noticed the pain, all her efforts and attention bent on getting back to the surface.

Once her head was clear of the water, she gripped the edges of the canoe with numb fingers. But the waves soon prized it away from her and dragged her back under. Flailing with arms and legs, she managed to resurface and take a water-sodden gasp of air before another wave lifted her and then threw her down. Pain stabbed in her side, making it hard to swim or breathe. The sea was like the raging monster from the nightmares of her childhood, but this time there was no waking up. She would be devoured by the beast.

Down again she was pulled and the controls that she kept around her mind dissolved. The whole world crashed into her, and her mind crumbled under the onslaught. Yet she fought her way back to the surface once more, managing to stay there for a few precious seconds before she went under again.

Desperately, she cast out a plea for help to the creatures of the sea. So long since she'd tried to exert control over nature, but she knew how to do it still. Only little fish answered her call, too puny to be of use. She pushed her senses farther, farther even than when she'd sought the mist eagles, and pain swelled in her skull. "*Help me!*" she cried. "*Help me!*" But no help came. She tried to struggle back to the surface again, but her strength was near gone. Then her mind brushed against that of another intelligent being, a vast creature whose nature and form she didn't know. It had never been to their islands and was surprised at finding her in its domain.

"*Please, help me,*" she begged. She wasn't sure it would answer. It was ancient, older even than the elders of the villages, a master of the seas.

"*Who calls me?*" They weren't words that he spoke. More like an impression in her mind that she was able to translate into speech.

"*Ina'Yakir'Suk. I am of Chelakan. I live on the island.*" She sent an image of it. "*Please, I will die. Can you carry me home?*" She managed to surface again, choking and spitting.

"*I am not a flyer! We do not carry your people.*"

The image that flashed into her mind was undoubtedly that of a drakir. But although she was able to identify it through the drawings that circulated among her people, these were nothing compared to the true splendor of the birds, their voluptuous, iridescent plumage, their proud necks and wise eyes. "*The drakiri are no more. I beg you, please take me home if you can. I'll die.*"

"*It is a long time since one of you has spoken to one of us. Why are you here?*"

"I was going to the island. There is a stone on its peak, put there by Chel. It calls me to it."

He was surprised and seemed to disappear. She panicked, trying to call him back, but there was nothing. She went down again, and this time, her arms and legs refused to respond as she tried to return to the surface. Deeper and deeper she sank, lungs heaving, demanding air. A sort of dreamy peace stole over her. This was it, her journey was over. She would open her mouth, and the water would return her to Chel.

"I will take you."

Something lifted her up and bore her to the surface, and as she broke the waters, her mouth opened wide to feed her starved lungs. Once she'd caught her breath again, she noticed that she was lying on a long, broad back. The skin was scaled but felt slick and smooth beneath her fingers. The creature sent a wordless instruction, and she found and then gripped onto a horny ruff at the base of the long, lizard-like skull. To keep her balance, she stretched herself out almost flat on her belly, using her knees to brace herself. The creature turned slowly and began to move against the current, back toward Lun'il. She could feel his muscles working beneath her as he strained against the churning waters.

The waves calmed when they escaped the current, but the rain continued to pelt down, each drop a stinging missile. "*Were we in the Maelstrom?*" she asked, thinking of the giant waves, larger than even the waves that rolled in on the northern sides of the islands during the summer storms.

"That was not the great storm. No living thing goes there, not even I."

He sent an image of a whirling funnel of water that went right up to the sky, so expansive that it would easily have swallowed up all the islands.

"But you've been there."

"I can go closer than any other creature, but I have only seen it from afar."

"What are you?"

"Your people called us leviathans."

"Are there others like you?"

She sensed a deep sadness. "*I am one of the last.*"

"How long have you lived?"

The leviathan didn't measure time as she did, but filled her mind with a rapid series of images that passed too quickly to isolate and understand. Her final impression was that he had lived for many centuries, certainly during the time of the first great war against the Eleusians, and then the second one that had led to the annihilation of her people and their exile to the islands. He filled her mind with a vision of the terrifying desolation that had struck several centuries later—of an enormous blast of power that had shredded the Cloth and sunk the continent her people had once shared with the Eleusians. Millions of living things had melted and dissolved as the threads that bound them were unraveled and sucked into nothingness. In its place came the Maelstrom—Sīut's Price, exacted on the Eleusians who had murdered her people.

"It was the landwalkers who caused the Unraveling," the leviathan said, clearly reading her thoughts.

"But their power came from Sīut?"

"I do not know about such things, I do not know this Sīut."

"Sīut is the Chaos Maker, enemy of Chel, who created this world."

"We do not think in such ways. I do not know why the creator-of-all-things made you landwalkers so restless and greedy, nor why you were granted such great power to pursue your desires. You are a danger to the world."

"So why did you save me?"

The leviathan said nothing for a few moments, then, *"A long time ago, one of your people saved a hatchling from death."*

As he spoke, Ina saw a young Chelak woman freeing a lizard-like creature from a tangle of fishing nets before returning him to the sea.

"In return, she asked us to watch for you."

Ina's grip on the leviathan tightened. "*Me specifically? Why?*"

"She said the creator-of-all-things wants you to fulfill a purpose. You were to be helped if you called."

"Did she say what the purpose was?"

"We did not ask, nor do we care. A life for a life, this is what was promised."

Ina said nothing, contemplating the leviathan's words. It seemed preposterous that he'd been told to look for her so many hundreds of years ago. Even more preposterous to think she'd been chosen by Chel. But then there was the Godstone, calling to her. If Chel had put it there, like the elders said, then surely the Godstone wanted to tell her something? But why would Chel choose a Cursed One, likely to be killed as soon as she was old enough to use her powers? What a terrible bet to make, that Ina would survive long enough to touch the Godstone safely. Why not choose someone untainted? Unless, of course, the elders were wrong, and her powers were not a curse and did not come from Sīut.

"Swim from here. I will not come too close to your land."

Ina peered through the sheeting rain, barely making out the island some fifty strokes away. "*Please, just a little nearer. I've lost my strength.*"

He hesitated, then said he would do as she asked. In the end, he brought her close enough that she would have to swim only a few strokes before she reached the shallows. She slid off his back and into the water. "*Many thanks, great one. If I may ever do something for you, call me.*"

"*We do not need the help of the landwalkers,*" he said with pride. His long, forked tail lashed the water as he turned, and for the first time, Ina realized how enormous he was—at least three times the size of the whales that sometimes came near the islands. His teeth could probably crunch through an entire hut.

When he disappeared, she began to fight her way through the water. Soon her fingertips brushed sand, and with relief, she got her feet under her and started to wade. But as she neared the beach, the waves caught her and dragged her down and back out to sea. She dug her fingers into the sand and began to pull herself along on her belly with shaking arms. At last, she broke the waterline and crawled onto the beach, then on up to the base of the dunes. It was here that the last shreds of strength deserted her, and she fell into unconsciousness.

She woke sometime later to the sound of her name being called through the rain. Opening her eyes, she saw Suni kneeling over her, long hair plastered wetly to her head, eyes wide with fear. "Thank Chel!" she exclaimed. "I feared the worst when I couldn't wake you." She put a hand to Ina's cheek. "Are you hurt?"

Thought was far away. Ina grasped for it, trying to make sense of what she saw and felt and heard. Wet skin. Dull pains. She shuddered out a breath.

"Ina! Speak, can you speak?" Suni's voice rose with alarm.

Ina found her voice. "I'm not hurt."

"But why are you here? What's happened?"

The fear and concern on Suni's face warmed Ina. "I went for a swim." Her breath shuddered out of her again. She was getting colder.

"I had this dream. You were far out at sea, near drowning in a storm. But it was a storm more terrible than any I've ever seen. The waves were the size of small mountains. You called out to me to save you. It was so real, so strong, that I woke and came to the beach. And here I find you, half dead." As Suni finished speaking, she lent over and pulled Ina up into a sitting position. Ina let her weight fall against the other woman, unable to keep herself upright.

"Tell me the truth," Suni murmured, her chin above Ina's head. "You didn't go swimming in a storm."

"There was no storm when I started out." Ina closed her eyes, listening to Suni's rapid heartbeat.

Suni pushed Ina away gently by the shoulders and raised her chin with her fingertips. "Was it true, what I saw in the dream?"

Ina's throat constricted, stopping her from speaking.

"You don't need to hide it from me," Suni said in a voice so gentle that Ina was overcome with an urge to weep. "I've been too close to you not to know that you have some form of the Cur— the old powers."

Ina began to shake violently and Suni wrapped her arms around her again. But despite the warmth of Suni's body, the trembling was so bad that she felt as if her bones would shake right out of her.

"Come, you're freezing and wet. I'll take you home."

Her legs wouldn't support her, so Suni put Ina's arm around her shoulders and then held Ina at the waist, half dragging her back to the Healers' Lodge, to a private room. Once inside, she helped Ina strip off her wet clothes before laying her down on a pallet and covering her with a double layer of blankets.

"Stay," Ina whispered. "Please."

Suni hesitated, but then removed her own wet clothes and slipped under the blanket, her skin warm against Ina's. Then she pulled Ina around so that her head was resting on her shoulder, after which Ina quickly fell asleep again.

Chapter 12

Fay

A Lumin priest may marry only with the permission of the archpriest overseeing their region. Their chosen partner must be as pure of heart and as chaste as any priest so they do not sully Lumia's name. Married priests may not reside in her temples but must live amongst the people they serve.

—The Lumin Priest's Handbook

Fay slid her copied key into the lock and turned. It wouldn't move. *Ruination, tell me this works.* She wiggled the key, tried again to turn it, and this time, the mechanism gave. Muttering thanks to Lumia, she pulled the door back and slipped into the Archpriests' Library, ensuring she locked it behind her. Her candle illuminated a small room crowded with book stacks. Two parallel rows of desks occupied the central aisle running between the stacks, each with a small lamp on a raised ledge in one corner. The only windows, two of them, were high in the left wall, so small they must let in only the tiniest sliver of light during the daytime.

The catalog, a huge, hardbound tome, was resting on a plinth by the door. She used her candle to light one of the oil lamps sitting on a little shelf above the plinth, then blew the candle out and dropped it into the pocket of her robes. This done, she opened the catalog to scan through its lists of books. Lots that looked boring, and she wasn't even sure why they were kept out of the main library. Some, however, caught her eye, and would no doubt catch Moth's if he were with her—for a thief, he was unusually interested in old histories. *History of Eleusia, Volume 1: From Ancient Times until the First Chelaki War.* Eleusia, wasn't that the land of the old people of Teleriol, lost when the continent sank during the Ruin? No one knew much about them except for legends and stories. But the Chelaki? Some race in the Federation lands? But how would they have warred with the Eleusians and why? There were two more volumes: *From the First to the Second Chelaki War* and *From the Second Chelaki War to the Reign of First Weaver Madagon*. Well, she didn't have time to look at them now. She needed books about the building of Lumia's temple.

The catalog, however, proved to be something of a disappointment, with only a single book that looked promising—*The Original History of the Temple of Lumia in Arindel.* She made note of the shelf and number and then, grabbing the lamp, hurried over to the book stacks.

She found the right stack, in the middle, and walked along it, squinting at the numbers on the spines of the books. Her nose filled with the smell of old paper, strangely soothing to her anxiety. The history turned out to be a hefty, dusty tome with crumbling paper, making her sneeze when she took it down.

Now, to read it here first, see if it had what she needed, or bring it back to her room? She decided to take the risk and stay. It might not have her answers, and then she'd have to trek all the way back here. She didn't have all night and she certainly didn't have all day.

So she dropped to her knees and began to flick through the yellowed pages. The writing was cramped, difficult to read, but it didn't take her long to realize it didn't have what she was looking for. The account started after the temple had been built. There were no plans, no mention of the actual construction. With a heavy heart, she returned the tome to the shelf and then sought out the catalog again. There must be something, some clue as to the contents of that hidden room.

She read the catalog more slowly this time, tracing each title with her finger, panicky frustration building in her. Then she saw it and almost laughed: Caris the Restorer's diary. Caris had founded the Lumin order, overseen the building of the temple. In her earlier frenzy, she had missed the entry.

With renewed hope, she made her way back through the book stacks, right down to the back of the room. But the diary wasn't in place. Fay swallowed and sucked in air. *Don't lose it yet. Books are put on the wrong shelves all the time.* She scanned the rest of the shelf, then the shelves above and below. No sign. Had she read the shelf number wrong? She returned to the catalog, leaden with disappointment, found the entry for the diary again. Perhaps that was a seven and not a one? New hope flickering, she made her way to a different stack.

And there it was, high on a shelf, right where it was supposed to be. A thrill of excitement ran through her. Not just at finding it. Caris had lived through the Ruin. Who knew what she'd written inside? Fay stretched up a hand to take the book, a slim volume, bound in dark, cracked leather. Etched into the front were the words, "Diary of her

Most Radiant, Caris the Restorer." Surely added later, after her death? Fay smiled in anticipation.

The sound of a key sliding into the lock.

Pits, pits, pits! She blew out her lamp as the door opened, leaving the room completely black. Impossible to find a hiding place.

But then the darkness became more transparent as the newcomer lit their own light. Fay remembered that in the alcove behind her was a glass case full of old maps. There might be enough space for her to squeeze under it. She looked for and found its dark bulk and tip-toed toward it. Dropping to her knees and then rolling onto her back, she squeezed in beneath the case, resting the diary on her stomach. The space was tiny and claustrophobic, and panic squeezed her chest. She closed her eyes and repeated a Lumin mantra she'd grown up with, one that still brought her comfort, despite everything. *Light burns away the darkness, conquers all our pain. Light burns away the darkness, conquers all our pain.*

The newcomer began to walk in her direction, then down through the book stacks toward her hiding place. She tilted her head sideways, widening her mouth and throat to make her breathing as quiet as possible. Faintly outlined beneath the map case was a pair of fine leather sandals, the feet and ankles most certainly female. Could it be Nuria? Hard to tell in this light, and it wasn't as if Fay spent her time studying the ankles of other priests. Certainly not Aniya. She was big-boned, and these ankles were slim. Marcie and Celeen were slender enough, but Celeen was black-skinned. So, Marcie or Nuria. If either caught her, she'd be in serious trouble.

The woman walked closer toward Fay, then paused, presumably scanning the spines of ancient books as she had herself. *And why is she here at this hour, when most people are asleep?* The archpriest found what she was looking for, removed it carefully, and took it to one of the desks in the center of the room, where Fay heard her sit.

Pits, now I'm stuck here. Determined not to think of Lothar, she let her thoughts drift to Moth. Hopefully, this diary would have his answers. But at least she had the key. The key had to be worth something—at least a few days of patience? There were surely many books in the library that would satisfy his curiosity. Oh, but to get his answers, to get into that hidden room. Then he might let her leave the temple. She could do some other work, maybe take over a jun shack or something, as long as it didn't involve whoring. She'd never need to see Lothar again ... *No, don't go there, don't think about him.*

Fay's fingers lightly skimmed the edge of the diary, feeling the softness of the old leather. How she longed to open it, to see what secrets it held. When would that wretched person go? There was movement from the desk, and Fay's heart leaped hopefully. The person walked toward the stacks and replaced the book. Fay expected her to leave, but to her dismay, she simply went to another shelf to take a different book back to a desk. Why was she reading in the middle of the night? *What* was she reading? *Well, it's not like she's breaking any rules, is it? Unlike me.* Unless it wasn't an archpriest. Maybe Fay wasn't the only key stealer around.

Her eyes started to grow heavy, but she didn't dare sleep. To keep herself awake, she pinched her skin, digging her nails in deep enough to draw blood, thinking about what Moth would do to her if she didn't come up with his answers soon. About what Lothar would do if she didn't find a way to satisfy him. Another age passed, and Fay began to worry that it would be daylight before the person left, making it much harder for her to sneak out unseen.

But at last, the unknown reader did return her book and leave. Total darkness followed her departure, telling Fay that dawn hadn't yet broken. Relieved, she crawled out from under the case, hitting her head against the leg of the map case on the way. Rubbing at the sore spot, she clambered back to her feet and felt her way through the darkness toward the door. She would take the diary back to her room. It was too risky to read here. At the last minute, she remembered to put the oil lamp back on the shelf by the catalog.

The hallway was equally dark, but Fay didn't have the means to relight her candle, so she used her hand to make her way along it. Thankfully, it wasn't far to the nearest main passageway, which was still lit with torches. After rekindling her candle from one, she returned to her room. She had fully intended to read the diary as soon as she reached safety, but she had barely opened the front cover when her eyes began to close. *Wake up. You need something for Moth tomorrow!* But this time no amount of pinching would help.

I'll just rest my head on the table for a few minutes. Just a few minutes. Down her forehead went, onto her hands, and she sank into a deep sleep.

Chapter 13

Alexios

I was taken across the Western Sea to a vast and terrible storm—a giant whirlpool that stretches all the way up to the sky. The clouds around it are purple and riven with lightning, and a furious wind whips and blows. The Lace there is torn and fragmented, allowing chaos to spill through, the power of Antiphos. This is what replaced Teleriol.

—The Visions of Keeper Alexios Arathraxis

Alexios was still walking when the sun peeped its head above the horizon again. The Ilk hadn't moved from their position of the night before, their presence warping the Lace and filling him with dread, a constant reminder of their wrongness.

The sun continued to rise, filling the day with new heat. Still, there was no sign of Nixos and Demeia. *I'd know if they died. I'd know.*

Children came with flatbread and honey for the guardians on the wall. Alexios forced himself to eat, though he had no appetite. He was swallowing the last of it when there was a stir among the ranks of the Ilk. He peered down—wondering, hoping. Then his attention was drawn by a blond youth running along the wall toward him.

"Keeper, please follow me, the Ilk mage has reappeared," he gasped.

Alexios's heart leaped at the expression on his face. "Nixos, Demeia?"

The messenger's face screwed up with anguish. "Alive, but he has them, and wishes to speak to you."

Alexios wasted no more time on words, running with him along the wall until they reached Theophila. She was staring grimly down at the Ilk, at the mage, masked again in bone. Flanking him were a pair of rippers. One each gripped Demeia and Nixos in its claws. There was blank terror on their faces, but they seemed unharmed. Even so, the sight of them in the enemy's hands made him want to vomit. *No, no, no. I should never have sent them out.*

The Ilk mage caught sight of him. "Keeper! I'm so glad you've come!"

"Will you return them to us?" Alexios said, trying desperately to think of a way to save them. *I can't let them die. I can't. Melissa, she'll never forgive me.*

The Ilk mage laughed. "You really thought these two would kill me? I'll admit they came fairly close, but my wards are strong."

Alexios stared at them dumbly. What could he do?

"As a gesture of goodwill, I'll return one," the Ilk mage said. "Which do you choose?"

Choose? *Choose?* How could he choose between his children? Nixos, clever and strong? Demeia, who had such courage and forethought?

"Take Demeia!" Nixos shouted. His voice was firm and carried easily.

Brave man, braver than I.

"No, let it be Nixos," Demeia said, voice ringing out strongly despite the fear that whitened her face.

"Hush now, let your Keeper decide." The mage sounded again like he was smiling under his mask.

Alexios realized that the mage knew—knew it was impossible for him to decide. How does one decide between one's children? Some of the souls began to cry. Alexios steeled himself. He couldn't show weakness. "I'll exchange myself for them."

"No!" Theophila hissed. "You're more valuable than both together."

But the Ilk mage only laughed. "I'm afraid you must choose," he said merrily.

Nixos had thirty years, Demeia only twenty-one. No, he couldn't choose. He looked at them helplessly, trying to think of some other bargain.

"If you don't choose, I'll take them both," the Ilk mage said.

"Demeia can train others to fight, take her," Theophila told Alexios. "And she has the power of a Keeper."

But Alexios couldn't utter the words.

Theophila huffed with irritation and then leaned out over the wall. "I am Theophila Sigon, ruler of this town. I make the choice."

"No, no. It is the Keeper's choice alone to make!"

But Alexios was paralyzed. His mind refused to even weigh up the choice, just circled blankly.

"Alexios, say something," Theophila said, fingers digging hard into his arm.

Alexios shook his head. "He knows," he whispered.

"Knows what?" Theophila demanded.

"He knows I can't, he knows." The souls cried but offered no answers. They could no more make the choice than he.

"You will not choose?" The mage's voice was laced with triumph.

"Will any other offer satisfy you?" Theophila asked despairingly.

The mage shook his head. "This is your last chance, Keeper!"

Alexios tried to break the loop of his paralysis. Nixos was a better illusionist, but only by a margin. Demeia was a Blade, able to train others, as Theophila had said. But he loved them both equally. How could he choose? How could he live with himself if he spoke a name so that the other might die?

"Fine." The Ilk mage gestured at Nixos. "He'll be first."

Alexios thought he would use the ripper to kill him. But that was not what happened.

What happened was much, much worse.

The Ilk mage removed a stone from his pocket. Alexios recognized it as the focus stone that Vycenian weavers used for their magic. So he was at least half Vycenian, this Ilk mage. As he held the stone aloft, Nixos's eyes sought Alexios, and in them, he saw love.

No, I don't deserve that. The souls wept in agreement.

A shaft of bright blue light leaped from the focus stone and into Nixos. He didn't even scream. His body turned rigid and shook for a few seconds before flopping in the arms of the Ilk, smoke rising from it. Immediately, the threads of his being began to detach from the Lace. As soon as they came loose, the Ilk Mage sucked them toward him. But he didn't bind Nixos's soul to his, as Alexios did, to preserve it and carry it with him until it was finally time to return to the Makers. No, instead he shredded it. He took the part he wanted, the part that would prolong his own life, and the rest he flung away like trash.

Alexios almost collapsed in horror. Nixos's soul could never return to the Makers in that state. Instead, it would wander the world, broken and fragmented, lost for eternity.

"Oh, he tastes good," the Ilk mage said. "The spirit of a mage is always strongest, is that not so, Keeper?"

All the souls attached to Alexios wailed and keened. "No," he whispered. "No, no, no." Demeia, he couldn't let her share his fate.

Then, somehow, she broke free of the rippers who'd been holding her, began to sprint toward the wall. The ripper charged after her. But she couldn't possibly outrun it, nor the Ilk spawner's magebolt, which was forming in his focus stone already.

A desperate plan came to him. He turned to the bowmen on his left. "On my count, shoot Demeia down, and make sure you kill her."

They stared at him like he was mad, the mouths of some forming the shape of an objection, but when they saw his expression, they swallowed their words and knocked arrows to their bows.

To the bowmen on his left, he said, "Shoot at the mage."

The Ilk mage was now aiming his focus stone at Demeia, who struggled uselessly against the grip of the Ilk, its claws drawing blood on her arms. "Now for this one!" he shrieked.

"Shoot!" cried Alexios.

The arrows hummed toward their targets, bearing all his hope.

The Ilk mage saw the missiles come and laughed as they hit his shield.

Demeia stood still in the ripper's grip, ignoring the arrows to look at Alexios with forgiveness. One punched straight into the middle of her throat. Another went through her eye. Three pierced her chest. The Ilk holding her stumbled back, letting her slump to the ground as blood welled from the deadly wounds.

Her body jerked as the threads of her soul began to unravel from the Lace, and Alexios reached out, hoping against hope that from this distance he could rescue it. But Demeia knew what he was trying to do, and with her dying breath, flung her spirit in Alexios's direction. Straining with all his might, Alexios reached for the threads. His head began to ache, but one by one, he gathered them up and bound them to his own. A few almost escaped him, but the Makers were watching and lent him a strength he didn't know he had.

And then it was done. The last flicker of life left Demeia, and the force that had sustained it crashed into Alexios. But Demeia's soul was much more vibrant than the elderly souls he usually absorbed, and he staggered under the weight of it. Someone grabbed him, but he flung whoever it was away and fell to his knees, screaming his torture.

Then he began to cry, helplessly, uselessly, and a woman dropped to her knees beside him and wrapped her arms around his neck, drawing him against her shoulder. He sobbed and heaved—at his own failure, at the loss of his children, at the loss of all his children through the decades, of all those he had loved who had gone on before him.

Finally, the pain and the sobbing died, and he became lucid enough to see that a circle of people had formed around him, stopping him from falling off the wall, from being seen by others. Their faces were twisted by dismay and disbelief.

Then the joy came, sweeping him away again. It was a terrible joy, given a sharp edge by what had happened, and he cried again, even harder.

After that came the vision.

This time he flew not to the cavern and breeding pit but instead across a huge expanse of salt water, past a great and terrible storm, a whirling vortex that bound sea and sky, the result of a great warp in the Lace. He'd been shown this before—it was the Great Maelstrom, which had swallowed Teleriol, the continent of his ancestors, after the Final Hundred had called up the power to destroy the Ilk Lord and his abominations. But this time, the vision took him beyond the storm, to five small islands that crouched alone amid the vast ocean.

He was dragged down to the most southerly island, passing through a dense canopy of trees to see a woman—a Chelak—with short black hair and amber eyes walking amidst trees the color of rainbows. Why was he being shown this? She seemed to sense his presence because she looked up, her eyes narrowing in confusion. Who was she? He tried to get closer, to speak to her, but he was pulled back to his flesh, and no amount of struggling would keep him with her.

When he came to, he found he was still encircled protectively by the bowmen. He tried to struggle to his feet, pushing up with his hands, but faltered halfway, dizzy and disoriented.

"Help him up," Theophila commanded.

Two men wrapped their arms around him and heaved him upright.

Theophila stood before him, her face stern but soft at the same time. "Keeper, are you with us?"

He tried to control himself, taking shaky breaths. It was humiliating to be seen in this state. For good reason, the soul bindings were conducted only in the Keeper's Sanctum.

"Take him to the Hall of Congress," Theophila said. "But keep him covered."

And so they bustled him away. He was only half aware of what was going on around him, his mind filled with the memory of Nixos and Demeia's deaths. Floating above that was the young Chelak woman in the vision. Why had the Makers shown her to him? To let him know that some Chelaki must have fled to those islands after the Protection War? Was it there that these new Ilk mages had arisen? Was he to take the war to them?

They reached the Hall and then the Chamber, and he was deposited onto a chair. Water was pressed into his hands and a damp cloth wiped across his heated face. Then the bowmen left.

"It wasn't a bad plan," Demeia said. *"We just didn't realize how powerful he was. His magic is great, much greater than ours."*

Tears sprang again to Alexios's eyes. *"I'm sorry, I'm so sorry."*

"I lived and died as I wanted to," Demeia said. *"Don't try to take that from me."*

It was small comfort to know she was with him still. She should be living and breathing. She'd been too young. And Nixos. Poor Nixos, the fragments of his soul doomed to walk the earth forever.

"We'll take revenge for Nixos," Demeia said with fury. The other souls echoed her anger. *"Maybe there's a way to restore his soul by killing that creature."*

Could that be? Perhaps. So much knowledge had been lost. But there was one place where he might get more answers, where he might get help for his people. Only he didn't want to go back there. It would be a bitter admission of defeat, proof that he had never been fit to lead, that his decisions had led to disaster.

Theophila, Castes, and Periklis filed in, made signs of respect to him, then took their seats. They regarded him with a curious wariness.

"I'm well," he said.

They relaxed a little.

"What did you see in the vision?" Theophila asked.

He told them briefly about the young woman in the trees.

"The last was a warning that came too late," Castes said, clenching his fist in frustration. "And this one tells us nothing about what to do next. What is the point of these visions? Are they given just to torment us?"

"The Makers send the visions, it is not for us to know their design," Theophila said quietly.

"But still we must know, what do we do?" Periklis said.

Silence as everyone stared at the table or at each other, waiting, hoping. Alexios could think of only one solution, but he hated it, and he knew they would hate it too.

"Is there any point in trying again to kill the Ilk mage?" Periklis said. "Maybe a larger force?"

"No," Alexios said. "No, that plan has failed." *I should never have sent them out. It should have been me. But maybe I* should *go. I might succeed where they failed.*

"Then what? We wait and starve?" Periklis said. "We need to fight."

We can't fight alone. The thought struck him hard, with more force than before.

"Yes, you must go and get help," Cassander said. *"The time for hiding is past. It hasn't served us well."*

For once, the other souls all agreed.

"We'll fight," Castes said. "We've already made plans for training. We continue with those plans. But we should try to send a messenger to Potas and Vonopoli."

Alexios made up his mind. "I must go to our old allies," he said. His voice was hoarse, and he took some more water. "I must go to our old allies," he said again, more firmly. "To warn them of what has happened and ask them for help."

"The Vycenians?" Theophila exclaimed, nostrils flaring, eyes and mouth wide with shock.

But Castes was nodding, looking vindicated.

"We can't defeat the abominations alone—and they need to know the Ilk have returned. We failed last time, we joined the war too late. We mustn't fail again." *Should have done that in the first place, not wasted their lives. Those weren't a price worth paying for concealment. I should have seen that before.*

Demeia stirred at this thought, but he didn't let her speak. Young and foolhardy. A Blade!

"Yes ... yes, someone must go," Theophila said, slowly at first. "There's no other real hope. But not you, you're the Keeper. We can't risk you. And you're the strongest illusionist and artefactor. We'll need you for the defense, especially now with Nixos and ..." She stumbled into pained silence.

"The honored ruler speaks wisely," Periklis said. "We'll need you here."

But Alexios was adamant. He had thrown away his children's lives. He must make amends. "I'm the only one who speaks the Vycenian language with any real fluency. I'm the only one who remembers anything, who remembers how it used to be. And I've spent time in their lands over the years."

"There are others, scholars who have studied their language and ways," said Theophila.

"As I've done," Castes said. "Why not let me go? I am a ruler of our people, and we need to send someone of authority."

"Unless you've learned how to spin illusions, you won't be able to pass through the ranks of the enemy," Alexios said. "It must be me, and the Vycenians have always respected the role of Keeper in our society." *And I can't stay here, I can't, not after having failed my children.*

"Really, father, stop that. You dishonor my sacrifice," Demeia snapped.

"He could help honored Castes go through the lines. We can't lose our only Keeper. Especially now," Periklis said.

But Alexios's mind was made up. "I exercise my sacred privilege," he said. "It is I who will go, and no one else." Despite his determination, he was reluctant to use those words. The Keeper was the ultimate authority, that authority granted by the Makers themselves. No one could countermand him if he insisted. But it was a privilege he had never before exercised, which few Keepers exercised in order to preserve the sanctity of their democracy.

Castes pressed his lips into a thin line, fury lighting in his eyes, but he bowed his head. “As the Makers will.”

“As the Makers will,” echoed Theophila in a choked voice. It had clearly cost her not to argue with him.

“I’ll go straight away,” he said, rising to his feet, grateful that they were steady.

“Are you sure? Don’t you need some rest?” Theophila said.

But despite his lack of sleep, Alexios had never felt more full of energy. Two fresh souls now sustained him, enough to add half a century onto his lifespan. He felt as brimful of energy as a boy of twelve—and just as driven to be doing, to be acting. “We can’t delay. Who knows what the Ilk mage will do next? He may choose to attack after all.”

“Very well,” Theophila said. “We’ll organize your provisions. Do what you need to prepare.”

There was no further disagreement.

Chapter 14

Mūak

How does Sīut select those he plans to curse? It's true that the curse often runs in families. But thanks to our diligence, few are born with it now. One day, we may finally be able to eradicate it entirely. That is our greatest hope.

—Teachings of Old Tsu

Mūak woke to cracks of thunder to find that Suni wasn't in bed beside him. He went to check on Tani. She was in her room, sleeping. It never ceased to amaze him how she could sleep through the storms like this. But where was Suni?

He pushed the door shutter aside and stuck his head out. The heavy rain instantly drenched him. It was too dark to see anything through the deluge, but a flash of lightning granted him a brief view of the huts around him. The only movement was the swaying of the trees at the edge of the village. Someone must have been hurt in the storm, Suni must have been called to tend to them.

He returned to their bed chamber. But he didn't sleep, listening instead to the sounds of the storm and wondering why it had arrived so early. Storm season was at least a moon away. A wild thought crossed his mind. If storm season had started already, they might delay the Test. He'd keep his girl for a few moons longer. And then he laughed bitterly at himself. What did it matter, in one moon or in ten? He would lose her, and then somehow he'd have to go on.

He fell back into sleep, but of the type where it was difficult to separate thought from dream. When he opened his eyes again, he found a dreary light outlining the window shutter. Outside, the storm still blew, a muffled roar that shook the walls of the hut. He got up and went to find Tani. She was in the main room, playing with her dolls. He caught a snatch of the dialogue between them. "Juji's been hit by a falling tree. Her leg is broken, and she can't walk. We need to make a stretcher."

"Good morning, monkey," he said, kissing the top of her head, inhaling her sweet, childish scent.

"It's not a good morning," she said reproachfully. "Silly Papi, can't you hear the rain?"

He chuckled. "Not, it's not that good, is it? But at least we're safe and dry here." The words were barely out of his mouth when the lie of them punched him in the gut. There was no safety for them. "You don't know where Mami went?"

She shook her head.

"Have you had something to eat?"

Tani nodded. "Some nuts."

"I'm going to the Healer's Lodge to see if Mami's there. Stay here—it's dangerous outside with the storm."

"I know."

He ruffled her hair and then retrieved his yaka-leaf cape from his clothing basket. He slung it over his shoulders and pushed the door shutter aside. The storm hit him with all its force, the wind so strong it nearly tore the cape off him. He clutched at the sides, pulling it tight around him, and ducked his head to walk into the wind. Warm rain stung his face and the exposed parts of his body.

The Healer's Lodge was quieter than he'd expected. Three people lay on pallets, the same ones he'd seen two days ago when he'd visited. Of the healers, only Enko was in the long room. He was squatting down next to old Gariku, one of the cooks, tending to a bloody gash on the man's head.

Mūak approached them. "Chel be with you both."

"And you, Mūak," Enko replied.

"Are you badly hurt?" Mūak asked Gariku, to be polite.

"A branch fell on me when I went out to check the pits this morning," he replied. "Head's spinning a little, but I'll live."

"What's a tree branch to the man who once survived a nouk goring, eh?"

"That beast tasted even better for it," Gariku chuckled. But he winced as he laughed, his hand going instinctively to his chest, where the wound had been.

"Are you looking for Suni?" Enko asked. "She's in one of the private rooms with Ina. She was caught out in the storm last night and has a fever."

"Thank you, I'll go find her."

"First room," Enko said.

He nodded in thanks and went out into the hallway. A small bell was attached to the door shutter, and he tinkled it. "It's Mūak, are you there, Suni?"

"Come in." Suni's voice was dull and tired.

He pushed the door shutter aside and found her sitting cross-legged next to Ina, grinding up paste in a bowl. Ina was on a pallet, unconscious, but thrashing and muttering deliriously.

"What happened?" he asked.

"She was at sea when the storm hit, and nearly drowned," Suni replied. "Now it seems she's caught a fever."

"What was she doing at sea last night?"

Suni shrugged. "She didn't say."

Suni was lying. He could tell from the way her eyes darted away from his as she spoke. He'd got used to her lying face, she presented it to Tani all the time. But what was she hiding?

He regarded Ina. She was obviously in the grip of some nightmare. Her distress was like a palpable force, pressing against him. He felt suddenly possessed by a terrible fear, a nameless, objectless dread. Then it struck him. He'd experienced this with Tani before, during her nightmares. He sometimes felt he lived them with her. Suni had noted the same. He'd always thought it was because she was their daughter, that they were just sensitive to her moods. But now he remembered what was said of those with Sīut's Curse. That the elkiri, the skyriders, could spirit walk. Old Tsu's voice echoed in his mind. *Don't be fooled by such a gentle term. Those we once called the elkiri are cursed, and they can fill your mind with their feelings, make you feel what they want you to feel, make you do what they want you to do. That's why they're so dangerous, for they can easily bend you to do Sīut's will.*

"She has the curse," he said to Suni. "Doesn't she?"

Suni started visibly. "Why do you say that?" she said, but the tremor in her voice betrayed her.

"She has the curse, and you know it already." He forced her to hold his gaze.

She rallied, placed her hand on his arm. "Mūak, please, you're talking nonsense. Your worry has got the better of you. Go and rest."

He shook her hand off. "I can tell when you're lying." He rolled his hands into fists. Had Ina infected Tani somehow?

Suni looked him squarely in the eye, said in a steady voice, "You know she can't have the curse—she passed the Test."

Yes, she had. And yet Suni was hiding something from him. He glanced back at Ina, sweat sticking her fine black hair to her forehead. Felt again that palpable, objectless fear. Could it just be his own fear for his daughter? He'd barely slept. Maybe his mind was playing tricks on him. He sighed. He didn't know what to think anymore. Every day had become a nightmare since he'd seen Tani throw that first stone through Sīut's realm. "Have you had breakfast?"

"No, I haven't left her side."

"I'll get you something."

"Thank you." She smiled at him, reached out a hand again.

He squeezed her fingers, then bent to kiss her cheek before going to the storeroom, where he knew the healers kept dried foods. The dread stayed with him, but it seemed to change in quality. No longer objectless, but fixated on what would happen to his daughter in but a few weeks. Whether there was any deeper meaning to the change, he couldn't rightly tell. But the more he thought on it, the more convinced he was that Ina had the Curse. She had passed the Test somehow, but she had it. And he would prove it and expose her.

Chapter 15

Ina

Nāit'Elkir murdered Gala Peacemaker to provoke the conflict with the Eleusians that led to the Great Slaughter. Some have said he was Sīut made flesh.

—Teachings of Old Tsu

Five days Ina spent in bed, recovering her strength after the fever left her. By then, the last of the rain had stopped, and the days were again bright and sunny. But while the weather diviners were still struggling to explain why the storm had come so early, they warned that another would come soon. As a result, everyone was occupied with the usual preparations for storm season. For the hunters, this meant taking in extra meat and fish to be smoked and preserved, and Ina spent her first healthy day out in the forest, tracking nouki. That night, though, she returned to South Beach to try to make a hole in the Cloth, and that way reach the Godstone.

The beach looked very different, the black sand covered with pebbles, shell fragments, and bits of broken trees, all flung there by the storm. The sea itself was relatively calm, with wavelets that glimmered in the light of the half moon. For some reason, she felt even closer to it than she had before her disastrous journey. The storm had almost killed her, but in a way, the sea had saved her by sending her the leviathan.

The leviathan, who'd told her she'd been saved for a reason. Could it be true that she'd been called to fulfill some great purpose of Chel's, or was it all a mistake? The whole episode now seemed like a dream. Why would Chel choose her, a Cursed One? Oh, to know more, to have a clearer sense of what she should do! She opened her senses, seeking the great creature, but instead found the Godstone's call. "I'll find out what you want of me," she said aloud. *And destroy you if I must.*

She took a deep breath and allowed Chel's Cloth to appear before her eyes. As always, her sensitivity to the world increased a hundredfold. Dealing with this was her first task. She needed to reduce the chatter while keeping the Cloth in view. It was too distracting and overwhelming for what she needed to do.

When she'd got it down to a low murmur, she looked out toward Uruk'il again. *Do I really want to do this? So much could go wrong.* The Godstone's call seemed to grow louder, as if in answer to her question. Well, if she was going to try it, she'd better do it soon, or she'd get no sleep. She took in a good lungful of air, then reached out with her fingers to part the fabric of the world—and clawed only empty air. She felt stupid. Had she really thought that would work? How had she done it before? Letting the Cloth wink out, she sat down on the sand and cast her mind back to her childhood, to those brief times she'd made a hole into Sīut's Realm. She turned the memories over and over. It had always been an accident, and she'd certainly never used her hands. What had she been doing when they appeared? Usually throwing something, a ball or a toy spear.

She picked up a pebble, then got to her feet and brought the Cloth back into view. Lifting the stone to head height, she fixed her eyes on a point in the sand. Like when hunting, she visualized a path for the stone through the Cloth, using her heightened senses to throw the stone with just the right amount of force and at just the right angle. It flew through the air, like any stone would, but landed in the sand precisely where Ina had intended. No holes in the Cloth. Part of her was relieved. The Godstone couldn't complain as long as she tried. *What am I thinking? Godstones don't complain.* She rubbed her forehead. *Stop being stupid ... stop being ...* Afraid, she was afraid. Her heart beat too fast and there was a sickly feeling in her stomach. *I won't give in to fear. I'm a hunt leader!* She picked up another stone and threw it. It remained determinedly in her own plane and landed next to the first stone. Seven more times she tried, but the only outcome was a growing pyramid of stones.

After the last attempt failed, she kicked at the sand in frustration, sending up a spray. She had no idea how to do this. Was there any point in going on? She dropped onto her knees and looked out to sea, thinking of not very much at all. Then she lay on her back and looked at the stars. By Chel, she was tired. She closed her eyes.

"Mami, look what I did." A grey, swirling nothingness by her sleeping mat.

Mami looked up from the beads she was polishing. "What is it my little berry?" Her eyes lit on the hole in the Cloth and she surged to her feet. "Oh, dear Chel! Stop it. Stop it now! Whatever it is you're doing, stop!"

Ina shrank under her fury. "I don't know how, but—oh, look it's gone."

Mami grabbed her by the shoulders, amber eyes boring into hers. "Never, ever do that again! It is evil and wrong. You must never do it. Do you understand?"

Ina began to cry.

Mami's face softened, and she pulled Ina into her arms. "That power comes from Sīut. You must not let him use you. If anyone else finds out, you'll be sent back to Chel."

"Will Sīut hurt me?"

"No. And neither will anyone else, as long as you don't use his power."

Ina jerked awake. How long had she been asleep? The moon had fallen behind the trees, the night was more than half done. She struggled to her feet. Just once more. She took a new stone and brought the Cloth into view. *I need to part the Cloth, push the threads aside. Maybe pull at it. Use my will.* Something felt different this time, as if the dream—the memory—had reopened some closed part of her mind. She reached out again, and this time her mental fingers snagged a thread. She pulled, ripping open a tiny hole, no bigger than a pebble. Behind it, the swirling nothingness from her childhood. She gulped, half afraid that Sīut would burst out of the hole and take her. The hole snapped shut. A breath later, a blinding headache stabbed up through the base of her skull and out her left eye. She clamped a hand against it, moaning in pain.

The pain died after a few more breaths, but enough remained to remind her of what would happen if she tried again. She wasn't quite ready to stop, though. She wanted to be sure she'd got it. Again, she snagged a thread and made a hole the size of her thumbnail. It closed before she'd even thought about throwing the stone through it. A fresh bolt of pain shot through the left side of her head, and she pressed both hands tightly against her ears. Her stomach rocked and rolled until she thought she would vomit, and she fell to her knees. *Surely, it wasn't this hard of old. I must be doing something wrong.* But when the pain and nausea finally passed, she found she'd lost the will to try again. *I've made some progress. It takes time to build up skill. Tomorrow.* But as she returned to her hut, she felt a niggling disappointment in herself for having given up so soon. Tani's very life depended on her, and she was giving into weakness. *Tomorrow will be better. It must be.*

The next morning her headache was so severe it felt like a sadistic spear-wielder had invaded her head to jab holes through her skull. Nevertheless, she returned to the beach that night and tried again. This time, she managed to get the opening a little wider, but her best attempt was only half a handswidth. Whenever she tried to throw a stone through it, she lost control and the hole would vanish again. The more she tried, the more her head screamed. But she kept going until the sick, burning feeling started to spread through her entire body and the holes started to get smaller rather than bigger. When she finally stopped, she was so ill and worn that she stumbled blindly back across the dunes to the village.

Despite the pain and exhaustion, she persisted for a third and fourth night. There was little extra progress with the size of the holes or the stone. When it came to the fifth night, she was sorely tempted not to go, exhausted from both lack of sleep and trying to use the magic. It seemed like an utterly futile task in addition to being a horribly dangerous one. But then she thought of Tani, and of how devasted Suni would be if she lost her child, and she dragged herself back to the dunes.

She used the same target as she had the night before, a large outcrop of rock at the east end of the beach. Then she palmed a chunk of pink quartz, ready to throw it.

Dearest Chel, if I'm truly yours, guide me in this. My intentions are pure. I'm not welcoming Sīut, I just want to protect Tani. A steadying breath, then she made the Cloth visible before her, hooked several threads, and pulled them all at the same time, forcing a hole in the Cloth.

Sweat broke out all over her body as she tried to stop the threads from coming back together. She gritted her teeth, her stomach already roiling. *I* will *do this.* She tossed the stone at the hole, and it vanished. Less than a heartbeat she heard a clunk as the stone struck the rock. Barely able to believe it, she ran over to the target, and there it was, her piece of quartz, glinting in the moonlight. But the pain was so bad that it sent her onto her knees, crying out and clutching her head. She waited until it subsided, then went back to her original position to try again. But she couldn't even manage to snag a thread this time, the headache blinding in its severity. Realizing she'd hit her limit, she reluctantly gave up. At least she'd made progress. And every step forward was a step closer to saving Tani.

Chapter 16

Alexios

The Keepers are the ultimate moral authority, so they must be completely untarnished. For a Keeper to deceive, steal, or murder is unforgivable, even if it is in the aid of a supposed greater good. This is why Keepers may never be political rulers but act only as advisers. They cannot sully themselves directly with the compromises that are so often required to rule effectively.

—The Keeper's Role, Alexios Arathraxis

Alexios decided to cross the wall midway between the southern and western gate, out of sight of the Ilk army and hopefully of the skreek. He went to the wall alone, under invisibility, having said goodbye to his family in the Hall. It was noon, and the midsummer sun burned relentlessly as he walked through the streets. Did heat affect the Ilk? Yet another question he had no answer to.

Once on the wall, he flung down a rope, then began the intricate work of recasting the threads to hide himself as he shimmied down.

The oppressive weight of the Ilk made it harder. They put a burden on the Lace, stretching and pulling it into unnatural shapes. It was like trying to straighten cloth once a thread had been snagged, resisting a return to its normal state no matter which way one tugged.

Despite his illusion, he felt terribly exposed as he descended, like an ant or a fly on a wall. But the skreek, a dark circling shadow over the western gate, didn't see him reach the ground. Then he was hurrying toward the forest, transformed from ant into mouse, terrified of the danger in the skies. With each step he spun and respun the threads, matching the changing terrain to keep himself hidden. It was agonizing work, sharp pains soon stabbing through his head from the effort. But he didn't dare make a looser illusion—it would have fooled ordinary people and even mages not actively looking, but not the Ilk mage.

He couldn't help but cast quick glances at the skreek, expecting at any moment to see it swooping down toward him. And a part of him wanted that. Wanted at last to be taken, to exit this world even if at the hands of the enemy. But it didn't come for him, and soon he was in the forest, able to release the illusion.

He knew the nearer parts well, having spent much time wandering them in his two centuries of life. The souls knew them too, in their different ways. He couldn't always tell one source of knowledge apart from another, couldn't see the tiny details of the lives the souls had lived. But they granted him an amorphous pool of knowledge, sparking him to recognize this fallen tree or that grassy clearing. And sometimes, of course, they spoke.

"We trained here," Demeia said as they entered a larger glade. *"See the markings on that tree?"*

Stab points, from a knife.

"How did you keep that from me?"

"It wasn't hard. You never took an interest in the Blades."

"I should have."

"I'll spare you the 'I told you so'."

The going was slow initially, for there were no paths, only wandering animal trails. And despite the time of day, it was dark under the trees. The canopy was dense, the air filled with the smell of moss and old leaves.

He picked up a large stick and used it to beat his way through, but soon grief was clawing at him. He should never have sent Nixos and Demeia out to kill the Ilk mage. It should have been him. And now they were dead, Nixos's soul shredded for eternity. The grief twisted and eddied inside him, and he bashed the undergrowth all the harder, trying to relieve the maddening pain.

"I'm still here, father," Demeia said.

"You should be living and breathing."

"Are you going to be tedious about this? If so, I might just relieve myself of you and head on to the Garden."

"You can't do that."

"I know, father."

As frustrating in death as in life.

"And now you're stuck with me," she said, laughing.

"*So it seems.*" He went on a bit, then sought out Epiktet and Cassander. "*Do you remember how far away Arindel is?*"

"We walked for weeks," Epiktet said. *"But it wasn't a direct journey."*

Cassander agreed with him.

He didn't have weeks. But he'd brought an extra glowglobe with him to exchange for money or a horse. They had only a handful of draft horses in Neopoli, not trained for riding, the rest donkeys and mules. And it would have been difficult to bring a horse out through the Ilk lines. He'd never ridden one. He had, however, learned to ride a single-horn when he was a child in Eleusia, a similar enough animal.

He wished now that he'd visited the Vycenian capital, kept abreast of changes in the world, made friends and allies. Isolation had killed his children and might yet kill the rest of his people. *But I argued for it, decade after decade, to preserve our ways.*

"And we succeeded in that," Doris reminded him. The other souls agreed, all save Lycurgus and Demeia. Both had itched to leave Neopoli, to see the wider world. As a future Keeper, Demeia had the right, the obligation, even, but he'd forbidden it until she was older, afraid that he'd lose her to the Vycenians, that she'd prefer that world to their own.

His avoidance of Arindel hadn't been based on hiding alone, though. Still today it was like a bane to him, and he felt nothing but leaden dread at the thought of seeing it again. He was only ten years old when his parents left him there so they could die in the war against the Ilk, and he still remembered vividly the day the Ilk Lord had marched in with his army of monsters. That, and the Ruin, when the whole world had been gripped by a violent seizure that had turned buildings to dust. But it was the tortured screaming of the Lace that he remembered most vividly, making him scream with it. *We can't let things get to that point again. The whole world could unravel, and then Antiphos will have won.* The thought made him push on harder.

He hadn't broken free of the forest when night fell but didn't stop even then—he was still full of energy from the soulbindings, and his glowglobe was strong enough to light the way. It was in the darkness of the early morning that he finally came upon a path that was more than an animal trail. He followed it past a log cabin, no doubt owned by a woodsman or hunter. That path led him to another wider one which angled toward the south. Now he was able to move much more quickly, and he escaped the trees as the sky was starting to lighten in the east.

The path he was following brought him through wild, rugged land covered with spiky yellow gorse and sweet-smelling lavender, and then down into a wide valley almost entirely given over to farmland. The sun was now a golden ball far above the horizon, threatening another stifling hot day. He came to a farmer's road, not much more than a dirt track, hard-baked and rutted with old wheel marks. But there were no signs of people, no one he could ask about how to get to Arindel, and impatience began to gnaw at him.

He'd been walking upon it for perhaps an hour when, in the distance, there appeared the outline of some low buildings with slanting Vycenian roofs. These soon revealed themselves to belong to a small village, lifting his hopes that he would finally find someone who would sell him a horse and tell him the way to Arindel.

He reached the village outskirts not long after and stopped the first man he met, a burly fellow with a thick brown beard and dull eyes. He stank of animals and old sweat. "I'm trying to get to Arindel," Alexios said in slow Vycenian. He'd learnt it well, but it had been a long time since he'd spoken it.

The man gawped at him, mouth hanging open. "Eh?"

Alexios realized he must look odd to the stranger. Trying to hide his discomfort, he reframed his words. "Could you tell me which way it is to Arindel? How far away is it?"

"You look like you've traveled far," said the man, scratching at his temple. "From Northland, are you?"

The northernmost province of Vycenia, if he remembered right. The man had probably chosen the most faraway place he could think of to account for his strange appearance. "Something like that."

"Long journey, that, eh." The man nodded a few times but said nothing more.

Alexios started to wonder if he was a bit dim. "The city of Arindel? How far away is it, please?"

The man blinked, frowned. "Well, now ... 'twould be a day's walk to Wren. And beyond that ..." He counted on his fingers, slowly and laboriously. "Walking ... er ... now, that would be, well ... two ... three weeks, I'd say."

Far too long. "And by horse?"

A shrug. "Don't know much 'bout horses."

Repressing an impatient tut, Alexios thanked him and continued through the village, stopping the next person he came across, a red-cheeked young woman carrying a basket of eggs.

She also seemed taken aback by his appearance but hid it behind a smile. "About five days on a good horse," she said. "This road will eventually take you there."

That was a lot better. "Where can I get a horse?"

"Village inn's your best bet. In the main square. Just keep walking straight and you'll reach it. Bigger building than the rest."

Alexios pressed on to the square. He passed a few people going about their daily business, all of them staring at him unabashedly. The Vycenians, they had no decorum, no sense of propriety. And they were loud, shouting and calling from one side of the road to the next, singing in their yards, screeching their anger and discontent. He'd forgotten how different they were to his own people. Perhaps he should have made better efforts to blend in. His facial features and skin coloring alone marked him out as a foreigner, particularly his eyes, much brighter in color than those of Vycenians. But those might have been overlooked if he were at least dressed like other men, in shirt and breeches or a worker's smock rather than his long Eleusian tunic.

He could have spun an illusion, but it was hard work, and he wanted to keep his energy for the journey, so he tried to ignore the stares, instead focusing on the buildings on either side of him. They appeared to be residences, two stories high and constructed of orange-brown brick. The doors were painted in bright colors—red, green, and yellow—giving the village a cheery aspect. However, the effect was rather ruined by the stench wafting out of the open gutter that ran through the middle of the road. Common enough in Vycenian villages. It seemed that no matter how many years went by, they never got around to building underground sewers.

He soon reached the square and spotted the inn on the north side. It was three stories high, the walls painted white and the shutters thrown open. Alexios stepped through the door and found himself in a half-full common room. He walked toward the counter being wiped down by the sole bartender. "I was told to come here to buy a horse."

The bartender's eyes betrayed a flicker of surprise as they took in Alexios. "A moment." Then he peered at the back of the room and hollered, "Ger, got a man looking for a horse here!" Then back to Alexios. "Drink while you wait?"

Alexios declined, and the bartender went back to his cleaning. Then something came to him. "Excuse me?"

The bartender paused his work. "Er?"

"You haven't heard anything about an army, have you?"

The bartender scrunched his brow in confusion. "Did you say army?"

"Yes, an army of ... monsters. Crossing the country."

His expression turned incredulous. "Monsters?"

If the Ilk had been seen, they would surely be the talk of the town. "Never mind. Just a rumor I heard," Alexios said. "Someone—"

"Horse, is it?"

Alexios turned to find a barrel-chested man with a square jaw and heavy brow standing behind him. "Yes, can you help?"

"Ger's the name. Follow me." He led Alexios back outside and then around to the side of the inn, where there was a stable with perhaps fifteen stalls. Fewer than half were occupied.

Ger went to one containing a white horse. "This one here, she's a fine filly, fully broken, not ridden much. She'll be eight consuls."

Alexios had no gold coins, but he had the glowglobe, which he now presented to the man. It was a small one, designed to be used as a torch, but was still probably worth more than the horse. Glowglobes were in short supply in Vycenia as few weavers could make them. They'd always been a specialty of the Eleusian artefactors. "I'll trade you this?"

Ger's eyes widened, then narrowed speculatively. "Show me it works."

Alexios rubbed his hand a few times across its milky surface. The weave inside activated, causing the stone to emit a bright, steady glow. Ger squinted at it. "Good quality," he said. "Let's see the license."

Alexios frowned. "License?"

"Papers to verify it's legal, where it was made, by who," Ger said impatiently.

Alexios had sold glowglobes in Vycenia before, and he'd never been asked to produce such papers. But it had been years ago. "I'm afraid not. I'm not from around here."

"Well, without a license, I can't take it. Where did you get it from?"

"I made it."

"You're a weaver?" Ger said skeptically, looking him up and down.

"Yes," Alexios said, deciding it was close enough to the truth not to count as a lie.

Ger's expression hardened. "Then you'll have papers for that glow-globe."

"Isn't there somewhere I can sell it without papers?" Alexios asked, daring.

Ger pursed his lips, seeming to weigh his answer. "There is a place," he said slowly. "Though you won't get full value for it."

"Where is that, please?"

"Take a right when you leave the stables, straight down that road, then second left. A small apothecary's shop. Tell them I sent you."

"Thank you. I'll be back for the horse when I have the money."

"It'll be here for you," Ger said.

"I don't trust him," Demeia said as Alexios left the stables.

"Neither do I," said Cassander.

"There's isn't much choice, though," Alexios said. *"I need this horse."*

The street in question was narrow, little more than an alley, and stank of urine. It didn't really look like the kind of place an apothecary might set up shop. He hesitated at the entrance to it. Something was definitely up.

"Hoy there, stop!"

Alexios turned and saw a pair of heavyset men in grey and brown livery, long batons stuck in their belts. Town guards. He let them approach warily, noticing Ger trailing behind them. "Can I help you?"

"We hear you're selling a glowglobe," said one, his mouth lost in a thick hedge of beard. "It might be of interest to us. Would you give us a look?"

Alexios took out the glowglobe uneasily and activated it.

"You made it yourself?" the bearded man said.

Alexios nodded. He was almost as good an artefactor as an illusionist.

"Let's see your weaver's token, then," said the other, who had squinting, suspicious eyes.

"What do you mean?"

The men glanced at one another, then at the same time, both stepped toward him.

"Sorry, but we're going to have to take you in. Impersonating a weaver, selling unlicensed glowglobes," said Squinty.

Before he had the chance to react, they had grabbed hold of Alexios by the arms and started hauling him down a neighboring street.

"I'm not from Vycenia," Alexios said. "I don't know your laws. Take it from me, but please let me go. I need to get to Arindel. It's an emergency."

"Well, you've picked the wrong place to sell illegal glowglobes, this is Wyven land, and Macio Wyven doesn't take at all kindly to people like you. We're going to have to lock you up until we get word to him," said the beard, gripping him harder and shoving him a little.

"We can get out of this," Demeia said. *"There's a trick I learned in training with the Blades for escaping capture."*

"Why didn't you do that when the Ilk mage found you?"

"We don't have time to talk about this now. Will you listen?"

"Tell me."

She did, and Alexios set about his work. He spun a double illusion—one of sensation and another of sight—to make it seem that he was struggling violently against the men's grip. As the men reacted to the illusion, he shrank in on himself, pulled his arms toward him, and shrugged himself free. Then it was a matter of spinning a quick and loose invisibility to slip away unseen.

The souls cheered, Demeia loudest of all. *"You'd have made an excellent Blade,"* she said.

"You'll have to teach me more of your tricks," he said, although he hated blood and violence, dreaded the idea of having to pick up a weapon and fight.

The men made a left turn down a wide street, and Alexios followed close behind, maintaining the illusion of his struggling self.

"Get the glowglobe back from them," Epiktet said. *"Don't let them rob you."*

"I won't," Alexios said grimly. He snuck up behind the man who had taken the glowglobe and slipped a hand into his pocket to retrieve it. It was laughably easy.

"We could steal all the money we need from them," Demeia said.

But Alexios knew she was joking. The Makers were strict about the evils of thieving, even if the overall purpose was good. Even if the men had wronged him.

Finally, they stopped outside a long, low building that appeared to be a guardhouse.

"Thanks, Ger, we'll take it from here," Squinty said, tossing the stableman a couple of silver.

"Always glad to be of service," Ger said, slipping the coins into his pocket.

Alexios waited until the guards had opened the door to the building before letting the illusion drop.

"Hey, what the pits is going on?" cried Squinty, his eyes widening to their fullest extent as he cast about him. "Where's he gone?"

"Magic!" said the other, spinning around, looking left and right.

Alexios smiled to himself and stole away. The smile soon left his face, though. It was quite clear that his plan of selling a glowglobe to get a horse wouldn't be carried out easily, if at all.

"Turn those Vycenian coppers into silver and gold," Cassander said. *"Or just steal a horse."*

"No," he said firmly. *"I won't stoop to common thievery."*

"Our purpose is urgent," Cassander replied.

"No, if we start now with this, we're on the road to damnation. No end is worth the villainy that purchased it."

"Yes, yes, I know the Makers teach that, and you're the Keeper and must uphold the laws to the letter, but I think even they would make an exception now," Cassander said.

Some of the other souls agreed with him.

"No," he said again. He couldn't bring himself to do it. For too long he had kept and enforced the laws. What a hypocrite he would be if he were to break them now, at the first sign of difficulty. But he did need to think of another way to get to Arindel at speed. At first, none came to him, and he started walking south, hoping to pick up the main road out of the village. He had reached the outskirts when a cart laden with barrels rattled past him, and he realized what to do.

"Good idea," Doris said.

Another cart appeared not long after, empty, driven by two young men and pulled by a pair of horses. The men had the same large ears and broad foreheads. Brothers, no doubt. Alexios called for them to stop, and to his relief, they did.

"Can we help you?" said the nearest one.

Reassured by his friendly tone, Alexios said, "I need to get to Arindel in a hurry. Could you take me some of the way? I'd be very grateful."

"We're only going down as far as Wren, but you can get the postal coach from there if you have the coin. Fastest way to travel these days."

Alexios's heart lightened. "Really? How long would it take?"

"No more than three days. I'm not sure how much it will cost, though. A few silver, maybe, to go the whole way."

He had that much. "And how far away is Wren?"

"Couple of hours. The evening post leaves at dusk, so you should make it. Hop into the back."

Alexios thanked them and walked around to the cart. However, when he climbed in, he realized it wasn't as empty as it had seemed. The bottom was covered in matted rushes and clumps of animal excrement and stank so much he had to breathe through his mouth. He found a spot at the side that was moderately clean and sat down as the driver whistled at the horses. The cart lurched into motion, leaping over every bump in the road and rattling his teeth. Still, he was so tired that he soon drifted off into a fitful sleep.

He woke to the voice of one of the men calling behind his head. "We're here. Down you get."

Alexios stirred and looked about him sleepily. He was in a market square already bustling with farmers and sellers.

As he clambered down, one of the brothers said, "You can find the post coach on the north side of town. Just follow that road and you'll come to the posthouse on your right. It's a big enough building, hard to miss."

"Thank you." Alexios went on up the road the man had indicated until he reached a large stable. Outside it was what he assumed to be a coach, a sort of covered wagon on four wheels, painted bright green with a white pigeon above the large back wheel. There were no horses attached to it, and no one inside. His spirits raised. Hopefully, he hadn't missed the evening service yet.

He went inside a low brick building next to the stables and found a man sitting behind a low counter, a large ledger in front of him.

"Post, is it?" he said to Alexios.

"I want to take the coach to Arindel."

The man peered down at the ledger. "Looks like I still have space on the evening coach. Goes on the strike of seven."

"How much is it?"

"Six vics a stage."

"And how long is a stage?"

"There's eight of them to Arindel. You pay fresh at each one."

Alexios counted the coins in his purse. He had enough for seven stages. And perhaps he'd be able to haggle the price down at the last one, or else get a ride on another cart. "I'll take the evening coach."

"Give us the coin and I'll put your name down."

Alexios put the coins onto the counter and was given a wooden token with a scroll on it in return, along with instructions to hand it over to the coachman.

As it wouldn't be long until the coach's departure, Alexios sat outside the post house in the shade and ate some of his rations. But inevitably his thoughts returned to Neopoli, to Nixos and Demeia, and his hunger died, making each swallow an effort.

As he ate, a stable boy led out the horses and began to harness them to the coach, while a burly man began to load the top of the coach with large sacks, presumably containing the post. A man appeared, wearing long white robes, a flaming torch printed on the front and back. When he crossed paths with anyone else, they pressed their hands together and bowed their heads, and he returned the gesture with some low words. A Lumin priest. The robes had changed. They had once been orange, but the flame, that was the symbol of their goddess. *A heresy born of the Ruin.*

Shortly after came a fair-haired townswoman of perhaps thirty years, and then a youngish man. He wore a sour expression that seemed to sour further when he caught sight of the Lumin.

Once the horses had been harnessed, the coachman called for the passengers' tokens and then loaded their trunks onto the roof of the carriage along with the postal sacks. While he was doing this, the passengers squeezed inside, two to a seat, facing one another. Sour Face sat next to him, and the Lumin priest directly opposite. There was little room and even less air, and his armpits, back, and neck were damp by the time the coach rattled down the paved road, drawn by its team of four horses.

The Lumin and the woman began to talk to one another, but Alexios was in no mood for conversation, and closed his eyes, resting his head against the side of the coach. Very soon, he was fast asleep, only waking briefly once to notice that the light had gone from the sky and that the other passengers had fallen silent. It was still dark when he was woken by the door opening and a voice calling for them all to get out.

Blearily, he stepped out into the warm night. The air smelled fresh, tinged with the scent of blossom. They were at a crossroads lit by oil lamps on long poles, in front of a posthouse. On the other side of the road was a sprawling, single-story inn. The woman and the Lumin made for the inn, while Sour Face went to a waiting horse and cart.

"What time does the next coach leave?" he asked the coachman.

"As soon as we change the horses," the man replied. "If you're taking another stage, pay inside."

Alexios went into the posthouse, but when he dug his hand into his pocket to remove his coin pouch, it wasn't there. Had he put it in his pack? He set it on the ground to look through properly. But there was no sign of it. Where was it? He searched all his pockets and then the pack again. No sign of it.

"Been robbed?" the postmaster said, with a shake of his head. "Happens all too often. I always warn them, don't lower your guard, don't fall asleep on the coach."

Robbed, yes, robbed. What a fool he was! He closed his eyes against his despair. This was what came of isolating for too long. He had thought himself knowledgeable and worldly, but he was like a child among these people. What could he do now? Go back out and try to find the man who'd been sitting next to him? But he was the one who'd got into the horse and cart, and it had sped off as soon as Alexios had entered the posthouse. Try again to sell the glowglobe? But he couldn't risk the chance of arrest. He must think of another way. He opened his eyes. "I need to get to Arindel quickly. My ... mother ... is dying. I'm trying to reach her to see her one last time."

The postmaster considered him, and Alexios let the full extent of his desperation show. He looked back down at his ledger, then back up at Alexios. "It looks like we're not full tonight. You can take the next stage to Preston. But that's as far as you'll get without paying. Coach is always full from there."

It was something. Maybe, when he reached Preston, some other plan would come to him. Or he could get a cart again. Every hour shaved off his journey was an extra hour of hope. "Thank you for your kindness," Alexios said. "I'll say a prayer for you to ..." He stopped himself. The Vycenians called the Makers by a different name—the Spinners. But he wasn't sure any of them even worshipped the Spinners anymore. The Lumin heresy was well entrenched.

"No need for prayers." The postmaster slipped him a token. "Don't tell anyone or it'll be my hide."

Alexios thanked him profusely again and went back outside, where the horses were still being changed. He handed the coachman his token and climbed back into the coach. There were two other passengers in there, two women of middle years, sisters by the look, with tired and worn faces.

They reached Preston at daybreak. It turned out to be another market town, similar in size to Wren. As the postmaster had predicted, there was no free ride for him this time, so he swung his bag onto his shoulder and began walking. But he was still exhausted, and realized that unless he found a cart, he wasn't going to get far. He berated himself again for having been so foolish as to let himself be robbed. There was almost no thieving in Neopoli, but he should have known that it would be different here, in a large country where some seemed to have plenty while others very little.

"Steal a horse," Cassander said.

"No," he said automatically.

"There are times when we must bend," Epiktet said to him. *"You do the Makers' work in saving our people from Antiphos and his slaves. The gods will forgive you."*

"It's not just our people we're saving," Doris said. *"It's the whole world."*

"Antiphos can't be allowed to raise an army of abominations again. We lost half the world last time," Cassander said. *"We lost Eleusia."* Grief, regret.

No, no, it was wrong. Stealing was wrong. No need was great enough to justify the crime. But what if the Ilk mage had already attacked Neopoli? How long could his people last on the food they had? Surely, this was an exception, a crime that was tiny compared to that of mass murder? But still Alexios couldn't bring himself to do it, and he kept walking, desperation fueling his steps, driving him beyond his limits.

He had left the main part of the town when he saw a man tie up a horse outside a forge and then go in. Alexios stared at the horse—hearty-looking, brown, with a white diamond on its forehead. All Alexios had to do was untie it, get onto its back, and ride hard. It would save him days and days of travel. He paused, agonizing. Who knew what this horse was worth to the man? He'd looked wealthy enough from his clothing. But what if he depended on it for a living?

"If Antiphos wins again, there will be no more horses. There will be no more people, or money, or forges," Cassander said.

Before he knew what he was doing, Alexios had ducked into an alley and spun an illusion to make himself invisible. When he walked back out, heart pounding, the horse was still there. *Dear Makers, please forgive me.* He went to the animal and, spinning an illusion to hide his actions, untied it from the hitching post.

Now he needed to work out how to get on it. He examined the saddle, noted the metal hoop dangling down the side, along the horse's flank. A vague memory stirred, and he put his foot in the hoop. It was a bit of a stretch, but the horse was a placid one, and only snorted as he grabbed the horn at the front of the saddle to swing his second leg up and over. Once mounted, he took the reins, then began to spin two illusions. One made it appear that the horse was still standing where it was while the other turned the real horse invisible, like he himself was. He nudged the horse forward with a press of his legs, old instincts kicking in. It didn't move. He leaned forward from the hip and flicked the reins, as he'd seen the coachmen do, and to his relief, it began to walk.

Once he was on the road, he spun an illusion of another man going to the illusory horse, untying it, and then hopping on its back. At that moment, the owner exited the forge, bearing a leather sack. "Hey, what are you doing?" he shouted, panic and anger in his voice.

Stabbed with terrible guilt, Alexios sent the supposed thief galloping off into the center of the town. The man ran after him helplessly, shouting "Stop, thief!" Alexios let the illusion disappear in the distance, then continued down the road, feeling sick to the stomach at what he'd done.

But soon he was occupied with his next challenge—the riding itself. He'd been very young the last time he'd ridden a single-horn, on his parents' estate outside Eios.

"It's not that hard," Epiktet said. *"You just need to get into the rhythm of it."*

That was easier said than done, and his legs and behind were hurting abominably by nightfall. Seeing then that the horse was as tired as he was, he reluctantly stopped to rest for a few hours in a field before continuing the journey.

On he continued like this for five days, resting only when he or the horse were in desperate need, until finally, he topped a low hill that gave him a view over a great plain bisected by a wide, slow-moving river. At its heart was the great, sprawling city of Arindel, and beyond it, a little farther to the west, was the blue expanse of the sea.

Chapter 17

Mūak

Everyone must choose at least one mate and bear children with them. Even better to choose more than one mate. This is how we can create a strong, healthy, and diverse population.

—Teachings of Old Tsu

The pipe bowl brightened as Mūak drew the smoke deep into his lungs. He held his breath for a few heartbeats before releasing it in little puffs that drifted toward the hunters' fire. Then he passed the pipe to Alisi on his right. She took it with a lazy smile, the color of her red-gold eyes enhanced by the flames reflected in them. He looked back to the fire, feeling the smoke expand inside him, soothing his harried mind.

Han's voice drifted over to him. "You and Ina need to work out whatever it is that's going on with you two," he was saying.

The mention of Ina's name roused him, and he glanced at Han to see he was addressing Oyu, who was sitting with his legs drawn up to his chest, his face set.

"I'd prefer not to come last in the Games this year," Han continued. "My reputation would be ruined."

He spoke lightly, but Mūak knew he was serious. Han was a ruthless competitor. He felt a surge of satisfaction to hear that not all was well with their team. They were the only threat to his own. But then he remembered that the Games would be held shortly after the Test, and suddenly, he no longer cared.

"There's nothing going on," Oyu muttered.

"Oh, come on, we aren't blind. You barely speak to one another. Ever since the Feast of Return. What happened?"

"He asked Ina to be his bondmate, more fool him," Ria said with an eye roll.

"You didn't?" Han said, wincing.

Oyu stiffened. "Of course not. I know better."

Han peered at Oyu, then said, "Ah, but she realized what you wanted, was that it?"

Oyu picked up a stick and tossed it into the fire. "I've never asked anything of her—never—but she's pushed me away like our friendship means nothing."

"And now you're just like the rest of us," Ria said ironically.

"She has to take a mate, those are the laws," Mūak interjected, irritation overriding the calm of the arrowleaf.

Han shrugged. "It's not my place to question our laws—"

"But you're going to do just that," Ria said. She smiled fondly, placing a hand on his arm.

"I mean, isn't it a form of violence, to force a person to lie with another?" Han said. "And doesn't that then break the Oath of Peace?"

"No one's forcing her," Mūak said. "She just needs to find a suitable man."

"Like Suni did, you mean," Han jibed.

Mūak's chest tightened. Couldn't Han take anything seriously?

"Some people are like that," Ria said with a shrug.

"Like what?" Alisi said, leaning over so that her arm brushed against Mūak's.

"They just aren't drawn to the other sex," Ria said. "Take Old Tsu, for example. He only ever liked to lie with men."

"He took a mate all the same," Mūak pointed out. "And raised five healthy children."

"Because he had no choice," Han said.

Mūak shook his head, too annoyed to speak. This was yet another example of how Ina flouted their traditions.

"Time for bed," Han said with a yawn.

Ria leaned into him. "Yes, bed is what I need now, with you."

Han smiled down at her head and then kissed the top of it.

"I'm going too," said Oyu. He got to his feet, his expression vacant.

"Would you like to share mine for a time?" Alisi said to Mūak, her eyes softly yearning.

He considered it. Alisi was passionate, and he'd had many a good tumble with her. It might make him feel better, ease him in a way the arrowleaf had not, despite all his attempts. But he quickly discarded the idea. It felt wrong to be away from his family. "Not tonight."

"Is it the Test?" she said.

"I just need some time to myself," he replied.

"Very well, see you in the morning." A note of disappointment in her tone, although she tried to cover it with a smile. "Do you want the rest of the pipe?"

Mūak took it from her and sucked in the last of the smoke. He wanted to stay where he was forever, to arrest time so that the inevitable wouldn't happen.

"Come on, Mūak," Han said. "We have to get up early tomorrow to fish."

"I'll stay here a little longer."

"Alright, but if you fall asleep in the canoe, I'm going to tip you in the water," Han replied, punching him lightly in the shoulder as he walked past him.

Mūak forced a grin. "You can try."

The hunters straggled off and Mūak stared into the flames, trying to think about nothing. But his thoughts soon darkened, turned toward the Test. Why had Sīut visited his curse on them? What had he done to offend Chel? Tani, poor, innocent, sweet little Tani, corrupted by the dark god. It wasn't right. It shouldn't be. He dug his nails into the dirt, trying to contain his rage even as it exploded from him in a strangled snarl.

It was time to go home, he realized, to be where his daughter was. Throat burning, he clambered unsteadily to his feet, tossed the remnants of the arrowleaf into the fire, and then kicked dirt onto that to quench the flames.

He took a few staggering steps that took him as far as the Hunters' Lodge. The world was careening wildly around him, and he could barely feel the ground beneath his feet. He seemed to be both heavy and light at the same time, victim of a pressure that dragged him to the earth while something else was making his limbs float and fly free. Before he knew what he was doing, he had sunk down against the side of the lodge, legs splayed out before him. Just a few moments' rest, and then he'd go home.

He drifted into a half-sleep, head on his chest, fragments of dreams chasing one another. It was the sound of someone exiting the lodge that brought him back to wakefulness. Blearily, he peered at the swiftly moving figure, outlined by the crescent moon, now high in the sky. Ina. He knew her stride well. She was going toward the path that led to South Beach—the beach where Suni had found her during the storm. What was she up to? A burst of suspicion cleared the fog in his head, and he pushed himself to his feet to follow her into the trees.

There was little light under the canopy, but Ina moved swiftly and soundlessly, as if she knew exactly where every twig and root and stone lay. As a hunter, he'd practiced that same silence and agility, even in total darkness. But her speed was unnatural. No one should be that good.

She completely disappeared from his sight, but he was certain of her destination, and continued until he reached the grassy dunes that lay between the forest and the sea. There was still no sign of her, so he walked halfway up the slope of the nearest dune before dropping to his belly to worm the rest of the way through the long grass. At the top, he was able to get a clear view of the beach. Sure enough, there she was, a dark shape against the bright sliver of moon. Her right hand was in the air, her fingers curled around something. He soon saw what it was—a stone—because she flung it into the empty space. It disappeared, and then almost instantly reappeared a little farther along the beach, raising up a halo of sand as it landed.

So she did have the curse. This was what Tani had done in her childish innocence. Had she infected Tani with it? And Suni had been lying to him. Lying and lying all this time, and saying nothing to the elders. Letting a Cursed One walk among them when so many others must die. His insides curdled, his fingers clawing at the sand. No, this wasn't Suni's fault. It was Ina. She was manipulating her, making her do Sīut's will. That was the danger of the Cursed Ones.

Ina was raising her hands again. He squinted but could see nothing. *Need to get closer.* He began to wriggle downslope, aiming for the rocks at the bottom, where the dune flattened out into the beach. He was most of the way down when she suddenly whirled around, looking in his direction. Had she seen him? She looked as if she would come toward him, but then seemed to think the better of it, going closer to the sea instead, removing her loin cloth and breast binding. Her body was lean and muscled, covered in hunter's tattoos. It had none of Suni's roundness or softness, but it was still womanly, and his own body stirred in response. He was furious, first with himself, then with her. This was some cursed magic she had used to beguile him! She was walking into the ocean, head high and proud. Both of her arms stretched up to the starry sky, and then she arched forward and dived under the surface of the water.

He watched some moments longer, fighting a desire to go down and grasp her body, to shove her head down under the water, to feel her flailing helplessly against his own strength. But he didn't want her to see him yet. He would need to be prepared. Even unclothed and unarmed she was dangerous.

He slipped away.

Chapter 18

Alexios

In this vision, I saw a huge new temple that had been built in Arindel. I didn't recognize the robes of those who went in and out of the temple. They were white, with an orange flame emblazoned on the front. Torches ringed the roof of the temple, and from its center burned a giant fire.

—Visions of Keeper Alexios Arathraxis

As he approached the city, Alexios's eyes were constantly drawn to the Spire, which towered above the other buildings on its high, weaver-made plateau. Despite the name, it wasn't one single spire, but seven shining, needle-like towers whose glittering tips pierced the hazy evening sky. The highest and widest of them rose from the very center of the hilltop, the other six circling it, connected to one another at each level by walkways of transparent crystal. A bird looking down would see the form of a spinning wheel, great symbol of the two Makers of the world. The Spire had been built by Eleusian artefactors, a gift to the Vycenian weaver Mages for their help in the Protection War against the Chelaki. Their weavers didn't have the skills or talent to construct magical stone. Their power was primarily a destructive one—which was why they were so useful as allies.

He joined a wide, paved road full of farmer's carts and merchant's caravans. The farmers were mostly leaving the city, their business done for the day, but the merchants were moving in both directions. Many of them traveled in convoys of four or more caravans, guarded by hard-faced men in mismatched armor. Most of the guards walked, but there were a few on horseback, and these looked better equipped too.

A multitude of shabby hovels had sprouted on the western side of the road, mostly constructed from interwoven sticks daubed with a mud mixture. A few were thatched, but others used timber or even tent cloth. There were no chimneys, and smoke from fires escaped through a hole in the roof. The narrow streets that wound between them didn't even deserve the name. Just hard-packed earth that must be near impassable on a wet day. Few people walked among them, but many did line the roadside, hawking pastries, ale, and wine, or more practical items like baskets or nails. A noxious stench drifted over to him, almost causing him to gag. Looking more closely, he realized the earth wasn't all hard. Especially between the hovels, the ground was churned up and muddy. And were those lumps of excrement? His stomach heaved.

Then he thought that this would be a good place to abandon his horse. One of these poor people could surely make use of it, and he couldn't afford stabling in the city. He dismounted and led it into the slum, stopped a bone-thin woman with reddened, worn hands. "Take this," he said. "I don't need it anymore."

She stared at him in shock, then suspicion. "You tryin' to set me up?"

"No, no, please, take it. I'm just going to leave it here, otherwise."

But she still wouldn't make a move.

"If you don't want it, I'll 'ave it," said a young man who was missing two front teeth. Before Alexios or the woman could react, he'd grabbed the reins.

"'Ey, 'e was giving that to me!" cried the woman. "Gi's it back!"

"Too slow, Mel. You 'ad your chance." The young man started to lead the horse away.

The woman launched herself at the man, scratching and spitting, but he flung her away. Others began to watch, some shouting encouragement at the woman. Alexios decided to slip away. *These people are mad.*

"No, they're poor and desperate," Epiktet said.

Vycenia, it seemed, was a place of extremes, the city he was about to enter forming a sharp contrast to the slum. The wall was as he remembered it from his childhood, entirely smooth. The white stone, he knew, had been melted and molded by the power of the Eleusian artefactors, using a now-lost technique. It rose to many times the height of a man and was circled by a wide, water-filled moat that he crossed by a wooden drawbridge. The water was greenish and thick with algae. Beyond the drawbridge was the first set of gates, forged out of huge slabs of iron. The guards didn't seem too bothered with checking who was going in, though, and were clearly used to foreigners, for they waved him by with only a cursory look. He passed into a dark, roofed passageway some ten paces long. At the other end was a second gate, this one a portcullis that could be swiftly lowered from above.

Once inside the city, he found himself on a straight, wide boulevard paved in the same white stone as the walls and buildings. All of it glowed in the evening light. The Spire lay to the northeast, its gleaming tips rising far above the other buildings. Would help be offered to him there? Were his people even alive? *They must be. The Makers will watch over us.*

He pressed on, but despite his weariness and worry, was unable to stop himself from looking around in fascination. The road he was on was lined with the shops of chandlers, tailors, cloth merchants, milliners, and leather workers, among others. Unlike in the smaller Vycenian towns, their wares were clearly displayed behind large, glass-paned windows, and people crowded in and out in an endless bustle of buying and selling. The density of the crowds was dizzying, frightening. Everyone pushing and shoving, shouting at one another to make way. So much louder than his own people, with no respect or poise. Where did they all live, he wondered. How could the city hold so many?

He thought of Neopoli's own little shops and workshops, everything so plain and ordinary. Then of his single memory of Eios. The Eleusian capital had also been crowded, it must have been, but he remembered sailing above the streets on a glider. Now *that* was a comfortable way of traveling. Clearly, the weavers had come no closer than Neopoli's artefactors had to rediscovering how to make them.

The boulevard finally took him to the River Arin, which divided the city in half. The sight of the broad, sun-touched river sparked another vague memory, of the Ilk Lord's troops marching across the wide bridge in front of him. *Where's mama?* He shivered. Would it come to that again? *Not if we can stop them now. And we must.* I *must.*

The entrance to the bridge was flanked by a pair of huge stone eagles that cast a shadow over the two human sentinels standing below them. The heads and bodies of the eagles were white and black marble, their eyes and beaks pure gold. On the livery of the guards were printed the same pair of eagles. They took little notice of him as he crossed, and he guessed theirs was a ceremonial position.

The road on the other side of the bridge was as expansive as the previous one, but while the former had been jammed with shops and trading points, the buildings here were wealthy residences that rose to three or four stories. They were all set off from the street by small, flourishing gardens, and silver birches lined the avenues. Refreshingly, there were no crowds, and elegant carriages often clattered past, drawn by teams of horses.

Straight ahead of him was the Spire, its towers glittering majestically against the blue sky. Seen from up close, the plateau upon which it was built was made up of a series of narrow, terraced gardens, with flowering vines falling from each level to give the impression of a wall of green and white. Each terrace had been planted with a particular scheme in mind—one was filled with flowers in shades of blue, the one above with variegated shrubs, and the one above that with reds and golds. It was a powerful reminder of the former greatness of Eleusian architecture, of the bond that had joined Vycenian and Eleusian more than once in the fight against Antiphos. Did that bond still hold, or had they doomed themselves with isolation?

He hurried on, doing his best to ignore his exhaustion and the heat until he finally came to the base of the plateau. An endless series of steps ran up from street level to the main gates of the Spire. He stopped and contemplated the climb with dread. Despite the soulbindings, he had precious little energy left.

Then he noticed that no one was on the steps, whether going up or down. Some people were walking around to the right of them, though. Curious, he followed them and came to a short tunnel carved directly into the hill. It was brightly lit by glowglobes and ended in front of a closed stone door carved with the symbol of the Vycenian weavers—a thread that spiraled around a high, needle-like tower. In front of the door stood a young man wearing a pale blue tunic emblazoned with the same symbol in silver.

Alexios knew what lay beyond the door—a levitator. Of course they would have installed one. He went to the guard, and mustering all the authority he could, told him he needed to go up.

"All are welcome to use the levitator, but if you want to enter the Spire, you'll have to state your purpose at the main gates," the guard said in a bored tone. He put a hand to the door and Alexios felt a brief hum of magic before the door slid open to the side. Beyond it was a small, circular chamber. "Go in, and I'll send you up."

He stepped through, and the door slid closed behind him. Alexios felt a pressure under his feet and knew the levitator was rising.

It soon came to a halt, and the door slid open again. He stepped out onto a grassy plaza. To his left, the city spread out below him, bisected by the wide band of the River Arin, while to his right rose the high, crystalline wall that surrounded the Spire. The gates were shining gold and wide open but flanked by four guards—three men and a woman. All wore the same livery as the levitator guard. However, while two of the male guards bore ordinary spears, the other two had weaver's battlestaffs—long wooden shafts that ended in curving steel blades, with the weavers' focus stones sitting in a metal cage between wood and blade.

The weaver guards moved to block his way as he approached. "State your business," said the male one, who had dark, bushy hair.

"Could you tell me how to find the First Weaver?" Alexios said, deciding it wiser to get that information first.

"At this hour, he might be in his quarters."

He was young, Alexios realized, no more than twenty-five.

"What business do you have with him?" said the woman at the same time, her eyes drawn together in suspicion.

"I need his help."

"What kind of help?" Her eyes narrowed even further, as if she were assessing whether he might be some kind of lunatic.

"That's not something I can share. I need to speak to him privately." But even as he said the words, he knew the guards wouldn't heed them. This wasn't Neopoli, where even the commonest workman could seek an audience with the Keeper.

"The First Weaver doesn't see just anyone," said the male guard haughtily. "You need a letter of invitation."

"Could you tell me how to get such a letter?"

"Write to him and send it by post," the woman said. She pointed at a large stone block attached to the wall to his right. There was a slit at the top and a hinged door beneath it. "You can put the letter in there or in another post box in the city."

But Alexios barely heard the answer. He'd had a much better idea and was kicking himself for not having thought of it first. "Where are the First Weaver's quarters?"

The man looked at Alexios like he thought he was playing a joke. "No need to write that on the letter. Everyone knows."

Alexios hazarded a guess. "The central tower?"

"Like I said, no need to write it on the letter," the man said.

But Alexios could tell from his expression that his guess had been correct. He thanked the guards and bid them good evening, then wandered off along the perimeter of the wall, pretending to admire the view. As soon as he was out of sight, he made himself invisible and returned.

It was easy to pass through. None of the guards were trained to spot illusions. And why would they be? His people were the only ones with the skills, and as far as the rest of the world was concerned, his people no longer existed.

Beyond the gates, the needle-like towers of the Spire rose imposingly above him. The grounds were extensive, dotted with clusters of outbuildings made from a different, grainer, stone to the towers. Evidently built later, by ordinary laborers, not artefactors. He went behind one of them to change his illusion, this time copying the livery of the guards he'd seen at the gate. Then he headed for the central tower.

The entrance door was polished silver, embossed with the Spire symbol and stretching to one and a half times his height. It was ajar and unguarded. Would they be open if the weavers knew the Ilk had returned?

He walked through and along a passageway that opened into a circular atrium of dazzling brightness. A hollow, crystalline shaft stretched almost to the top of the tower. It was surrounded by a shallow pool tiled with a bronze mosaic of a spinning wheel, the shaft at its hub. Four narrow bridges spanned the pool, and tilting his head back, he saw that they repeated themselves on each floor at different points, giving the impression that the whole formed the spokes of a wheel. The clear crystal at the top of the tower allowed the sun to shine through almost unhindered, but some magic or trick of the construction blocked out the sun's heat, keeping the temperature pleasantly cool. What marvels his people had once been able to construct, how much knowledge they had lost!

Feeling small again, he crossed the pool on one of the bridges, finding as he expected that the hollow shaft contained a levitator. Carved into the stone to the left of the shaft entrance was a map of the tower's seven levels. It told him that the First Weaver's quarters were on the sixth. He stepped inside the levitator, pressed his hand against the activation panel, and went up.

There was only one door on the sixth floor. His heart beating faster, he knocked on it. Would he get the help they needed? A few anxious moments, and then the door opened to reveal a young man of about eighteen years with a bearded chin and chestnut brown hair that fell below the ears. "What is it, guard?" he said stiffly.

"I must speak with the First Weaver. It's urgent."

The youth's mouth curled with disdain. "You can't just come to his quarters and expect to be seen."

"Someone is dead."

"Someone?" he said skeptically. "Who is this *someone?*"

"A mage," he said. *Come on, boy, I don't have time for this.*

"The *name*?"

Alexios picked the first Vycenian name that came into his head. "Loris," he said. Loris, leader of the Final Hundred who defeated the Ilk Lord and destroyed Eleusia.

The name had a greater effect than he had expected, causing the youth's scorn to turn to open shock. "Loris! How—"

"Please, just fetch the First Weaver," Alexios said.

"Yes, yes, of course."

The door closed in Alexios's face but reopened a moment later. This time, it was a man who stood on the other side, with silvering hair and a slight stoop. His close-set blue eyes were creased with worry. "Did you say Loris Sturn is dead?"

Alexios let his illusion fall away, and the glow of the threads leaped up around the old weaver. "I am Keeper Alexios Arathraxis of Eleusia. I must speak to the First Weaver—is that you?"

The other took a half step back, his brow furrowing in confusion. "Yes, I'm the ... did you say ... Eleusia?" He formed the last word awkwardly, as if he'd never uttered it before.

"Yes, and we have great need of you."

The weaver shrugged off his confusion, his voice hardening as he spoke. "Is this some kind of joke? Who are you?"

Alexios dug into his pocket and produced a bronze disk. On one side was the old symbol of Eleusia, a web of lace, and on the other, the symbol of the Spire. "I come in the name of our old alliance." Alexios held it out to him.

The grey-robed weaver hesitated, then took the disk. His eyes widened as he beheld it. "Where did you get this?" he asked, turning it over, mouth tightening in suspicion.

"I am of Eleusia," Alexios said.

"Impossible," the other said, still peering intently at the disk, rubbing his thumb over its engraved surface.

"Not all of us died in the Ruin," Alexios said. "There were a few, including me, who were children at the time. We live in a small town in the forest to the north, which you call the Deepwood."

The First Weaver fixed his gaze back on Alexios. "You do look like the drawings," he said slowly. "Eyes shaped like those of a cat ... and the color ..."

The color of Eleusian eyes, brighter and more vibrant than those of any Vycenian. Were his people not the most beautiful who had ever lived? "You saw my illusion," Alexios said. "You know that has always been an Eleusian magic."

The other man nodded. "Yes, yes, that's true," he murmured, seeming to unstiffen a little. "But then, why have you come?"

No time to waste words. "The Ilk have returned, and they have besieged my town."

The man's chin jerked forward. "What? Ilk? A town—of Eleusians? But—" He turned suspicious again. "This is some joke. The Ilk Lord is long dead. No one knows how to make Ilk now."

"Dead he may be, but someone is making the monsters again. There was an Ilk mage leading them."

The weaver blinked rapidly, appearing overwhelmed. Then he looked at the disk again. "I ... well ... perhaps you should come in and tell me more." He stepped aside to let Alexios through, but the glow of the threads did not dissipate.

Alexios didn't move. He needed to know he was talking to the right person. "You *are* the First Weaver?"

"Yes—Elwin is my name. Elwin Morgan. Please ... enter."

Satisfied, Alexios passed into the room beyond and took it in with a single sweep. It was a reception area, with walls of white crystalline rock like the rest of the Spire. But the outer wall was transparent, like a window, overlooking the grounds of the Spire. The floor was reddish wood, covered by a fine white rug with the tripartite symbol of the Spire woven in silver.

Elwin bade him sit on one of a pair of leather couches by the window. "Wine?"

Such a normal thing to say in such extraordinary circumstances. He had to give credit for the man's composure, better than that of most Vycenians he'd met. "Certainly," he said, thinking it politer to accept. His back thanked him as he eased himself down, and he fought back a sudden desire to close his eyes and sleep. Instead, he looked down at the grounds, at the people hurrying about, some obviously weavers, others attendants or servants of various sorts.

The old weaver returned with a goblet of water and poured red wine for himself. Then he sat on the couch opposite Alexios. "Tell me."

Alexios leaned forward and began. "The Ilk arrived a week ago, without warning." *A week already!*

Again, the suspicion. "But how did the Ilk get to you? How could they cross our country and we not hear of it?"

"Some magic of Antiphos," Alexios said.

"There were always stories about that," Epiktet said. *"The Chelaki mages could travel long distances at speed and without being seen."*

"Antiphos—the Eleusian name for the Shadower," Elwin said with a questioning note.

"Yes, the dark god of the Chelaki," Alexios said.

"Chelaki," Elwin repeated, shaking his head. "We don't know anything about those."

"In that case, you have lost much history," Alexios said. "They lived with us on Teleriol, a murderous people, and you Vycenians helped us destroy them many hundreds of years ago. But some of them lived and took their revenge in the Ilk War."

"We've lost much indeed," Elwin said. "Much magic and technology as well as history. We barely even know anything about the Ilk or how they were made."

"We too have lost much," Alexios said sadly. There had been no one to teach him. Everything he knew, he'd learned for himself.

"We taught you," Cassander reminded him.

"Yes, you did, to hunt, to smith, to build and mend." But Epiktet and Cassander had known little about music or magic, even less about the role of a Keeper.

"How large was this Ilk army?" Elwin asked.

"We counted around six hundred."

"Which could mean that someone has been breeding them again for some time," the other said, running a finger along the lip of his glass. "Do you know how long it takes to make them?"

Alexios sighed, feeling even more tired. "No. As I've said, we too have lost much. Those who survived the Ilk War were nearly all children, like me, or else did not fight." Lines of monsters, trampling through broken buildings, over the bodies of dead men and women. Blood and screaming. Endless screaming. Alexios drew in a breath against the sharp vividness of the memory. *Where's mama?* He blinked rapidly, drank from his glass. Then noticed Elwin frowning at him.

"You say you survived the war?" he said.

"I'm a Keeper. We live for many hundreds of years."

"I thought that was only a wild tale," Elwin said, suspicious again. "How is it possible?"

"I'll tell you, but please, let me know, will you help?"

Elwin considered him, then seemed to decide something. "I'll send for Danial Thane and Arianna Velden, our two most senior weavers. Let them hear your story." His tone was firm and determined. "And Danial is a great scholar of the time before the Ruin. He may know more about the Ilk."

"So you'll help?"

Elwin fixed him with a piercing gaze. "I make no promises. I'm not sure yet if you're a liar or not. But if you speak the truth, then we must act. We can't let things go like last time."

No, we can't. "I can't offer any proof, but I can conjure an image of the monsters we saw."

"That may help when the others arrive."

W*hat if they're all dead already? Like Nixos, like Demeia.* The souls wept, but Demeia, if she'd had a body, would have stamped her foot in annoyance. "*I'm still with you,*" she said. "*We'll find a way to help Nixos, maybe when we kill that Ilk spawner.*"

Elwin went to a door behind Alexios, opened it and stuck his head through. "Horace," he called. "Summon Magister Thane and Magister Velden. Tell them to drop whatever they're doing and come now. No excuses."

Alexios didn't hear the answer, but as Elwin was walking away from the door, the youth who had initially opened the door to him emerged and hurried out into the hallway.

"My apprentice," Elwin said with a wave of his hand. He went to the transparent wall and pressed his hand against it. It activated a weave within that made it opaque, closing off the outside world. Glowglobes mounted on lamp stands around the room sprung to life at the same time, providing a cozy light.

Elwin returned to the couch. "Tell me more about the Ilk and your current defenses."

In as few words as possible, Alexios described the situation to him, and the more he spoke, the more Elwin seemed to believe him.

"Not all of us specialize in warcraft, but everyone learns basic skills," the First Weaver said once he'd finished. "We would be able to gather an attack force of at least fifty within a few days. The great limiting factor, of course, is the Tapestry itself. There's only so much weaving we can do without causing greater disturbances than the Ilk themselves create. It would probably be best to bring the regular army. And for that, we'd need to go to the ruling Consulate of Vycenia."

This wasn't what Alexios wanted. "I'm not convinced that's the best solution. An army will move slowly, especially once we reach the woods. The enemy may see us coming and decide to launch a pre-emptive attack. The town could fall before it even arrived."

"Yes, you have a point there." Elwin looked up at the ceiling behind Alexios, clearly thinking.

Horace came then to tell them that the other two weavers had been summoned.

"Thank you, Horace, you may return to your tasks."

The apprentice nodded and went back into the room from which he'd initially emerged.

"I suppose we could send a smaller number of weavers in advance to bolster your defenses. But we'd still need to cross the lines," Elwin said.

"I can hide at least ten with my own illusions. There are other illusionists in our town, though, and they'll be able to hide more." Alexios felt himself grow hopeful. Maybe it wasn't too late. Maybe they could still save his people.

Elwin nodded, opened his mouth to speak.

Then the lights went out.

"What's going—" Elwin's outraged words were cut short in a strangled cry.

Blinded by darkness, Alexios flung his goblet aside and jumped to his feet. But suddenly he couldn't breathe, as if all the air had been sucked out of the room. His lungs heaved and heaved but nothing came in. He couldn't breathe. He couldn't see. Cold panic washed over him.

The crackling of magefire, a blue bolt shooting through the darkness. A scream ripping the air. Then another scream, from the other room.

Who was there? He could see nothing. He couldn't breathe. His limbs were growing heavy. He was falling to the ground. A shooting pain in his skull. His cheek hard against the floorboards. The smell of burning flesh. Like the cook fires of the Ilk. Nixos. Demeia. Dead. He was dying. The Ilk had come again.

I can't breathe. I'm dying. I can't breathe.

Chapter 19

Castes

The Ruin was the greatest cataclysm ever inflicted. The Final Hundred no doubt knew they were taking an enormous risk, but I can't believe even they knew how terribly it could go wrong. All of Teleriol, with its millions of people, wiped out in an instant.

—Eleusia After the Ruin, Alexios Arathraxis

All around Castes, flames sprang up, licking at the walls of his bedroom. He tried to get to the door, but the fire was faster than he was, engulfing it and then reaching out to seize him. He screamed.

And woke to find himself in his bed, beside his sleeping wife. His room was not on fire, but there was a fire somewhere, the acrid smell of smoke wafting through the half-open window. For a moment he lay unmoving, paralyzed by dread, his heart a loud thudding in his ears. But then a greater fear impelled him to rise and discover the source of the smoke.

Doing his best not to wake his wife, he slipped out of bed and threw on a robe before going out to the living area.

It was lit by a pair of standing glowlamps, and he was arrested by the strangeness of it. Bereft of the illusions that had disguised it for so many years, it did not seem to belong to him at all. He'd been reluctant initially to accept the privilege of cloaking, granted only to the rulers and representatives of Congress. He didn't want to feel like the illusionists controlled what he saw and heard. But his wife had insisted. She loved beautiful things. And it had been beautiful—floors of brilliant mosaic and walls papered in rich design instead of slate tiles and dun wattle and daub. It was the furniture he mourned most, however. The couch and chairs had once appeared to be upholstered in fine violet damask, edged with gilt leafwork. The illusionists had even been able to make him feel like he sat on feather cushions. But now it was all revealed as plain oak wood, and just as hard and uncomfortable to sit on.

He went to the window and pulled back the shutters, poking his head out to find the dawn sky obscured by billowing black smoke. It seemed to be coming from more than one direction. Had the Ilk attacked already? Fresh terror waking in him, he hurried to the front door. Despite the early hour, the street was full of people, some exclaiming and pointing at the sky, others running in one direction or another.

"What's going on?" he demanded of Gatos, one of the house guards who was standing outside.

The man snapped to attention. "Fire, Honored Ruler, from all directions."

"We go to the Hall, we'll have a better vantage point," he said. "You two, follow me." He pointed at Gatos and his brother Janius.

The men obediently fell in beside him. He repressed the urge to run, knowing that it would fill others with fear if they saw their ruler behaving like a frightened lamb.

The journey to the Hall was chaotic, people swirling about in all directions, knocking each other over in their haste to find out what was happening. Some were shrieking that the fire had taken the city and that they were doomed. Others shouted it was nonsense, that the alarms hadn't rung.

The entrance to the Hall was manned by four harried-looking guardsmen who were trying to stop citizens from entering. But as soon as the saw him, they saluted and let him through.

He entered and turned right to get to the upstairs gallery. Repressing a fresh urge to run, he took the stairs two at a time, striding across the gallery to another, narrower set of stairs that would take him to the roof. When he reached it, his heart was pounding as much from exertion as from fear.

With Gatos and the guardsman flanking him, he swung his gaze about. The horizon to the south, east, and west were flaming orange and red, black smoke rising thickly into the sky like R poison. He went to the southern edge of the roof and confirmed that the fire wasn't in the city but beyond it. At first, he was relieved, but dismay followed quickly.

Gatos gave voice to his thoughts. "They've set fire to the fields."

"So it seems—but I want to be sure. Let's go to the wall to see."

In the street, they joined a flow of people all going toward South Gate. His guardsmen called sharply for people to get out of their way, pushing them aside if they didn't move quickly enough.

But Castes was barely paying attention. Circling in his mind was the report his daughter Ianthe had delivered the night before. Food enough in the city for three weeks, and that on half rations. Alexios would have to fly like the wind to get back with help before Neopoli began to starve.

When they reached the top of the wall, it was easy to see that the fields were indeed ablaze. The Ilk appeared to have retreated into the woods, for he couldn't see them, only the raging fire that had once been golden wheat. Periklis was on the wall, glaring at the destruction as if it were a personal affront.

"Yesterday the livestock and today the crops," Castes said, recalling the scenes that had greeted him the morning before, of Ilk slaughtering sheep and cattle, ripping out throats and entrails that they consumed before dragging the carcasses off into their camp.

"Honored Ruler." Periklis turned and made a short bow, then with a glance at the flames, added, "The enemy means to demoralize us."

"No, the enemy means to annihilate us," Castes said. "No harvest means we will not be able to endure the winter, even if we defeat his army." Which meant Neopoli was doomed one way or another.

"Then we'll fight them!" Periklis said. "I won't just stand here and waste away, doing nothing."

"We'll fight them when we're ready," Castes said. "This morning, we'll go see what your Blades can do."

He spotted Oxil farther along the wall. The High Artefactor was kneeling, hands planted on the wooden rampart, eyes closed. To his right and left, guards were stopping people from getting close to him.

Curiously, Castes approached and asked what he was doing. Oxil didn't answer and Castes forced himself to wait silently while he finished.

At last, he opened his eyes and let out a sigh before standing and answering his question. "Honored Ruler, we're strengthening the ramparts to protect them against fire."

Castes realized there was another artefactor, a young woman whose name he didn't recall, about twenty paces away, kneeling just as Oxil had been. "How long will it take?"

"Most of the day," Oxil replied.

"And what progress on new weapons?"

"We've had little time to discuss those," Oxil said. "We spent much of yesterday learning how to strengthen the walls adequately. But at dusk all the artefactors will gather with the smiths and carpenters of the city to hear proposals. A message has been sent to you at the Hall."

Castes bid him farewell and began to walk along the walls, staring out at the flames, seeking inspiration that would help them escape this hell. His mind returned to the conversation he'd had with his wife the night before.

He'd come home to find her in the reading room, silvery head bent over a book.

She'd risen when she saw him, greeted him with a kiss on the cheek. "So, he's gone," she'd said.

"He's gone."

He'd sat wearily on a chair as Pandora went to pour him a brandy.

"It should have been me," he'd said, thinking it again now. He should have gone to the Vycenians. He was by far the better politician than Alexios. He imagined himself riding at the head of the relieving army, triumphantly bringing them victory. Alexios dragged a sense of depression with him wherever he went. He was more likely to make the Vycenians cry into their cups than come to their aid.

But his wife had spoken wisdom. "It should have been you," she'd said, placing the brandy before him. "And you would have done a fine job. But his absence presents an opportunity."

He'd been too tired to follow her meaning at first, sipping at the brandy, barely noticing its taste.

She continued, "Alexios is gone—and we have grave need of a leader, someone who can carry us to victory."

Then his eyes had fallen on the book she'd been reading. "What is that?"

"Cassander's account of Eleusian army formation."

Cassander, minor noble of Eleusia, founding member of Neopoli. One of Alexios's souls and distant blood relatives. "Have you learned anything of use?"

"In the past, there was always a supreme commander for war," she said. "It might be the king, but as often, it was the highest general of the land, and he was given almost equal power to the king in all matters, as long as martial law had been declared."

"You're not suggesting Periklis? The man's a fool!"

"Of course not, he might be an able captain, but he has no vision, and he's rash. No, that commander must of course be you."

He'd felt a deep rush of affection for his wife. This was why he'd married her.

His mind returned to the present and the burning fields. Periklis hadn't been wrong. They couldn't sit here like ducks while the Ilk spawner starved them. And there was no guarantee that Alexios would have any success in getting help. They'd need a bold and daring plan, something the enemy wouldn't guess at. The first step was to go see the Blades, though, find out what they could do, before he went to oversee the training of their citizen army.

They were warming up in the yard when he arrived. Some were running laps, others swinging swords at wooden posts or firing at archery targets.

They stood to attention upon the arrival of Periklis and the rulers.

"As we discussed earlier, divide into your groups, and we'll show what we're made of," Periklis told them.

Castes watched as the seasoned Blades demonstrated their skills. There were four illusionists in total. Two of them—Tanos and Mithral—had barely reached adulthood. The third, Arguea, was in her middle years, while Pintokule was as white-haired as Castes himself. They all wore swords and knives at their belts. Each illusionist was matched with a group of ten guardsmen.

The four groups stood at one end of the practice ground. As he watched, guardsmen poured out onto the ground from the barracks, running at the Blades with spears and drawn swords.

Immediately, the defenders vanished from sight, hidden by invisibility illusions. The attacking guardsmen slowed, looking around, trying to sense their opponents. A handful lashed out wildly and seemed to strike flesh, for there were yowls of pain. But within minutes, most had been felled by unseen blows, many of them coming from behind. Or they were tripped or pulled to the ground.

It struck him as a cowardly way to fight. But it was how they had fought in days of old, he knew. Should he have joined the Blades when he was asked so many years ago? Perhaps he should have, to be of more use now. But deep down he knew he'd made the right decision. He wanted to lead from the front, not sneak and hide, dependent on the illusionists.

"Impressive, but these tactics won't serve us well against the Ilk mage," Theophila said to Periklis standing between them. "Not after what he did to Nikos and Demeia."

Periklis stiffened. "The Ilk mage can't be everywhere. As you've seen, a small group can fell many times their number."

"Agreed," Castes said. "The Ilk seem to be little more than beasts—they're probably not so clever."

"Assumptions," Theophila said. "In the end, we know almost nothing about the Ilk. We don't know how intelligent they are, whether they can act independently, and whether they can see through illusions."

"So we test them," Castes said. "We send out a small attack party."

"And have them taken by the Ilk mage like Nixos and Demeia?" Theophila scoffed. "No, we can't take such risks."

"We distract the mage," Castes said. "We call him for a parlay while the group attacks some of the Ilk from the rear. Yes, it's dangerous. But isn't this what they've trained for?"

Periklis nodded. "Yes, it could work. I'll lead the party myself."

"Absolutely not," Theophila said. "We need you here as commander."

"If a commander can't show the same bravery as those he leads, he will not command their respect," Periklis replied, his face reddening.

"Nonetheless, we need you here, training our people to fight," Theophila said.

"But I can't train them to fight against an enemy I've never fought myself," Periklis said.

"Periklis is right," Castes said. *And if you do perish, there will be no one to stand against me in my bid to become supreme commander.*

"I seem to be outnumbered in this," Theophila said with a sigh. "But let's take a few more days at least to train them. We have time, after all."

"The longer we wait, the more time he has to prepare," Periklis objected.

"I think he's already far ahead of us in that," Castes said. And he needed more time himself, to figure out his plan, relearn how to use a blade in case it came to fighting. He would lead, but he wouldn't let himself be slaughtered like a sheep either. "No, let's take time to think carefully about how we'll approach it. And let's assign every illusionist we have to train like this with all our guardsmen."

“It can take years for illusionists and soldiers to learn to work together effectively,” Periklis warned.

“Perhaps before, when they trained part-time, as a hobby. Now they train for war, and they will dedicate themselves day and night to the task,” Castes said. “And there must be more ways we can use our illusionists to our advantage,” he added. “The Ilk mage can’t be everywhere at once.”

“We see the artefactors later today,” Theophila said. “Let’s see what proposals they have for us in weapons.”

Chapter 20

Fay

Lumins serve in many ways. We offer succor to the sick and food to the hungry. We pray to Lumia to protect us all against the Shadower. We guide rulers and shape laws to ensure society is just and fair to all. But above all, we spread word of Lumia's great gift of light and hope.

—The Lumin Priest's Handbook

Fay dreamed of the Lady. She appeared as a black marble statue with eyes of blazing fire. Then she spoke with Nuria's voice and said that Fay must be purified. The fire in her eyes jetted out and Fay screamed as the flames seared her, melted away her flesh to reveal the rotten core beneath, the liar she was, the whore.

She woke to find her head on the table and her tongue thick with thirst. She sat up, stretched her neck left and right, then dazedly rose to pour herself a cup of water from the ceramic jug on her side table.

What time was it? It didn't feel like she'd been asleep that long, but she vaguely remembered bells, so she'd probably missed morning prayers. And that meant she was expected in New Arindel. The desperate dying needed her to light their path to Lumia, who would in turn guide them to the heavens—if they were worthy. *Are lecherous archpriests allowed into the garden? If so, I don't think I want to go.*

Before she went to New Arindel, though, she needed to leave a message for Moth. That meant a detour through the Rainbow Quarter on the west side of the city, which in turn meant she would be late to the slum. And she still didn't have Moth's answers, still hadn't had a chance to even skim through the diary, which was on her desk, looking at her accusingly.

She pulled off her smelly, sweaty old robe, sponged herself with water, dressed, and scribbled her note for Moth. Without further delay, she left the temple, making her way toward Temple Bridge to cross the river. The sun was already a furnace that beat down on her uncovered head, sucking out even more of her energy, and her steps soon slowed despite her urgency.

She had gone two blocks when she remembered with a cold pang that Lothar had discovered her past. Which meant he might be having her followed. *Pits!* She glanced back—a couple of men behind her, each walking alone, wearing a non-descript shirt and breeches. Following instructions given long ago to her by one of Moth's earwigs, she took the next right turn, looked again. One of the men, the thinner one, was still behind her. She took another right turn, walked for a bit, stopped and looked around as if unsure where she was. The man had disappeared. She continued down the road, turned right twice more. No sign of the man. Either she was safe, or he was very skilled. She started making her way toward the river once more, but looked behind her compulsively—and more often than she should have, making it obvious she was nervous and on her guard.

She was nearly at the river when she realized a woman had been following her for two blocks. *Pits, I'm going to be so late.* But she couldn't take the risk, and so repeated the circling trick again, losing the woman.

Finally, she was crossing the river. Even then, she paused midway across the bridge, checking again for a tail before gazing downriver at the docklands and the forest of tall sailing ships that punctured the skyline. After a final glance to her left and right, she finished the crossing and turned south toward the Rainbow Quarter. Once in its thronged streets, she had less fear of being followed, so she took a direct path to The Goat. Just in case, though, she occasionally checked behind her but saw nothing or no one untoward.

The Goat, as usual, was full of hustlers and drinkers. As she pushed her way through the crowd, she caught snatches of conversation. At first, she paid no attention, but then she realized they were all talking about the same thing, and her ears pricked.

"... First Weaver's dead. Right in his bedroom."

"... Velden bitch done it ..."

"Danial Thane, he's saying ..."

"... burned to a crisp ..."

She resisted the urge to stop and ask someone what was going on but pushed through with more urgency until she reached the room she was looking for. Pie, Hook's second, was with him, and they were both counting and bagging coppers. There were also a couple of boy maggots polishing silver on the ground in the far corner.

"Alright, Fay," said Pie, scratching at a pudgy arm.

"Have I heard it right, the First Weaver's dead?" she said.

Pie's eyes brightened with excitement. "Jus' this night gone," he said. "Killed with magefire. Danial Thane says 'e come in and sees Arianna Velden standing over the stiff, her magic residual in the room."

"Magical residue?"

"Is that how you say it? Anyway, he says it's her done it. Course she's sayin' it weren't her. But I bet you it was, I bet you it was."

The First Weaver, murdered in the very heart of the Spire? And Arianna Velden behind it? Yes, the Veldens were greedy and power hungry, but murder, when Arianna was already Guardian of the Spire, outranked only by the First? It seemed—too obvious, too stupid. But then, people were often stupid, the most powerful particularly so. They thought they didn't need cleverness, that everyone would automatically bend to their will.

"You got somewhat for the boss?" Hook said.

She dragged herself back to the present and dug out the note she'd written. It was tightly wrapped with string and sealed with wax, meant for Moth's eyes only. "Give him this."

Hook tucked the note into a pouch at his waist.

"Anything for me?" Fay said.

Hook grinned humorlessly. "He says he hopes you have answers as he's been waiting long enough. I hope that note's got you covered."

Fay's stomach flipped. She wasn't at all sure that Moth would be happy with her news. Yes, a key to the Archpriests' Library, the diary. But also a plea for more time. *He'll punish me, make me stay in the temple just to spite me if I don't find something fast.* But she said nothing of this to the men, only bid her goodbyes and made her way out. The two maggots she said nothing to, and they said nothing to her. Maggots were expected to be quiet unless spoken to.

After that, she went to South Gate and into the stinking pit of New Arindel. She always felt like a fraud when she went. Light wasn't going to feed the wretched and keep their children from getting sick and dying, and the food she brought would only stave off the inevitable. She was assigned to the western part of the slum and going through it called up images from her childhood, of grubbing through trash piles and begging for crusts—until the day her first blood came, and Pa decided she was old enough to be sold, to replace her ma as his personal coin creator. She passed women like her mother, still trying to tempt men with bodies broken and rotted. A copper vic for a hand. Two for a mouth. Three for a hole. Sometimes the women got lucky and pulled the trick into the narrow, shit-filled lanes to finish their business.

"Alms, priestess." The boy was filthy, dressed in rags, oozing sores all over his face.

"Come to the soup kitchens," she said. She knew better than to give him anything. As soon as the slum dwellers saw money or food, they would swarm her.

But as she'd guessed, he wasn't looking for food. He wanted money to buy some cheap bliss mix. He melted away into the crowd, and she continued on her way, trying not to let herself be overwhelmed by the stink of shit and unwashed humanity. How was it that she had never noticed the smell as a child? Or maybe she had, and had forgotten it.

The soup kitchen was a wooden shack with a fenced yard. In the yard was a large fire over which a huge cauldron of soup bubbled. Maev and Jon were standing inside the shack, out of the sun. Maev had covered her head with her white Lumin scarf, edged with orange embroidery to complement the burning flame printed on her robes. Jon's head was bare, though, his curly mop clinging damply to his high forehead.

In front of them was a table bearing a large soup cauldron. They ladled the soup into bowls presented by the starving wretches who queued for an hour or more to receive what might be their only meal of the day. Fay remembered being in that line, when Pa had spent all the coin on bliss or jun, remembered the painful hunger and humiliation of it.

Fay took a deep breath, put on a friendly face as she approached her fellow priests. "Light shine on you," she said.

"Fay! We were wondering if you were coming today," Maev said brightly.

How could she be so cheerful when faced with this horror of half-dead humanity? "I had to give last rites, his wife came to me as I was leaving the temple."

"Someone you knew well?" Maev said. She filled another bowl, smiled at the little girl, or was it a boy, holding it.

"I've been to see him a few times. He was a good man, a cobbler." Fay affected a sad look, and Maev put a sympathetic hand on her arm. Fay stretched her lips into a faint smile, to show Maev she need not worry, that she was a strong priestess who could bear the weight of the world's miseries in the name of her goddess. "What can I do?"

"Take a turn at the ladle?" Jon said. "I need to check the soup out the back."

Fay nodded, and he ducked into the shack while she took his place behind the table.

The next person in line was a woman who could have been twenty or thirty or forty. It was hard to put an age on New Arindelers—they burned up life much faster than others. She had the twitching look of a bliss addict who'd been without her fix for too long. Fay knew that feeling and repressed a shudder. At least she had freed herself from that particular prison. She took the woman's cracked wooden bowl and filled it to the brim with the soup—itself little more than water with barley and root vegetables. "Light shine on you," she said as she returned the bowl, putting on her kindly priestess's smile.

"Thank you, Your Light." The woman's words were slurring, her teeth black, half-rotted. Fay gave her a year before either the bliss or something else snuffed the last of the life out of her.

"Did you hear what happened?" Maev said.

Fay didn't answer her straight away, trying to think what she meant. Then it came to her. Of course, the murder. She'd been so caught up in her worries she'd almost forgotten about it. "The First Weaver, you mean?" Fay took a tankard from a man, this one grey-haired and scrawny, with most of his teeth intact. A more recent pauper, she guessed.

"Shocking, isn't it?"

Fay filled the man's tankard with soup and returned it to him. "Light shine on you."

"I'm hardly surprised that Arianna Velden's behind it," Maev said, stretching her hand out for a bowl, still looking at Fay.

"Have they found proof, then?" Fay took another bowl, dipped the ladle into the steaming soup, now running low.

"Well, Danial Thane says he came in and saw her standing over the body."

"Words aren't proof, though."

"He said he could sense her magic in the room. Did you know they could do that? I never knew."

"Yes, there's always a trace," Fay said. One of Moth's men had told her that. Usually, only other weavers could sniff it out. But he had claimed he could do it too even though he was no weaver. She'd never been sure whether to believe him.

"Bloody Veldens," spat the bony man whose bowl she was filling. "Used to work their lands years back, kicked us off for not paying the rent. Didn't give a shit my pa'd just died, and ma was sick, so's couldn't get enough of the wheat in."

"She's a cold one, too, isn't she?" Maev said, casting him a sympathetic eye.

"They're all cold. Don't care 'bout nothin' but lordin' it over the rest of us," he said, taking his soup.

Could it really have been her? Had she expected to become the First in his place? Political assassinations were rare, the punishment for them harsh.

"I heard Archpriest Nuria is negotiating to have her locked up in the temple," Maev said when the bony man was gone, this time keeping her voice low.

"Really?" Fay needed to get onto this. Was Nuria using her connections with Danial Thane? But then she remembered that she'd betrayed Nuria to get Lothar on her side. When would he call her again? It must surely be a "when" and not an "if." The thought of him touching her made her want to stuff herself into the smallest hole she could find. She could probably put him off for a while, avoid being alone with him. But there was another danger, that once he'd had her, he'd expose her anyway.

"Where you drifted off to?" Maev said, nudging her with an elbow.

Fay started, realized there was a tiny girl in front of her, missing half her teeth, her belly swollen under her dirty smock.

"Soup please, Your Light," she said in a quavering voice.

Fay filled her bowl. There were too many children like her. But what could she do about it other than be glad she had managed to escape herself? Half of them would be dead before they reached puberty. And maybe they were the lucky ones. The girls, at least. *Girls are only good for one thing,* Pa had said. *Now go you in there and lie with him or I'll beat you bloody.*

She shoved the memory aside. She was out of that now. But no, Lothar. She must solve the mystery at the heart of the temple. Yes, that was her best hope. She needed to please Moth, make him see that she could be useful in other ways. Maybe she could do some bliss runs. The sea would take her far away from Lothar.

"Nuria's been taking an interest in our work here," Maev said.

It took a few moments for the words to cut through the circling of her thoughts. "What do you mean?"

"The soup kitchens. She visited yesterday, asking how many people we served every day."

"Really?" It seemed Nuria was serious when she said she wanted to do something about the slum. Normally, the archpriests didn't involve themselves directly with New Arindel. Nobody really cared about its people. Yes, the priesthood did the minimum, serving soup, dispensing blessings that wouldn't heal their hurts. But it was less about concern and more about easing the priests' guilt over their own well-fed bellies. After all, none of these slum dwellers would ever even be considered for entrance to the priesthood. They were unclean, unlettered, unworthy. Fay herself had escaped only through determination and luck—a lot of luck. An escape that Lothar now threatened to put an end to.

"... hundreds, we can't count them all. Thirty cauldrons is about right, isn't it?" Maev was saying.

"Lissie, is that you?"

The name, unheard and unspoken for so long, hit Fay like a slap to the face. Heart thumping, she eyed the man who had spoken. A bald pate, most of his teeth rotted or missing, but she recognized the face. One of *them* her pa had sent her to.

"Excuse me?" she said with feigned politeness.

The man peered at her with sunken eyes, licked his shriveled lips. "Nice little thing you were. Nevil's girl."

"I'm afraid you're mixing me up with someone else," she said, smiling at him benignly.

The man cocked his head, frowned, then shrugged his shoulders. "Sorry, priestess. Course you're not Lissie. Just reminded me of 'er. Years since she disappeared." He held out his bowl for soup.

With shaking hands, Fay took it from him. It was the first time anyone had recognized her from those days. Who would associate the scrawny, barely budding Lissie with Fay the priestess? Slum rats did not become shining paragons of virtue and light. She ran her tongue over her teeth, remembering the pain when Moth's firefly had used his magic to straighten and shine them, hiding one of the most obvious signs of her background.

"Hey, would one of you come help me bring the next cauldron?" Jon said from behind her.

"I'll go," she said, grateful for an excuse to step away from the line, if only for a few moments. She thrust the bowl back at the man, who took it with a mumbled thanks.

"Great." Jon wiped sweat from his brow with the back of his arm, and Fay followed him out the back.

Jon unhooked the cauldron, and together they lugged it back to the front, soup splashing out to burn their fingers when they went too quickly. Once they'd got it onto the table, Fay said she'd make the next soup and took the empty cauldron. She needed some time to think, about how to please Moth and escape Lothar, about Nuria's connection with Danial Thane in the light of the First's murder. About what to do if all failed and she needed to concoct her own escape.

Chapter 21

Ina

Long ago, only men went out to hunt. But after the Exile, when there were so few men, women took up the duty. Now, we choose the best from among the men and women of each village. But while a woman is with child, she must lay down her bow and spear to protect the new life she carries.

—Teachings of Old Tsu

Ina's father, Naku, surprised her with a visit on the seventh day after she started trying to make holes in the Cloth. He arrived at lunchtime, alone, and sought her out at the fire as they were eating. She immediately knew something was wrong because her father rarely visited. A hunter like her, he lived with his new mate and their two children on Yon'il, the northernmost island. It was a half day's sailing in good wind, but distance wasn't the reason he stayed away. He had been strange with her ever since he had learned she had the curse.

And Mami could barely look him in the face without making a biting comment.

"Do you have duties after?" he asked as he sat next to her, cupping a bowl of broth.

It had been at least a year since she'd seen him last, and she noticed that his hair, near black like hers, was liberally sprinkled with white. His face was still almost entirely unlined, though, and he appeared strong and healthy. "Not until later," she said, searching his eyes to learn why he was there. There was concern, and perhaps fear too.

"Good, we can talk." His voice had changed too—it was rougher, deeper. He didn't say much more to her while they were at the fire, instead answering the questions of others about family or friends they had on Yon'il, and how they had survived the unseasonal storm. But once people started drifting off to their various tasks, he suggested that he and Ina go for a walk.

"Why are you here?" she asked once they were in the shelter of the trees.

Naku winced. "Straight to the point, eh?"

Ina cracked a twig between her fingers but said nothing. She wasn't going to pretend they were a normal father and daughter. Normal fathers didn't act like you'd never been born.

"Your mother sent for me," he said. "She's worried."

Great Chel, Mami, really? "There's no reason for her to worry."

"You look terrible. As if you haven't slept for weeks."

"How nice of you to say." She picked a trail at random that would lead them deeper into the woods.

"Your mother isn't the only one who's worried."

A spike of fear. "What do you mean?"

"The elders have spoken to me. Mūak has complained about your relationship with Suni. You know it's wrong to come between mates."

"I haven't come between them," Ina said. "I barely see Suni these days." She was unable to stop a sullen note from creeping into her voice. As if she had come between them! She knew the rules, she never demanded too much.

"The elders are also concerned that you haven't chosen a mate yet."

"I don't want to bond anyone. And I won't!" *I just want to be with Suni.*

"No one is exempt from the law."

"To Sīut with the law!" she exclaimed. "The elders force us women to bear children whether we want it or not, and then kill the children if they aren't exactly what they want."

Naku came to a halt. "Ina! You can't speak like that!"

She glared at him. "Why don't you leave me alone, go back to your island and your other children? You never wanted me anyway."

"That's not true," he said. He placed a hand on her shoulder. "You are a fine young woman. You've done well to ..." He looked away. "To deal with things as you have. But why don't you come back with me?"

Ina's mouth dropped wide in shock. "What!" He seemed to wither under her stare, and she could see him mustering the courage to speak again. It was almost funny.

"It will do you good to get away," he said. "Maybe on Yon'il you'll find someone suitable."

"I'll never find a man I want. I wasn't made for women's duties." She kicked at the undergrowth and then felt like a child. This made her angrier.

Naku shook his head. "No one is exempt."

"In the past they were."

"These have been our laws for centuries."

"Leave me," she said, shrugging free of his hold on her shoulder. "I won't talk about this anymore."

"If you don't do find someone yourself, he'll be found for you."

Disgust and rage made her dumb. She wouldn't take a mate. She wouldn't be forced to bear a child. Never. *Never.* They could send a man to her pallet, but she wouldn't part her legs for him. Let him try.

"It's not so terrible, to have children."

Ina laughed bitterly. "Really? Then why do you avoid yours?" *And why does Mami remind me over and over of the amount of suffering I cause her?*

Naku looked pained. "Ina, daughter, I left because your mother and I ... and—"

Furiously, Ina cut across him. "No, don't bother. I've heard it all before. I know why you stay away from me. And you must know why I can't have a mate. Even if I wanted one, I couldn't. Don't you understand? Don't you know what would happen if I had a child, if I let anyone get that close?" *Suni knows and I already see her looking at me strangely, like she's wondering who I am.*

Naku stood helplessly in response to her outburst, mouth opening and closing like a fish. She left him, ran off into the forest, hot with anger.

She was still in turmoil when she went out to practice the magic that night, so much so that she moved without her usual caution. And she paid for it, because as she neared the beach, a heavy weight landed on her from above, sending her tumbling to the ground.

She knew at once who it was. Mūak, his aura seething and livid. She wriggled under him and onto her back, then froze when she felt the press of a blade against her throat.

"Go on, Cursed One, use your magic against me," he said in a harsh, low voice.

Suni's betrayed me. The realization crushed her.

"It was you, wasn't it?" Mūak growled. "You infected Tani. I knew there was something off about you. I should have done more to keep Suni away from you."

Ina tried to speak, but his hand pressed down harder against her mouth, mashing her lips against her teeth. What to do? He hadn't restrained her arms. If she could hook one of hers quickly through his elbow, she could perhaps get the knife away.

"I'll tell them. They'll see you for what you are. I don't know how you passed the Test, but you shouldn't have."

A sting as the knife broke the skin of her throat. Ina began to fear he really did mean her harm. She needed to move swiftly, before he had time to react. Opening her mouth wide, she snapped her teeth around his little finger and bit hard.

He snatched his hand away. "Sīut's pawn!"

"Have you forgotten the Oath?" she spat.

Mūak flinched, and she knew she had struck home. But then his expression hardened. "You are cursed. We must send all Cursed Ones back to Chel."

"It isn't for you to make that judgment." This time she kept her voice as calm as she could, but sweat popped out on her brow and all the moisture had left her mouth.

"Stay away from them. I don't want your sickness infecting them anymore."

You can't stop me.

"I want to hear your promise, Cursed One. Promise to stay away from them."

She stayed silent.

Mūak pressed the knife harder against her throat, and she felt it prick the skin. "Promise it or I'll make sure the elders learn the truth."

"Go ahead." She fueled her voice with contempt. "Tell them that the Test is a lie. I'm sure they'll listen to you." In a single move, she twisted his arm around and heaved her weight to the side, forcing his knife out of his grasp. She wasn't strong enough to shake him off completely, but she was able to get her other arm around his neck, pinning him down against her chest while she tried to free her legs. Even so, the effort caused black spots to dance in front of her eyes. She was weak from lack of sleep and too much magic use.

He tried to prize himself free, pushing his arm against her chest to break her grip. But Mūak had never been much of a grappler, and she hadn't been beaten in three years. He was big and strong, though, and she was tiring much more quickly than usual. This had to be finished soon.

She managed to free her left leg from under him, raising it up and wrapping it around the back of his neck. He tried to wriggle out, but her right leg was free too, and she swiftly joined the triangle around his neck. He grunted, his breathing coming harder as he struggled against her.

Then he changed strategy, shifting his weight to try and get her off her back. She knew a moment's worry as they began to tilt sideways. But she managed to execute the next moves of the choke, switching her grip to tighten the screw around his neck. The next part would be the hardest. As she expected, he resisted her fiercely as she began to rotate her body around with her free leg, making her work for every step. Pain stabbed into the sole of her foot, and she cried out. The knife.

Mūak took advantage of her distraction, almost succeeded in shrugging his head out of the tightening noose. Yet she held on grimly, continuing to push herself into position.

Long moments of excruciating, exhausting effort. Her breathing turned ragged, her muscles burned, pushed to their limits. Drawing on a deep well of strength, she heaved and strained until at last, she had it. His head was lodged in the crook of her knee. One more squeeze and he'd be unconscious.

"I'm not cursed, and I don't need magic to protect myself against you," she spat between breaths. "What kind of a man jumps on a woman from a tree?"

Mūak tried to speak but could emit only a hoarse rasp.

"For Suni's sake, I'm going to let you go. You'll get up and walk away. You won't touch the knife. If you attack me again, I'll choke you out and report you. Tap your hand if you agree."

He rapped three times with his free hand, the signal in a match that the opponent had submitted.

Ina released him, and he stood up. To her relief, he made no move toward the knife. "I'll prove it to them," he said in a voice tight with anger. "And then you'll be sent back to Chel." He stalked off into the night and she lay back on the ground, gulping in deep breaths, her exhaustion absolute.

Chapter 22

Fay

Caris the Restorer was only twenty-one years old when Lumia appeared to her. She was the daughter of a blacksmith and a candlemaker. Both her parents died in the Ruin, along with her two brothers and sister. Some speculate she founded the priesthood to replace the family she lost. One thing is certain—she wanted to ensure the Ruin could never happen again.

—The Lumin Priest's Handbook

Fay went back to The Goat after her day at the soup kitchen, dreading Moth's answer. It came from Hook. "He wants answers, not excuses. You have three more days. If you haven't got what he's looking for, he says he's going to put someone else in there and send you back to where he found you."

Fay's stomach flipped at that. Back to Madame Sisi's. Back to the brothel. No, anything but that. She would run away, die before going there again.

She dragged her tired feet back to the temple, choked with a cloying sense of dread. There wasn't just Moth's anger to contend with but also Lothar's lechery. She contemplated skipping evening prayers to avoid seeing the archpriest, but that would have invited comment given she had also missed the morning service. Instead, she ensured to arrive at the very last moment, slipping into a seat right at the back of the worship room, out of Lothar's sight.

But he arrived even later than she did, and their gazes crossed as he was walking along the aisle on his way to the dais. His fleshy lips parted into a fleeting smile, and she shuddered, cold waves of panic starting to swell in her belly. She had to get out fast. She had to. She would read the diary, and if it revealed nothing, return once more to the Archpriests' Library. There had to be something somewhere.

Fay clung to these thoughts as the prayers progressed, mumbling words and refrains without effort or meaning. She carefully avoided Lothar's eye but noticed that Nuria was missing. That was unusual, maybe related to her negotiations with Thane over Arianna Velden's imprisonment. But Fay didn't spend too much time thinking about it, preoccupied as she was with Lothar and the diary.

As soon as prayers were over, she hurried back to her room, keeping her head down. She locked the door behind her, then removed the diary and apricot brandy from her chest and took them to her desk. A swig of brandy to warm her, and then she began to read.

Restday, Fifth Moon, 1 AR (After the Ruin)

This is the first time I've written the new date. It feels right and correct. The world has been changed forever, and the weavers are no more. Let us always remember the cataclysm they unleashed on us. It will serve as a warning. No mage will ever rule over us again. The time of Lumia, Lady of the Flame, has come.

This journal will be the chronicle of our journey back to civilization, to a new world free of magic.

That was the very first entry. Fay slumped with disappointment. She'd hoped for an account of how Caris had founded the priesthood, of the first time Lumia had appeared to her. A description of the goddess, perhaps. *But maybe it's all how the Founding Book recounts it. Lumia, a young woman who walked out of a fire in the aftermath of the Ruin and told Caris to found a religion in her name.* Of course, it would have made no sense that Caris would have started her diary on the very day of the Ruin. She was probably too busy trying to stay alive. But maybe there was more later? Fay took a sip of brandy and read on.

Marketday, Fifth Moon, 1 AR

Today, I walked around the whole city with Matheu and Johann. We're trying to decide on a location for the new Temple of Lumia. It's about time we had a true place of worship, a place for Lumia's followers to gather in her name. And that will bring hope, a way to cope with our dreadful losses.

It's been three moons since the Ruin, but the city is still shattered. Other than the walls, the only buildings in full condition are the weavers' Spire and the Temple of the Spinners. How ironic that the buildings belonging to the harbingers of our doom are the only ones to withstand the cataclysm. Both places have been locked up, and no one is allowed inside. Who knows what monsters still lurk there.

We did find that the other buildings east of the river weren't too badly damaged, and most major repairs have been finished. But West Arindel is still little more than rubble. Of course, much of that damage dates back to the Great Siege. It will take many more moons, if not years, to restore it to its old glory.

East Arindel, then, is probably the best place for the temple. But we haven't decided for certain yet.

Lumiasday, Fifth Moon, 1 AR

Finally, I've received reports on the effects of the Ruin on the country as a whole. The news is shocking. The sea has advanced and is now only a half hour's ride away from the city! No wonder the river has swelled so much. I suppose it will be good for trade. Small blessings.

However, the White Coast has disappeared, allegedly swallowed by a giant wave that was higher than the walls of Arindel. Harport is under water, and no town or village on that coast was spared. South Vycenia has also suffered land losses, and the Middle Passage has widened so much it may now be possible for large, keeled ships to pass all the way from the Western Sea to the Myrnian Ocean. However, a number of port towns and villages to both north and south have been submerged.

I dread to think of how many died in the convulsions. More than those who died at the hand of the Ilk Lord and his fiends, I fear.

Famine and plague are also rife. I'd hoped we would source more food for the city, but there is none to be had. We will have a bitter summer. I can only pray that the harvest can be saved, or we will all perish come winter.

Solday, Fifth Moon, 1 AR

It's been confirmed that Teleriol is gone, sunk into the ocean. A vast, spiraling storm has replaced it. It is being called the Great Maelstrom. We can be pretty certain, then, that none of the Hundred survived the Ruin their magic unleashed on the world. We must be thankful for such mercies. Lady Lumia has watched over us.

The only mages left alive are children, and we will ban them from the weavers' Spire, stop them from developing their dangerous gifts. Magic <u>*must*</u> *be outlawed*

What must it have been like, Fay wondered, to see the world so changed? And so many dead—in the war, in the Ruin that ended the war. All because of magic. She shuddered. Surely, the priesthood was right to oppose the weavers, even if it did mean putting up with candles and smoke. But how had the weavers become so numerous again? There must be hundreds of them. Why hadn't the priesthood been able to stop them from returning to the Spire? But that wasn't her concern now. She continued to read, skimming those parts that concerned themselves with more mundane details, or with people that Caris knew but who had no place in history.

Solday, Fifth Moon, 1 AR

Our followers are growing. People are abandoning the Spinners in their thousands, whose own priests brought this destruction down upon us. We need to hurry and decide where to build Lady Lumia's Temple.

Tomorrow, though, we start tearing down the Temple of the Spinners. The weavers' evil gods must be erased and forgotten lest they lead us to destruction again.

Restday, Fifth Moon, 1 AR

We've tried hard to destroy the Spinners' temple, but the weavers have infused it with some magic that makes it indestructible. And there is a lingering evil inside. So we'll seal it with nicoleum. There is plenty of it around now that the war is over. We just need to melt the armor down.

Lumiasday, Fifth Moon, 1 AR

The Lady came to me in a dream last night and told me to build her temple around the Temple of the Spinners. This makes sense. Envelop the darkness with light.

Her temple will be a great and vast complex, large enough to house all her priests, and it will contain a place of rest and succor for the sick and the poor. It is a great ambition, but we <u>*can*</u> *do it.*

Fay stopped reading in shock, then reread the lines again to be sure she had understood correctly. The Temple of Lumia, the very temple in which she was standing, *contained* the old Spinners' temple? This was her hidden room? It had to be! No, it was framed as a suggestion. They might not have built it that way. With mounting excitement, she continued to read. The next few pages mentioned various other restoration projects in the city, along with growing unrest in the countryside, but at last she found another reference to the Spinners' temple.

Laborsday, Sixth Moon, 1 AR

South Vycenia has entered full-scale rebellion. The rebels reject Arindel's authority and have raised a dic-

tator. We don't have the troops to bring them to order, as they clearly know. And the Middle Passage has widened so much that the south is now completely separated from the rest of the country. So we'll have to abandon it to its fate. It's hard enough to keep the peace here, with food growing short.

But at least the plans for the new temple are complete and the Spinners' temple has been completely lined with nicoleum. Next week, we follow the Lady's bidding, and build her temple around that of the weavers' gods.

So the Spinners' temple *was* still there! And it sounded very much like that was what was in the secret room. At last, something for Moth. Did the archpriests know? They must, if they had access to this diary. But what a thing if it were true! She took another swig of her brandy, then continued reading, looking for a way in.

Marketday, Eighth Moon, 1 AR

I've left all the weavers' books inside the Spinners' temple, bar a few which preserve the history of the Vycenian Republic. These we will keep safely in our new library. I tried to burn the other books, for they contain knowledge that should not be shared with the world again, but the weavers put some enchantment on them, and the flame dies as soon as I try to set it to the pages.

Hide them in the darkness, away from her eyes, and those of the followers of light. That will do.

Restday, Ninth Moon, 1 AR

Our numbers have grown to two thousand, and our priests now walk the land, spreading the good news of our Lady of the Flame. They report positive responses from most. But others cling to the old gods. For these, we'll have to find stronger means of persuasion.

There is also much banditry, with people complaining they can't take produce to market without the fear of being robbed or worse. We'll need to create a civil guard of some sort to protect the roads, or Arindel will starve.

Solday, Tenth Moon, 1 AR

At the Lady's bidding, I've left a single access point between the old and new temple. The location will be secret. We don't want just anyone straying in there. But perhaps there will come a day when the Lady wills one of her priests to go and retrieve some ancient piece of knowledge. If that is you, dear reader, then here be guided by her flame.

Fay looked at the last lines again. A way into the Spinners' temple? Old books filled with lost lore? Moth would love this. Surely enough to get her out of the temple and away from Lothar. Or maybe not. Maybe he'd need more. What if she were to find the way into the old temple first? What if she brought him some old, hidden-away artifacts that no one had seen for two hundred years? Yes, he'd be pleased with that. He'd reward her for that.

She scanned through the rest of the diary, looking for more clues about the tunnel entrance. Nothing. Caris clearly hadn't trusted this to be put into words, or hadn't bothered. She sagged. This was ridiculous, impossible. She should just give Moth the diary. After all, it answered his question. And she was exhausted. She needed sleep.

She closed the diary and got to her feet. But then an image of the old maps in the Archpriests' Library jumped into her mind. Maybe *they* would hold the answer? It was worth at least investigating. Fresh excitement banishing her weariness, she slipped the diary into her pocket, picked up her candle, then made her way back to the library. It was easily three o'clock in the morning, perhaps even later, so there was no one in the darkened corridors. The first prayers of the day were at dawn, though, and that was only a couple of hours away, so she walked as quickly as she could.

It was only when she got back into the library that she wondered if the map case might be locked, and it was with added anxiety that she hurried through the book stacks. But her fears were unfounded. There was a lock, but the key was in it, so she had only to turn it and lift the glass cover.

The maps inside were fascinating. Some even showed the world as it had looked before the Ruin, with cities and towns that had been drowned in the flood. Teleriol was there too. And one map answered her question from the day before: the Chelaki were from Teleriol too. It seemed they had occupied the southern part of the continent, their lands divided into twelve or so tribal regions. The map seemed the oldest of the lot and began to crumble when she touched it. She snatched her hand away.

There were also plans for old Arindel, sketches of the original city before the Spire had even been built. And then, finally, what she was looking for—a plan of the new Temple of Lumia. But it was like all the other plans. There was no indication of the old Spinners' temple. And the measurements looked off, as if falsified to hide how large a space it took up.

Not ready to give up, she looked around the library in search of more maps but was disappointed. She even leafed through the catalog again, hoping to find other books from the time of the Ruin. But again her efforts were in vain. Maybe there was a clue buried in the diary somewhere?

She went back to her room and began to go through the diary more methodically. But it revealed nothing new, and her eyes grew heavier and heavier until they began to close of their own accord. At last, she gave up and dragged herself into her bed, mulling over the words she had read until sleep took her.

Chapter 23

Castes

I was taken to a strange city in South Myrnia. It was in the eastern part of the continent, and it was under siege. A vast army of men wearing the livery with a pair of crossed spears surrounded the city, which had high walls of stone.

—Visions of Keeper Alexios Arathraxis

Six men together lifted the huge wooden bars that reinforced the East Gate and carried them to the side. Then they returned to drag the gate itself open, grunting with the exertion. Castes stood still, keeping his chin up and his breathing deep and even. It wasn't enough to quell his rising terror, but enough, he hoped, to conceal it. He glanced up at Theophila, who was watching with the illusionist Thais from the wall. She raised a hand in salute when she caught his eye, but he didn't reply.

The men who had been working the gate stood aside, having opened it enough to allow him and Hereia to pass through to meet the Ilk mage.

"Let's hope our enemy is in a merciful mood," she murmured as they walked toward it, Janius following them with a white flag, the ages-old sign of truce.

If the enemy wasn't merciful, it would be Hereia's job to cloak them all with invisibility illusions while they tried to escape. Given how successful the Ilk mage had been at unraveling illusions so far, though, he had little faith in her ability to hide them from him. His right hand twitched, aching to drift to the sword he now wore at all times, but he forced it to remain at his side. Let his people see him as the fearless leader who would march out to meet the enemy. Let them see that he, of them all, had the courage and foresight to take them to victory.

But he felt far from fearless once they exited the confines of the town. The blackened fields were a stark reminder of the enemy's ruthlessness and an all-too fitting backdrop for the army of monsters that lurked ahead of him. He also regretted that they'd waited until sunset to ride out. They'd thought it would benefit the attack party, which should already be on its way to the Ilk lines to the south. But with darkness claiming the skies, he found himself thinking it would be of more advantage to the enemy than to them.

The hundred paces from the gate were the longest he'd ever taken. With each step, the fear crept higher until it infected every part of him. When they finally came to a halt, he was thoroughly soaked in sweat, and his hand was wrapped firmly around his sword hilt.

The only relief was that the Ilk had not stirred and had made no threatening movements. Most were sitting, but he spotted some walking slowly but purposefully toward the south gate, as if on patrol.

"Time to see what he has to say," Castes said.

"I'm ready," replied Hereia.

Castes inhaled deeply and then hurled out his opening words, pushing them out with all the force in his chest. It was Hereia's spinning, though, that ensured they would reach the Ilk mage, wherever he was. "We wish to negotiate! Come forth and tell us what you want!"

No reaction from the Ilk, no sign of the Ilk mage. They waited silently as the last of the light drained out of the sky, Castes wondering if the attack party had already been spotted, if that was why he didn't come.

"Let's try again," Hereia said.

Castes repeated his words, but despite his attempts to sound strong and commanding, his voice had a shrill edge to it.

Again they waited. Again nothing. Castes judged that the attack party should have reached the Ilk lines by now. Their ploy wasn't working. He was about to ask Hereia to raise his voice a third time when he spotted movement from among the Ilk. It was the Ilk mage, marching forth from his army, wearing his gruesome mask. There was an odd jerkiness to his walk, as if he were perhaps trying to hide a limp. And as he got closer, Castes realized that he was more robes than man. They hung on him loosely, hiding a frame as skeletal as the mask he wore.

He came within ten paces of them before stopping. "My, my, aren't you brave, coming out here, all defenseless!" he exclaimed. "What is it you wanted to discuss?"

Castes wished he could run at the wretch, tear him to pieces with his bare hands. He was short as well as thin, and in a physical contest, it was clear who'd win. It infuriated him that he could do no such thing, that the mage could kill him where he stood with a wave of his hands. So instead, he spoke. "We've come to find out if there's anything that would persuade you to leave us in peace."

"Peace, you say? Ooooh, I can offer peace. Yes, all the peace that can be gained." He gesticulated wildly as he spoke, and used a strange sing-song voice, like that of a puppeteer at a children's theatre.

Castes felt foolish, as if he were trying to play a game whose rules he didn't know. "So you'll go—leave us alone?"

"I'll go! Yes, yes, yes, I'll go! I'll go! I'll go." He spun around in a crazed circle, robes flapping about him.

"Then go!" Hereia cried.

He stilled, faced them head on. "I'll go—once you feed my pets. They're hungry for flesh. Come feed them and you can have peace in the next world—if it exists." He shrieked a laugh.

Castes ground his teeth. He was toying with them. "You know that's not what we seek," he said. "Tell us what it would take for you to leave us alone."

The Ilk mage stopped laughing abruptly and cocked his head. "Maybe—maybe if you give me ..." He paused dramatically. "Your Keeper!" Then his tone turned sly. "Oh, but he isn't with you, is he? I wonder where he is now. Did he run away?"

Did he know, then, that Alexios had slipped out? Had the Keeper even made it past the lines?

"Tell you what, why don't you give me all your mages. Mage souls taste so much better," the Ilk mage said, "And I could do with a little pick-me-up." He rubbed his belly theatrically.

"If we gave you all the mages, would you leave our town and promise not to attack again?" Castes replied.

"Surely, you're joking," Hereia hissed.

"We need to keep him talking," Castes murmured. Aloud, he added, "Can't we just let the past lie? You've already avenged your people. Teleriol is no more. There are only a handful of us in this town."

"I count hundreds of you, thousands!" he shrieked. "It is we who are but a handful because you murdered us all. And we can't abide being less than you. No, no, no." He abruptly broke into a cavorting dance, robes fluttering in the stinking air. "We will not be less," he crooned. "Noooo, we will not be less, not be less."

"He's insane," Hereia said.

It was clear that the man was indeed mad, and it gave Castes cause for hope. He might not be as fearsome an enemy as they'd thought.

The mage stopped dancing as suddenly as he'd begun. "Would you like to come and see my Ilk? They're so beautifully made, a true marvel of creation."

"We can see your abominations well enough from here," Hereia replied.

"But some of your people wanted a closer look, did they not?" He giggled.

Cold certainty filled Castes.

"They looked quite closely, but I'm afraid they lost their eyes."

Five rippers emerged from the Ilk lines, shambling toward them with a body in hand each. Up close, the monsters appeared even deadlier. He didn't reach past their midsection, and their canine jaws were filled with long, pointed teeth that looked strong enough to bite off a human head with a single snap. They wore no clothing and had no genitals that he could see, but their scaly hides looked as tough as armor, and he was quite certain that they could slice him in half with a single rake of their claws.

Castes clenched his teeth against the numbing fear that came with the monsters, but then was forced to breathe through his mouth when their putrid stench became too much for his stomach to bear. By the time they had reached the Ilk mage, his whole body trembled with the urge to run. It was pride alone that kept him in place. He heard the creak of armor behind him, but Janis too held his ground, as did Hereia.

When the rippers were within five paces, they dumped their load on the ground, then returned to flank the Ilk mage. Castes gazed down at them with dread, but soon realized it was not the attack party as he'd feared. Two of the dead were young children. Two others were young women, evidently related. One was a man, perhaps husband to one of the women. Their eyes and hearts had been ripped out, leaving gaping, bloodied holes. The gorge rose in him, and it took every ounce of his discipline to keep his face blank.

"You know they gave us so much information before they died," the Ilk mage said. "The children couldn't talk quickly enough."

Castes stomach twisted, his mind filling with images of screaming, tortured children, the images refusing to leave him even as he tried to focus on what the mage was saying.

"You're already hungry, aren't you?" the Ilk mage continued. "Not enough food to last very long, really. You could always try eating your dead, I suppose." He giggled. "But perhaps your Keeper will return in time with help."

They have him, Castes thought dully. *There'll be no hope from that quarter.* He groped for something else to keep the creature talking. "Will you at least tell us your name?"

"My name. Hmmm, what is my name? You could call me Deathdealer or Flesheater. Or even better, Soulstealer! That one I've always quite liked—your people were so inventive in the last war. But why not prove yourself even cleverer and find your own name for me?"

"Apt names indeed," Hereia muttered.

But Castes' attention was on another detail. "Were you alive during the Ilk War? Are you Ilis'Elkir?"

"You murdered him! You killers! You think yourselves better than us, but you're all *murderers*!" His voice rose with each sentence he spoke, the last word a long screech.

Castes couldn't tell if he was genuinely angry or still playing a game. But perhaps it was time to retreat rather than risk provoking him further.

The soulstealer wasn't done, however. "Well done on strengthening your walls. I wasn't sure you'd manage that. You've lost so much knowledge, haven't you? I'm sure you'd love to know everything I do. You might even have had a hope of winning if that were the case."

Castes steeled himself to speak. The attack party was still out there, there was still a hope for this mission. "If you're so confident of your victory, why not come and get us?"

"Don't encourage him," Hereia muttered. "We're far from ready."

Castes ignored her. "It must be lonely out there with all those abominations. They don't seem like terribly interesting company."

"My pets provide me with all kinds of entertainment," he said, giggling again.

"How about a challenge?" Castes said with sudden inspiration. "A hundred of your monsters against a hundred of our people. Out in this field. Winner takes all."

"Have you lost your mind?" Hereia exclaimed.

"That is a most intriguing proposal, most intriguing indeed! Your townsmen would have no hope, though. There are women learning to fight too, aren't there? Training every day in the main square. How brave of them."

How did he know? The skreek? "So do you say yes?" It was a mad gamble—yet, with the Blades, maybe with the Blades.

But it was as if the enemy could read his thoughts. "Oooh or perhaps you plan to cheat, to use some of your illusionists to make things harder for my Ilk, even tip the balance a little? That could be quite fun." He giggled.

"Will you agree, then?"

He cocked his head. "Tell you what, let's do a hundred of your best against these five rippers? That would be a much fairer fight. That could be amusing!"

"And you'd leave if we won?" Castes said.

"Pack up and leave, oh yes. Ohhh, we'd go on a looooong walk."

Castes stared at the creature, trying to determine if he was lying. So hard when he couldn't see his face. Everything he said sounded like a joke.

"It's a trap," Hereia murmured. "If we lost the fight with such odds, the whole town would be demoralized."

"I accept!" Castes said. Maybe it was a trap, maybe the wretch was lying. But it would serve as a distraction.

The Ilk mage clapped his hands. "Oh, marvelous. Shall we start now?"

"In five days," Castes replied. "At noon. We need time to prepare."

"Oh alright, I suppose we can wait. In the meantime, I have the pleasure of watching you slowly starve. You know, it's very interesting to see the madness that overcomes a starving population. Especially when the Ilk are around. People start to do all kinds of strange things, things you'd never expect them to do. You must be sure to share your tales with me."

"He's just taunting us," Hereia said disgustedly.

Castes was still considering what to say when the mage spoke again. "Well, I'll leave you to go burn your dead. Or eat them." He giggled. "But don't worry, I'll still be here when you're ready to fight." He turned and skipped back to his army, robes flapping about his bony frame.

"Call for guards to take them in," Castes said to Hereia with a brisk wave at the bodies.

She did as he asked, using her powers to carry her voice, and by the time they were halfway to the gate, it was opening to allow the assigned men out.

Theophila was waiting on the other side of it, her face pale and grave.

"We need to ensure that no one else goes over the wall," Castes said. "He probably learned much of our plans from those fools."

"They can hardly be blamed for trying," Theophila said, shaking her head. "I'm only surprised that more haven't."

"We double the guard," Castes replied. "And try to find out where they went over and if someone allowed them to do it."

"Do you think he has Alexios?" Theophila asked.

"You were able to hear what he said?" Castes replied.

"Thais could, and relayed the words to me."

Hereia answered before he'd time to draw breath again. "It's possible he has Alexios, but seeing that it was Castes and I who came to speak, he may have been trying to trick more information out of us."

Castes shook his head. "I'm certain that even if he doesn't have Alexios, he knows where he is or where he's headed."

"What makes you think that?" Theophila said.

"The way he spoke—we have to assume that Alexios won't return with help. We need to make other plans," Castes replied.

"Falling into his trap seems like a poor plan to make," Hereia said sourly.

"Trap it might be, but we might find a way to outsmart him," Castes said. "I won't discuss such things in public, though." There were too many ears about, too much danger that another fool might cross the wall and reveal everything.

"Let's wait for the attack party to return, and then we'll talk further," Theophila said. "We need to hear what they've learned."

They spent the long wait in the Chamber, poring over reports and consuming their meager allotment of food. At last, a runner came to announce that the attack party was on its way, all members still alive and largely uninjured. They went out into the Hall to meet them.

Periklis strode at their head, looking exuberant. Some of the others wore hopeful expressions, but the illusionists seemed less pleased.

"Speak, captain," Castes said.

"We found a few of the abominations lurking near the trees," Periklis replied. "They neither saw nor heard us attack, so we can be confident that our illusions will work against them."

"And did you kill any?" Hereia asked.

"Five," said a young,e blond fellow proudly. "The small ones. Their hide is tough, almost as tough as leather, so it wasn't easy to penetrate with blade."

"It's easiest to take them down at the leg and then hack their heads off," added Periklis. "And you have to take their heads off before they'll stop. Critical wounds have virtually no effect on them."

"And the rippers?" Castes said.

They shook their heads. "We didn't get close enough," said the first soldier.

"It's very hard to maintain illusions near the Ilk," Pintos said. "The Lace frays and is unstable. It's possible that if we are near too many, the illusions would collapse entirely, like they did when the army arrived."

"If we were to surprise them with a two-pronged assault, do you think it would work?" Castes asked.

"What do you mean exactly?" Periklis said.

Isn't it obvious? Makers, he's slow. "We distract them with an attack from the front while the Blades harry them invisibly from behind."

"Too dangerous," Theophila said. "We don't have the numbers. It should be a last resort only."

"But we've proven that with the Ilk mage distracted, we can get people through the lines," Castes said. "And he's agreed to a fight. While his attention is on that, we could at least start evacuating the women and children."

"But where would they go?" Theophila said. "We don't know if Vonopoli and Potas have been hit or not. And who knows if there are Ilk in the woods? They'd be defenseless. And we can't provide them with food."

"We won't be able to feed everyone through the winter anyway," Castes pointed out. "There's no harvest, the livestock have been slaughtered. We'll need to seek help from outside one way or another."

"Let's give Alexios time to return," Theophila said.

"A vain hope," Castes scoffed. "You heard how the wretch spoke. We'll have to attack, and sooner rather than later, before we grow even weaker."

"So you'd have us all perish in a futile assault?" Theophila snorted.

"Hardly futile if it can cover the evacuation," Castes returned. "And he agreed to a fight of five on a hundred."

"A fight he surely means to win," Hereia said. "If our soldiers see one hundred of us dying against such a small number, they'll be completely demoralized."

"I fear you're right," Theophila said. "He might be mad, but I doubt he's a fool. He no doubt plans some trick."

Castes controlled his temper with an effort. What a lack of imagination and daring! Couldn't they see that they had to be proactive, force the Ilk mage to react to them rather than waiting around like sheep for slaughter?

“We can have the new missile weapons ready in two days,” Oxil said. “They won’t be expecting that.”

“Excellent,” Castes said. “All the more reason to strike.”

“If we evacuate, we’ll have to think about how to avoid a mass panic,” Theophila said slowly.

“But we try it?” Castes said.

“Let’s vote,” Theophila responded. “Who wants to attempt an evacuation while we distract the Ilk mage with a frontal assault?” She raised her hand.

Castes and Oxil promptly joined her. Seeing this, Periklis also raised his hand, but Hereia shook her head, repeating again that it was a fool’s idea.

“Very well, let’s make plans,” Castes said.

Chapter 24

Fay

The Ilk Lord was responsible for the Gloom. His Ilk brought it wherever they went. We don't know how he created his abominations. But the power he used was dark and dangerous.

—The Ilk War: A History, Carolin Morgan

The morning after she'd read the diary, Fay returned from breakfast to discover a note under her doorway.

I expect you tonight with your latest report. On the strike of nine. Don't be late.

It was unsigned, but Fay knew the hand, and a chill ran through her. She'd hoped for a few more days' reprieve, but now she was going to have to find some way to avoid the disgusting beast. She thought of the diary, made up her mind to take it directly to Moth. Maybe it would be enough for him to know what the hidden room was. Maybe he didn't actually expect her to find a way in. At the least, she could use her discovery to ask for restationing.

Without delay, she left the temple and made her way to the back room of The Goat, finding both Hook and Pie there again.

"Moth ain't seein' no one today," Pie said. "Not unless it's proper urgent."

"I've got something good for him," she said desperately. "He'll want to see it straight away."

Pie scratched his belly. "What is it?"

Moth had told her to keep any discoveries strictly to herself. "Not something I can share with you."

"Well then you ain't seein' 'im," Pie said, crossing his hands over his chest.

"Oh come on, it's urgent. I swear. Just let me talk to him. He can decide for himself and punish me if I've wasted his time."

Pie looked at Hook. "You tell 'er."

"Just give us the message," Hook said. "We'll see it gets to him this morning. You can come back after noon for your answer."

Fay swallowed her frustration. *To the pits with Moth, and Lothar, and all bloody men!* She had prepared a note, and now thrust it at Pie. Then she left for the soup kitchen in New Arindel, her head aching.

"You don't look well," Maev said to her with concern when she arrived.

Neither would you if you hadn't slept properly for days. "The heat is getting to me," she replied. *And that bloody diary. And bloody Moth. And piss-stinking Lothar.*

The day was long and torturous, the heat even worse than in previous days, and she longed for a cold bath. When her shift was finally over, she returned with some hope to The Goat. But there had been no reply from Moth.

"I passed the note on, but he wasn't there," Hook said with a shrug. "Try again tomorrow."

With a rising sense of despair, Fay took some vegetable stew in one of the quiet side rooms. She would avoid the temple and Lothar until long after the strike of nine. As she spooned the food into her mouth, tasting nothing, she thought again about the diary. She should read it again. Maybe she'd find some new message she had missed yesterday. So she pushed her half-empty bowl aside and dug it out from her satchel, opening it on the very first page.

It took her a few hours to go through the whole thing, but the final mention of the old Spinner's temple was the line she'd read the day before: "If that is you, dear reader, then here be guided by her flame." There were no other clues. *Pits. I'll never figure this out.*

With a defeated sigh, she pocketed the diary and made her way back to the temple. She needed some sleep. And who knew, maybe her dreams would have answers.

But as she walked the darkened streets, mulling over all she had read, fresh inspiration struck her. "Then here be guided by her flame." She'd interpreted it as a priestly saying, but maybe it had a more literal meaning? "Then here be guided." The "here" seemed to suggest something more. Otherwise, why not just write "be guided by her flame"? As she recalled, the rest of the page was entirely blank, and Caris had started the next entry on a new page. This was unusual as she always began a new entry directly below the previous one. Could there be some hidden message on the blank part of the page? Some inks, she knew, were visible only when heated or treated in some other way. Moth sometimes used these to encode especially important messages. She picked up the pace, walking so fast she almost tripped over herself.

She slipped into the temple by the side entrance, taking a winding back route to her room to avoid anyone else who might be awake.

She half expected to see Lothar stalking the corridors, watching her door, although it was ridiculous. He wouldn't be so obvious. And sure enough, there was no sign of him outside. However, when she got to her room, she found another note.

Don't think to avoid me forever.

Fuck you. She burned the note with her candle clock, watching it curl and crisp and then crumble into ashes. *One day, you'll be ashes too.* But she was shaking, and it took her a few breaths to compose herself enough to sit down at her desk and take out the diary again.

She opened it to the blank page, then, holding her breath in anticipation, put it close to the glass of the clock. After about half a minute, she looked at the page. Nothing. Maybe it needed to be closer. She pressed the diary right up against the glass, uttering silent prayers to the Lady.

Her prayers were answered. The next time she looked, the page had changed, brown letters unfurling themselves. Catching her breath with excitement, she returned the diary to the glass. When she looked again, the full message had been revealed.

CHILD OF FLAME AND FIRE,
HEED WELL THESE LINES,
ALLOW THEM BE YOUR GUIDE.
TO LIGHT UPON THE VAULT SO DIRE,
YOU ARE TO START UP HIGH,
GO ACROSS THEN DOWN TO FIND
A ROOM AND LATCH OF WIRE.

A poem. No, more than a poem. There was another message hidden in there, she was certain. She pondered the words blearily. "The vault so dire" must surely be the Spinners' temple. She was to start up high, but up high where? In what room? "Go across then down to find a room and latch of wire." Was the poem trying to tell her where the room was? She doubted the room was the same as the vault. Could it be the tunnel? Or the place where the entrance to the tunnel could be found?

She squinted at the words again, her eyes burning. Rubbing them only made them burn more. She squeezed them tightly shut for a few breaths, then went to her jug and basin and splashed water onto her face. The burning died, and with a small sigh of relief, she returned to the diary.

It was hard to think straight. The lack of sleep and the long day had left her bone-tired. But she wanted to solve this. *Needed* to solve this. A job in the Spire like Tom, that would be nice.

She shook her head. *Focus.* Instead, a craving for apricot brandy hit her. *Might as well, might wake me up a bit.* She took out the bottle from her chest, a fresh one she'd bought earlier that day. Uncorking it with her teeth, she returned to her desk. She took a few swigs and closed her eyes as the soothing liquor ran down her gullet.

Dear Lady, if you really care for your children, if you are watching over me, please show me how to solve this puzzle so I can escape that disgusting man. He's not worthy of you. I could be. A short laugh burst out of her. *Me, worthy? I'm nothing more than a murdering spy and a whore. I probably deserve Lothar.*

Eyes open, back to the poem again.

CHILD OF FLAME AND FIRE,
HEED WELL THESE LINES,
ALLOW THEM BE YOUR GUIDE.
TO LIGHT UPON THE VAULT SO DIRE,
YOU ARE TO START UP HIGH,
GO ACROSS THEN DOWN TO FIND
A ROOM AND LATCH OF WIRE.

"You are to start up high." Maybe that referred to the lines themselves? Start with "CHILD" then go across to "OF" then down to "WELL," then across to "THESE" then "BE YOUR" and "VAULT SO"? "Child of well these be your vault so" made absolutely no sense. Maybe she'd picked the wrong words. Maybe instead of including "OF" she should follow the directions and pick only one word from the next line: "Child well be the high." Equally meaningless. She tried different words, tried starting farther down the poem, but nothing worked. She leaned back in her chair and allowed herself a screech of frustration. Then she took a mouthful of brandy. *Lady, please guide me.*

Back to the poem again. It was written very precisely, every letter placed exactly beneath the one above, the large letters made smaller and the small letters made larger to fit. A new idea came to her, and her heart leaped. What if it wasn't entire words she was supposed to choose, but letters? She rubbed her eyes. First letter, "C." Then across. The "H" of "CHILD" or the "O" of "OF"? If she chose "O" and then went down, she got "COE." That didn't sound hopeful. So "CH" and then "EE" from "HEED" and then "OW" from "ALLOW." No, that clearly didn't work.

Just one letter per line? So, "C" from "CHILD," then across and down to get the "E" from "HEED," and again to get the "L" from "ALLOW," a second "L" from "LIGHT," the "A" from "ARE" and the "R" from "ACROSS." The last line yielded only a blank space. But that didn't matter. She had her word. She had her room. CELLAR.

She could have wept for joy. Of course, what a perfectly logical place for the tunnel entrance! She looked at the last line of the poem once more: "FIND A ROOM AND LATCH OF WIRE." The latch probably referred to some trigger for a door.

Her tiredness gone, Fay scraped back her chair and hopped over to her chest to take out a map of the temple. She unrolled it on the desk and looked for the kitchen in the Temple of Lumia, which was above the cellar. It looked like the entrance to the old temple might be somewhere in the eastern wall of the cellar. Satisfied, she returned the map to her chest and put the diary in her pocket. She would go now. The kitchen staff weren't due for hours yet to bake the morning's loaves.

The kitchen was as empty as Fay had expected, the fire reduced to glowing embers in the cavernous hearth. The room smelled of smoke and herbs and the venison stew they'd had for dinner. She carefully edged around the huge wooden table that occupied the center of the room to a door she knew to be located in the left wall. But that one brought her into the pantry, so she went back out to the main kitchen to look again. This time she found the door she wanted, a little farther along the same wall. It opened directly onto stairs leading down.

Fay had never been in the cellar before, but soon discovered that it was divided into two parts. The first was filled with food and drink in sacks, barrels, and boxes, and smelled strongly of root vegetables. But if her understanding of the map was correct, it was the second part she needed to access. That was through another door and down a short set of steps. Her mouth fell open when she realized what was in it—bottles of wine, rows and rows of them, lining every wall. At first, she marveled that they weren't kept under lock and key. All this wine, and she could simply go and get a bottle and no one would notice? But then she remembered that priests were not expected to steal. *Not wine. Not women's bodies either.*

The bottles presented a problem, though. She'd have to take them out from the racks to get to the wall behind, and they stretched up to head height. The thought of all the work almost sent her back up to her bed. And then what if someone came across her? What excuse could she possibly make? She'd have to feign sleepwalking or some form of madness. But there was nothing for it. So she gritted her teeth and forced herself to go on. She'd start right in the left corner. If there was a secret door, it was likely to be in the darkest part.

She put her lamp on the ground and set to work, stopping to examine each bit of wall and floor for a hidden trap door or mechanism. Soon, her back and arms were aching, and she was cursing herself for ever having started. She kept going, though, finally reaching the opposite corner of the east wall. But even here, her investigations led to nothing. She groaned and was about to slump onto the ground in defeat, but something skittered over her foot, causing her to jump in fright. Rats. *That's it, I'm done. Maybe Moth will have some ideas.*

But first she had to put all the bottles back. *That* thought made her want to cry. Even so, she took a lungful of air, rolled her neck and shoulders, and got to work again. She had replaced the first few bottles when the lines of the poem returned to her, causing her to stop in her tracks: "Look up high, go down and across to find a room and latch of wire." Could the door have been set high up? The foundations of the old temple might not have run as deep this cellar. *Fuck me, why didn't I think of this before?* She returned to the steps to fetch a ladder she had seen on her way in and dragged it back one-handed. It was heavy enough, and by the time she'd set it against the wine racks in the left corner, her hair was sticking to her forehead and her breathing was hard. Holding her lamp in one hand, she began to climb up, peering carefully at the wall to her left and right.

And finally—finally—her efforts were rewarded: a black metal ring protruding from the brickwork, buried in the corner right up near the ceiling. Where no one would ever see it unless, like her, they were shining a lamp right at it. Grinning with delight, she pulled and heard an invisible mechanism spring into action. A large flagstone at the level of her chest moved backward and to the side, the action surprisingly noiseless for a door that had presumably been shut for the past two hundred years.

The opening was barely large enough for her to crawl through, but the lamplight showed that it soon opened into a larger area with a door. She pulled herself into the opening and shuffled along on her elbows and knees, nudging her lamp ahead of her. The air was flat and stale, but the fresher air of the cellar quickly rushed in, as if the tunnel itself were gasping for breath.

There was another hole in the ground just in front of the door, partly covered by a square piece of wood. She lifted the wood and shone her lamp down into the hole. Another tunnel, burrowed animal-like into the earth. *Where does that go, and who made it?* But the door was her priority, so she re-covered the hole and stood to examine it. It was made of blue-tinged metal—nicoleum, no doubt—and almost perfectly sealed into the metal around it. Then she noticed an oddity. A hole in the door where there might once have been a lock. There was a script etched into the metal above the hole. She crouched and held her lamp close to it. *Seek the key in the Lady's flame.* Another puzzle set by Caris, perhaps. But it seemed someone had found a way around the puzzle and removed the lock.

Fay put her eye to the hole. Total darkness. But there was something in there, something malignant. "There is a lingering evil inside," Caris had written. She straightened. She should wait for Moth. Maybe he'd have a weaver in his employ who could help. Then she thought of Lothar. The better the prize she delivered to Moth, the more likely he was to reward her. But this door was surely enough? She'd solved the puzzles for him. *What if it's not enough? What if I can tell him what's in there, maybe even bring him some of those old books that Caris spoke of in her diary?*

Fay steeled herself and gently pushed the door. It opened on squealing hinges, revealing a deep, sinking darkness, entirely unpenetrated by the light of her lamp.

The thought hit like a hammer blow. She must not go beyond the threshold. She must not. The place was evil and wrong. Demons lived there. She must leave now and never return.

She slammed the door shut, and with pounding heart and shaking limbs, scrambled back through the tunnel into the cellar. Let Moth himself go in if he wanted. She would not.

Chapter 25

Alexios

Raging storms, all across Myrnia. Homes destroyed. The sea engulfing coastlines in giant tsunamis. Was that the Ruin? Or is it some other cataclysm that is yet to strike?

—Visions of Keeper Alexios Arathraxis

Alexios opened his eyes. Then wondered if he had opened his eyes. He could see nothing, not even the faintest outline. His wrists were weighted, bound in cold metal. He reached for the Lace to help him see. But the threads wouldn't appear. The metal around his wrists—nicoleum, it must be—was blocking him from the Lace. Where was he? He seemed to be lying on a bed, a soft one, the linen fresh and scented. The air in the room was neither hot nor cold.

Then he remembered the attack, the smell of burning meat. The First Weaver hit and probably dead. Bitter despair seeped through him. *I've failed. There'll be no help. The Chelaki have won before the battle is even started.* But then he roused himself. No, he must keep thinking.

Find out why he was here and why he was still alive. That must be a source of hope. "Is anyone there?" he called, although he sensed no other presence.

Silence. So total that his breathing sounded loud and harsh to his ears.

He returned to his last impressions. There had been blue magebolts, so it was a Vycenian weaver who'd attacked them, or at least one who had their powers. But why? Was it a coincidence, and he was caught up in some political plan already set into motion? Or could the Ilk mage be involved? If so, how? Had he followed Alexios? Guessed his intentions and sent someone here to capture him? But then why imprison him? Why not kill him too?

"Whoever killed the First Weaver is working for Antiphos," Cassander said. *"It's too much of a coincidence. They don't want us getting help from the weavers. They don't want word of the Ilk spreading."*

"You're probably right," he said. But if the weavers were implicated, was there any hope of defeating the Ilk at all? Had things already gone too far?

He needed to get some idea of where he was, but getting up without the use of his hands wasn't easy. He slid one leg over the side of the bed, then pushed against it to shift his body around before bringing the second leg down. His two feet now on the ground, he used momentum to get himself upright, then stumbled as fresh pain burst in his head.

The ground beneath his feet was soft. A rug. Then harder ground, then a wall. He raised his manacled hands and brushed them against it. Crystalline rock. Was he still in the Spire, then? That would indicate it *was* a weaver who'd taken him.

He walked along the wall, counting his steps. Ten paces by eight. A door of polished, varnished wood at the shorter end, opposite the bed.

Also, a metal box, locked. He returned to the bed and slumped wearily onto it. He was convinced that he must still be in the Spire, but why, and would someone come for him? Surely, they would, eventually?

Despite his anxiety, he fell asleep again, and his dreams were shot through with memories of the past. The Ilk Lord marching his army through Arindel after it had fallen. The Ilk mage murdering Nixos.

He was finally stirred by the sound of an opening door. It allowed no light into the room, but there was someone there, in the threshold. "Who are you? Why have you taken me?" he said into the darkness.

No answer. Only the rattle of metal on the wooden floor. Alexios tried to swing himself out of the bed, to get to the door and whoever was there. But before he'd made it to his feet, the door had closed and the key was turning, locking him in once more.

He awkwardly dropped to his knees and then felt along the ground. His hand first brushed a pewter plate. There was food on it. Some meat, venison from the smell, and bread. Next to it a tankard and a full skin. He used his teeth to remove the stopper in the skin, sniffed. Water. His mouth was furry, his tongue thick, and he held the skin between his manacled hands and tipped it over. Water rushed down his throat, cooling, relieving.

He forced himself to eat the food, although he had no appetite. Until he learned what had happened and who had imprisoned him, he intended to stay alive, and he needed food for that. He clambered back to his feet, returned to the bed. Not long after, a deep lethargy came over him. It struck him, as he fell into unconsciousness, that something must have been put into the food or water to make him so tired again.

But the thought came too late. He was already overcome.

Chapter 26

Castes

I saw a Chelaki woman giving birth in a rocky chamber. I don't know who she was or what the significance was. Surely, between the Cleansing and the Ruin, there can be no Chelaki left alive in this world?

—Visions of Keeper Alexios Arathraxis

Castes faced the assembled men and women under the morning sun. One hundred in all—ten fully trained Blades, fifty town guards, five hunters bearing bows. The rest, men over forty who'd received no more than two weeks' training with a spear. Many of them grey-haired and balding, they stood in the front ranks, ready to die so that their families could escape. On their gaunt faces, Castes saw fear, determination, and desperate rage. But he found, to his surprise, that he himself could feel nothing. So often, he'd imagined what it would be like to march at the head of an army, to lead his people to victory in war. But now that the time had come, it felt unreal, much less real than those dreams of glory. He opened his mouth to speak, but nothing would come to him, the words he'd prepared entirely lost.

"Honored Ruler, shall I say something?" Periklis prompted.

Damn you, you're not taking this moment from me. He cleared his throat, made a sign at Hereia, standing in the front, to raise his voice. "Today, we fight!" he began. Too weak, much too weak, and his uncertainty was mirrored in the faces before him. He filled his lungs with air. "Today, we march against the enemy!" Better. "An enemy that our people have fought throughout time!" Still not enough. He firmed himself, spoke from deep in his chest. "Today, we march against Antiphos!" Grips tightened around spears, mouths became set and hard. His confidence gathered. "We fight for our children, for our brothers and sisters, for the people we love—for those we do not even know!" Now energy sparked and surged through him, bearing his voice on a wave. "Today, we fight for our people!" He drew his sword in a grand sweep, and a roar exploded from the assembled troops.

Castes turned to face the eastern exit of the town. "Open the gates—we march!"

As the gatekeepers worked, he went to take his position to the right flank, next to Hereia. Periklis went to the left with Pintos, as they'd agreed.

Castes sheathed his sword. He'd practiced nearly every day with it since the Ilk had come. As a result, his arm was tired and heavy, unused to the exertion and the weight. But he wouldn't fight at the front. He had little desire to die, and he would need to lead the retreat when the time came.

They waited until the gates had been fully opened, then sallied out into the ruined fields. The air still stank of burning, a sharp contrast to the blue beauty of the sky and the wisps of cloud that trailed across it. Too glorious a day to die. Terror assailed him, banishing the exuberance that his own speech had lit in him. The enemy was overwhelming in force. The Ilk mage wouldn't have offered to fight with only five of his rippers if he didn't have some other trick up his sleeve. What chance did they have? But he was their leader, he couldn't turn away now.

They kept going until they were within firing range. The Ilk made no move toward them. Perhaps the Ilk mage wasn't with them? A fragile hope flickered in him, that they could somehow achieve the evacuation without any blood being spilled.

"Come out, Soulstealer!" Periklis roared, his voice carried by Pintos. "Where is the fight you promised?"

There was still no movement from the Ilk, no sign of the rippers who were to fight them.

"To the pits with him, let's sting these creatures," Periklis said.

"Patience," returned Hereia.

But Periklis behaved as if he hadn't heard her. "Archers, fire at will!" he cried.

"Dammit, no!" Castes said. "That wasn't the plan!"

It was too late. The first volley of flaming arrows soared into the sky and fell among the ranks of the Ilk. The creatures scattered but made no other move. A second volley caused them to fall back out of firing range. It was like they didn't want to fight. Or had no commander at their head. Despite his anger at Periklis for his disobedience, his hope strengthened.

"We should press the advantage," Periklis called. "Look at them! They're like helpless children."

"No, we wait for the soulstealer to make his move," Castes replied firmly.

But nothing happened. The Ilk stayed out of firing range, but none came forth to meet them.

"Let's go get them!" Periklis said. "We can kill some at least."

Castes gripped the hilt of his sword, indecisive. What was the soul-stealer playing at? Was he trying to lure them into a trap? But if they didn't distract him, the evacuees would be more vulnerable. "Forward march!" he yelled at last.

They advanced, and when they were in firing range again, sent another volley. Again, the Ilk fell back, and again his soldiers marched. But then Castes realized that they had moved quite far from the walls, farther than they had intended to go. "Halt!" he cried.

"Why? Let's take them," Periklis urged. "They're clearly leaderless."

Castes shook his head. "If we advance any farther, we'll be caught from behind by the other army. This might be a trick."

"We can't just sit here," Periklis said.

"Yes, we can," Castes replied. "Because while they're paying attention to us, they aren't watching what's happening at the West Gate."

"Look!" Hereia said. "They're coming out."

Five huge creatures, coming to the front of the line, moving toward them.

"Archers, ready," Periklis said. "Fire!"

Arrows rained onto the five rippers, many bouncing harmlessly off their scaly hide. Even when the shafts did penetrate, they just yanked them out and continued forward.

Leaden despair invaded Castes. How were they to kill these creatures if arrows barely even slowed them? When the monsters were close enough that he could smell their stink, Periklis called for the archers to fire again. More sank into their flesh this time, and they halted to pull them out.

"Let's go and strike them down while they're distracted!" Periklis said.

But Castes hesitated. What was the soulstealer playing at? Even as he was thinking this, a low rumbling began to sound, deep in the earth. At first it was only a light buzz against his booted feet, and he looked down in puzzlement to see nothing untoward. Soon though, the very earth started to shake, so violently that it threw him to his knees. Men and women fell around him, knocking each other over, yelling in surprise and fear.

Magic, Castes realized. Powerful magic. "Fall back!" he cried, scrabbling to stand again. "Fall back to the walls!"

They'd planned for an orderly retreat. But that wasn't what happened. No, his people turned tail and ran like bleating sheep, staggering and falling and staggering again as the ground shifted beneath their feet.

"The Lace!" Hereia exclaimed. "They're tearing the very Lace!"

Her words released something in him. This was no foe that he could see, let alone defeat. "Run!" he shouted, "Get to the gate!"

The few who had stayed with him didn't need to be told twice. He sprinted to the gate on legs born by terror, no longer conscious of anything but a desire to get away from thef shattering earth.

The ground behind him split open with a groan, those closest tumbling down into the yawning crack. Castes' foot gave way beneath him, and he fell heavily. One of the soldiers stopped to help him up while earth and stones spewed down on top of them.

Finally, he was on his feet again, running for his life, not even daring to look behind him at what was happening. The gate was open for them by the time they arrived, and they poured through, those coming behind shoving those in front when there wasn't enough room. It was only once the gate had shut behind him that Castes was hit by the shame. He'd run. He'd run like a frightened sheep. There had been no choice, but how pathetic they must have looked. A glance at Periklis told him that the captain felt as he did.

Furious with himself, Castes made for the ramparts, followed by some of the soldiers, to see what was happening. The crack was spreading in both directions, ringing the town.

Theophila was there, watching. "You were right to flee," she said.

Castes didn't respond. Instead, he strode along the top of wall, following the crack as it lengthened, the Ilk to one side of it, the town to the other. It continued right to the south gate and then beyond. "The evacuation!" he said, realizing what it meant.

"We've already called a halt," Thais replied.

"Did many escape?"

"The first three groups got out, so three hundred in total," she said. "When the earth began to shake, we paused to see what was happening. But I'm afraid we lost some thirty people to it."

"Do they have an illusionist with them?"

"Pintos."

Enough to start a new enclave if worst came to worst. Their people had been whittled down to fewer than that after the Ilk War. And they had grown and prospered. They could do so again. He had to believe that.

The crack came into view, continuing to spread northward until it reached the ravine that bounded the northern side of the town.

"That wretch is still playing games with us," Castes said. He resisted an impulse to strike the wall with his fist. Already, shame filled him because of the fear he had shown, along with rage at men and women they had lost. He would not allow emotion to escape him again now.

Once the crack had stopped its progress around the town, it began to widen, more earth and stones vomiting out of it, all on the Ilk side this time.

"The power they're using is incredible," Thais said.

"They?" he said.

"There's more than one of them."

Great Makers. "Can you see them? Do you know where they are?" he pressed.

"I can't see them, but I can sense the source of the spinning," Thais replied.

"Can you stop it?"

"No, they're tearing the Lace itself to do this. But even so, I probably wouldn't be able to see clearly all the threads they're using. Their power is of a different type to mine. I'm an illusionist," she replied.

"Do you know how many there are?"

"Two, I think. They're under the cover of the trees."

"If they can do this, they could bring the walls down," Castes said with sudden realization.

"We've already got artefactors strengthening the foundations." These words from Oxil, who had appeared seemingly from nowhere.

Theophila had come too, and Periklis.

"There'll be no easy way to attack them now," Periklis said. "And no easy way out for us."

Damn the Ilk mages. They seemed to always be several steps ahead. Meanwhile, his people did nothing but react. Then inspiration struck him. "A tunnel," he said. "A very long tunnel that takes us north of the forest, beyond their lines."

"Oxil, how long would it take to create this tunnel if your artefactors were put to work?" Theophila said.

"Depending on the length of the tunnel, weeks at the least," Oxil said. "Months even."

"Then we get everyone on it," Theophila said. "Now."

"With respect, we need artefactors working on weapon design," Periklis said.

"The artefactors will need to alternate," Oxil replied. "The work will be exhausting. They'll only be able to do a couple of hours before they'll need a rest from using their powers. But while they rest, they can still contribute to the weapons projects."

"It's settled then," Castes said. "Let's get started." He was relieved to have a plan, another stratagem to use again the enemy. But the shame still burned brightly in him.

Chapter 27

Ina

The Test is a terrible, dark thing. No one can deny it. But it is also our duty and our burden to bear. We must remain true to Chel and protect the world she wove for us and all her creatures.

—Teachings of Old Tsu

A new storm arrived the day after Mūak's attack, the wind so strong and the rain so heavy that Ina was forced to abandon any further attempts with the magic. It also meant that she and Suni had to postpone their plan to go and harvest the clawtongue. Indeed, they didn't see each other at all, as Ina was expected to wait out the storm in the Hunters' Lodge while Suni spent her time in the hut she shared with her family. The storm did at least make her rest and recover some of her strength, but as the days dragged by and the Test got closer, she began to sleep less and fret more.

The storm finally began to die on the third day, the wind dipping enough to make it possible to go outside for urgent repair tasks. But two more days passed before Ina and Suni could make time to meet. By then the sun was shining in a clear sky, and the Test was only one day away.

Their meeting point was the beginning of the path that wound its way up the steep sides of Ilij'ai. They would need to follow it for close to two marks to get above the tree line and reach the nearest patch of clawtongue, so they met in the early morning. The afternoon would be taken up by preparations for the Ritual of Exile that would take place that night.

As Ina made her way to the meeting point, she debated again whether to tell Suni about Mūak's visit. Telling her meant revealing she had been practicing her powers, and she wanted to keep that secret. But she also wanted to know if Mūak had followed her because Suni had said something to him. In the end, she decided to wait and see whether Suni herself would bring it up.

Suni was already at the meeting place when Ina arrived, looked wan and drawn. Her smile, though, was hopeful. Ina kissed her on the lips, wanting to take her time, but Suni soon pulled away. "I don't want to be gone from Tani too long."

So Ina led the way onto a barely visible animal trail that took them through dense fern into the highlands. They walked largely without talking, the humid heat causing sweat to prickle on their bodies. In some parts, Ina had to use a stick to beat back the ferns and other growth so that they could pass through. The way was made even more difficult by fallen tree branches, and sometimes also by toppled trees. As a result, her breath was harsh and ragged by the time they broke out of the tree cover and onto the rocky upper half of the mountain. Here she changed direction, going east a short distance to reach the clawtongue, which was spread out in a large, irregular patch.

It was a squat little plant, named for its fat, glossy leaves, a pair of which sprouted from the central stem. The leaves were oval-shaped, each one covered in tiny curling needles, making them extremely painful to walk on or grasp hold of. It was the roots that they needed, though, and these were tenacious and strong, so they had brought special leather gloves to protect their hands as they pulled them out.

It didn't take them long to fill up a small noukskin pouch with enough roots for several weeks' worth of tea. They worked in silence, but when the digging was done Ina repeated her instructions about the tea. "Boil a root for a mark and no more. That was the dose my mother gave me. But be careful. If the dose is too strong for her, she might not be able to walk, and they'll see that something's wrong with her. She'll probably also feel very sick, so don't give her any food beforehand."

"It *will* work, won't it?" Suni was holding the pouch and peering down at the thick, white roots.

"It worked for me."

Suni nodded and then tied the pouch closed before hooking it around her belt of twined grass.

As they made their way back to the village, Ina started to think about Mūak again and to wonder what Suni had told him. The thought that Suni might have betrayed her was agonizing, and some part of her didn't want to know the truth. But another part of her would not rest until she knew. She was so conflicted that she opened her mouth half a dozen times before finally plucking up the courage to speak "How's Mūak?"

Suni pulled a leaf from a nearby snail fern and began to tear it into smaller pieces, letting them fall to the ground as she went. "He's anxious," she said at last. "I haven't told him about the clawtongue."

"You're sure he won't work it out?"

"He's not always that perceptive," she said. "But even if he notices something, I'll say it was all me."

Ina swallowed dryly. "He realizes more than you think."

"What do you mean?"

"My father told me that he's made a complaint to the elders—about us."

Suni sighed. "Yes, I know. I was going to talk to you about it, after the Test."

Ina's heart lurched off-beat. She could tell that Suni had something difficult to share and that it wouldn't be something she'd like. "We might as well talk about it now."

"Let's wait. There's too much going on."

This only frightened Ina more. "Mūak attacked me the night before the storm."

Suni came to a stop. "What! Why?"

Ina told her what had happened and what he'd said.

"I didn't tell him anything," Suni said. She took hold of Ina's hands with both of hers. "Please believe me."

"Well, he's worked something out," Ina said. "He's threatened to report me to the elders for having the Curse." Seeing how crushed Suni seemed, Ina regretted having told her, and felt selfish for having added a fresh burden.

"I think he's just worried about Tani," Suni said. "He's not very rational these days. If he's complained to the elders about our relationship, it's because he's trying to protect her, and probably me too. It's best we stay away from each other for the next while, until the Test is over at least."

"I don't know if I can bear to stay away from you," Ina said.

Suni stroked Ina's cheek. "I know," she said. "I'll miss you. But Mūak and Tani have to come first."

"Even before your own happiness?"

Suni looked away. "I'm not like you, Ina. I like having a family. Mūak is a good man, and I love my daughter."

More than me. A thought came to her, that if Tani failed the Test there would be no more reason for Suni to stay with Mūak, and they could spend their nights together. She immediately banished it, ashamed it had even come to her.

"It would be better if you didn't come tomorrow."

Ina was stung. "It's my duty."

"You could get Kinuk to go instead of you."

But Ina wasn't missing this opportunity to get near the wretched Godstone. "I'm going."

"You'll only make him angrier."

"I don't care about him. I'm not afraid of him," Ina said, although this wasn't true.

"Stay away from us then," Suni said. "Don't provoke him."

"I'll keep my distance. But I'll come."

Suni started walking again and Ina followed her. They didn't speak again for the rest of the journey.

Ina walked at the head of the hunter column, flanked by Kinuk, the other hunt leader of her village. Directly ahead of her walked the twenty-four elders in male and female pairs, one pair for each village on the four inhabited islands. Their long ceremonial headdresses of red and black feathers trailed down the length of their backs—red to symbolize blood and the drakiri, black the loss of the birds and of the original Chelakan and its people. Ina was also in full ceremonial garb, in her case, a heavy necklace of whale teeth to symbolize her standing as hunt leader and a band of woven anan fiber around her head, from which three bright yellow achak feathers stood upright. A length of soft, red barkcloth was wrapped around her hips. It fell all the way down to her ankles but was split at the sides to make movement easier.

Behind her, the hunters drummed out a steady beat for the march through the trees to South Beach. Ina would not drum that night. Instead, she carried her long, ceremonial spear, whose shaft was inked with drawings of her mascot, the stiku lizard. A piece of purple stiku skin was also wrapped around the shaft, at the base of the blade. The stiku was a symbol of luck, and Ina had chosen it because she'd always thought it was something she particularly needed. The lizard was also tattooed in black ink on the inside of each of her forearms. Like every hunter, she'd had the tattoos done at the Ritual of Acceptance, which marked both her official entry into adulthood and the beginning of her days as a hunter. The ritual they marched to now was a far less joyous one, however.

It took half a mark before the entire village was assembled on the beach. A large fire had been lit in its center and the twenty-four elders split into two groups to stand on either side of it, their backs to the sea, as the villagers poured down from the dunes. Canoes had been laid out close to the seashore and were filled with the salted fish and water they'd consume that night to commemorate the landing of the exiles almost five centuries ago.

When everyone arrived, they stood grouped according to their social function. The exception was the women with children, who stood farthest away from the fire. The children who would do the Test the following day also had their own place, and both parents stayed with them. They had come with their elders from all the islands earlier that day, as they would rise early on the following one to make the trip to the Godstone.

Once everyone had assembled, Alik'Ri, an elder of Ina's own village, began to speak. "We, the people of Chel, are gathered together to fulfill her purpose and keep her world safe from Sīut. We remember our failures past, when we let those tainted with Sīut's Curse rule over us. We warred against other peoples, we created chaos and destruction, and Chel's creatures died." He stopped speaking, and the drums rolled. Four shaven-headed fire dancers took burning wood from the bonfire and began to caper backward and forward, waving and thrusting the burning torches as if attacking one another. All wore a cape of dried grass that covered them from neck to foot. Underneath it, Ina knew, was another layer of fresh yaka-leaf to protect them. One by one, they set each other on fire, causing the assembled villagers to gasp and the children to scream as flames billowed around them. Once a fire dancer's entire grass cape was in flames, he or she dropped to the sand, where the flames were extinguished.

When all four dancers were lying prone, Alik'Ri took up his narrative again: "Few of Chel's people were left alive when Chel finally intervened to save us. Chel blessed Takan'Ri, the Landfinder, with a vision of these bountiful islands, which have now sheltered our people for 519 cycles."

He paused, and the drummers rapped a sharp pattern of beats as the fire dancers leaped back to their feet and ran off into the darkness. Ina glanced over at the group of children to be tested. All were huddled close to their parents. Suni stood behind Tani, her arms wrapped protectively around her child. Mūak was next to Suni, an arm around her waist, and Ina felt a stab of jealousy.

The rhythm of the drums changed, extending to a long roll as six bare-chested male hunters slowly marched through the center of the crowd with a towering statue of Chel on their shoulders. Runners had been attached to its underside so that it could be carried more easily, but it was almost as big as the statue in the grotto, and the men were hunched from the weight. They stopped when they reached the bonfire and slowly turned so that the statue was facing the people. Framed by a halo of firelight, it cast a long shadow over those assembled. The drums stopped and the elders took a few steps forward until they were level with the statue.

Naomi'Ri, the second elder of Ina's village, now spoke: "As Chel bid, we swore the Oath of Peace—to never cause hurt or harm to another person, Chelak or other. And so we speak again the oath, and remember the three hundred who first landed on this island."

Three booms from the bass drums, and then everyone spoke in unison: "I do swear this oath—to never raise a hand against another person in violence or anger, to never kill or hurt except in defense of my life or of that of another person.

"I will accept the sacrifice of lower creatures according to my need, but I will not hunt for sport or game, nor show cruelty to any of Chel's creatures high or low. If I break this oath, I will make amends to the one I have hurt, and if I fail to do so, I understand that my immortal soul will be banished from Chel's Haven to spend eternity in Sīut's dark realm."

Ina shivered as she spoke the final words. Had she already earned herself a place with Sīut? And, so far, it had all been for nothing. The Test was only hours away, and she would face the Godstone again, but with the elders in attendance. Tani's fate was in the hands of the clawtongue. *The tea will work for her, no reason it won't.*

Naomi'Ri was speaking again, giving instructions for the next part of the ceremony. Ina barely listened. She knew already what she had to do. As Naomi spoke her last words, Ina raised her spear in the air, along with the other hunt leaders, and the drummers beat out a final rhythm. Then she pointed the spear westward and the hunter columns followed her to another, smaller bonfire that had just been lit. Once they were settled around the fire, designated hunters ran to fetch fish and water from the canoes.

There was no singing that night, nor dancing. Instead, small groups of people sat around their fires on the beach to eat and drink and remember their ancestors. Once everyone had finished eating, the fires were extinguished, and they returned in a silent procession to the village. No one stayed late at the main fire, as happened on other nights, although some of the hunters played stones or talked quietly in the lodge's common area.

Ina herself went straight to bed. Although she was bone-weary, it took a long time for her to fall asleep. When she did, she dreamed that Suni had been judged as cursed by the Godstone along with Tani, and both were made to drink the starweed poison that would send them back to Chel while Ina watched.

Chapter 28

Fay

The weavers still worship the old gods, whom they call the Spinners. But that is a false name for the Shadower. Are the weavers therefore evil? Their magic certainly is, even if they don't or won't recognize it.

—The Lumin Priest's Handbook

The next morning, Fay left another note for Moth at The Goat to tell him that she had got his information for him. He'd told her not to write down any details, so she'd have to wait to find out if he'd speak to her directly. She hoped he would, because that gave her the chance to request a new position outside the temple. But she'd have to wait until that night, when she could pick up his answer at Papa Julia's, another of his businesses in the Rainbow Quarter. It was one she much preferred to The Goat, and where she'd promised to meet Tom.

It was after ten o'clock by the time she slipped out of the temple, wearing underneath her robes a blue silk dress. She removed the robes in an alleyway and stuffed them into her satchel, then put on a pair of dangling silver earrings before continuing to the Rainbow Quarter.

The area was even more chaotic and frenzied at night, music pouring out of the alehouses, taverns, and dancehalls to mix with the chatter of the street. Heavy in the air were the smells of food and drink, of perfume and tobacco, barely masking the stench of sweat and reek of piss from the alleys. Nearly everyone, highborn or low, was doped or drunk. She passed men and women in embroidered silks with flushed faces and sparkling eyes, sometimes tailed by watchful men with swords. But also plenty of ordinary sorts in homespun cotton, staggering about, laughing and shouting. And then the destitute—dirty, dressed in rags, missing teeth, even fingers or limbs. They were there to beg or to steal, and Fay tightened her grip on her satchel whenever they came near.

As always when she went to the Rainbow Quarter at night, her eyes were drawn to the glowglobes that crisscrossed the main thoroughfares. Red, yellow, blue, green, and white, they bobbed and sparkled like jewels in a necklace. Or like stars. Like someone had plucked the stars out of the sky and hung them up and shot them with color. Fay laughed at her own fancy and pressed on. Too much apricot brandy.

Her destination was on a quiet side street. It was a plain, brickwork building from the post-Ruin era, with no windows or markings to show what was inside. She banged on the narrow door, and a small shutter slid open. Two light brown eyes peered through, widened in recognition. Pep? The door swung open, belching out music and tobacco smoke.

She stepped through into a tiny hallway, empty except for a chair. It *was* Pep, wearing tight black breeches that made his legs look all the skinnier. "You're not usually on tonight. Or have I got the day wrong?" she said, kissing him on the cheek in greeting.

"Argie's sick. Well, that's what 'e says. Saw 'im leave last night with some new boy. You know what 'e's like when 'e gets a new one."

"You shouldn't put up with it."

Pep shrugged. "Could do with the extra coin."

"Is Tom here?"

"Came in an hour ago with Silk." Pep opened a second door for her as the front door banged shut. This one brought her into a different world—her world.

A stranger would look upon it all and think that everything had turned upside down—for the men here were not like men elsewhere. They didn't push and shove, they simpered and strutted. They didn't grasp tankards of ale in meaty hands, they balanced long-stemmed glasses between elegant fingers. They didn't fight, they kissed.

And the women. Well, they were fewer, as in all taverns and alehouses. But they were also of a different sort. Some wore men's clothes—tight-fitting breeches and shirts, their hair cropped short or falling below the ears in a masculine style. They slouched on chairs and couches, cigars between their lips, other women on their laps. But many wouldn't have looked out of place in any ordinary locale, their hair long, their dresses brightly colored, their ears and necks strung with pendants.

There were whores too. The female ones were off duty but were easy to spot by the gaudiness of their clothing and the glint in their eye, often sparked by bliss or skybark. Only the prettiest and healthiest were allowed into Papa Julia's. It was, after all, a place that people visited in order to look and be looked at—although it wasn't attention the whores wanted. Rather the opposite. Here, they were neither bothered by the desires of men nor judged for the work they did.

The male whores, on the other hand, were busy. They too could easily be recognized. Many were young—too young, maggots who'd decided they'd rather turn tricks than turn flea. Most people knew them, for they would ply their trade here almost every night of the week.

Fay looked at the stage, directly ahead of her. A slender man in a long, blonde wig and sparkling, sleeveless red dress was singing. Fay didn't recognize him. He had a fair voice and did a passable imitation of a woman's way of moving, but Papa's often had better performers, so she gave him only a minute's attention before making for the bar to her right. Behind it was Brice, his eyes rimmed with black kohl, his lips and cheeks flushed with rouge. He wasn't wearing a shirt, and a heavy silver chain rested on his hairless chest. Who had given him that, she wondered. It looked expensive.

"Alright, Fay," he said, a bright smile dimpling his cheeks. "The usual?"

"To start with."

He nodded and turned to the bottles of bright liquor lining the back of the bar. She dug out some copper vics and put them down on the counter. Moments later, he was handing her a large, bowl-shaped glass filled with a liqueur so red it glowed in the light of the glowglobe floor lamps.

Fay took a sip, sighing as it flamed across her tongue and down into her belly. Then she stood on her tip-toes to survey the room, looking for Tom.

"He's with Silk and some others, down in the left corner there," Brice called behind her.

She raised a hand in thanks and wound her way across the room. People greeted her, for she too was well known here. When she had first come, she was still a whore, turning tricks in New Arindel, hoping to rise higher. That was how she'd first met Tom, who'd put her in touch with Moth and helped her get into Madam Sisi's brothel. Eight years now, from frightened girl-child to ... *what am I now? A bad priestess, I suppose.* But not a whore, never again.

She spotted Tom, exactly where Brice had said he'd be. He was handsome in his white calfskin breeches and blue silk shirt with its wide sleeves and tight cuffs. No doubt bought for him by his highborn lover, Silk, standing next to him. As always, the young man looked like he was in a sulk, with pouting lips and haughty eyes framed by styled blond locks that fell to his ears. Silk was every spoiled rich boy rolled into one, and Fay was convinced Tom kept him only for the money.

"Fay! Gorgeous as always!" Tom exclaimed, holding his arms out wide to welcome her.

"And you. We should get married." She leaned in to kiss him on the cheek. He smelled of spicy cologne.

"Not unless you leave the priesthood. I'm not spending the rest of my days on some farm in West Vycenia."

"We might get lucky, I could be sent somewhere dazzling like Pitstown. Think of all those northern miners, just pining for a bit of Arindel glamour."

"Oh, I *do* love a bit of rough," Silk said. "Take me with you, darling." He pecked Tom on the cheek.

Tom squeezed his round buttock. "And let them ruin you? Not a chance."

"Oh, you're so commanding. I love it," he simpered.

Fay restrained an impulse to roll her eyes.

Silk pulled a small leather pouch out of his breech pocket and dangled it before them. "Who's in?"

Fay knew what was in it, and her heart beat a little faster. Skybark. Silk could always be counted on.

"Get your pipe out." Tom winked at him.

"Oh not here, there are ladies present!" Silk said with mock outrage.

Tom smirked and stuffed a hand into Silk's pocket. The blond youth grabbed his other arm, drawing their bodies close together. A moment later, Tom took his hand out, planted a kiss on Silk's lips, and then gently pushed him away. He held up a carved silver pipe. Silk snatched it off him and began to pour light brown powder into the bowl while Tom got a red candle from the table. He used it to light the powder, and Silk put the pipe to his lips and inhaled, eyes closed.

Fay knew she should get her work out of the way first, but what was the harm in a toke or two? So she took the pipe when it came to her, sucked in deeply. When it came to her a second time, a giddy wave swept her away, freeing her from her worries and fears.

"Come, Fay, future wife!" Tom cried, grabbing her wrist and pulling her toward the dance floor. A band of musicians had joined the singer—fiddle, flute, and drum—to play lively folk tunes.

She let herself be taken, ignoring Silk's protests at being left behind. This was their moment. "So, tell me, the First Weaver," she said as Tom led her to the middle of the dancefloor.

He took hold of both her hands and drew her in close, a grin on his handsome face. "Whole place has turned mad since he was murdered," he said without dropping the grin. "They've doubled guards everywhere and set some where there were none before. It's making my job hard."

She smiled back. "I'm sure Moth's gonna love that."

Tom pushed her back out, swung her round in a circle. Lights fizzed past in a streak of yellow and red, making her dizzy. Then he brought them both to a stop, pulled her closer again so that their noses were almost touching. "I'm doing my best to make sure he gets what he wants. But it's more dangerous than it was."

"Be careful. I don't like dungeon rats."

Tom grinned again, and this time it was genuine. "Neither do I. But speaking of dungeons, I heard they handed Arianna Velden over to your lot this morning."

"Nuria's doing. Did she meet with Thane this week?"

Upon the mention of Thane's name, Tom took on a dreamy look. Fay knew he was obsessed with the handsome weaver. But Tom had told her that Thane only liked boys. Not children exactly, rather youths who still hadn't come to their full growth. At twenty-two, Tom was too much a man.

"Hello?" She tugged on his hand.

He snapped back. "Sorry, yeah, usual place, yesterday evening."

Lothar would love to know that. But she wasn't going to spy on Nuria for him anymore. "She's stormed this one. All the priests are saying it's a great victory. First time anyone has successfully enforced the rule." *And Lothar will hate that, but even* he *has to commend her for this.* They swung around again, avoiding other dancing couples. "Have you had new instructions from Moth since the murder?" she asked him when they came close again.

"Nothing I can share," Tom said with a wink. "And you? Any luck with the Archpriests' Library?"

Fay hesitated. She was dying to tell him what she'd discovered—the diary, the old temple. But she needed to talk to Moth first. "Nothing I can share right now either."

The song ended. "C'mon, then, let's get more skybark." Tom pulled her away from the dancefloor, and she went willingly. A toke was exactly what she wanted. The initial rush had already started to die, leaving room for her worries to crowd back in.

The maggot came not much later. This one she recognized—Nim—a scrawny youth who looked several years younger than he was. His brown, puppy dog eyes darted left and right as he squirmed through the crowd, and she saw him try to avoid more than a few groping hands. Men!

"Come this way," she said when he arrived, taking his elbow and hauling him toward the bar.

"I don't like this place," he said with a furious look at the man who'd most recently tried a grab. "Why the pits do you come here?"

"Because the men don't touch *me,"* Fay said. "And I get enough of that the rest of the time."

"I don't like 'em touchin' me."

"Now you know what it feels like. When you grow up, you remember that before you start hassling girls."

"I isn't gonna do that," Nim said. "I don't care 'bout girls."

"Well don't hassle boys either."

"I isn't no breech puller!" he cried.

How had she managed to get herself into *this* conversation? "What have you got for me?"

"A note."

She held her hand out, and a moment later it was tickled by a folded piece of paper. She curled her fingers around it. "What will you drink?" she said when they reached the bar.

"Sweet wine."

"Is he old enough?" Brice said, frowning at Nim when she ordered.

"I got seventeen years," Nim said with outrage.

He looked little more than fourteen, barely reaching to Fay's shoulder. "I can vouch for that," she said.

"Well I'm putting water in it," Brice said.

"I can drink a proper drink!" Nim's face screwed with anger.

"Darlin,' trust me. Your size, you'll be on your ear after half a cup and I'm not wastin' my strength draggin' you out of 'ere," Brice said.

Nim said something else, but Fay didn't hear it. She was scanning the note he'd given her.

I want to meet with Arianna Velden in her cell. Organize this meeting by the end of the week.

That was it. Fay stamped her foot in frustration. Nothing on the diary. Nothing on Lothar. The prick was deliberately ignoring her success. And why in Lumia's holy name did he want to meet Arianna in the first place? Everyone knew Moth hated the Veldens. If the stories were right, he'd even killed Eduar Velden, Arianna's elder brother. Did he want to gloat?

"Two vics," Brice said, resting their drinks on the counter.

Distractedly, Fay paid, and they returned to Tom. "Is that all he said?" she asked Nim.

He walked close to her, snarling at any men who looked like they were getting handsy. "He said to make sure and tell you there'd be consequences if you don't do what you're told."

"Consequences? What bloody consequences?"

Nim shrugged.

"Anything about a diary?" she asked desperately.

"Nah."

A pox on Moth's poxy bloody ass! How in ruination am I going to get into Arianna's cell? And avoid Lothar for another Ilk-damned day?

"Get your hands off me!" Nim spat at a man who had approached him.

"Come with me," she said, grabbing Nim by the arm again and steering him to a quiet corner. "Tell me what Moth said."

"I've told you," Nim said. "What's bugging you so much?"

"I can't tell you."

Nim drank half of his wine. "No one ever tells me anything," he said sullenly.

"That's because you're a maggot." As soon as the words left her mouth, she felt guilty. "We all start somewhere. And anyway, you know how Moth is, all secrets. I'd be in trouble for telling."

"Yeah, whatever." Nim drank the rest of his wine, put it onto the nearest table. "I'm out of here. Don't like this place."

He was dodging away before she even had the chance to react. She shouted a goodbye at his back, her mind already elsewhere. How was she going to get into Arianna Velden's cell? It wasn't just a matter of walking down there and asking to see her. Drug the guards and slip past them? No, far too obvious. They'd be wondering afterward what had happened. She was friends with some of the Defenders. Could she flirt her way into the cell? But then, questions. She needed a good excuse. But why would a lowly priestess like her want to see a weaver prisoner? Ruin and bloody ruination, to the pits with Moth, really and truly.

Tom appeared in front of her, looking worried. "I was starting to think you'd gone," he said. "Is everything alright?" He handed her a full red dragon, holding another in his hand.

Maybe she could share this with him, he might have some ideas. "It's Moth," she said, showing him the note.

"He wants you to set up a meeting with Arianna Velden?" Tom said incredulously. "Why?"

Fay shrugged. "I've no idea. I also don't know how I'm going to arrange this bloody meeting. Moth seems to think I have a lot more power than I do."

Tom's pursed his lips. "You said Archpriest Nuria is the one who got Velden transferred, right?"

"Yes."

"Could you speak to Nuria, ask her if you can visit?"

"But what reason could I give?"

"Hmm, yes, fair enough." He frowned, then his face cleared. "Velden's got an advocate. You could try meeting with her first, see if she'll arrange the meeting for Moth."

Fay brightened. "That could work—who is it?"

"Her cousin—Galinda Velden, another weaver. Makes Arianna seem positively sunny."

"Can you set something up with her?"

"I surely can, first thing tomorrow." Tom knocked back the rest of his drink. "Come on, let's get more drinks and more skybark. We can worry about the rest of it in the morning."

But Fay found it hard to relax, even after several pipes of skybark and more red dragons than she could count. She staggered back to the temple in the early hours of the morning and fell deeply asleep, not even stirring when the morning bells sounded. When she finally did wake, though, she found a message from Tom in her mailbox.

Galinda will meet you at Beryl's Grace coffee house on South Street, tomorrow on the strike of eight.

Chapter 29

Fay

As of 200 AR, Lumia's light shines most brightly in the Vycenian provinces. In Arindel, the picture is more mixed, where people still like to use weaver-made objects, particularly the wealthy. But we have made inroads into Sorin, Ferin, Tarsis, and Yaro, as well as the northern states of the Federation.

—Lumia in the World, Archpriest Herman Mill

Fay arrived early for her meeting with Galinda Velden. The coffee house was already crowded, but not loud, everyone too asleep still to raise their voices. Right in the middle were two big rectangular tables crowded with newspapers and pamphlets. Fay had sat at such tables before, to share news with strangers. Not why she was here now, so she went for a small table in the corner. She caught fragments of conversations as she walked past. Wool and iron prices, the weather, the First Weaver's murder, Tarsis warring, all the usual.

Moments after she'd sat down, a young male server dressed in black came to take her order. He'd just come back with a cup of steaming black coffee when the door opened. In stepped a tall woman wearing a wide-brimmed blue hat over her long auburn hair. She looked around with sharp eyes, her gaze stopping on Fay, sharpening further. From the descriptions Fay had received, this had to be Galinda Velden, and she raised her hand in a wave.

With the barest nod, Galinda glided toward her. People seemed to automatically give way to the weaver, and their eyes, if they lit on her, quickly found some other target. Despite Fay's determination to put up a shield of cool authority, she was struck by darts of fear. This was a woman used to being obeyed. And she was a *weaver*.

When Galinda reached her table, Fay rose on shaky legs to greet her. "Alinne Fuller at your service," she said formally, inclining her head a fraction more than she would have if dressed in her priest's robes.

Galinda raised her chin in acknowledgment, then looked around the room and down at the cracked blue tiles beneath their feet. "They won't be winning any prizes for this floor."

"Well, thankfully that shouldn't disturb our meeting," Fay said with forced brightness.

Galinda sat down but kept to the edge of her chair, as if she might take off at any moment. While Fay took her seat, the weaver removed a silver-trimmed handkerchief from her purse. She ran it over the polished wooden table, then raised it to her eyes. Her mouth curled. "Dirty too."

Fay would have sworn there wasn't a speck of dust on the table. "I'm glad you agreed to meet with me," she began.

Galinda put her handkerchief away. "As long as you don't plan to waste my time. Between my cousin's case, the whining of our tenants, and the mulishness of my father, I have little time for games."

"I won't keep you long."

Galinda raised her eyebrows as if to show *she* would make this judgment. The server came to take her order. "Ginger tea, not too hot." She barely glanced at him.

Fay ground her teeth together. Arrogant bitch. She might have been more polite if she knew Fay was a priestess, but she'd decided to dress like a merchant. Well-off but not wealthy, offering a deal to a highborn lady.

"So, you claim to be able to assist my cousin with her case?" Galinda said.

"Are you familiar with Moth?"

Galinda's cold, blue eyes drew together. "I know *of* him."

"I'm here on his behalf, he can help your cousin."

Galinda stiffened. "We have no interest in the aid of a scoundrel."

Fay decided to risk an aggressive play. She needed to appear strong with this woman. "Do you have a choice? She was seen over the body, her magical residue was in the air. She's even been handed over for imprisonment in the Temple of Lumia. The Conclave of Weavers wouldn't do that if they didn't think she was guilty."

The serving man appeared with a white porcelain teapot and cup. "Allow a few minutes for the tea to brew, milady," he said. Galinda ignored him, her sharp eyes fixed on Fay, dissecting. Determined not to be intimidated, Fay thanked the server on Galinda's behalf, and he nodded at her.

Galinda sipped at her tea and winced as if the taste offended her. "The residue was the result of her attempt to save Elwin, it's not proof of a crime. You'll have to do a lot better than that, girl."

Fay bristled at the implied insult in her use of the word "girl" but clamped her teeth around her tongue. "Everyone loves Danial Thane, but your cousin, not so much. Not even a little, truth be told. They'll be far more likely to believe him."

Galinda's scorn showed itself in the arch of her eyebrows. "The rule of law still presides in this land, and that law says my cousin cannot be hung on the words of a man, no matter what the priests desire."

"It's not just words, though, is it? You advocates are well able to spin hazy circumstances into iron proofs." Fay had seen it done many a time. Clever talking could get you far in a court, especially when your audience was predisposed to listen to you.

"The best of us are well capable of demolishing such 'iron proofs'," Galinda replied, making it clear in her tone and expression that she considered herself among this select group.

Fay raised her eyebrows a fraction to show skepticism, but then moved to her next tactic, thinking it wiser. "Moth might be able to find out who really killed the First, if not your cousin."

"It is the job of the investigators to do that," Galinda replied. "They hardly need the help of a criminal."

"Investigators don't have access to the same networks that Moth does. There are people who would tell him things they would never tell a spi ..." Fay caught herself. She'd been about to say spike, but that was thieves' talk. "A member of the Watch."

"I think we've spoken quite enough," Galinda said. She called for a server with a click of her fingers.

"It's only a conversation," Fay said. "At least tell your cousin what we're offering."

The server appeared. "This tea is undrinkable," Galinda said. "Take it back."

The server turned red. "Apologies, milady, we're sorry it isn't to your taste. Can I bring you something else?"

"No, I'm done here."

"Yes, milady." The server bowed and removed the teapot and cup.

"Please, at least bring the message to her," Fay said, no longer trying to hide her desperation.

Galinda rose to her feet. "Good day."

Fay thrust a note at her. "Details on how to contact me with your cousin's reply." That was Eleine's wineshop, which was close to the Temple of Lumia.

Galinda regarded it as if it were some filthy rag Fay had proposed she wipe her face with. Still, she reached out to pinch the note between the tip of her thumb and forefinger and lift it delicately out of Fay's hand. She placed it into her purse, and without another word, turned and swayed elegantly out the door.

Fay groaned into the remnants of her coffee. To the pits with the woman and her highborn arrogance. Why did they think they could treat everyone like dirt just on account of how much money they had and who their parents were? *Although she probably could smite me down with a wave of her hands. That's a good enough reason to think you're better than others. Certainly a reason to think you're more frightening than others. What's more frightening than a weaver?* But Fay had an immediate answer to that—the darkness locked in the old temple.

Shivering at the memory, she signaled for the server and asked him to bring the bill. When she'd settled both her own account and Galinda's she stepped outside into the warm morning sunshine. New Arindel beckoned again, but it was the very last place she wanted to be. It reminded her too much of what she had to lose. *Please agree to the meeting, Arianna Velden, or I'm fucked.*

Although she wasn't confident Galinda would reply, Fay went to Eleine's wineshop on her way back from New Arindel that evening. She was pleasantly surprised.

"Yes, this was left for you not half an hour ago," said Eleine.

She handed Fay a folded paper, sealed with red wax and stamped with the Velden coat of arms, a ring of slender trees. Fay's heart leapt into her throat. So Arianna had agreed to the meeting after all? She unrolled the note.

We have no interest in speaking to your associate.

G.V.

Fay stamped her foot. *Ruination! What now?* She couldn't just give up. Moth didn't tolerate failure. It wasn't going to be enough to say she hadn't convinced Arianna's advocate. For all she knew, Galinda hadn't even brought the proposal to her cousin. *I'll have to go into her cell myself.* But how? The old ideas came back—flirt with the guards, put the guards to sleep, ask to see Arianna and have them all think her in league with the weaver or worse. Was there *anything* she could say to Nuria?

"You look like you're in a spot of bother," Eleine commented.

The woman was clearly fishing for gossip, but what Fay told Tom she would tell no one else. "Wasn't the answer I wanted." She looked at the note again, wishing the words would rewrite themselves.

Then it came to her. Forgery. A note from Nuria saying she was to speak to the prisoner. It was risky, but there was no plan that wasn't risky, and this one probably had the best chance of success. Fay was a fair forger, another reason she'd been able to escape the whorehouse. That and her ability to mimic the speech of the better-born. "I'll take some of your apricot brandy, though." Fay handed over her flask, and Eleine refilled it from a barrel behind the counter.

Fay paid and returned to the temple. It was time for evening prayers, and she shouldn't miss them to avoid drawing attention to herself, especially with Lothar keeping his greedy eye on her. She'd get a sample of Nuria's writing from her secretary's desk, but as always, she'd wait until the middle of the night.

Fay beelined for her room once the prayers were done, while the rest of the priests went to the refectory for their evening meal. She was hungry, but she would wait until later to get some food. The archpriests ate at their own table with other high-ranking priests, but it wasn't uncommon for one to decide to share a meal with the lower ranks. These were the priests they needed to influence if they were to be made High Luminate, so it paid to be friendly. But she didn't want Lothar using it as an excuse to get near her.

While she waited, Fay thought about what she would say to Arianna, trying to anticipate the weaver's various responses and how she might counter them. She couldn't let herself fail. That meant angering Moth, and if Moth was angry, he'd throw her to Lothar simply to punish her.

At last, her candle burned down to the midnight mark, and Fay left her room. Her nerves had killed most of her hunger, so she went down to the administrative office first. It was a large room filled with rows of desks and the smell of paper and ink.

Fay made straight for the desk belonging to Nuria's secretary, having already been there many times during her spying. As always, there were large stacks of paper on the desk, many in Nuria's handwriting. Fay rifled through them, scanning their contents. Mostly instructions, letters to be copied. Nothing too sensitive. Those would be kept locked in the two drawers.

Fay took a note near the bottom of the pile. It was just a few lines, reminding her secretary to deliver a report on the number of dwellings in New Arindel. In fact, Fay saw quite a few instructions related to New Arindel. Nuria really did seem to be serious about doing something.

Fay folded the letter and slipped it into her pocket. Now to get the seal. That was in the righthand drawer, but it was one that Fay had opened many times. Crouching, she took her set of picks out of her pocket and inserted the first into the lock.

A noise. She froze. Footsteps, coming toward the office. *Pits!* She blew out her candle and crawled under the desk, heart hammering violently.

Whoever it was had brought a small lamp that barely lifted the darkness. But the footsteps were coming her way. What if the person were coming to this very desk? She needed to move farther back. Holding her breath, she inched her way around the side of the desk, matching her movements to the sound of the footsteps.

The person stopped and seemed to raise their lamp in the air, for the circle of light extended. Fay stilled. Had she been heard? But then the footsteps started again, and she crawled to the next desk as fast as she dared. She kept going until she was right at the far end of the room.

The person stopped at Nuria's desk, and a fresh bolt of fear struck her. Had she left her pick in the lock? She put a hand in her pocket, counted the picks with her fingers. No, they were all there. *At least I had some sense. And what is that person doing at Nuria's desk? Another spy? Or is it her secretary? What would he be doing here at this hour?* She risked peeking above the desk she was hiding behind, but the light was too poor and the person's face too indistinct. All she could say with certainty was that it was a small man or a woman, going through the documents on the table, pulling out several to read through. Next, they checked the drawers, but clearly didn't have the keys or the ability or tools to trip the locks. After that, the person went to the next desk, which belonged to another archpriest, Marcie perhaps?

Fay began to despair of ever finishing her mission. Did this spy, for spy it must be, intend to go to every single archpriest's desk in here? Oh, to be able to see the face and know who they were working for! But did she dare get closer to find out? After a few moments, she was decided. The news could be useful, sellable. She began to crawl silently in the direction of the spy as they went to a third nearby desk. At last, she got close enough to tell it was a man with short fair hair. But he had his back to her so she couldn't see the face. She crawled around to a different part of the room, hoping to get a better view. But then he straightened and went toward the entrance. Fay glimpsed a clean-shaven cheek with a weak chin and jutting nose. Nobody she recognized. After he'd left, she counted three hundred breaths just to be sure, then returned to Nuria's desk.

Her hands were still shaking, so she fumbled her first attempts with the lock, but it finally gave to her, rewarding her with the seal. She was tempted to go through the documents in the drawer but told herself she could return another night. She wasn't going back to Lothar, and Moth's priority was Arianna, not information.

She passed by the kitchens on her way to get some food and thought again of her trip through the secret tunnel to the old Temple of the Spinners. What evil magic lay in there? And with the door unlocked as she'd found it, could it get out somehow? She shuddered, but then put it out of her mind. That was something to share with Moth, and she needed to get this job done first.

Once she'd returned to her room, she began the task of writing her note. Her plan was to go to Arianna's cell before dawn prayers. It might make the guards a bit curious, but she reckoned Nuria was unlikely to make a trip to the prison at that hour herself. She rewrote the note several times until she was satisfied that the writing was a close match. Only an expert would be able to tell the difference, and the Defenders probably couldn't even recognize Nuria's writing anyway. When the note was ready, she dripped some candle wax onto it and stamped it with Nuria's seal. Then she slipped back down to the office to replace the seal and letter.

She still had a couple of hours of waiting left. Should she go to the Archpriests' Library? She might find other books that Moth might be interested in, and it was something to do. But if she were trapped like she had been before, she might not get down to the cells on time. No, it wasn't worth risking her mission.

So she returned to her room, took some apricot brandy, and reread Caris the Restorer's diary yet again. But her eyes kept closing, and in the end, she was forced to splash water on her face and then pace the room. Skybark would have been the perfect solution, but the smell was strong and would have carried out into the hallway even if she had some to smoke.

Finally, it was time to descend into the bowels of the temple to the prisons. In the guardroom, four sleepy-looking Defenders of the Faith were sitting around a trestle table playing a board game—Conquest, by the look of it. Unlike normal priests, they wore chainmail under white tabards emblazoned with a golden torch. Stacked against the wall were their long-bladed spears. But they weren't just warriors, they were fully trained priests, so Fay had no rank on them. She recognized none of them, which was maybe for the best. She was less likely to be remembered. "Brothers, I've come from Archpriest Nuria," she said. "She wants me to deliver a message to the prisoner, Arianna Velden."

"Uh, just a moment," said one, frowning down at the brightly colored chips on the board.

"Give up, Jos, you're done," said the man opposite him, smiling smugly.

"He's right, nowhere for you to move, might as well give it up," said the third, a skinny fellow with a very long nose.

Fay sucked in a frustrated breath. Bloody men. "Could one of you please open the prisoner's door so I can speak to her?" She forced a smile. By Lumia, she was tired.

The fourth man looked up at her, scratched at the stubble shading his gaunt face. There was a lightning bolt on his shoulder—a lieutenant, great. "Her Radiance said no one was to see the prisoner, except her advocate." An officious one too, even better.

"Alright, fine, I yield. I'll never get the hang of this game," Jos said, smashing a palm down on the table. The chips on the board jumped.

"Wise," said Smugface as he cleared the blue chips and put them in a pouch.

"I have a note from Nuria herself," Fay said to the lieutenant.

Now they all looked at her. Their eyes traveled from her face along the length of her body then back up again. Male priests were no better than other men. Fay held the note out and the lieutenant took it. Although she was confident in her forgery and it was marked with the seal, her mouth dried as he reviewed what was written. Then he shrugged. "Looks in order." To the man, Jos, who'd just lost the game, "You take her. It's my move."

Jos scowled but got to his feet, chair scraping loudly against the stone floor. He went first to take down a large ring of keys from a hook in the wall, then beckoned her to follow him with a grunt.

"Thanks," she said, smiling her special smile at him.

He softened. "Sure, no problem. Game's over for me anyway."

"Better luck next time."

"I'm always overeager," he said. "Gets me every time." He brought her down a poorly lit passageway that smelled of mold and damp. There were heavy-looking doors in the walls at even intervals, each one closed. He stopped at the third one on the right, which, unlike most of the others, was made of blue-tinged metal—nicoleum, to stop Arianna from weaving. He slid back three huge bolts before turning a key in the lock. It swung open with a squeal.

The room beyond was dark, but Jos handed her a torch. Her heart leaping into a faster rhythm, Fay stepped through.

"Bang when you're ready," he said.

The door slammed shut behind her, and she had the sudden irrational fear that she wouldn't be allowed to leave.

"Who's this?" came a sleepy voice from the dark.

Fay thrust her torch in the direction of the voice. It illuminated a woman stirring herself from a pallet on the floor. "I'm Fay," she said, suddenly awkward.

"Why have you come?" The woman got to her knees, dragging her blanket around her shoulders. She blinked at Fay with bleary, shadowed eyes.

"To talk, to offer you a deal." Fay shivered. It was colder in the cell than in the hallway, probably because of the nicoleum that lined the walls. *No chance she'll try magic on me at least.*

Arianna Velden got to her feet, still clutching the blanket around her. Beneath it, Fay could make out rich weaver robes of dark green, hemmed with silver scrollwork. She was tall, at least two hands taller than Fay herself, taller even than Galinda. Slender rather than thin, her long, red-brown hair shot through with silver. Fine lines webbed from the corners of her eyes, and a crease marked her brow, but her skin was still relatively smooth. Was it the face of a murderer? Not the kind Fay was acquainted with.

"I'm sorry I can't offer you a seat," Arianna said with a wry twist of her mouth. "They don't really encourage visitors." Her voice was low and resonant but not exactly warm.

Fay resisted the urge to bow. Even sleep-filled and off-guard, Arianna had a commanding presence, but priests of Lumia did not offer honorifics to weavers. "I've come on behalf of Moth," she said.

Arianna's eyes hardened. "So he's sending priests now too. I thought I'd already made it clear I have no interest in speaking to him."

So Galinda *had* brought her message to Arianna. "He might be able to help you. He has more influence than you might guess."

"I really don't see the advantage of getting involved with a crook," Arianna said. "Association with him is only likely to increase the suspicion on me. Please leave, this conversation will bear no fruit for you."

"No one need know you've been speaking to him," Fay said. "I can sneak him in as a priest." The weaver's eyes narrowed. She was thinking about it. Fay pushed on. "You could at least hear him out. It won't cost you anything."

Arianna rubbed a thumb on her elbow, still frowning. "Surely he's given you *some* indication of how he can help?"

Your guess is as good as mine. "Moth is powerful. His networks are wide. They go beyond this city, beyond Vycenia even. He can find out who did kill the First Weaver. And he has more than one judge in his pay. You'll need their favor when the trial comes. Danial Thane is well loved. Many will listen to his word over yours."

"Can he find mysteriously disappearing Eleusians?"

"I'm not sure what you mean." *Did she say* Eleusians*?*

Arianna waved a long-fingered hand. "Never mind." She went silent, her gaze turning inward.

Fay began to feel even colder and tried not to shiver. *What does Moth hope to achieve here?* Long moments of silence passed, but

Fay didn't dare disturb Arianna while she was thinking. Instead, she prayed to Lumia that the weaver would agree to Moth's request.

At last, Arianna opened her mouth to speak, and Fay caught her breath. "Fine, I'll talk to him."

Relief flooded her, weakening her knees.

"But only if he lets me see his face."

And with that, the relief ebbed away. "Is that really necessary?" she said. "Can't you speak to him first?"

But Arianna's voice only firmed. "I don't want him coming in that ridiculous mask."

So she knew about the mask. There was definitely some kind of history between them. Could the rumors be true, about her brother? "The mask would be conspicuous," Fay said. "But I really doubt he'll show his face."

"That's the deal. I want to know who I'm talking to." Arianna tugged the blanket around her more tightly.

Fay ground her teeth but could tell the weaver wasn't going to budge on this one. "Very well, I'll tell him." This wasn't going to work. There was no way Moth would reveal his face. No one had *ever* seen his face. Fay doubted his lovers had even seen it, if he had lovers. She'd never seen him with a woman—or a man.

"When will he come, if he comes?"

"Soon, the next few days, I imagine," Fay said. "I'll need to get word to him." Her eyes met Arianna's for a heartbeat. Was that fear she saw beneath the stony determination? "I'll probably have an answer by tomorrow." She went to the door, raised her fist to bang on it.

Arianna's voice trailed after her. "I didn't kill Elwin and his apprentice. But I want to find out who did and why. Tell him that."

Fay stopped mid-bang, looked back at the weaver. Her expression was more animated than she'd seen it yet. Fay realized she believed her, but answered with only a nod before striking her fist against the door. *Hopefully, once Moth has seen her, he'll get me out of here. He's going to be pissed about the mask, though.*

Chapter 30

Ina

We discovered what the Godstone could do by pure chance. A child touched it when some of the exiles were exploring Uruk'il. It burst into light. Six months later, the child showed early signs of having Sīut's Curse. It then became clear why the Godstone had been placed there.

—Teachings of Old Tsu

The morning of the Test dawned hot and humid. The skies were clear, but the weather diviners said a fresh storm would reach them by the following day, bringing an added sense of urgency to the proceedings. Twenty-one children would go—Tani and two others from Ina's island, with the rest coming from other villages on the four islands of Chelakan'ili. The Test was traditionally conducted island by island, and those from the northernmost island, Yon'il, went as soon as the sun has risen so that they could return home by nightfall. The children from Ina's own island, Lun'il, went last, and the sun had reached the fourth quadrant in the sky by the time they had gathered by the seashore to board the large canoe that would take them to Uruk'il, the island of the Godstone. Among their number were the three children to be tested and their parents, the six Lun elders, the eighteen rowers, and then Ina and her five hand-picked hunters. The hunters had a specific job, although as far as Ina knew, they'd never been called on to perform it. If any of the children or their parents refused to go through with the Test, the hunters were to take charge of the child in question and restrain the parents. Ironic, too, that it was her responsibility.

When Mūak saw Ina, his face darkened. Ina matched his stare with one of her own, silently daring him to speak. Suni put her hand on his arm and murmured something to him. He said something but didn't take his eyes off Ina. Ina looked at Tani, who seemed pale and sick, and was clinging closely to Suni. The two other children were crying loudly into the arms of their parents, none of whom looked as if they had slept much the previous night.

The rowers boarded the canoe first and took up their paddles. The elders went next according to village. Like the night before, they wore their red and black headdresses.

When all were aboard, the rowers put their might against the paddles, and the canoe began to cut through the ocean. The swell was slight, but Ina thought she could sense the gathering storm—even out at sea the air was still and humid, pressing heavily on them. She wondered if the leviathan were anywhere near but resisted an urge to reach out for him with her mind. He might not appreciate the contact, and the last thing she wanted to do was make him angry.

As they neared the island, the canoe began to shudder in the grasp of the currents, but the rowers were fresh and strong and kept the course true. The closer they got, the more the Godstone seemed to call Ina, making her feel like there was an itch in her brain that she couldn't scratch. She stared at the tiny island, a dull, black hump against the horizon. Almost nothing grew on it, and steep cliffs of bare rock dropped down to the sea on nearly every side. They were aiming for a landing place on the opposite side of the island to the one Ina had tried to reach. It had to be carefully approached, for there were many rocks lurking beneath the water. Elder Naomi was an expert navigator, though, calling out a succession of sharp instructions to the rowers as they maneuvered the canoe to shore.

The canoe landed safely, and once they had dragged it onto the beach, they began the steep ascent to the Godstone, at the top of the island's lumpish peak. It would take them little more than half a mark to reach it. The elders led the way, the parents and children following. Mūak carried Tani in his arms, speaking in a low voice to his daughter in a way that seemed intended to comfort. The other parents also tried to soothe their children, but other than that, no one spoke.

Ina inhaled the island's strangeness as she walked. It smelled completely different to Lun, more strongly of the sea, without the scent of green things and flowers to soften the salt tang. There were birds here that were never seen on the main islands. They clearly preferred the rugged barrenness of the island and the isolation from people and predators. The most distinctive kind walked on long, stick-like legs and had white plumage with a yellow tuft on their chests. They passed a flock of them in the shallows near the landing place, many of them with their long narrow beaks thrust into the turquoise water to search for food. A few turned their heads to look at their grim party, unafraid of their presence.

Soon, though, all of Ina's attention was drawn to the Godstone. It was calling her insistently, tugging her forward, making her want to run to it. The strain of resisting the impulse made it harder for her to block out the thoughts and emotions of the others, and the anxiety of the parents and children caused her insides to knot. She looked often at Suni, who kept her gaze trained on Mūak and Tani, walking ahead of her on the narrow path.

At last, they climbed over an outcropping of rock, and there it stood. It was half the size of a man, white and perfectly smooth, rounded at the top like an egg, but swelling at the base to root itself firmly in the ground. It pulsed faintly with inner life, proving that it was no ordinary piece of rock. Unable to repress the instinct, Ina reached out to it with her mind. It flared with a bright white light, and the group fell back with cries of astonishment.

She almost fled in panic, certain that the elders would discover the reason for the Godstone's reaction. But instead, all eyes went to the three children. Tani remained silent and dry-eyed, but the other two began to wail loudly. Some of the adults began to whisper and murmur, casting their eyes back and forth between the children and the Godstone. Suni glanced over at her, and Ina could see the unspoken question in her eyes. She gave her head the slightest shake, pointing a finger briefly at herself to try and communicate what had happened. Suni seemed to understand and gave a faint nod. Mūak saw the exchange, and his thick eyebrows drew together. Ina looked away from him and at the elders, now standing three on each side of the Godstone, facing the rest of the group, their faces grave and solemn. Ina suddenly hated them, hated them so much that her teeth ground together. *They* were the reason that this awful ritual was repeated, year after year.

"Bring the children forward." It was Elder Noruk who spoke, a short, stocky man from the northern village. He was known for his fairness, but his voice was as cold as the grave.

The first of the children stepped forward, Nuni, daughter of two cloth-makers who had once lived in Ina's village. She was led to the Godstone by her father, a man taller than most, but with stooping shoulders, as if he were apologizing for his height. At his gentle urging, the girl placed a hand against the Godstone's surface. It didn't react. Yana, the girl's mother, looked as if she would faint with relief, bundling her child into her skirts when she returned.

The next child was a boy, this time accompanied by his mother. She was shaking visibly, the dark purple stain under her sunken eyes making it plain she hadn't slept. They reached the Godstone, but the boy kept his hands firmly down by his side.

"Go on, Uki," the woman said, trying to take hold of his right hand.

"I don't want to," he said, wriggling out of her grasp.

"You have to," his mother said, reaching for him again.

He dodged away. "No! I don't want to!"

Ina signaled at her hunters, and they quickly formed ranks to block off escape. She was about to go for the boy herself, but his father was already striding toward him, his face dark as a storm cloud.

"You will not shame us!" He grabbed his son's wrist and yanked him back to the Godstone.

The hapless child tripped over an outcrop of rock and fell headlong against the Godstone. Ina winced at the sharp crack as his forehead smacked against the stone's surface. The boy began to screech, but the Godstone stayed dark and quiet. His father pulled him away roughly, ignoring his cries until they were back in the ranks of the watchers. His mother fell to her knees, tears falling as she scooped her screaming child to her.

Ina realized she had chewed her lip so hard she had drawn blood. She tried to relax, but even her hunter's training couldn't relieve her of the maddening itch of the Godstone. Mūak stepped forward with

Tani, and she dared to send out a plea to the Godstone. *Please, let her pass. She's just a child. I'll come to you if you let her pass.*

Ina held her breath as Mūak gently took hold of Tani's hand and placed it against the Godstone. For a moment, it was as if time had stopped, and Tani's hand seemed to stretch out with infinitesimal slowness.

It has to work, it has to work.

Tani's hand reached the stone. The reaction was instant, a glaring white light that told the watchers unequivocally that she was cursed, that she could not be permitted to remain in Chel's world.

Ina saw clearly what happened. The Godstone tried to form a connection with Tani through her mind. She could see the sparking of Tani's network, her instinctual reaching toward the magic of the Godstone, even through the clawtongue. But why? Why hadn't the clawtongue worked? They had given her the same dose as Ina had been given, she'd even checked it with her mother. Why? Why?

Suni sagged and, thinking she might faint, Ina leaped over to her and put an arm around her waist to keep her upright. "I'm sorry," she said, but the words seemed so inadequate. "I don't understand it."

Tani began to cry. Mūak took her in his arms, and she was startled to see that he too looked as if he were about to cry, his mouth twisted and his eyes pinched.

"The Godstone has spoken," Elder Alik intoned. "The Purge will be conducted three days hence as the laws dictate."

Suni leaned against Ina as if she were unable to trust her legs to carry her. "You said it would work," she said, disbelieving rather than accusing.

"I'm sorry, I'm so sorry. I don't understand it."

Nobody spoke to comfort Suni or Mūak. Instead, they all took a step or two away from the family, as if afraid that the taint would spread to them. But there was compassion in the faces of a few, mingled with the fear. The elders, for their part, remained cold and expressionless. Ina hated them, more than she ever had. This was all their fault. They called it a curse, but it wasn't a curse. It couldn't be. *I'm not evil. Tani isn't evil. She's the sweetest little child, she doesn't deserve to die. Her life has barely begun.* Rage and grief brought tears to her eyes, and she tried to blink them free.

"Let us return to Lun," Naomi said. "This Test is done."

To Sīut with you, Ina thought savagely.

But no one spoke a word as they began the descent, Mūak walking with Tani in his arms, Ina behind them next to Suni, feeling her beloved shaking—Ina shaking herself. But she'd barely taken a few steps before she was hit by a surge of demand from the Godstone. It filled her with fresh fury, and she continued down the path without a backward look. *You seek to betray me. I won't fall for your tricks.*

She expected the Godstone to become quieter as she descended, but if anything, it became more insistent, tugging at her mind, causing the hairs on her arms to prickle. Grudgingly, she began to think, *maybe there's something else to it. Maybe I* should *go back and find out. Who put it there and why? I don't believe the elders. I don't.*

She remembered what the leviathan had said, that she had been expected. It still seemed ludicrous. But would the Godstone reveal Chel's purpose for her? *Maybe it's just a trick. Maybe the Godstone does want me dead.* She walked on, and the Godstone's call became ever more maddening. By the time they were halfway down to the cove, it was so strong that her feet began to drag, to refuse to take her further. *I need to find out. I can't hide and pretend anymore. Not after this, not when we'll lose Tani.*

"Suni, I have to go back," she said quietly.

"What for?"

"The Godstone."

Suni shook her head. "No, don't, I don't want to lose you both." Tears shone in her eyes, threatening to spill over.

"I have to go. I have to find out what it is."

But Suni just looked at her, silently pleading.

Ina firmed herself. "I'm going no matter what. But they're less likely to catch me if you create a distraction."

Suni blinked rapidly, trying to hold back her tears, but then finally, she said, "What do you want me to do?"

"I'll go back to the end of the line. Maybe you could pretend to fall or something?"

She nodded, wiped at her eyes with the tips of her fingers. "I'll try and hold them off as long as possible."

Ina squeezed her waist. "Wait until we're at the part where the path curves around sharply, just before we go down to the cove. I can run back out of sight."

"What will you do then?"

"I don't know."

"Are you sure?"

"I have to." Suni nodded, and Ina stopped and removed one of her sandals, as if to shake loose a stone. She waited until the last person in the group had passed her before putting it back on. Then she continued down until they reached the curve in the path. Suni disappeared around the bend and Ina prepared to run. Would Suni do as she'd promised? The people continued to file down the path, and Ina was almost at the bend herself. *Come on, Suni.* One more step, then another. If Suni didn't stop now it would be—a cry of pain cut through the humid air.

She didn't wait to see what happened next. As those in front of her hurried forward to investigate, she turned and scrabbled back up the path. She ran as fast she could, tripping and stumbling but not slowing, ignoring the burn in her muscles and chest. At last, she reached the Godstone, breathing heavily and drenched in sweat. She stared at it, both dreading and craving the moment she would feel its smooth surface again.

Then she took a step forward and grasped it firmly between her two hands.

Chapter 31

Alexios

My duty is my faith, my faith is my duty. I am the servant of the gods and of my people, and so I must carry my burden through the centuries. To willfully set it down is the greatest of sins, the most intolerable of disgraces.

—The Role of the Keeper, Alexios Arathraxis

Alexios woke again in a place of even deeper darkness. He was lying on cold stone, the chains still on his wrists. The smell was different too—musty and airless. And the darkness seemed to have an oppressive weight, reminding him of the Ilk. That realization jerked him to full wakefulness. He strained his ears but heard nothing that indicated they were nearby.

"It's the Gloom," Cassander said.

"I thought that only came with Ilk," Alexios said.

"Usually. But the Gloom isn't caused by the Ilk themselves. It's a by-product of the Lace becoming overly warped. Or so the magi used

to say," Cassander replied. Then after a brief pause, *"I can't be sure I understood it correctly, though."*

"Get up, father," Demeia said. *"Let's see what we can learn of this place."*

She was right. But something about the darkness, the Gloom, was making it very hard for him to sit up, never mind stand. It was as if it interfered with the connection between his will and his body. Instead, he longed to give himself over to sleep, to find an escape, even if his dreams were likely to be just as fearful.

"Now isn't the time for dreaming," Epiktet cautioned. *"You need to resist this."*

But he still couldn't muster the ability to move, nor even the desire to do it.

The muffled sound of metal against metal, a door opening, a faint beam of light slicing the darkness. At the sight of it, Alexios finally found the energy to push himself into a sitting position. The light entered the room and moved toward him, illuminating dark robes and a bone mask with ram's horns. The Ilk mage had followed him to Arindel. He crouched and placed a plate of food and a drinking flask on the ground next to Alexios.

But Alexios had little interest in them. "Where have you taken me?" he said, the words slow and difficult to produce.

He'd spoken in Eleusian, but his captor answered in Vycenian, speaking like a native. "Where you won't be found."

Not the mage at Neopoli, then. This voice was higher in tone. The youth in the vision? No, his captor sounded more mature. But, of course, he still didn't know if that vision had been of the past or present, or even future. "Who are you? What do you want of me?"

"It isn't really a matter of what *I* want."

As Alexios watched, the ram's horns seemed to move, to reach down to spear him. He instinctively shrank back, but then marshaled the will to speak. "Did you kill the First Weaver?"

"Regrettable but necessary."

"Why not kill me?" Death would be better than this prison.

"You're no true Keeper," hissed a voice in his mind, not one of the souls. *"A Keeper is tested, chosen from the best of the best."*

"She doesn't want you dead. Not yet, anyway."

"Who is *she*?"

"Mother. You'll meet her, no doubt."

Mother. Hardly that Chelak woman he'd seen in the second vision? She was far too young to be the mother of the man before him. "So she's behind all this? The attack on my town?"

"She intends for you to be finished, this time."

Alexios laughed bitterly. "You've already succeeded. Teleriol is no more. My people are a bare candleflame to what they were."

"Yet some of you remain. And the Vycenians grow ever more numerous and more prosperous."

"The Vycenians destroyed you before, they'll do it again." Alexios tried his hardest to sound defiant, to believe what he was saying, but he was filled with crawling doubts. It seemed these Ilk mages were everywhere. And from what the First Weaver had told him, the Vycenians had also lost much of their technology and knowledge in the Ruin. How could they hope to stand against this new invasion? "Did you steal the First Weaver's soul too?"

"Souls give life and power, you know that, Keeper."

The souls bound to Alexios screamed their rage. "You violate them," Alexios growled, the sudden violence of his emotion surprising him. "It's evil what you do. They can't return to the Makers."

"Oh, religion is so trite. There are no gods. Those are stories people tell themselves to feel better about their own mortality. A soul is nothing more than a piece of the elemental power, temporarily granted to a living being until its time has ended. The true gods are us, Keeper. You and me. The mages who can wield the elemental power, who can live forever. We don't have to tell ourselves such silly stories."

Alexios almost choked in outrage. "You aren't gods! You're slaves of Antiphos."

"Antiphos, Sīut, Farax—names that mortals give to the elemental power because they're afraid of it."

"I saw how you use it to spawn the Ilk. It's wrong, that power belongs to the gods. Your abominations warp the Lace. Don't you see how dangerous it is? You could cause the whole world to unravel. You nearly did."

"We understand the limits," the other said calmly. "The Ilk, as you call them, are but a means to an end. A very effective weapon. And don't you agree that we save many human lives by using them?"

"But still you murder many," Alexios said. Ilk tearing heads off farmers. Cook fires and the smell of roasting meat. Nixos and Demeia.

"Oh, come now. If we were to use a human army, many thousands more would die. The Ilk kill efficiently and undo armies before they have even joined the combat. If you're so concerned, why not make your own creatures? We could see who makes the best ones!" He laughed, the sound muted by the bone mask.

"And destabilize the Lace even further? You're mad!"

"Not I. But Inyaki is a little."

"The one who came against us in Neopoli?"

"The very one. He's quite brilliant, despite the madness." The Ilk mage tipped his head to the side. "Maybe because of it."

Fresh rage boiled up in Alexios. "You're nothing but death-lovers," he spat.

"Believe it or not, Keeper, I don't have much taste for killing. I merely like to win."

Alexios glared at him, but his anger drained away as suddenly as it had appeared. In its place, cold fear. How could they hope to prevail if the enemy were in the heart of the weavers' Spire itself?

"I will take my leave now. Duty calls me elsewhere." Words laced with irony, perhaps a hint of weariness.

"What are you going to do to me?"

"Leave you here, of course."

The Ilk mage turned his back to Alexios, opened a door he could not see. It shut quietly behind him. Muted squealing as a bolt slid home.

Alexios slumped back against the wall behind him. What was he to do now? He was stuck, imprisoned. He had failed. Tears leaked out of his eyes.

"Eat something," Epiktet urged.

Alexios didn't even look at the food. He had no appetite, and there was no point. If they wanted to keep him alive, it was for no good reason. Maybe they planned to torture him. They already *were* torturing him, leaving him in this place. *"I won't give them the satisfaction. I won't take their food, or their water."*

"Don't give in, father!" Demeia said. *"It's not over yet. It's not over until you give up."*

The other souls chimed in agreement.

"Leave me alone!" he cried. "I want peace." He shoved them away, forced them into the deepest recesses of his consciousness. How he hated them, hated that he was never free of them, never free of the crippling weight of his burden. His body tipped sideways, his head hitting the ground. Drawing his knees close to his body, he closed his eyes. *This will be the end of it. This will be the end.*

Chapter 32

Fay

The only reason weavers were allowed to remain in the Spire after the Ruin was by agreeing never to serve on the Council of Twelve (now Eleven) again and to allow any accused of committing a felony to be jailed in a Lumin temple pending their trial. Weavers found guilty of murder are subject to capital punishment, to be carried out by a Lumin-appointed executioner.

—The Lumin Priest's Handbook

The evening after her success with Arianna, Fay was summoned to meet Moth in a warehouse at the docks in New Arindel. It had been a long time since Fay had met Moth face to face, and she was nervous. He could be unpredictable. But at least it would give her the chance to talk to him about the diary and about Lothar.

The warehouse was full of cotton, and a boy maggot led her on a winding path through stacked bales to a door at the back. Two scorps were standing guard outside it, practically the only men Moth trusted to protect both him and his secrets. She recognized them both from a distance: Ruadh, with his enormous bulk, flaming red hair, and thick carpet of a beard, a Northlander who always had a smile at the ready; and Vigo, almost as big as Ruadh, his arms marked with jagged black and red tattoos in the Yaro warrior style.

"Been too long since I've seen your pretty face," Ruadh said with a wink. "You should get yourself into trouble more often."

"I'm not in trouble, am I?" she said, her nerves jangling at an even higher pitch.

"Nah, how should I know? But he expected you an hour ago, and you know what he gets like."

"I couldn't come any sooner. Go on, tell him I'm here." She almost knocked on the door herself in her anxiety.

Ruadh seemed oblivious to her impatience, though, and moved slowly, as if he had all the time in the world. Was he hungover? His eyes were bloodshot. At last, his knuckles struck wood, and he opened the door and put his head through. "Fay's here." There was a muffled answer, and Ruadh jerked his chin at her to go in.

The room beyond was small and empty of cotton. Just a large desk, behind it a half-man, half-insect. His iridescent head rippled green, yellow, and blue, and two curling antennae twitched between a pair of burnt-orange globes set over a ridge-like nose and lipless mouth. Covering his lean torso was a finely cut, black silk shirt, buttoned with pearls. The sight of Moth always made Fay uncomfortable, probably the reason he wore his weird magical mask. He was talking to a couple of men sitting in front of his desk, flanked by four burly wasps who gave her searching looks.

"Wait here 'til he's done with them," Ruadh said behind her.

She strained to hear what the men were talking about but caught nothing more than the odd word. Drug smuggling it sounded like, maybe bliss. They were dismissed, and Fay stepped aside to let them through the door. Moth started scribbling in a large book, the only sound for a couple of minutes the scratching of the quill and the odd shout from outside.

Finally, he put the quill aside and looked at her. "Come forward." Sounded as ever like the highborn Vycenian he was rumored to be.

She walked up to the desk.

"Sit."

She sat on one of the chairs opposite him, trying to conceal her nervousness.

"Well done on organizing the meeting with Arianna Velden, and so quickly. You'll be rewarded," he said.

Fay leaped at the chance. "I need to get out of the Temple. The Archpriest, Lothar, he wants me to fuck him. I can't—"

"You'll be rewarded when you've finished your work," Moth said coldly. "I want to see Arianna tomorrow. There's a preliminary hearing the day after, and I don't want to risk her being released before I speak to her. Tell me how you propose to get me in unseen."

Fay swallowed her frustration. "Novices often come from other parts of the country to study for a time in the main temple here in Arindel. No one will question you if they see you with me." She removed black robes from the sack she was carrying and put them on the table. "Novice robes."

Moth touched them lightly and the iridescent mask rippled, conveying dislike.

Fay could guess why. "Novices are expected to put up with some difficulty," Fay said. "The priest robes are much softer."

"When?" Moth said, removing his hand from the robes.

"The best time is after evening prayers, when most are eating," Fay said.

Moth fixed his globular gaze on her, waiting.

"Seven o'clock," she clarified.

"Very well. We'll meet in Eleine's wineshop at half past six."

"There's one other thing," she said, heart beating faster again. He was going to hate this.

The antennae twitched. "Yes?"

"The mask ..."

"I won't wear the mask, of course," he said. "Is that it?"

"She says she ..." Fay swallowed.

"She ...?"

"Wants to see your face." She half winced, expecting something cutting.

"Fine. Is that it?"

Fay blinked in surprise. "Er, yes, I suppose so."

"Good." Moth looked down at his book.

Ruination, no that's not it. Gathering her courage, she said, "The diary, the hidden room, you got my message?"

Moth's antennae waved as he looked back up at her. "That isn't a priority now."

What the pits? Three days ago you made it seem like it was the most important thing in the world. "I have more to share," she said, her voice shaky. She rolled her hands into fists to firm herself. She needed to convince Moth of the worth of her findings.

There was a knock at the door, and Moth called for the person to enter.

Ruadh stuck his head in. "Janis to see you."

Moth turned his creepy orange back eyes on Fay.

"It will only take a moment," she said, allowing a note of pleading to enter her voice.

"Tell him to wait," Moth said to Ruadh. When the big man had left, Moth said to her, "I hope your tale is an entertaining one."

Only marginally relieved, Fay told him about the tunnel she'd found, how she'd opened the door to the old Temple of the Spinners and felt the evil inside. Moth listened intently, and she hoped that the vibration of his antennae meant he was interested. She could never read the bloody things.

When she finished speaking, he was silent for a moment. Then he said, "I suppose we'll have to send a wasp in with you."

"A firefly would be better," Fay said. "Someone who might be able to deal with the dark magic in there." She knew Moth had a weaver or two in his employ. Surely, he could send one with her?

Moth's antennae bobbed. "I'll think about it. First, I want to meet the Velden." He pointedly looked down at his book.

But Fay couldn't leave yet. She swallowed, choked out the words. "Lothar—if I don't do what he wants, he'll reveal me as a spy."

Moth's globular eyes snapped back up. "What do you mean?"

"The archpriest I stole the key from, to get into the Archpriest's Library. He wants to fuck me. He thinks I'm spying for the weavers."

"Then do what he wants," Moth said, the globular eyes flaring bright orange. "Surely, I don't need to tell you that."

"I can't, not that. Not again." Her voice cracked over the words.

"Did you want to go back to Madam Sisi's instead?"

Fay hung her head. "No."

"Then do what you must." A second's pause. "If things work as I wish with the Velden woman, I'll see about setting you up elsewhere, a jun shack maybe. Now go. I'll see you tomorrow."

Fay went out, simmering with frustration and fear. She couldn't let Lothar touch her, she couldn't. Not now, not after she'd been free for so long.

In the end, though, Lothar wasn't at evening prayers, nor at dawn nor at morning prayers, which meant he had to be out of the city on some business. Gladdened by the unexpected reprieve, Fay went to New Arindel with more cheer than normal, sparking a comment from Maev. But as the time to meet Moth drew closer, her nerves rose again. This was going to be even riskier than going to see Arianna on her own had been. What if the Defenders asked about him?

She arrived at Eleine's before Moth and waited in a room above the shop, squinting out at the bustling street. But she didn't have to wait long before he came in to find her, already wearing his novice blacks. He wasn't wearing the insect mask but had the hood of the robe pulled right over his head and a black scarf over his mouth and nose.

They entered the temple through the side entrance and went straight down to the cells. The corridors were empty, everyone eating as she'd expected. There were four Defenders in the guardroom as before—Jos and the lieutenant and two others.

"Here to see the prisoner again?" the lieutenant said, casting a curious look at Moth, obviously wondering why a novice was being taken to the prisoner.

Fay dug a freshly forged note out of her pocket.

But the lieutenant waved it away. "Jos, you take her."

Fay almost laughed at the ease of it. They had no sense of danger at all, these Defenders. No idea about the games being played beneath their noses. But then, priests were often quite a literal bunch. They liked rules and to follow them, and didn't consider that others might be different. The archpriests, of course, were a whole other kettle of fish.

Arianna was sitting on a chair reading when they entered, an oil lamp at her feet. She had the blanket on her knees, but when she rose, she transferred it to her shoulders. Her eyes, when she fixed them on Moth, were cool. "What do you want?"

Moth regarded Fay. "Turn and face the wall. Do not look if you value your life."

Fay didn't need to be told twice. She walked right up to the wall of the cell and pressed her nose against its cold, metallic surface. But her ears pricked, listening for clues.

"You," Arianna gasped.

"I want a pardon."

"I could have you arrested," Arianna said.

"I don't think you're in much of a position to do that," Moth said. "Face it, your brother was a sadistic little prick."

What did that mean? Was it Moth who had killed Arianna's brother, all those years ago? Was that the reason he'd gone underground?

"Eduar was ... difficult," she said. "But if you think my father will award a pardon ..."

"How much does your father love you?"

"How dare you—"

"I merely meant that if your father would like to keep your head attached to the rest of you, then he may want to consider this pardon," Moth said. "I can help you get out of this."

"There'll be a trial. There's no concrete evidence against me. I don't need your help."

"If you believed that, you wouldn't be talking to me."

Silence.

"You're not particularly loved, are you?" Moth continued. "Do you know what they're saying out on the streets?"

"There's no proof," Arianna said.

"*Did* you do it?" Moth asked. "I'm curious. I don't care if you did or didn't."

"I did *not* do it," Arianna snapped. "Why would I?"

"Power. You want to be First Weaver."

"If I had, I'd have been a lot more careful," Arianna said. "To be caught over the body, with my residue in the room? Come on."

"Indeed, you're known to be a cold bitch, but not a stupid one."

Fay wondered at Moth's boldness. Surely, this wasn't the way to win Arianna over? But the weaver surprised her again.

"I'll get you your pardon," she said. "If you can help me. But it's the truth I'm after. I want to know who killed Elwin, and I want you to find the killer."

"Tell me what really happened, and I'll do all I can," Moth said, his tone dry and ironic.

"I was summoned to Elwin's rooms the night he was murdered, perhaps less than a half hour before. When I got there, he was dying, burned by a magebolt. I tried to do an energy transfer to save him, but it was too late. Then Danial came in and, as you know, accused me of the murder. But I found this in Elwin's hand." A rustle as Arianna reached into her robes and pulled out something.

"What is it?" Moth asked, sounding puzzled.

"A very old token of the alliance between Vycenia and Eleusia. Whoever bore it was to grant aid to the bearer."

So that's *why she asked about Eleusians yesterday.*

"What would the First Weaver be doing with this?"

"I suspect someone came to see him, bearing this token."

"But there are no Eleusians left alive."

Exactly.

"It might not be an Eleusian. Elwin was definitely with someone, though. There were two glasses of half-drunk wine."

"You think this visitor killed the First?"

"Maybe, but I've been able to find no other evidence that someone came to see him." Arianna's voice was tight with frustration. "We've asked the Spire guards and the Watch, but no one reports anyone strange entering or exiting either the city or the Spire that day."

"I'll track down this visitor, whoever it was. And if not, there are other ways to help you."

"How?"

"I can get you out of this cell."

"And what, make me a fugitive for the rest of my life?"

"Like me, you mean?"

Fay imagined the frosty look Arianna might be shooting him now.

"It would be a last resort," Moth said. "I plan to uncover the truth."

"You get your pardon only when you do," Arianna said.

"Fay here will be our go-between. I won't risk coming again unless necessary."

But Fay was thinking that this wasn't such a good idea. Stepping away from the wall while keeping her eyes firmly on it, she said, "I can't be seen coming in here too much, either. Eventually, someone might talk to Nuria and she'll know I've been using her name."

"My advocate, Galinda Velden. You can also leave word with her," Arianna said. "Your priestess has already had dealings with her. She can be trusted."

"Very well." Sounds of Moth pulling his scarf around him again. "Turn around, Fay," he said.

She did so, and found his features once more fully hidden from her. Still, she knew more about Moth now than most. She could probably find out a lot more by investigating Eduar Velden's death and learning who the prime suspect had been. She really hoped he wasn't planning to have her killed.

"We're going," he said.

Fay went to bang on the door for the Defender to let them out.

They walked in silence until they were back out onto the street, then Moth spoke. "Tomorrow, you'll meet a firefly called Zethir. He'll go with you into the old Spinners' temple. I suppose you can give him these. We're a similar size." He plucked at the novice robes he was wearing with evident distaste.

"You expect me to go in, too?" she said, her voice little more than a squeak. This was not what she had intended. She didn't want to go into that evil place.

"I thought you were all eager to uncover the secrets inside," Moth said sardonically.

Fay knew better than to push the subject. If Moth intended her to go in with Zethir, she'd have to do as he said. At least she wouldn't have to go in alone. She swallowed the cold, hard lump of her apprehension, tried her voice again. "What next with Arianna?"

"I'll do as I said, and see if we find this mysterious visitor," Moth said. "If we don't find him or her, we'll go to the second plan."

"Break her out?"

"She can flee south to Federation lands or to Tarsis. They don't have many weavers of her caliber there. And she's a fully trained war weaver, she'll find employment easily."

Moth was right. Arianna Velden would have no trouble getting protection in Tarsis if she needed it. The kingdom made a sport of tearing itself apart and was ever hungry for weavers as well as weapons. Although she'd heard the other day that one of the warlords was getting the upper hand. Not that Fay cared much about what went on there. She had her own troubles. *I'll get out soon. Lothar won't have me. He won't.*

She returned to the temple and found a note waiting in her postbox. It was from Nuria, instructing her to attend her office the day after tomorrow. Fay's stomach flipped. Nuria had never summoned her for a personal audience before. Had she learned that Fay had been using her name to get access to Arianna? Surely, if that was the case, Fay would have been summoned sooner, or even taken by the Defenders? Unless Nuria was playing a game, waiting to see what Fay would do next. She put a hand to her face, suddenly overcome with exhaustion. It seemed like there was just one thing after another. Would it never end? Would she never find peace?

Chapter 33

Castes

I saw a man being crowned like the kings of old. It was somewhere on South Myrnia. Inside a great palace of marble, gold, and lapis lazuli. Thousands crowded into a vast square, cheering when the king came out to greet them. Why I've been shown this, I have no idea.

—Visions of Alexios Arathraxis

Castes woke to gnawing hunger, as he had the past two days. But it seemed different now, easier to bear, somehow. He dressed and went out to the living area. A handful of nuts rested in a bowl on his place at the table. He reached out to take them but stilled his hand. No, let him wait until he'd conducted the morning's tasks. He could master his appetite. He could do what it took to win.

He summoned Gatos and Janius, and they flanked him as he strode to the Great Plaza. The gong rang out as they walked, summoning the people to witness the sentence he was about to pass. But word had already filtered out, and the plaza was full of people when he arrived.

Three pillories of wood had been constructed on a stage in its center, guardsmen keeping the immediate area clear.

Castes went to them, Theophila there already, early as always for any appointment. She seemed tired, the skin below her eyes dark and puffy. He probably looked much the same.

"I wish we didn't have to do this," she said with a sigh.

"There are always weak fools," Castes replied. "And they must be more afraid of us than their empty bellies."

"Hunger has a powerful voice," Theophila responded.

Castes made no response. Hunger called him too, but he'd resisted it. They must all do the same if they were to endure until the tunnel was built.

They waited a quarter of an hour until the plaza was full to bursting before motioning for the prisoners to be taken out of the Hall. Two men and a woman—grain merchants. The fact of their hoarding was plain in their still-plump cheeks. In contrast, those who watched were wan and drawn, bones already starting to stand out. Idiots. Well, they would suffer now, and know true hunger.

"For hoarding, you have been sentenced to one week at the pillory by a jury of your peers," Castes told them, to roars of approval from the crowd. "You will be bound here day and night, with no shelter from the sun, and receive only sufficient water to keep you alive."

He noted with satisfaction their shock and despair at the sentence. The heat alone might kill them. It was a summer to beat all summers, the sun like a furnace more days than not.

Guardsmen fastened their heads and wrists to the pillory in a standing position while the crowd hurled insults. Those were soon followed by stones, one that almost caught Castes in the face.

Periklis roared at them to stop, but more stones came.

"Honored Rulers, you must go, it isn't safe," he said.

A stone landed at Castes' feet.

Guardsmen closed around him and Theophila, hustling them toward the Hall while guardsmen dispersed into the crowd under orders to arrest the perpetrators.

"People are losing their reason," Theophila said once they were safe inside, the doors closing behind them to drown out the mob.

"Let's speak in the Chamber," he said. He dismissed the men who'd accompanied them. These days, the only ones allowed in the Chamber were the High Council and four designated illusionist-artefactors. And there was a good reason for it.

They continued silently and he unlocked the door with the key he kept on him always. Outwardly, all appeared as normal, but his eyes went straight to the far end of the room. Incredible, how well the illusionists worked. The old discontent flickered deep in him, but he pushed it aside. Mages were useful for certain things, but they weren't all fit to rule, as he was. "It's Castes and Theophila," he said loudly.

A yawning hole appeared in the floor at the back of the room. He stared down into the depths. Thais was there, holding a globe torch.

"I'll leave you to it," Theophila said. "I have reports to read." She took her usual seat at the table, where slate tablets had been stacked. They had no more means of making paper and had been reading from the tablets for several days now, reduced to primitivism.

Castes descended via the rope ladder that hung from the lip of the hole. The hole resealed as soon as his head was under the ground.

"How goes it?" he asked Thais.

"Our progress was slow this night," she said. "The rock is hard and difficult to break, and we're afraid of taking down the whole tunnel. But we managed to clear all the debris."

That had been the trickiest part to work out. They'd settled for moving the rubble at night, using illusionists to cover up the cart that transported it to the wall, ready for throwing onto the heads of Ilk should they try to storm the walls. Both carts were stored in a pair of alcoves by the tunnel entrance, empty for the moment.

He walked five minutes, then ten, before he reached the front line of the works. Two artefactors were on duty, hands pressed against the bedrock. Near them rested ordinary tools—picks, shovels, and spades. He watched silently as the rock slowly began to crack, tiny fractures spreading like questing roots. Although he couldn't see them work the Lace, he could feel it—a sensation of wrongness, of things pulled out of place. But not as bad as the feeling that had come when the Ilk mages had split open the ground, using the expelled earth and stone to build themselves high ramparts to protect the Ilk from attack.

Tiny fragments of stone broke loose and skittered down to the tunnel floor, but the artefactors remained as they were. It was only as larger chunks of stone began to fall that they stepped back. Two men, ordinary laborers, took up the picks and hacked at the rock. It came loose easily, sometimes falling onto the hard boots they wore. When the laborers could do no more, they stood aside and the artefactors took up their work again. Castes noted that the rock seemed slick with moisture.

"I think there's water nearby," said one of the artefactors, echoing his thought. "We need to be careful."

They continued their work, but there was a greater tension to them.

Distantly, Castes heard a rushing sound, then a rumbling coming from somewhere in the rock before him. The noise increased and he felt the ground move beneath his feet. His mind went to the day the Ilk mages had opened the earth. "What's happening?" he demanded.

"Get away!" cried Theia, stumbling several paces back.

A large hunk of rock broke from the end of the tunnel, and water jetted from a hole the size of his head.

"We've hit an underground stream!" Theia exclaimed.

"Hurry, we need to block it!" said the other artefactor, Kavistes.

But the water was crashing through with surprising speed, taking down more of the weakened rock. The stream became a torrent.

"We can't," Theia said. "There's too much water. Go! Go!"

The water was already swirling over his feet. He turned and walked quickly back to the entrance, the others following closely.

"Run, Honored Ruler, the water rises too swiftly!" Theia cried.

Humiliating to do so, but she was right. The water was already above his ankles. He broke into a run, but soon that turned into a dreary and difficult sloshing as the water reached his calves and then his knees.

He began to panic. He couldn't swim, none of them could swim. There was no body of water large enough for his people to learn how. The water reached his waist, then picked him up and carried him. It was cold, full of stone and mud, but it brought him flailing and gasping to the tunnel entrance. Thais had already climbed out, and was standing at the top, staring down anxiously. He grabbed onto the rope ladder and hauled himself out as quickly as he could, the others following.

"We need to block the hole, stop the water," he said.

"Upturn the table for now," Thais suggested.

They worked together to remove the chairs and then turn over the huge oak table to cover the entrance. Water seeped out beneath it, but only slowly.

"There must have been an underground stream that we didn't sense," Theia said in dismay.

"Is there any hope of salvaging the work?" Castes asked.

"I don't know," Kavistes replied. "We need to call all the artefactors together. Maybe, if we can find a way to pump out the water or divert it somehow. But it will mean days of delays at the least. Weeks, more likely, if we need to bore a tunnel elsewhere."

As if reminding him of how little food was left, Castes' stomach rumbled. They didn't have weeks, not before people started dying in earnest. Already, hunger and disease were claiming the oldest and frailest.

"Summon all the artefactors," Theophila said. "And see what can be done."

While they waited for the artefactors to come, Theia and Kavistes knelt around the seeping hole, hands on the ground, eyes closed as they stretched out their senses.

"The water has stopped rising," Theia said eventually. "Which means it must have another, greater channel that it flows through."

"Is there any way to map it?" Castes asked.

Kavistes winced. "It would be difficult. Unless it's close enough to the surface, we won't be able to sense it. We can't reach that far."

Other artefactors began to file in, barely hiding their dismay when they learned what had happened. But to their credit, they soon turned to practical matters and possibilities.

In the end, they opted for a two-pronged solution. They would try another tunnel in the crypt of the Temple, one that ran in a different direction. At the same time, they would take turns to dive into the water and carve out another tunnel in the hope it would siphon some of the water away, reducing the water level enough so they could swim through the tunnel to find its source.

"We need Alexios and the Vycenians," Theophila said quietly as they watched the artefactors disperse.

Castes wanted to deny it. Wanted to save his people. Wanted to *fight.* But Theophila was right. They were out of time, foiled at every turn. Alexios should have returned by now. That he hadn't spoken of his failure. But they needed the Vycenians. They needed an army.

Chapter 34

Alexios

Over time, I stopped thinking of my birth parents so much. I was so young when I lost them. Losing Epiktet was worse in many ways, although my comfort is to have him with me always. My comfort and my curse.

—Memories, Keeper Alexios Arathraxis

Alexios dropped fresh hazelnuts into his basket and then ran over to Epiktet, who was doing the same. "My basket's full," he said.

"That was quick! You have nimble hands."

"Shhh, I hear something," cried Agaue, just a few paces away.

They froze, straining with all their senses. Sounds of breaking twigs and slapping branches. Loud, made by a large animal. Heartbeats later, a roar, and then a hulking shape of black fur crashing through the undergrowth.

"Bear!" yelled Eurin, who was closest to the animal. He began to run, but the bear was already on him, swiping him with a paw and sending him screaming to the ground.

"Here, you beast!" cried Epiktet, running forward with his spear. The bear lumbered in his direction.

"Run!" cried Epiktet, planting his feet and pointing his spear at the onrushing animal.

Agaue didn't hesitate, throwing her basket on the ground and clawing her way through the undergrowth.

But Alexios didn't move. "What about Eurin?" The man was lying on the ground, unmoving, blood welling from a wound in his chest.

"Just run, I'll take care of him!" cried Epiktet, his attention all on the bear.

But Alexios couldn't run, not with Eurin on the ground, bloody, and Epiktet alone against the raging animal. He called the threads to him and then spun an illusion, turning Epiktet invisible as the bear reached him. It wasn't as good as he'd have liked, but it was enough to make the animal stop in its tracks. It raised its snout to sniff the air. Alexios worked another illusion to mask Epiktet's scent. That was harder, he'd only started to figure out illusions of smell.

Realizing what Alexios had done, Epiktet backed away, slowly and quietly.

The bear gave up on Epiktet, but its nose led it to Alexios, and it lumbered forward again.

Alexios frantically spun another invisibility illusion to hide himself, breath coming fast. Again, the bear stopped and snuffled in puzzlement. He needed to send the bear away. But his head was starting to hurt, and he could feel the illusions starting to slip. Epiktet was flickering, bits of him briefly appearing and disappearing. He needed a distraction. An illusion of sound. But could he manage it? Painfully, he worked the threads again. But then Epiktet picked up a rock and hurled it with all his might.

The bear looked in the direction of the sound, then ambled off to investigate.

All of Alexios's illusions collapsed at once, and he fell to his knees, clutching his head against the blinding pain.

"Are you alright?" Epiktet said.

"Eurin," he said faintly. "What about him?" He struggled to his feet, eyes squeezed half shut against the pain. Eurin was still lying where he'd fallen, his chest a red stain.

It turned out that the bear's claws had missed his gut, that he might live. Epiktet removed his shirt and used it to bind Eurin's chest, but the blood quickly soaked through.

"You saved ... my life," Eurin said to Alexios the effort clearly paining him. "My thanks." He reached up and briefly clasped Alexios's hand with his much bigger one.

"I did what needed to be done," he said, thinking of how easily the bear had wounded Eurin, of how helpless Epiktet had been, even with his spear.

"That's my boy," Epiktet said, ruffling his hair. "Saved all our lives, you did."

"The future ... of our people is ... safe with you," Eurin added.

"A cool head, I've always said it," Epiktet said, nodding. "Exactly what we need."

Alexios jerked free of the memory. The Gloom was forever taking him into the past, bombarding him with feelings and memories he'd thought long buried.

"You couldn't save them in the end, though, could you," said the voice in the darkness. *"They all died, didn't they? They always die."*

"Who are you? Who's speaking?" The words came out as little more than a croak. He'd had nothing to drink since he'd been put in this new prison, and his throat felt like sawdust. But death continued to elude him. How long had he been here? There was no way of measuring time.

"Everyone else dead. They're all dead. But you're not allowed to die. Even your enemies won't kill you. You'll live forever, live forever with your failure," said the voice.

He tried to pull his fists apart, forcing the manacles to cut into his wrists so that blood leaked around the mage-metal. The physical pain distracted him, and he yanked harder, wishing he could free himself of the tormenting metal.

"Drink," Epiktet urged. *"Don't give up, son."*

"Come on, father," Eliana urged. *"The flask is there beside you."*

"Leave me!" he cried.

But they kept pushing him, and he didn't seem able to shut them up any more than the strange voice of the Gloom. Furiously, he picked up the water flask, uncorked it. The water smelled sweet and delicious, and he almost put it to his mouth.

"That's it, father," Demeia said.

"It's over, let it be over," the voice of the Gloom said.

"Yes." He turned the flask and poured the water onto the floor.

"No! Alexios, stop!" cried Cassander.

The souls shrieked at him, but Alexios felt a grim satisfaction in defying them. Now, there was no choice but death. Once he'd emptied the water, he closed his eyes, sinking into his memories once more.

Chapter 35

Ina

The drakiri are no more, and while we mourn their loss, it's for the best. They always bonded with the Cursed Ones, bearing them on their backs when they would bear no one else. Most of them died in the Slaughter. The remainder vanished across the ocean.

—Teachings of Old Tsu

Ina touched the Godstone and a spark leapt between them, forging a vital link.

"Blood of my blood, open yourself and learn what you must."

Unthinkingly, Ina dismantled the barricades around her mind, and the spark lit a raging fire that tore through her entire being, blasting her consciousness to pieces and sending her spinning into dreams.

The escarpment was right at their backs, the Eleusian unit bearing down on them at full speed. Dust flew out from the hooves of their mounts and swirled into a thick, yellow cloud that half obscured their charge. Behind Ina and to her right, lacquered wood clacked as soldiers shifted restlessly in the shield wall. No one liked feeling trapped. Even worse to face down a charge of heavily armored single-horns and their armed riders. Her hand tightened on the grip of her spear and sweat broke out beneath her helm of hardened grikar skin. She breathed deeply, and as she exhaled, made her muscles relax and her mind re-embrace the Stillness. Then she linked to the Cloth, pushing a sense of calm to her troops. The noises of movement dampened but didn't entirely abate.

It had been a long time since she'd stood in a shield wall, and again she wished she were flying with her drakir, Moondancer, wreaking death from the skies. But they'd left the drakiri behind the lines. For the ploy to work, their foes needed to believe they had no skyriders with them. She glanced down the line to her right, seeking Toku. He was staring impassively at the oncoming Eleusian riders, and she could feel the soothing pulses he sent to his unit. Stretching her consciousness out, she sensed Ani doing the same in the back line.

She could not only see the oncoming enemy but also feel the thundering of their mounts' hooves. Sunlight sparked off metal armor through the dust cloud. The air stank of sweat and fear. She mindcast to Ani and Toku, *"I'm ready to splice."*

"Ready," echoed Ani.

"On my count," said Toku. *"Three. Two. One—now."*

Without turning her head, Ina parted the Cloth along the left flank of the shield wall, widening the tear until it stretched back three ranks. Then she extended a passageway through Sīut's Realm to the place they had agreed. Pain stabbed up through her skull and out her left eye, and her insides roiled, but she grimly pushed through it to stabilize the pathway.

When she was finished, she focused on the charging enemy. The Eleusians were so close she could see the faces of the men at the fore. Ina hated looking at those she killed, the bulging of their eyes and the skewing of their mouths as she plunged a blade into their flesh. Even worse hearing that last plea for mercy and ignoring it as she twisted the blade. But she never turned away. She owned their death, and it was her duty to acknowledge the bitter prize.

Her eyes caught those of the Eleusian leader beneath his gold-plated helm. They were haunted, wounded. He'd killed too much. They were all creatures of Chel. Why did they continue the killing? She lowered her spear, wanting to embrace him and tell him she wasn't going to take his life. He held her gaze, recognized her thoughts, and raised one hand in salute.

A sharp blow to her arm. "Lin, you're being entranced."

She blinked at her second-in-command, Rak. "It wasn't an illusion. He—"

Rak struck her hard on the face and her cheeks flooded with warmth, less from the slap than from the shame. The eyes of the man she'd nearly embraced now gleamed like hard, polished gems. The salute had been a signal to engage, and the lances of the Eleusians were leveling toward them.

"Order your units to move now," Toku mindcast.

Ina gave the order, and her section of the shield wall side-stepped into the opening she'd created. Even as they moved, she pulled the opening toward and around them so that they were swiftly sucked through. The passage through Sïut's Realm always felt longer than it should, but barely three heartbeats had passed in their own plane before they emerged behind the ranks of their enemies. Ani and Toku reappeared to her right, leading the center and right flank. All around her, shields clattered into place.

"Forward march!" Toku shouted.

They began to walk slowly, in time, intending to trap the Eleusian cavalry between the escarpment and the shield wall. But the Eleusians were continuing straight toward the escarpment—they weren't slowing, and they weren't turning away. It was as if they hadn't realized their enemies were gone. Then, moments before they reached the escarpment, twenty or so of them suddenly wheeled around and charged back toward the Chelak lines, shrieking war cries. The rest simply melted away to nothing.

Another illusion.

There must be a whole circle of illusionists for them to have succeeded so thoroughly in deceiving them, and skilled half-bloods able to spirit walk too, to have fooled her lifesense, make her think they were real.

"Behind us!" Ani cried.

Ina stood on tiptoes and craned her neck around. Enemy infantry—not one unit, but at least six—all running at a charge. They threw their spears, and screams filled the air as some found their mark in the backs of the Chelaki ranks.

"Ranks five and six, about-face!" Toku cried.

Rattling and cursing as two lines of Chelaki troops turned to the new threat.

Ina swung back toward the charge of single-horns, now almost upon them. Arrows sang through the air from the mounted Eleusian archers. "Ranks two and three, shields up!" she shouted.

As one, the soldiers in the second and third rows raised their shields, covering the line in front from the rain of arrows. At the same time, the front line ducked down behind their own shields. More than one arrow thunked into the shield above her head, but none pierced through. Ina peered between a gap in the shields and saw that the single-horns were only a few paces away, their riders extending long, blunt lances to smash through the shield wall.

"Front rank brace!" Ina shouted.

Again, a clattering as the soldiers readied themselves to absorb the impact. The air around them began to prickle. Ina opened her mouth to cry out a warning, but it was swallowed in an explosion of blue fire. When she could see again, half the unit to her right had been reduced to hunks of charred, smoking flesh.

The Eleusian lances smashed into her shield, forcing her back a few paces, but the line held. She thrust her spear into the throat of a single-horn, twisted and pulled out the blade, blood spraying over her arm and face. The wretched animal squealed in agony as its legs folded under it, spilling its rider off its back and into the shield wall. She dispatched the man with a downward thrust to the neck. A serrated cavalry blade swept down at her head, and she ducked behind the shield, the wind of its passage stirring her cropped hair.

"Center close ranks!" Ani cried. "Center close ranks!"

Another volley of arrows, singing death. Screams of wounded soldiers echoing around her, more than before. Ina blocked another downward blow, felled a single-horn with a slash to the hamstrings. Its rider fell beneath it, his cries quickly silenced by the crushing weight of the animal. Ina caught a spear on her shield, thrust forward with her blade, but it slipped on armor. She sliced again, ducked a sword blow, caught another blow on her shield, and then her blade found home in a groin. Hot gushes of blood spurted out.

A horn rang out. The Eleusian cavalry pulled back. "Close ranks and stay put!" she cried. What now? The air changed, became charged. Instinctively, she spliced, emerging on top of the escarpment even as another explosion rang through the valley. When she looked down, the bodies of her soldiers were burning, and shrieks of agony filled the air. She should have taken them with her. She should have, but there had been no time.

Toku's unit, still holding up the right flank, was struck by the blue fire next. When the light died, she saw that the shield wall was completely broken on all sides. The remaining troops fought bravely, but they were vastly outnumbered, and it didn't take the Eleusians long to cut them all down. Three units of their finest soldiers destroyed in moments—the most efficient display of killing she'd seen in the whole year of the war.

Toku appeared beside her, her own feelings mirrored in his silver-flecked blue eyes. "Our orders were to save ourselves if it seemed hopeless." There was a question beneath his words.

"It was hopeless," Ina answered. "But it doesn't make the shame any less."

Toku said nothing, watching as the last of their people were massacred below. His voice was rough when he spoke again. "We'd better go and warn Anya."

Ina stretched out her lifesense, listening for the tell-tale thrums of a hidden sentry. She used her eyes and ears too, just in case, but the Eleusians used illusionists to guard their camps and lifesense was more reliable. There had been many reports of non-elkiri scouts being captured by invisible sentries and then tortured to reveal the location of their camps. So the elkiri were now sent to do the scouting instead, using their lifesense to find what their eyes could not.

That lifesense told her that she'd almost reached the outer circle of sentries. She could feel them and even see a couple—black shapes against the glow of the campfires. Her task was to count how many warriors they had, and whether they had any single-horns with them. That meant she had to at least penetrate the first circle while staying out of sight of the inner circle, who were always positioned more closely together.

She crawled through the grass toward the nearest sentry, stopping when she was a dozen paces away. Then she tapped into her own lifeforce, summoning the power for a stun strike. Carefully, she traced the threads that bound the sentry to the Cloth, then propelled the strike through it. When it hit him, he stiffened for a heartbeat and then crumpled to the ground. Keeping low, Ina ran toward him and removed his helmet and cloak to put them on herself. He would be unconscious for perhaps half a mark. Enough time to do what she needed to do.

Ina climbed onto the back of her drakir and clipped the straps shut around her legs, securing herself to her seat. When she was done, Moondancer launched herself into the air with a few quick steps and a double flap of her great, red wings. She climbed high into the sky, riding the winds. It was a fine spring day, warm enough for Ina to leave her face exposed and feel the air against her cheeks. The usual heady rush ran through her as the land shrank beneath them, and for a few moments, she was free of the dread that had clouded her since the defeat at Suk'an. Again, she thanked Chel that she had left

Moondancer behind that day, that her beloved drakir was still alive to bear her.

Anya had sent them to see how far the Eleusian lines had advanced so that they could find a way to slow them while the rest of the army regrouped. They were being pressed hard. Even with the land working in their favor, they couldn't defend against the ever-larger number of barbarian mages that had crossed the seas to join the enemy against her people. These would quickly target all the skyriders with their blue fire before they could splice or take their armies to safety. Then the Chelaki fighters were incinerated or buried beneath mountains of falling stone, or once, swallowed by the very earth.

Moondancer reached the height she wanted and then coasted eastward. Ina could see the land beyond the forest, sloping gently and green with new growth, free of Eleusians. Where were they? In the forest already?

Lightning streaked across the clear blue sky. Moondancer banked sharply to avoid it, and Ina would have fallen if it weren't for the seat fastenings they'd developed for the war. Other crackling bolts followed. Ina swallowed one with a quick splice, while the other fizzed above her. She swung her head around to look for the source of the attack.

"From the north, there," Moondancer said. Even as she spoke, a spray of blue fire flew toward them.

"Go down into the trees," Ina said. *"We need cover!"*

Moondancer dropped toward the thick canopy of the forest, but as they came closer, Ina realized the first attack had been a ploy. A group of barbarian mages was hiding among the trees. She could see the tell-tale glow of their auras. But it was too late. They joined their forces to launch a powerful single strike, an electrical sheet wide enough to envelop at least five riders.

Moondancer angled upwards, flapping her mighty wings with all her power. For a moment, it looked as if they would escape. Then Moondancer screamed as the electrical charge caught her left wing and breast. A smell of charred meat came to Ina's nose. *"I'm going to fall! Save yourself!"* Even as Moondancer spoke, she dived toward the ground, trying to use her good wing to break the fall.

"I'll take us both." Ina began to splice but another sheet of electricity was coming at them.

"There's no time, and I'm too badly injured. Go!"

Ina would have allowed the fire to consume her too, but Moondancer would never have forgiven her for breaking her vow. With a cry of despair, she kicked free of the seat fastenings and spliced into Sīut's Realm, flinging herself high into the sky so that she could see what would happen to her beloved drakir. Moondancer rolled to try and avoid the attack, but she was too slow, and it passed right through her. Afterward, nothing was left but a blackened ball that fell straight down into the trees, heavy as a stone.

Ina kept her mind linked with Moondancer as she died, to share the pain of her passing and to make that passing less lonely. And because she wanted to take the death for herself, to treasure it and keep it from the enemy until she gave it up to Chel along with her own.

"I'll wait for you." Those were the last words. Then the mind of the drakir blinked out and Ina's own mind tore and nearly broke. But the vow they had sworn together forbade madness as well as death. How could she have known then how impossible it was to keep? She spliced again, this time to the camp.

When she arrived, she fell to her knees and wailed, tearing at her hair and banging her fists on the ground until they were bloody. Other skyriders tried to comfort her, but they knew as well as her that words would not help. A part of her was lost and she would feel that loss during every moment left to her on Chel's world.

This is not me! These are not my dreams! Ina clawed and struggled through the cobwebs of memory, which parted only to cling to her again. She tried to scream, to move, to do something that would bring her back to her own body, her own world.

"She's awake."

"Make her drink."

Strong hands forced open her jaw. Tepid liquid slid over her tongue and down her throat, familiarly sharp.

Ina stared down from the cliff top at the assembled boats. Thirty in all, but sturdily made while the shreds of their armies had stalled the Eleusian advance. They were the last of her people, no more than three hundred, most of them mothers and children. The last three drakiri circled overhead, checking for danger. Unusually, she had bonded them all, for she was the last remaining skyrider on this side of the world. She allowed her mind to drift through each bond, one after the other, to see through their eyes. There were no Eleusians nearby.

Ina turned to the Foreseer standing beside her, a woman with piercing, pale green eyes and long, thick silver hair that spilled around her slender shoulders. "What's the point of fleeing our lands," she said. "Chel doesn't want us in this world or they would have stopped this war. And if we're no longer able to inhabit their lands we're no longer their people." Ina was never really aware of the bitter taste in her mouth because it was always there, but now it came stronger, pushing itself into her consciousness. It almost turned to tears, but she had long ago stopped crying. There weren't enough tears for all the sadness.

"Chel can't control what happens in the world they made. They gave their people the freedom to do that for themselves. But their power lies in you, skyrider, in your ability to manipulate the Cloth and ride the winds with the drakiri. And a fragment resides in me, so that I may perceive some inkling of their will and help to preserve their world."

The last of the provisions were being loaded onto the boats. Barrels of salted fish, cured ham, and fresh water. There had been little enough to eat in recent weeks. All the wildlife had fled the war, and something in the air was causing plants and fruits to sicken.

"You'll have to be careful when you reach the islands. Many blame the elkiri for this tragedy. They'll turn on you once they reach safety."

Ina knew that many held the elkiri responsible for what had happened. It made her angry because not all elkiri had welcomed the war. And when it had come, they'd put themselves at the forefront of the battle, using their power to protect their people until it flayed them. "Maybe they don't deserve to be saved," she said at last.

"You must make sure that your knowledge is passed on to your descendant. If it isn't, Chel's Cloth will one day be torn to pieces, and our world end."

"Can one person really make such a difference?"

"It's the passing of your knowledge that's essential. Much will be lost, much has already been lost."

"When will this happen?"

"I've told you before how my foresight works—flashes and dreams. This nightmare comes to me many times, but I can't locate it in place or time."

Two boats were full. Not much longer before they were ready to cast off. Ina stared up at the sky, achingly blue, then at the sea beneath it, stirring under the breeze. She looked at the trees beyond the dunes, where death was marching. She thought of Moondancer and then of her bondmate Seniku, dead early in the war, like their first son. She opened her mind to the Cloth and its shimmering magnificence and embraced all the sound and color of the world until it hurt.

Then she turned to the woman who had found her after the final defeat. "I'll do as you say."

When the tunnel through Sīut's Realm spewed Ina out onto the tiny island, she knew she was about to die. The distance had been too great, even for her. But she had completed her mission. There was a waygate between the two lands, and her divided people would be able to come together once more. Her last task was to ensure that her knowledge did not die with her, for she was the last elkir, and the last skyrider. The waystone would serve as a memory stone too. Perhaps Tsuk's child would be a girl, and she would come. And if it was a boy, then his daughter, or his child's daughter. There was only one task left—it was time to dig her grave.

Ina woke. *A lie, it's all a lie! They've been murdering children for no reason. It's not a curse. Liars, liars, liars!*

Chapter 36

Fay

Lumin priests must wear their robes at all times, unless they are performing a service that requires discretion or travelling in an area where Lumins are not tolerated. In such cases, and where it is essential for safety, they may choose other clothing.

—The Lumin Priest's Handbook

A broad-shouldered man peeled away from the late-evening flow and walked toward Fay. He was wearing the black robes of a Lumin novice, the hood pulled up to hide his face. This must surely be Moth's firefly, wearing the robes Fay had passed to him.

"May the Lady be with you," he said with irony.

She opted for a pious tone. "And you, child of fire." She wondered what he looked like behind his hood. All she could see was brown skin over a strong, clean-shaven jaw. It suggested he wasn't Vycenian, as did his name—Zethir. It triggered her curiosity, but one didn't ask questions of Moth's people.

Without speaking further, they walked toward the Temple of Lumia, a few blocks away. It reared up over the surrounding buildings, its golden crown shining brightly against the darkening sky. A hundred braziers provided this light, their flames kept alive by Lumin novices day and night. Fay remembered the bitter cold of winter nights on that rooftop, and the crueler bite of the night she'd been made to serve in nothing but her shift as punishment for falling asleep. The summer nights would be a blessing to the novices up there now, though. Solaris was burning hotly this summer, more hotly than she'd ever remembered. Even a child of Lumia must find the heat intolerable during the day.

The building itself, with its large, unadorned slabs of grey-white stone, wasn't particularly lovely. There hadn't been much money around after the Ruin, Fay supposed, so they had kept it plain and turned it into a virtue. And it was vast, taking up an entire four blocks—but she knew why, now. A shiver ran through her at the thought of what lay deep in the temple's core.

They didn't go in by the main entrance, mostly used by members of the public who had come to pray or visit one of the priests. Instead, they went through a locked door on the east side that served as the priests' entrance.

Still without speaking, they moved through the identical, grid-like passageways that divided up the different sections of the temple. The regular construction reflected the Lumin commitment to order and logic, a counter to the chaos of magic and war.

They reached the kitchen without meeting anyone she knew—there were few people in the hallways at that hour and none with any interest in her or Zethir.

As Fay had expected, the kitchen itself was dark and deserted, the main evening meal having been consumed two hours earlier. Zethir took out a glowglobe, and she led him into the wine cellar, pausing on the way to pick up the ladder.

His glowglobe illuminated a good portion of the wine cellar, and this time Fay saw the rats as they scampered for cover. Some were nearly the size of a small cat, and she swallowed back a scream.

Zethir gave the rats only the briefest of glances, though. "Go in, and I'll lock the door," he said.

"There's no key."

"I don't need one."

So she dragged the ladder down the steps while he put his hands against the door. Was he doing something with magic? She shivered. What would the other priests think if they knew magic was being performed in the temple? A few heartbeats later, he finished and walked down the steps toward her.

"The catch is up there," she said, pointing to the far corner.

They went over, and Zethir sent the glowglobe drifting through the air to attach to the corner wall. She propped the ladder against the wine rack, taking care not to disturb the bottles. Then she climbed up and pulled the metal trigger to open the hidden door. Zethir followed her once she'd wormed through the tunnel. He paused at the entrance, and she thought she heard the ladder being moved. Then the hidden door closed, sealing them both in. A moment of claustrophobic panic seized her, and she gulped stale air.

Zethir squirmed through the tunnel on hands and knees, an incongruous sight. When he reached the hole in the ground, he paused to lift the wooden covering and peer down. "Have you gone through it?"

"No."

"We'll see where it leads later." He got to his feet and dusted his robes off, then regarded the nicoleum door, his glowglobe flickering as it got close.

Fear hit her as she remembered what it had been like the last time. "I don't want to go in," she said. "There's something in there. Something evil."

He was unmoved. "You'll be with me," he said, putting his hand to the door.

"I don't think I can." Her voice came out strangled. *Please, don't make me go.*

But Zethir ignored her and pushed the heavy door open. He was swallowed by the darkness as soon as he stepped through, the light of his glowglobe vanishing entirely.

Fay stood at the threshold, staring at the blackness. Tendrils of doubt slithered through her, coiling around her lungs, her heart, her throat, squeezing and crushing. She couldn't go in. She couldn't.

But she had to follow. Moth might be angry if Zethir told him she'd refused. Might not help her afterward. She shuffled forward. Then shuffled again, until she was in the doorway. Terror assaulted her like a physical force, and she shrank back. *Come on, one more step.*

She plummeted into the abyss. Darkness folded around her, choking, smothering, suffocating. Then it began to speak, to hiss in her ear. "*No one loves a liar or a whore, not even your goddess. Loves a killer even less. You're alone here, all alone. All alone and alone. Godless, motherless, loveless. Just filth, lies and filth, a filthy lying whore. Godless you are, and loveless and motherless. Give up, give it all up. Give up, give up, you filth. You filthy, lying, killing whore.*"

Images appeared. The shrunken face of her mother on a rickety bed. The man who had taken her virginity in a cold room in winter. Her knife, carving a red line across her father's throat. Snarling, open-mouthed anguish as he died. Other men, wearing his death mask. "Leave me alone!" she screamed. "That's over!" "*No, it's not,*" whispered the voice. "*It's never over.*" Lothar, eyes hooded with lust as he commanded her. "No! Away from me!" she cried again, scrabbling to push the archpriest away. Her hands found fabric and flesh. A spark of light, and then the outlines of Zethir's face appeared in the blackness.

"This feels like the Gloom," he said, his voice muted and hollow. "How it was described."

The Gloom. Dark magic. Killing magic. She noticed that Zethir's light was coming from a candle rather than the glowglobe. Didn't *his* magic work here? Or was the Gloom feeding on it? Was that how it worked? "We need to go back." She clawed at his arm. "We need to get out of here." The voices of retribution rang out more insistently, and now they had more to say. *"Unwanted. Unloved. Uncared for. The priests would never keep you if they knew."* Flat on a bed, too weak to resist him, his stabbing insistence. "No, no," she mumbled. She tried to go back to the door, but Zethir grabbed her arm and held on tightly.

"Don't listen. The Gloom sees the darkness in us and turns it against us. This is known."

Fay remembered that the Gloom also sucked up life. *The Ilk will come and take us. We need to go. We need to go!* Words lashed her like whips. "*Murderer. Liar.*" More men came at her, faces rotting, worms crawling out of their eye sockets. She twisted free of Zethir and stepped toward the door. Where was the door?

Zethir grabbed her again. "No. We continue."

"I can't." Her heart was going much too fast, tripping over itself in its hurry. Her mind seemed to have disconnected from her body. It was as if she was floating, unmoored, in the darkness.

"We'll continue." Zethir held her arm so hard it hurt. But the strength of his grip gave her reassurance. She took a step closer to him, fixing on the warmth of his presence.

"Come now. Be strong." He pulled her on.

Again, she noticed that his voice was oddly muffled, as if the Gloom had eaten some of the sound. It was the same with their footsteps. She began to recite the Lady's mantra in a low voice, barely more than a mumble, "Light burns away the darkness, conquers all our pain. Light burns away the darkness, conquers all our pain."

Zethir didn't join her.

They walked slowly around the room, Zethir using his candle to illuminate walls and corners. The walls were lined with strips of nicoleum, but the ground was paved with slabs of stone. Had they run out of the metal? Or had they decided that the Gloom wouldn't be able to get out through the earth? There was something else odd, but she couldn't quite place it at first. Then it came to her. No dust. There was no dust anywhere. After two hundred years it should be inches thick. Did the Gloom eat dust too? "*Murderer, liar, whore.*"

They followed two walls around, then came upon a narrow stairwell from which the darkness seemed to pulsate with even greater intensity. Fay would not go there. He would have to kill her first.

As if sensing her resistance, Zethir gripped her arm harder and pushed her up ahead of him. A moan of terror escaped her. Something up there was going to kill them.

They emerged from the stairwell into more darkness. But here, Zethir's puny candle illuminated the outlines of blocky furniture. Chests and a wardrobe, even some chairs and a low table. All made of wood. All strangely preserved from rot. There was no nicoleum on the walls. Instead, they were paneled with wood, perhaps old oak. When she remarked on it, Zethir told her that the nicoleum was on the outside. "I can sense it," he said, his hand flat against one of the outer walls.

"Why on the outside here and not downstairs?"

"We're above ground here. Easier to line the outside."

Of course. Stupid of her. They would have covered the outer walls of the old temple with the nicoleum before building Lumia's temple.

They came across a solid wooden door locked with a steel bolt. The bolt seemed out of place, as if it had been added at a different time. Zethir let go of her arm to grasp it.

"Don't." The word escaped her, small and desperate. But Zethir didn't even glance at her, the bolt making a muffled screech as he pulled it back. Fay braced herself as he opened the door, but nothing jumped out to attack them.

They stepped through, and Fay heard a rustling and clanking. Someone was in there. She stumbled back a few steps, heart skipping off beat, hands rising in panicked defense.

Zethir stood his ground. "Who are you?"

What are you? Fay wondered. Her legs shook so badly that she sagged against the doorway.

A man's voice traveled out from the darkness, rasping and hoarse. "Have you come to play with me again, Ilk spawner?" He spoke with a strange, lilting accent. Fay peered into the darkness but saw nothing. Was this another trick of the Gloom?

"*Killer, loveless whore,*" muttered the darkness.

Zethir moved farther into the room, and his candle revealed a huddled figure in the corner.

"Not him," said the man, voice barely above a whisper.

"No." Zethir stood still, regarding the shadowy figure.

"Are you another of them, then?" The words were spoken so breathlessly that Fay struggled to understand them.

"I don't know of whom you speak. Who are you?" Zethir said, crouching to shine the candlelight on the stranger. He was wearing a dirty, white tunic, and his wrists were manacled with nicoleum. Some kind of mage, then. His nose and face were long, his cheekbones high and prominent, but it was his eyes that made him different—wider apart than normal, slanted and narrowing at the edges in an almost feline way. His fair hair fell in waves around his ears and neck, and his cheeks were covered in a fine stubble. But while he was handsome in an exotic way, he also looked extremely ill, his bones pressing tightly against his skin.

"Another dream," the man muttered, then coughed drily.

"This is no dream," Zethir said. "Do you need water?" He unhooked a flask from his belt.

"Leave me," the prisoner rasped.

"You should drink," Zethir said, holding the flask out to him.

The prisoner made no effort to take it.

He wants to die, Fay realized. And could she blame him, trapped in here, in this horror? "We can free you," she said on impulse.

A twitch. The words had had an effect.

"Drink and tell us your story," Zethir urged. He brought the flask to the man's mouth, but it remained closed. "Help me," he said to Fay.

"You want to force him?"

"He's on the verge of death," Zethir snapped. "He needs to drink."

She couldn't disagree with that. "What should I do?"

"Take the flask, I'll get his mouth open."

Fay took it from him while Zethir prized the prisoner's jaws apart. He tried to resist but was far too weak, and Fay tipped the water into his open mouth. The man swallowed reflexively.

"Again," Zethir said to her.

This time, the man didn't resist, the needs of his body overpowering his will. They gave him four more swallows before Zethir told her to put the flask aside.

"Tell us who you are if you can," Zethir said to the prisoner.

This time, he answered, the word almost inaudible. "Alexios."

"An Eleusian name," Zethir observed.

"Eleusian am ... bassador."

This must be Arianna's Eleusian! So what she'd said was true!

"The Ilk ... have returned. I came ... for help," Alexios said, sounding as if each word were a supreme effort.

Ilk! Surely, he was lying or at least mistaken? No one had seen Ilk since the Ruin. But then, no one had seen any Eleusians either.

"How did you end up here?" Zethir said.

"Attacked," Alexios said, the word dissolving into a cough. "In the Spire."

"Were you with the First Weaver?" Fay asked.

"Asked him for help, he was hit by magefire. Is he dead?"

"Yes. Do you know who killed him?" Fay said.

"Some Chelaki beast, no doubt." Alexios's voice stronger now, fueled with hatred.

Fay remembered the books she'd seen in the Archpriests' Library about a war between the Eleusians and these Chelaki. *Are they still around too?*

"*Kill, kill, kill. Kill them all, kill the beasts who torment you,*" muttered the voice.

"Describe him," Zethir said.

Alexios's mouth twisted. "I never saw his face."

The darkness began to laugh shrilly, and Fay put her hands to her ears, trying to block it out.

Alexios looked at her as if he knew exactly what she was hearing. A clanking as he shifted, bringing his knees closer to his chest.

"You must have seen him before he took you here," Zethir said. He still sounded calm, as if the Gloom didn't touch him. Or was it for show?

"But you're just a pathetic little lying whore, no mother, no father, no brother. No one."

Fay swallowed and squeezed her hands together.

Alexios was speaking again. "He visited me once. He wore a mask made of bone, that is all I could see. And a robe, maybe a weaver's robe. His voice ... that of a man in his prime." The Eleusian took a ragged breath and shifted again, encircling his knees with his manacled arms.

"Why did he bring you here?" Zethir said.

"Because he wishes to torture me." Alexios said this as if this were self-evident and the question pointless.

Torturing me too. I can't take much more. Her heart was thudding so loudly in her ears that she could barely hear anything else.

"Why does he want to do that?" Zethir pressed.

"Have you Vycenians forgotten already?" Alexios said, fury and hatred mingling, lending greater strength to his voice.

"Yes, we have. So why not enlighten us," Fay snapped. Then she caught herself. "Sorry, I didn't mean to speak so sharply."

The Eleusian's mouth formed a rictus of a smile. "The Gloom makes us all cruel." He sat up a bit straighter. "You know what causes it?"

"She's a worshipper of Lumia, the Lady of the Flame," Zethir said. "Dear sister of Lumia, why don't you tell him what she teaches about the Gloom?"

Zethir's tone was mild, but Fay could hear contempt buried in his words. It made her feel both ashamed of herself and angry with him. She didn't want to answer, but his hooded face was turned toward her, demanding that she speak. "The Priesthood of Lumia says that the Gloom was caused by too much magic and that the Ruin was the result. Solaris, the sun, and Lunaris, the moon, sent their daughter

Lumia into the world to restore light and life afterward. She is fire made flesh, the light of the world."

"And what does the priesthood say about Eleusians?" Zethir said, goading.

"I—" Fay cleared her throat. "The Eleusian continent was sunk in the Ruin because Eleusians used so much magic, used it to run their—your—cities. It was a punishment of the gods."

To her surprise, Alexios laughed. But it was harsh, cackling laughter echoed by the voice in the darkness. Fay pressed her hands tightly to her ears again, trying to block it out, but it was no help.

"What a tale," he said at last. "Taken from our own book. We blame the Chelaki, and you blame us." He shook his head, the awful rictus still on his lips. "The weavers, they say that, too?"

"The weavers know that the Gloom was—*is*—a consequence of creating Ilk," Zethir said. "And, of course, the Ilk were created by the Ilk Lord so that he could conquer the world."

"Closer to the truth." Alexios reached for the flask, his movements slow and sluggish.

Zethir handed it to him, and the Eleusian drank.

"Not too much," Zethir warned him. "Or you'll be sick."

Alexios put the flask down. "Do they say that the one you call the Ilk Lord was Chelaki?" He practically spat the last word.

"Who are the Chelaki?" Zethir asked.

"Enemies of the Eleusians," Fay said.

Zethir looked at her in surprise.

"That's all I know," Fay said. "No one talks about them. I just saw an old book."

"We did our best to rid the world of their foul race many centuries ago," Alexios said. "Unfortunately, the one you call the Ilk Lord has survived to inflict another terrible war on us. Or has been born again. Such is the power of Antiphos."

"Who's Antiphos?" Fay asked.

"The Great Unraveler, enemy of the Makers and their creation."

"The Makers?" she repeated, unfamiliar with the term.

"Our name for the Spinners," Alexios said.

Oh, the old gods still worshipped by the Weavers.

"Did this Antiphos cause the Ruin?" Fay asked.

"Indirectly," Alexios said.

"How?" she said.

"He tricked the Last Hundred," Alexios said. "Who summoned a great power to defeat the Ilk but instead unraveled the Lace and destroyed Teleriol."

"You said the Ilk have returned?" Zethir said.

"They have besieged our town," Alexios replied. Then, showing more animation than he had, he added, "Please, release me, come and help us. Before it's too late."

"First, we need to know who your captor is," Zethir said.

"Find out quickly. Or stand by and see the world crumble again." Alexios sank back, clearly exhausted once more.

"Do you think your captor was from the Spire?" Fay asked.

"I was kept in a room there at first," Alexios said.

"Has he said he'll visit again?" Zethir asked.

"He said they didn't wish me to die. He left food and water, but that was some days ago."

Fay noticed the plate of uneaten food next to Alexios. Had he been starving himself, too? No wonder he was so thin.

"Will you release me?" Alexios said.

"Not yet. Not until we know who your captor is," Zethir said. "We need to know if he's one of the weavers in the Spire. The next time he comes, ask him questions. Get his name, try to find out if he lives in Arindel."

"I'll try, but if you really want to know who he is, wait here with me." Alexios laughed his horrible, despairing laugh again.

Fay shuddered, knowing she wasn't brave enough to wait with him. Zethir wouldn't make her stay, would he? *I'll die of fear if I stay here. How is that man not dead already?*

"If you won't free me, then at least send an army to my people, help us defeat the Ilk before the Chelaki have created even greater numbers of them."

"We have only your word about the existence of this Ilk force," Zethir said. "Where is it?"

"The forest you call the Deepwood. We hid our town with illusions so no one would find us," Alexios said. "Little good it's done," he added bitterly.

Zethir picked up a flask that was lying next to Alexios and peered into it. "I imagine this is empty?" But he didn't wait for a response, taking the flask he'd brought with him and pouring the water from it into the other. When he'd corked them both, he got to his feet. "We'll return soon. Help us discover who your captor is, and we'll try to free you."

"Do you want me to beg you to take me now? I'll beg if I must."

Fay's impulse was to release him. Nobody could stand this. How he wasn't already completely mad, she didn't know. To Zethir, "Can't we …"

But Zethir gave a sharp shake of his head. "No. We need to know who the Ilk mage is."

And so they left the Eleusian to his awful prison. To her relief, Zethir led her back to the stairs rather than continue their explorations of the temple. She didn't ask him why in case he changed his mind.

Once they were safely back out in the tunnel, though, she thought of something else to ask him. “If the Gloom is caused by Ilk, why didn’t we see any in there?”

Zethir pressed his lips into a thin half smile. “You priests may have been right about one thing—the old Temple of the Spinners is still tainted. We know that the Ilk Lord made it his headquarters once he had conquered Arindel.” His smile widened, but there wasn’t a trace of humor in it. “Or else there is a horde of Ilk lurking in the main worship room, which we didn’t enter.”

Fay shuddered. “Shouldn’t someone go and find out? I mean, Ilk, right in the middle of the city, they could ...”

“Are you volunteering?”

“Of course not! I’m just ...”—a whore, she was going to say—“a priest.”

“If there are Ilk up there, then they must be attached to an Ilk mage or mages. They can’t function without a master. It’s the Ilk mage we need to find,” Zethir said. He looked down at the hole in the ground. “Time to see where this leads,” he said. “I’d bet it was made by the Eleusian’s captor.”

Fay didn’t want to go down. Not in the slightest. “What if we meet him?”

“Then we’ll learn who he is.” Zethir stooped and dragged the plank of wood off the hole.

“What about the door you locked in the cellar? They’ll be suspicious.”

“The weave will wear off, and I’ve moved the ladder away from the entrance. No one will know we’re here.” He took out his glowglobe, then snuffed out his candle and put it in his pocket. This done, he lowered himself into the hole.

Fay reluctantly followed, and Zethir used his magic to put the wooden cover back in place. Then they began to walk. The new tunnel was low and narrow, and Zethir had to crouch a little. It smelled of earth and living things, and she noted that there weren't any struts to keep it from caving in. "Is it being held up by magic?"

"Yes, this is the work of a decent artefactor."

Artefactors, that rare breed of weaver who could make glowglobes and heatstones. It significantly narrowed the number of possibilities for who the Ilk mage might be. She wondered how easy it would be to get a list of all artefactors in the Spire. Not that she was planning to investigate. The less involved she was in all this, the better. She was a priest, not a hero.

The tunnel dropped steeply for perhaps five or so paces, then straightened for another ten before rising steeply again for another five. It ended in a hole like the first. Zethir went first, pushing himself up with his arms. He then squatted to help her out. When she was through, she saw that the glowglobe now showed a very different tunnel, paved in stone. The near end was blocked by a brick wall.

"The foundations of Lumia's temple," Zethir said, a faint thrum of excitement in his voice. "I suspect this tunnel has been in existence since before the Ruin."

"So the Ilk Mage who imprisoned the Eleusian dug the tunnel we've just come through? To get under the foundations?"

"That would be logical."

Zethir began walking again, and she followed him, her anxiety mounting, making her feel breathless. Surely, they would meet the Ilk mage?

They'd been walking for maybe twenty minutes when the tunnel divided into three. One branch continued in the same direction in which they'd been traveling. The others angled off to the left and right.

"I imagine that way leads to the Spire," Zethir said, pointing ahead.

Fay didn't like this reminder that the Ilk mage was probably living and working in the Spire and prayed Zethir didn't suggest they go that way.

Her prayers were answered, and he selected the right branch. "I have a feeling this one might take us outside the city walls."

This seemed a much safer option, and Fay followed him with relief. The tunnel had a slight leftward curve, although it was hard to tell whether this was just her imagination because of the darkness. After another half hour or so of walking, it began to slant upwards before ending abruptly, the way blocked by a large stone. Zethir put his hands against it, and again she thought she could feel the power gathering around him, creating a disturbance in the air. The stone slowly moved aside, and fresh air poured through. The scent of woodlands came to her nostrils. They must be in Arindel Woods, beyond the eastern wall of the Spire.

Zethir pulled himself up and out with his hands, and Fay quickly followed, half certain that it would be now, just as they had escaped, that the Ilk mage would confront them. But there was no mage, only trees. They threw long, grotesque shadows in the light of Zethir's glowglobe.

She looked back at the entrance to the tunnel, which Zethir was already re-covering with a large, moss-covered boulder. He used magic to do so, his fingertips barely touching the boulder before it moved back into place. When he had finished, the tunnel entrance was completely invisible.

"What now?" she said, eyes still darting around, looking for the Ilk mage.

"I'll speak to Moth. Say nothing of what you have seen or heard here," Zethir replied. "We can't risk the Eleusian's captor hearing of it."

"Don't worry, I'll keep quiet." And she meant it. She didn't want to tell the wrong person and end up dead, or worse, in that Gloom-filled prison.

Zethir began to walk in the direction of the Spire, whose shining towers could be glimpsed through the trees. "Count the number of paces," he said.

She did as she was told, counting over a thousand before they hit a narrow track that wound its way north–south. Zethir pointed to a large oak. "Remember this tree if you need to return." He scratched an x-shaped mark low down on its trunk using a tiny stream of blue light.

Then he motioned her onto the track leading south, which soon brought them to the edge of the woods and the main road in and out Arindel. They turned toward the city, and Fay glimpsed the line of glowglobes that lit the road for the first mile outside the city walls. They reached the road a few minutes later, continuing a short while until they reached a crossroads. One branch of the road curved south, the other continued straight west to Spire Gate, visible in the distance.

"It's best we're not seen entering the city together. Go that way to East Gate," Zethir said, indicating the southern road. "I'll go through here."

Fay cursed him silently. That was the long way back to the temple.

"Pick up Moth's message tomorrow evening." With that, he left her.

Fay walked quickly, eager to be back within the safety of the city walls, her mind churning over all she'd seen and heard. The Gloom, alive at the heart of Lumia's Temple. The Ilk back in force again.

Ilk mages walking the land. This dark god that the Eleusian called Antiphos perhaps returned to flesh. And Lumia? Where was she? What *use* was she? The candle flame had been tiny, almost swallowed by the living darkness in the old temple. If Lumia's very fire didn't work, what *could* banish the Gloom? One thing was certain, she was caught up in an extremely dangerous game, and if she didn't figure out how to escape soon, she was going to end up dead, or worse.

Chapter 37

Alexios

When the burden becomes too heavy, I pray to the Makers. I don't ask them to take it from me, but to give me more strength to carry it. And often, they respond. A Keeper must always retain his or her faith. That is what shields us and sustains us.

—The Role of the Keeper, Alexios Arathraxis

When Alexios heard the door shut the energy that had fueled him through the conversation drained away. *They've left me. To think I was foolish enough to hope.*

"*There* is *hope,*" Demeia said. "*You just need to stay alive. We'll find out who the Ilk spawner is when he comes back.*"

Were his people still alive or had the Ilk finished them already? How could he have been stupid enough to let himself get captured?

"*Failure, failed, failing. Worthless as a Keeper. Chosen from a pool of one,*" said the voice.

Had his mind finally cracked? It happened to some Keepers, he'd heard, when they had too many souls.

"The Vycenians will come back. The weavers will help," said Cassander. "*They know they must.*"

"*No they won't,*" said the voice. *"They've left you here, haven't they? Never should have been made a Keeper. Not strong enough. Not brave enough."*

But Alexios found himself thinking about the Eleusian priestess. There was something about her that drew him, made him want to protect her. She'd known great suffering too, but she was a survivor. No, more than that, a fighter.

"Isn't she a bit young for you?" Demeia said. If she'd had eyes, she probably would have rolled them.

"Stop reading my thoughts," Alexios said. "*And that's not how I think of her.*"

"If that's not how you think of her, then clearly I can't read your thoughts," Demeia said.

Alexios, infuriated, didn't respond. But then he realized that he wanted to live. He wanted to bring help to his people. He wanted the priestess to free him.

"She'll never come back," the voice said.

But if there was even the tiniest chance that she would, that he'd still be able to rescue his people, then he had to take it.

"Oh, they'll be dead already. You've been gone too long."

To try and shut out the voice, Alexios began to recite one of his favorite dramas, the Legend of Araphiel. But that brought him to the Fall of Mataios and Demeia's brilliant rewriting of the songs. Then to her death, along with Nixos's. His ears filled with the cries of Nixos's fragmented soul, begging to be saved, begging for him to choose. But he had made no choice. *How could I choose between my children?*

He thought of his lyre, focused on the feeling of the strings beneath his fingers. But what was the use of music and poetry in a world like this? He should have learned to be a warrior instead. They all should have. *An artist has no place in such a world. I've failed my people. Too cowardly even to make a choice. Afraid of the sight of blood. Easily captured, like Nixos, like Demeia. Our people will fall, and no one will even remember us.*

The screams of dying farmers rang in his ears. The stench of Ilk filled his nose. Blood poured from the walls around him and across the floor. Everything was death. And yet he could not die.

"Be strong, my son," Epiktet said. *"This is the Gloom. We'll resist it together."*

"It's just so ... hard," Alexios said, squeezing his eyes shut, finding only more darkness. *"It's taking the life out of me."* He felt like a child, wishing for Epiktet's strong arms around him, comforting him after yet another nightmare.

"The priestess will come for you," Cassander said. *"The Makers are still with us."*

"We're all with you, father," Eliana said. "We'll endure this trial together."

"Let's pray to the Makers," Achaikos said, startling Alexios. He almost never spoke, but he'd been an intensely religious man.

What would the gods think of him, a Keeper who lost his belief in their greatness and goodness? No, this couldn't be. He must hold to his faith. Through the Makers they would prevail. They had sent the Lumin priestess here, and he could save his people yet. *"You're right. Let's pray together."* He began to recite the Daily Prayer, and the souls joined him, and it seemed that the Makers did answer and took away some of his agony for a little while.

Chapter 38

Fay

New Arindel is a dreadful shame on this city. But what is to be done? We need bold ideas. But bold ideas are in short supply in the priesthood. We look too much to the past.

—Letters, Archpriest Nuria Garibaldi

Fay slept badly, and when she checked her appearance the next day, found her eyes puffed, the skin beneath them dark, as if bruised. She'd been summoned to Nuria's office straight after morning prayers, and the closer the time came, the more she worried that the archpriest had learned of Fay's betrayals. So it was with dry mouth and pounding heart that she finally knocked on the door to Nuria's office. Her voice came through the door, clear, confident, instructing Fay to enter.

She pushed the door open to find Nuria standing in front of her huge oak desk. The archpriest looked as tired as she herself felt, her movements slow, her skin off-color. She was still attractive, though, her long, chestnut hair wound in a complex knot at the back of her head, her white, gem-encrusted robes falling in perfect folds, somehow accentuating the curves of her figure rather than hiding them.

Fay bowed her head and pressed her palms together. "Light shine on you, Your Radiance."

"And you, daughter."

Warmth in those words. And she was smiling. Just a little smile, but one that reached her dark eyes. So maybe Nuria didn't know what she'd been up to? "What is it I can do for you, Your Radiance?"

"Please, daughter, sit." She gestured at the pair of chairs in front of the desk. "There are matters I wish to discuss."

Fay froze for a second. So Nuria did know. And now she couldn't remember a single thing she had prepared in her defense. *Shit, shit, shit.*

"Is something wrong?" Nuria asked.

Fay jerked back to the present moment, saw the archpriest was already moving to sit behind her desk.

"I'm fine, Your Radiance. I just remembered something I need to do," Fay said. *Idiot. She wouldn't be smiling at you like that if she knew, would she?* Fay sat in one of the chairs and looked at Nuria with what she hoped was expectation rather than fear.

"How are you, daughter?"

"I'm well, Your Radiance. Thank you for asking." What would Nuria say, if Fay told her the whole truth? Would she lock her up, exile her, give her to Lothar out of spite? But Nuria had never struck her as a vengeful sort.

"Have you been getting enough sleep?"

A fresh blast of cold through her insides. What did Nuria mean by that? Had she heard about Fay's night-time trips? "Y-yes," she said, and cursed the traitorous quavering of her voice.

The archpriest leaned forward a little, frowning, and Fay swallowed hard. "Are you sure you're alright? Have you been troubled by recent events? There's no need to worry we'll be attacked here. It's strictly a weaver's affair."

What? Oh, that. Fay latched onto the lifeline. "Yes, I suppose I've been a bit worried. It's quite frightening to think someone could murder the First Weaver right in his chambers."

Nuria smiled reassuringly. "Many people are worried, but we do have Arianna Velden safely in custody here. Our prison cells for weavers are all lined entirely in nicoleum, did you know that?"

Fay's heart skipped a beat. "Em, I've never been there. I wouldn't know." *Great Lumia, can she tell I'm lying?* Nuria cocked her head slightly, as if wondering, and Fay braced herself.

"Do *you* think she's guilty?" Nuria said.

Is this another test? Sweat was starting to pop out on her brow, hidden under her curls for now, but would Nuria notice? "It's not for me to say, Your Radiance. There'll be a trial, won't there?"

"Of course, of course. We must wait for the facts to emerge," Nuria said. "But many already think she *is* guilty." She fell silent, stroking a scroll on her desk with a slender finger.

Fay sensed she was deliberating over something. *Where is this going?*

Nuria looked up from the scroll, sought and met her eyes. "For my part, I'm not so sure."

Fay twitched. Could she be an ally? *Do I dare tell her about Alexios? No.* Fay realized that Nuria was looking at her expectantly, as if she wanted her to say something. Stumbling, unsure of what the archpriest wanted to hear, she said, "She ... em ... she was caught in the act, though, wasn't she?"

Nuria nodded slowly. "Danial Thane says so." Another pause, another uncertain look, then, "What is your opinion of the weavers?"

Fay blinked at her. *Oh great Lumia help me, is she laying traps?* But she had to say something. Better to play it safe. "Well, I don't know any so I can't make a personal assessment. But as we all know, their power is dangerous and must be curbed."

Nuria pressed her lips together, gave a slight nod. "Of course. However, there are some who say we should work with them rather than against them," she said. "What do you think?"

Why was Nuria asking her this? Was she trying to get Fay to betray herself in some way? "I'm only an ordinary priestess ..." she began.

Nuria waved an impatient hand. "I want your opinion."

Her mouth drying even further, Fay hazarded an answer based on what she knew of Nuria's activities. "I think it could be ... advantageous ... to try and work with them. Keep your friends close and your enemies closer, as they say."

A triumphant glint in Nuria's dark eyes. "My thoughts exactly." She rested her elbows on the table, bent her head toward Fay's. "Can you keep a secret?"

How many secrets am I already keeping? "Of course, Your Radiance," she said weakly. Why did the woman undo her like this? She was usually a much better liar.

"It's not much of a secret, truth be told. I plan to tell everyone soon."

Fay held her breath. What was this about?

Nuria drew herself up straight. "I've been meeting with Danial Thane to form a plan to help New Arindel."

The words were like a gut punch. She'd known what Nuria was up to but would never ever have thought she'd declare it publicly. It was professional suicide.

Nuria's lips twitched into the hint of a smile as she took in Fay's reaction. "I know it's unprecedented, but it's been two hundred years since the Ruin. Isn't it time we moved on from old feuds? We're stronger together than apart."

Fay opted again to play it safe. "If you say so, Your Radiance."

"It's because of my cooperation with Thane that he agreed to have Arianna Velden imprisoned here," Nuria said. "He's now poised to become First Weaver. We would have an ally at the very top of their hierarchy. Of course, we can never entirely trust them. But some things can only be accomplished with money, and the weavers have that."

The great weaver families she meant, surely, who controlled most of the land and wealth of the country. It gave them de facto power, even if no weaver could sit on the Consulate by law.

"I have an ambitious plan." Nuria's entire body now vibrated with excitement. "I want the Consulate to extend the right to vote in Delegate and Consulate elections to all adults."

Fay couldn't hide her astonishment. Only those who owned property had ever been allowed to vote. Surely such a plan would be vigorously opposed? How did Nuria think to get it voted through?

"Danial Thane is in agreement. He himself is an outsider. He understands how difficult it is to succeed without property or a name behind you."

It was common knowledge that Thane didn't belong to a weaver family. He wasn't even from Vycenia, but from Tarsis. His rise had been as unprecedented as it was spectacular.

"Are you still with me?" Nuria's words cut through her thoughts.

Fay felt herself grow red. "Sorry, yes, of course."

A nod, a half-smile. "As I was saying, I've been trying to convince the consuls for a long time that we must do more for the people of New Arindel. But half of them want to solve the problem by tearing down their hovels and sending them away."

Just like Lothar did. "What about the other half?"

A little huff of annoyance escaped the archpriest. "Generally, they prefer to ignore the slum and let us deal with the worst of it. But the First Consul has approved the plan I've prepared with Thane. We've designed an expansion of the city—real buildings, a sewage system, lighting, policing by the Watch. I'm trying to put together some people who are familiar with New Arindel who can help finalize and implement it. Your friend Maev recommended you. Would you lend yourself to our efforts? It would take quite a lot of your time over the coming months."

Fay would once have been excited to work closely with Nuria just for the sake of it, to have a purpose, do something that could actually make a difference, make her feel less like she was being slowly suffocated. But instead, she could only think that she was betraying her. "Of course, Your Radiance. It sounds like a marvelous plan."

Nuria nodded with satisfaction. "Danial Thane has the ear of the Wyven family, and they've agreed to front some money. He's also assembling a team of weavers who will help. In four days, there will be a rally on New Arindel Common where we'll make a public announcement. I'll need your help in the organization of that too."

"Of course," Fay said, feeling more than a little wrongfooted.

Nuria's smile now broke fully. "Wonderful. I'm having a preliminary meeting with those interested the day after tomorrow—after evening prayers in the Torch Room."

"I have no duties," Fay said. "I'll be there."

"Good, I'll see you then. You may go."

Fay wandered out in a daze. She wasn't sure if Nuria was greatly daring or impossibly foolish. Certainly, her ambition extended much farther than Fay had ever imagined. Was she really going to go public about Danial Thane? Maybe she knew that Lothar had already got wind of it. This would be a way of making sure he couldn't use it against her. But still, a risky move. A very risky move.

"My sweet Fay."

The sound of his voice caused every muscle in her body to lock into paralysis.

"You've been avoiding me." Suddenly he was there, his bulk pressing her against the wall. He stank of sweat beneath his cologne.

"I've been busy," she said, the life and breath draining out of her as she looked into his pale blue eyes. They shone with anger and greed.

"Your report is overdue." Puffing breath hot on her face.

"There's nothing to report, really."

"Don't play silly games. It won't go well for you." He pressed against her, squashing her against the wall.

Fay said nothing, trying to breathe.

"My chambers, tonight, or there will be consequences," he said. His hand squeezed her buttock.

She didn't dare deny him outright. "I'll try."

"Don't *try*. Be there." Another squeeze and then he waddled off, leaving his cloying scent in her nostrils.

She stayed where she was, her legs unable to support her, feeling as if she would vomit. Tonight. No, she would not go tonight. She'd go to Papa Julia's or lock herself in her room. He wasn't going to have her. She'd rather be exposed, thrown out of the temple in disgrace. And to the pits with Moth.

Shakily, she pushed herself off the wall. She needed to go see if Moth had instructions for her. On trembling legs, she made her way to the side exit and then into the Rainbow Quarter. She walked blindly, Lothar dominating her thoughts, and was surprised to suddenly find herself in front of The Goat. It was only then that she realized she'd been careless. She'd done nothing to ensure she wasn't being followed.

She glanced down the street behind her, saw no one conspicuous, but then if the tail was any good, they wouldn't *be* conspicuous. *I'm an Ilk-damned fool.* Still cursing herself, she opened the door into the alehouse. It was already crowded, and she danced around the groping hands of men as she made her way to the back room. Pie was on his own for once, counting coin.

"Moth wants to talk to you direct," he said to her. "He's in The Merchant's Daughter. Password's 'Mirella'."

The Merchant's Daughter was a high-class inn off River Street. She knew Moth sometimes held court there, although she'd only ever seen it from the outside.

"Thanks, I'll go out the back," she said. Just in case someone *was* waiting to follow her.

"It's open."

Fay crossed the room to another door which opened into a stinking alleyway. Wrinkling her nose, she stepped through piled-up refuse and into another alley. It would take nearly twice as long to get to the Merchant's Daughter through the back ways, but she'd be in terrible trouble if she were ever followed to one of Moth's hideouts.

The sun was high and burning hot by the time she got to the inn. It was a vast place, with stables even larger than the main building, able to cater for entire teams of horses. The common room was busy but clean. Many were eating lunch, and the smell of roasting meat made her stomach complain loudly. But she needed to get business over with first. She went to the nearest barman and asked for Mirella.

"She's in the Blue Room, top floor," the barman said. "Stairs is through there." He pointed at a door in the far end of the common room.

She hurried up, found Ruadh standing guard outside in the hallway, along with another wasp she didn't know.

Ruadh knocked on the door and announced her, then told her she'd have to wait. It was at least half an hour later before an unfamiliar woman exited the room. She had a hard face, and her eyes glimmered with barely suppressed anger. Fay hoped it didn't bode ill for her.

Moth was sitting behind a desk in the middle of the room, wearing his mask again. The colors of the walls gave the room its name—deep, almost marine blue, decorated with gilt-framed landscapes. Large windows let in beams of summer sunshine.

"Zethir filled me in on what you found, but I want to hear it from your lips," Moth said as she sat before him.

Fay recounted all that had happened.

"This supposed Eleusian is either telling the truth or totally cracked. Which do you think it is?" Moth said.

"The way he looked and spoke—he's not Vycenian. And it all sounds like something an Ilk mage would do."

Moth's antennae vibrated. "We're going to break Velden out," he said. "And that man too."

"What? But ... can't she prove her innocence with the Eleusian?" Fay assumed that was what would happen. They'd break Alexios out, tell the weavers, send an army to save his people. Something suitably heroic that she would have no part in.

Moth's orange globes flared. "Who do you think would believe him? As *everyone* knows, all Eleusians died in the Ruin."

"But his looks," Fay said. "He had an Eleusian face."

"Have you ever seen an Eleusian?"

"No, but—"

"So how do you know?"

"Drawings, there must be drawings somewhere, in a book," Fay said, thinking of the Archpriests' Library. "He didn't look like we do. I'm sure ..."

But Moth was shaking his head impatiently. "It won't work. No Eleusians have been seen for two hundred years. And no Ilk have been seen either. The story is more likely to send her to the gallows than to save her from it."

"The disk," Fay said. "That disk she found, with the Eleusian mark on it."

"A relic from the past. It could have been picked up anywhere. If she wanted that to help her, she should have handed it over to her questioners straight away."

Fay realized with a sinking heart that Moth was right. Who *would* believe Alexios's story? "So what's your plan?"

Moth's antennae twitched. "That's what we need to decide now."

Fay went later that evening to relay the plan to Arianna. Despite the agreement to go through Galinda, he'd insisted that she speak directly to the Guardian to ensure his words were transmitted correctly.

To her surprise, though, Galinda was already in the cell with Arianna. She regarded Fay with all the haughtiness she'd displayed on their first encounter. And if Fay had thought she'd be more polite toward her if she knew she was a priest, she was roundly disabused of the notion.

"So, Moth's little girl turns out to be a heretic too. How nice."

Don't let them get to you. She took a deep breath, smiled at them through gritted teeth. "You'll be pleased to learn that we've made some discoveries." She began to tell them about Alexios and Moth's plan.

"Absolutely not!" Galinda cried when Fay suggested they break Arianna out rather than go through with the trial. "It will make everyone think she *is* guilty."

"As things stand, she doesn't have much of a chance of being found innocent," Fay said.

"But we have the Eleusian," Galinda said, looking at Arianna. "We free him from that prison, and he gives testimony."

Fay made the same point that Moth had made, and even as she spoke the words, she realized how true they were. No one would ever believe Alexios's story.

Galinda mentioned the disk, and again Fay echoed Moth's words.

"It was too risky to hand it over," Arianna murmured. "Not until I'd learned who'd brought it. Elwin's murderer could have been anyone in the Spire. To be able to walk into his chambers like that ... for all we know it was Danial Thane himself."

Danial Thane? Surely not? And hadn't he found Arianna with the body? Would he have had time to kill Elwin and get out before she arrived?

"If we free the Eleusian, then whoever imprisoned him may decide to act in some other way. There may be dangerous consequences we can't foresee. We need to find out who his captor is first," Arianna continued.

"But the trial is in two weeks," Galinda replied, shaking her head. "There's little—"

Fay broke in, meeting Arianna's eyes. "It means we still have time—which is why Moth proposes to break you and the Eleusian out. Then you go to the Eleusian's town with some other trusted weavers and see the Ilk for yourself, bring back evidence."

But Arianna didn't seem convinced. "I want to try and find out who his captor is first," she said. "We *need* that information. We need to know if it's one of our own."

Fay was inclined to agree, although it wasn't the answer she wanted to hear. The sooner she got Arianna and Alexios out, the sooner she got herself out. "A delay could cost us—we don't know what the Ilk mage will do to the Eleusian in the meantime. He might be dead by tomorrow."

But Arianna was unmoved. "Go back and ask him if he's been able to find out who his captor is. Then we'll discuss what to do."

Fay really didn't want to return to the Gloom-filled prison. The very thought of it caused her stomach to churn. But someone had to, if even to bring the poor man food and water. And going there would help her to avoid Lothar that night. So, reluctantly, she agreed.

Chapter 39

Ina

Every village is ruled by two elders, one male and one female. They are guardians of the laws and it is their role to resolve disputes in a fair and impartial manner. For great crimes that involve more than one village or island, a full council of may be convened in the village where the defendant currently lives.

—Teachings of Old Tsu

Ina opened her eyes to darkness and the roaring of the wind. She was lying on her back, on a pallet. Her feet and wrists had been trussed together, as if she were a slaughtered animal. There was a sour taste in her mouth and a sick, hollow feeling in her stomach. The dullness that pressed on her mind told her she'd been dosed with clawtongue. Even so, fragments of memories that were not her own continued to cross her consciousness.

Where was she? She tried to open herself to the Cloth but was rewarded with only brief sparkles that soon blinked out. She could guess where they'd taken her, though—to the Elders' House. That was where they kept those who were called to answer for their actions. They must have found her after she went to the Godstone and brought her here while she was still dreaming. And what dreams!

A stirring outside, and then the darkness faded as the door shutter was rolled up. Someone entered the room, bearing a small candlenut lamp in a familiar, red-stained stone bowl. The flickering flame cast light on the slender nose and high forehead of her mother, framed by the hood of her waterproof yaka-leaf cape. Rivulets of water streamed down the cape and onto the ground, and her mother removed it carefully and laid it out flat before coming to sit next to Ina. She set the lamp down, then reached to her belt, from which she unhooked a waterskin. "A drink?" she said as she held it out before Ina.

"Please." Mia helped her raise her head, and she gulped greedily, suddenly aware of how thirsty she'd been. When she'd had her fill, she lay her head back down, feeling too dull and heavy to sit upright.

Mia set the skin down next to the lamp and put a cool hand over Ina's bound ones. "They said they found you lying near the Godstone. It was broken into pieces." Her words had a questioning note.

"I went back and touched it. I had to—I know you said not to, but I had to." Ina blinked back a wave of dizziness. "I suppose we're in the Elders' House?"

"They brought you straight here. Mūak has told the elders he's seen you practicing magic. You're to be brought before the full council soon to explain yourself."

"The full council? How long have I been here?"

"Two days." Mia leaned over her and gripped her forearm hard. "Tell them nothing."

"If Mūak has spoken and they found me as they did, then I don't see how I can pretend," Ina said. *And I don't want to pretend anymore. They've been lying, all these years.*

"They have no proof that the Godstone reacted to you because you have magic. You passed the Test, after all."

"They've given me clawtongue, though," Ina said.

"Mūak told them about its properties."

"Not Suni?" Ina held her breath for the answer.

But Mia just shrugged. "I can't be sure. It wasn't me."

Ina managed a weak smile. "I wouldn't blame you even if you had. The elders can be persuasive."

"I won't have you sent back to Chel now, after everything!" Mia said fiercely. "We need to make a plan, decide what you'll say."

"You haven't even asked me what happened. Don't you want to know?"

"You can tell me later. First, we need to work out how to get you out of this."

Ina shook her head. "No, you need to hear this. It's ... it's ... it will sound like madness. When I went and touched the Godstone I ... I was filled with the memories of Lin'Elkir, the last skyrider. Somehow, she stored her memories in the Godstone before she died."

Mia's brow wrinkled in confusion. "But she disappeared, she went east with the last of the drakiri to look for those of our people who fled to the barbarian lands."

"Tsu says that in his stories, but the memories tell me she returned secretly to Uruk'il to put her memories in the Godstone. She was told to do it by a Foreseer so that one day the memories would be passed on to one of her blood descendants. And it was she, not Takan'Ri, who led our people to these islands."

"One of her blood descendants? But we have no blood relationship with her."

"Maybe on Papi's side?"

Mia shook her head. "The stories all say she died childless. Her sons were killed in the war."

"Lin had a son called Tsuk whose amiki was expecting a child. I'm sure of that memory."

Mia clasped both her hands together over her knees. "There's no Tsuk in my ancestry, maybe your father's ... But let's not distract ourselves with this. When you go before the Elders—"

"There's something more important. The Foreseer told Lin'Elkir to put her memories in the Godstone because one day the Cloth itself would be threatened by some great war, like when the Great Maelstrom swallowed Eleusia and old Chelakan." Ina remembered the visions of the Unraveling, shown to her by the leviathan. Was that what was coming for them again?

"That was Sīut's doing. It wasn't a war."

So Ina told her about the leviathan, how he'd shown her that the Maelstrom was a result of dangerous magic used by warring magic-users.

"You're full of secrets!" Mia exclaimed. "What else have you hidden from me?"

"You would have been angry at me for trying to go to the Godstone."

"I *am* angry! How could you have been so foolish? There was no need to—"

"You don't know what it was like. You don't realize how it called me—" A shock of intense heat caused sweat to break out all over her body and she shuddered. Moments later the muscles around her gut clenched and spasmed and she rolled onto her side. She heaved once, twice, and a dribble of water leaked out of her mouth and onto the floor.

Mia loosed a soft, wordless exclamation of dismay. When Ina's heaving subsided, she used a corner of her dress to wipe her mouth. "More water?"

"Please." Her voice was as dry and cracked as she felt, but she took only a small mouthful in case she vomited it out again.

When Ina was done drinking, Mia spoke again, this time more thoughtfully. "You talk of war, but our people have sworn an oath of peace that very few have broken in five centuries. The Eleusians are all gone, the barbarians are on the other side of the Great Maelstrom. Who would we go to war with?"

"I don't know. But I've learned that the Godstone is also a waygate. It can be used to travel to the eastern lands through Sīut's Realm. Some of our people went there in exile. There may even be drakiri still alive. Imagine—drakiri!"

But Mia didn't look convinced. "The Godstone is broken. If it ever was a waygate, I doubt it's one now—but this *is* madness, Ina. At least wait and learn more from the memories before you say anything to the elders. Mūak had nothing concrete, he just said he followed you onto the beach and saw you using your powers. It's your word against his. You can concoct a—"

The shutter rolled up again and Ina peered at the growing sliver of light. She soon recognized the first person to enter—Mūak. He was closely followed by Jiu'Ri. Jiu'Ri was the youngest of the elders, his hair still falling to his shoulders brown and thick, his face clear of lines. He was a former hunter and only recently Elder of Hiku, the northernmost village on the island. Both he and Mūak were armed with nouk spears and wore belt knives.

"We're taking Ina to the hearing of the elders," Jiu'Ri said to Mia. "As her mother, you may attend, but you may not speak." He glanced only briefly at Ina. Mūak fixed her with a hostile stare, his lips pressed together in smug self-satisfaction.

"We're going to untie your legs," Jiu'Ri said to her. "Don't try to run. All the elders are armed and will strike you down you if you do."

Once they had finished removing the bindings, they helped her to her feet. Weak and faint from clawtongue and lack of food, she almost fell over, but they grabbed hold of her elbows and kept her upright. Mūak's grip was so tight it hurt, but Jiu'Ri's was gentler. They made their way out of the room and into a small passageway that led directly into the elders' meeting hall. The shutter was already up, and she could see some of the elders standing on the other side.

They passed through the doorway and Ina counted the full complement of elders—twenty-three plus Jiu'Ri. They were standing in a semi-circle in male-female pairs according to village and island. All were wearing their ceremonial red and black headdresses. Unusually, most of the men held loaded spear throwers over their shoulders. Others stood with long-bladed nouk spears, even those who had never been hunters. A couple of the women were also armed. No one smiled when they saw her, not even Naomi'Ri, who had always been kind to her.

Mūak and Jiu'Ri walked her to the center of the room and then took a step back. They angled their spears toward her, the sharp tips of the black firestone blades a bare fingerswidth from her flesh. Why had they let Mūak stay, she wondered. There should only be elders here.

"Ina'Yakir'Suk, you have been brought before the elders to explain yourself. Why did you go to the Godstone, and why did we find it broken while you lay before it?" It was Alik'Ri who spoke. His tone was wary rather than hostile, and Ina dared hope.

But she hesitated before answering, her mother's words echoing in her mind. The elders could prove nothing. She could deny it all, walk away free. The Godstone was broken, it couldn't betray her. But what of the Foreseer's warnings to Lin? What of the leviathan's task to save her so that she in turn might stop a second great unraveling, ludicrous as the possibility seemed? In saving herself, she might doom them all. But she was tired of the lies, and she didn't want to see Tani die. "I've discovered the Godstone's true purpose," she said boldly.

"What do you mean by that?" Alik'Ri said, more sharply this time.

"It has long been said that the Godstone was found by Takan'Ri the Landfinder, but that isn't true."

A stirring, looks of consternation and anger.

"What nonsense are you speaking? Have you gone mad?" Naomi'Ri demanded.

Ina braced herself. "The Godstone has called me for many years. I was always afraid to answer that call because I thought it meant death."

"She's plainly cursed!" cried Niak'Ri, a round-faced, round-bodied Elder from Kan'il.

"Cursed or mad or both," agreed his fellow elder, Kiasi'Ri, a slender woman with more brown than white in her hair.

"Give her the starweed potion now before it's too late!" said another woman, this one from Olon, although Ina couldn't remember her name.

"Let her finish!" Jiu'Ri said. A couple of others took up the call, and a grudging silence fell. "Continue," Jiu'Ri said to Ina.

"When I put my hands on the Godstone, I was filled with the memories of my ancestor, Lin'Elkir, the last skyrider."

A few looked like they wanted to say something, but they held their tongues, frowning and shuffling instead.

Ina gathered her courage. What she was about to say would surely break the temporary truce. "It was Lin'Elkir who put the Godstone there because she knew what our ancestors would do. She knew what *we* would do—that we would murder all the elkiri that were born after. The great irony is that she didn't know you would use the Godstone itself to do it. It was never meant to lead to the murder of children. It was created to protect us from a terrible future harm."

"Blasphemy, you've lost your mind!" shouted Niak'Ri.

But Ina shook her head. She wouldn't back down now. "Another great war is coming, and without the power and knowledge of the elkiri, we'll be consumed by it. Lin'Elkir spoke to a Foreseer, and another unraveling will come to pass, like that which caused the Great Maelstrom. I've been ..." She paused, realizing how mad she'd sound next. "I've been called by Chel to lead us against this war."

"Again, an elkir speaks of war!" cried Naomi'Ri, stabbing the butt of her spear hard against the ground. "Send her back to Chel now, before she bends our minds with her cursed powers."

Many other voices chimed in agreement, and wood rapped sharply against wood.

"We have no evidence yet that she's cursed," interjected Jiu'Ri. "She passed the Test, and the Godstone is broken."

That quieted most of them.

But Naomi's eyes had hardened to chips of rock. "She's already admitted as much. Who else but Sīut's pawn could break the Godstone? And listen to her words—war and death is what she speaks of. She pretends to be chosen by Chel, but it is Sīut who speaks through her."

Murmurs and nods of agreement.

"The elkiri didn't cause the genocide, they fought to prevent it," Ina said. "It isn't the power itself that is evil, nor the people who are born with it. It's what is done with it that counts. You elders have been lying to us, all these years. If anyone is working for Sīut, it's you!"

A roar of angry voices rang out, some challenging her, others challenging each other. Some were stunned and speechless. Others spat and choked. A couple looked like they wanted to stab her.

Alik'Ri, red-faced, finally spoke to her. "Our people ..." He choked off, evidently overcome, then composed himself. "Our people have had five centuries of peace with the elkiri gone," he said. "We elders have kept our people safe."

Ina's own anger sparked and flamed. "You murdered every elkir who has entered the world since that day—innocent children. That's not peace!"

"The elkiri are cursed. They brought the destruction of our people," said Kouna'Ri. She was an old, bent woman from the next island, Olon'il, but her tone was as sharp as her mind.

"The Eleusians and the easterners destroyed our people," Ina said. "And the elkiri died to defend them. I saw what happened."

Kouna'Ri shook her head. "It is well known that Ilis'Elkir started the war," she said. "And the elkiri—the Cursed Ones—followed him." She spat those last words out, five centuries of hatred in them.

Hanuk'Ri, a tall, measured man who came from her father's island, held up his hand. Slowly, the voices quietened. "I say we discuss our decision in privacy."

"The Cursed One has already told us all we need to know," said Alik'Ri in a tone of agreement.

No one dissented, and they commanded that Ina's mother leave the room with her. Mūak and Jiu'Ri took hold of her arms to steer her out. Mūak's grip was hard, bruising, but Jiu'Ri touched her only lightly, as if leading her in a dance. When she was back inside her prison, Mūak bound her feet but allowed her to sit up with her back against the wall.

"You'll be back with Chel soon," Mūak said to her triumphantly before he left.

Jiu'Ri said nothing, his expression blank.

Chapter 40

Fay

Light will keep the Shadower at bay. Ordinary, non-magical light. The light of the sun is the most potent. But when there is no sun, we must rely on the moon, and torches, candles, and lamps. For this reason, the fires of the Temple to Lumia must never go out.

—The Lumin Priest's Handbook

Fay stared at the door to the old temple. If only Zethir were with her again, or anyone, anyone at all. She didn't want to face the Gloom alone. And what if the Ilk mage was in there at this very moment?

Taking a deep breath, she put her hands on the door and pushed. It opened noiselessly, revealing the same total absence of light as before. Another long breath to stem the rising panic, then she stepped over the threshold. The darkness swallowed her instantly, choking out most of the light of her lamp. The voices began to whisper to her again, bringing with them memories. "*Filthy, loveless whore. Liar, liar, liar.*"

She turned in the direction of the stairs and went up. It took a bit of searching before she found the door to the cell. It was still bolted shut, and she felt a tiny measure of relief. At least the Ilk mage wasn't already inside. When she had opened the door, she spoke into the darkness. "Alexios, it's Fay."

A rustle of fabric and the clinking of chains. "Have you come to free me?" His voice sounded weaker than the last time.

"No—not yet, I'm sorry. But I've brought food and water."

She approached him and knelt, putting her lamp down in front of her. The light was barely enough to outline his features. He looked as terrible as he had before. Horribly thin, his skin almost papery, blue veins standing out starkly on his hands and at his temple.

She unhooked two waterskins and removed the roast chicken, bread, and apple she had stashed in her satchel. "We'll free you, very soon," she said, handing him the waterskin and setting out the food in front of him.

Alexios put the skin to his lips and drank. Fay noticed his hands were trembling. After taking a few mouthfuls, he set the skin down and began to eat the food in small, careful bites, starting with the meat.

"I've told the Guardian, Arianna Velden, that you're here, and she'll help you and your people. She's still imprisoned, but we're working on a plan to free you both." It involved sleepfast and a lot of clever talk on Fay's part that she would much rather avoid. But it was the best they could come up with.

"I can help you free her with my invisibility illusions," he said.

So those rumors were true, about Eleusian magic. "That could be really helpful," she said. "I'll pass it on. The plan we have is quite complicated, but it would make things much easier if you can do that."

Alexios swallowed his food. "I can. But please, don't delay," he said, his voice hoarse. "My people could be dying as we speak."

The despair in his eyes was unbearable. "*Filthy, loveless whore,*" said the darkness. "It will be very soon, I promise," she said, leaning over to place a reassuring hand on his arm. He flinched, and disconcerted, she removed her hand. "But we really need to know the name of your captor first. Arianna is insisting. She's afraid it's a weaver in the Spire."

"He hasn't returned yet," Alexios said.

Pits, would Arianna delay more now? She couldn't leave this poor man in here any longer. And she had to get out of the temple. "Very well, if he does come, try, won't you?"

"I will try."

She started to get to her feet, to make her excuses.

"Stay, please, a little while. Tell me about yourself."

Fay stilled. She wanted to say no. What if the Ilk mage came? But the man seemed so desperate.

"*No one loves a whore, a liar even less,*" muttered the darkness.

Trying to ignore the needling voice, she sat back down, folding her legs underneath her. "I'm a priestess of Lumia," she said. "But you know that. Do you know anything about the priesthood?"

A ghost of a smile. "Only what you told me before, but I would hear more."

Fay decided to start at the beginning. "The priesthood was founded in the wake of the Ruin by Caris the Restorer. She saw Lumia stepping out of a fire during the cataclysm, telling her to abandon the worship of the old gods, the Spinners, as it was they who'd caused it. Caris built the Temple of Lumia around the old Spinners' temple to contain the evil in here."

Alexios twitched, chains rattling. "We are now in this Temple of the Spinners?"

"Yes."

"An almost perfect prison," he said. "But not a perfect one." A full, genuine smile, surprising—no, shocking—in that place. "The Makers are with us."

"What makes you say that?"

"They led you here so you could find me. They haven't abandoned us."

Fay didn't want to stamp out the spark of hope that lit in his haunted eyes, so she didn't say what she really thought—that it was all coincidence, that it was only because Moth was obsessed with old books and artifacts that she was here. Or—maybe it was *Lumia* who had led her here. Hadn't Fay solved the riddle in the diary? No, *I can't be Lumia's chosen one. I'm a fake, a whore, a priestess only because Moth wanted to make me one.* She groped for something else to tell him about the priesthood, something uncontroversial. Her thoughts went to Nuria, and then Lothar's scheming.

"He'll have you soon, show you you're still nothing but a filthy whore," the darkness said.

Fay gritted her teeth. *Go away, shut up.*

"Are you alright?" Alexios said, chains clanking as he shifted again.

Fay stared at him. It sounded like he actually cared. *No, probably just a game to keep me here so he's not left on his own.*

"Go if you can't bear it. There's no need for both of us to go mad." A weak chuckle, more of a cough.

Yes, I should go. Instead, words burst out of her. "The priesthood is ruled by seven archpriests." She would *not* let the Gloom eat her up. If he could survive it, so could she. And she'd already endured worse. "The head of them is called the High Luminate. Every five years, elections for High Luminate are held. The next one will be held the day after the winter equinox, which we call the Dawning. The current High Luminate isn't running again this year. He's served two terms, the maximum. There are two archpriests seeking election. One is called Lothar and he's ..." Fay couldn't bring herself to tell Alexios about Lothar and what he was doing to her. "I don't think he'll make a good High Luminate. He's greedy and self-centered. I think he cares only about the power for its own sake. I prefer the other one, Nuria. She wants to help the poor of New Arindel. That's the slum outside the city walls."

"Yes, I saw it on my way here," Alexios said. "It seems a wretched place." He shifted, and his handcuffs rattled in the dark.

"I grew up there," Fay said impulsively.

A deep compassion in those hollowed eyes. "That must have been hard. Would you tell me about it?"

Fay didn't want to think about that time, certainly didn't want to say anything about it. And yet Alexios seemed to genuinely care. So much so that she couldn't look at him as she spoke. "I had a little brother, Art. He ... died when he was still a little child. A fever took him. My father ..." *Sold me, took my money. Until I killed him.* "Died when I was young. My mother when I was a bit older, a few years ago now, she was a ..." Fay couldn't say it. *My mother was a whore.*

"A filthy, dirty whore," whispered the darkness. *"Just like you."*

Fay tried to silence the voice, but it became more insistent, listing her sins relentlessly. It was too much. "I have to go," she said. "I'm sorry. I can't stay any longer. It's dangerous. If I'm caught ..."

"You're right," Alexios said. "It was wrong of me to keep you."

Don't look at him. "Try to get your captor's name. I'll be back tomorrow," she said, getting to her feet.

"Thank you," Alexios said.

Still not daring to look at him, she left the cell. But as she finished sliding the bolt across the door, she heard a sound downstairs. She froze, hoping it was a trick of the Gloom. But no, those were definitely footsteps, coming in the direction of the stairs.

The Ilk mage!

She scurried about frantically on tiptoe, looking for a place to hide. There, a cupboard. She hurried over, got the door open, and squeezed in amongst hanging cloth, nose filling with the musty smell of it. As the footsteps began to sound on the stairs, she blew out her lamp, and was plunged into total, suffocating darkness. Her instinct was to close the cupboard door, to lock herself into a safe cocoon. But she needed to see who it was. For a long, frozen moment, panic fought curiosity, until finally curiosity won, and she left the door open a crack.

The footsteps reached the top of the stairs. Fay hardly dared to breathe as a figure bearing an oil lamp passed her in the darkness. The voice of the Gloom needled at her, but she firmly ignored it to study the figure. Male with those shoulders, medium height, blond hair, weaver robes. Her heart skipped several beats. Danial Thane? Could it be him? She had only ever seen him from afar. And it was hard to make out anything in the weak lamplight.

The newcomer pulled back the bolt, which emitted a thin screech, and Fay prayed that Alexios had had time to hide the water and food she had left for him. The Ilk mage didn't close the door after him, and she strained to hear what he said.

"So, you finally dare to show your face." That was Alexios's voice.

"The mask wasn't terribly comfortable, truth be told." The voice, neither high nor low, sounded like it belonged to a man in his forties. The right age for Thane. As she listened, she tried to imprint the sound of it in her mind, that she might recognize it if she heard it again.

"You're one of the weavers, aren't you?" Alexios said. "You kept me in the Spire at first. Then moved me here."

Rustling noises and a dull thunk as the newcomer presumably deposited food and water in front of Alexios.

Ruination, answer!

"Are you one of those the First Weaver called for before we were attacked?"

Good, Alexios. Now, let him answer.

"Would it please you if I was?"

Ruination.

"Why not tell me your name? You've told me the name of the one who attacked Neopoli—Inyaki, I remember."

"There's so much power in a name, isn't there?" the other said. "Names give us our place in the world. They make us and break us, tell us who our enemy is and who our friends are—or do they? Can you ever really know another person, Keeper? Can you trust even those closest to you?"

He speaks the truth there.

The darkness whispered, "*Liar, liar, liar.*"

"If you won't tell me your name, will you at least tell me how long you plan to keep me here?"

"For as long as she wants."

The accent, what accent is it?

"Who is *she*? The mother?"

"Mother to us all," the other said sardonically.

The mother? Had Alexios mentioned a woman? Who in Lumia's holy name was the *mother?*

"Your mother was a filthy whore, all rotten at the end. Let him sell you so she didn't have to do it anymore. Let them take you, steal you."

Fay tried to shut the voice out, to focus on what Alexios was saying. But she only caught the last part of Alexios's next question.

"... the Spire?"

"You're full of questions. I suppose I'd be the same in your position. But I've been instructed to say very little to you."

The man's Vycenian was flawless, but there was a hint of something foreign, a slight clipping of the vowels. Thane was originally from Tarsis. Was it a Tarsis accent? It wasn't strong enough for her to tell for sure.

"I'll take my leave now."

"When will you come back?"

"I've left you enough food and water for several days. We don't plan to starve you—yet." With that, the Ilk mage left Alexios, shutting and barring the door behind him. Fay peered at him from her hiding place, trying to memorize how he walked and held himself. If only it weren't so dark!

She waited ten minutes after he had gone down the stairs before daring to come out of her hiding place. Then she went back in to Alexios.

"He didn't find you," the Eleusian said with relief. "When he first came ..."

"I was able to hide."

"I'm sorry I wasn't able to get his name," he said, shifting to lean against a wall.

"Danial Thane—you didn't see him before you were captured, did you?"

"No. I know only that the First Weaver summoned him to join our meeting."

"It might have been him," Fay said. "How would you describe the man who just came?"

"It was hard to see his features. But I had the impression of a fine-boned face, no hair on it, the chin perhaps a bit narrow, the hair very blond, almost white, curling slightly."

"Would you say he was handsome?"

Alexios's chains rattled slightly. "I could ... yes, you might say that from your perspective."

Ruination, that really does sound like Thane. And if it is, we're in deep shit.

"When I asked if he was one of those the First had summoned during our meeting, his expression told me I'd struck the mark."

Oh Lumia, an Ilk mage in the very Spire. Then another realization. Nuria. Could *Nuria* also be working for the Ilk mages? No, surely not. Surely not? "I'm going now. But I promise, I'll be back tomorrow to see how you are. And we'll free you soon."

She felt awful, leaving him in that Ilkhole. But her relief when she finally emerged into Arindel Woods was immense. It wasn't as late as she'd expected, and there was still a hint of twilight in the sky. She didn't go back to the temple, though, but to The Goat, which was at its noisiest and most raucous. She had left a message before for Moth to tell him Arianna was sending her back into the temple to talk to Alexios. Now she sent another relating her suspicions about Danial Thane and her intention to return to Arianna with the news. Then, determined to avoid Lothar and receive Moth's reply as soon as it arrived, she went up to one of the free rooms and sank onto a bed.

It took her a long time to fall asleep, her mind racing with all she had seen and heard that day. But sleep she finally did, until she was woken in the morning by Nim. He had instructions for her from Moth, some amendments to the break-out plan, and an exhortation not to take no for an answer, or else. *To the pits with Moth. And Arianna too. She'd better agree, this time. Danial bloody Thane. And Nuria maybe too. Oh Lumia, please let it not be true.*

She sent Nim to Galinda Velden to propose another meeting with Arianna that evening. Then she went to New Arindel to attend to her priestly duties. It was the last thing she felt like doing, but if she went missing, it would be noticed. And it kept her out of Lothar's way. Nim found her there a few hours later with confirmation that Galinda would meet her in Arianna's cell after evening prayers.

To Fay's relief, there were new guards on duty in the dungeons when she went. She'd been coming rather too often and was worried the other guards would start to ask awkward questions. *At least, this will be the last time.*

Once more, Galinda was already in the cell, and Fay quickly told her and Arianna everything that had happened the night before.

"If it *is* Danial Thane, we can be sure he'll work against me in some other way if I'm freed," Arianna said, her expression grim. "I see no choice but to escape and go to the Deepwood."

Galinda stared at her with open-mouthed horror. "Think of what it will do to our name! And our businesses, our political standing! There are Delegate elections in a few months."

"There are much bigger things at stake," Arianna said. "Do you think business will continue as normal with an Ilk mage, or mages, in charge of the Spire, and Ilk over-running the land?"

"But we don't even know for certain it is Danial. We can't make such a decision based on mere conjecture!"

She might as well have added "from a heretic and whore" from the way she looked at Fay when she said those words. Breathing deeply against her anger, Fay said, "Both the Eleusian and I are convinced it was him. I've seen him before."

"It makes sense," Arianna said to Galinda. "Danial has always been fascinated by the time before the Ruin. Maybe his studies finally led him to the secret of Ilk making."

Galinda shook her head. "If we leave, we practically hand him power in the Spire. If he's framing you, this is why. We'll be doing exactly what he wants."

"He won't expect this," Arianna said. "These Ilk mages clearly don't want the news that the Ilk have returned to spread. Their army might still be small. If we can defeat it in the Deepwood, then maybe we can stop this war before it's really begun. The enemy has been ahead of us, now let's get ahead of *them.*"

"You hope to *defeat* the Ilk army?" Galinda exclaimed. "We don't have the numbers! We don't even know how!"

"That will be your job," Arianna said. "We have friends and allies. Convince them to join us."

Galinda opened and closed her mouth like a fish, shook her head.

Arianna's sea-green eyes fell on Fay. "If I'm to turn myself into a fugitive, how do you propose we do it?"

Fay let out a relieved sigh. "Moth wants to break you out in three days' time. That day, Archpriest Nuria and Danial Thane have organized a rally at New Arindel common to share their new scheme for improving the slum."

Arianna nodded approvingly. "Yes, Thane will be distracted with the preparations."

"To make him even more distracted, Moth's people are going to start a riot and a fire during the rally. He'll have to stay to deal with the fire."

"That seems rather excessive," Arianna said with a frown.

Fay had thought the same. Fires easily got out of control. And they didn't even know for sure that Danial Thane *was* involved in Alexios's capture. But Moth, as ever, had his own reasons. "This suits Moth too."

Arianna looked unhappy but motioned for her to go on.

"I'm to help organize your escape from this prison. I'll free Alexios first, and then he can spin an invisibility illusion to get us into your cell and the three of us back out together."

"Will you be coming with us to the Deepwood?"

Fay's stomach curdled. She hadn't wanted to join the escape, had hoped instead that Moth would keep his promise and get her out of the temple. But he'd been adamant—she was still needed where she was, to get more books from the Archpriests' Library and investigate the old temple further. She had begged and pleaded until he'd threatened to return her to Madam Sisi's instead. "No. Once you're free, I'll take you to a stable where carriages will be waiting to take you out of Arindel. If you have any friends that you trust to go with you, tell them to meet us there. Moth will send one of his wasps—I mean, soldiers—with you. Apparently, he's had a lot of experience with sieges." That was Ruadh. But Fay reckoned the real reason he was going was to spy for Moth.

"Tell Moth we'll do as he suggests," Arianna said. "He'll get his pardon tomorrow."

Some of the tension eased out of her. At least Moth would have no cause to punish her. "Good, I'll let him know."

Chapter 41

Ruadh

New Arindel came into being some fifty years ago, after the city had been rebuilt and its population restored. But it is especially in the last ten that its population has swelled, largely with immigrants from Tarsis, or people from Northland seeking a better living. The Council should have moved to integrate it immediately rather than pretend it didn't exist. The conditions there are beyond shocking.

—Letters of Archpriest Nuria Garibaldi

Ruadh climbed up the rickety ladder that had been set up along the wall of the shack. "This better not bloody fall in on me," he said to no one as he put a tentative foot on the rough-cut planks that served as a roof. It was one of the few buildings around that even had something close to a proper one. Many were covered in canvas, not little of which had probably been beetled from the docks. He walked gingerly over to the north-facing side of the shack, the planks groaning and creaking under his weight. It gave him a clear view of New Arindel common, a large stretch of grassland that marked the west end of the slum. The common was usually used as pastureland by the few New Arindelers lucky enough to own a sheep, pig, or goat. But there were no animals now, just people, so many of them that not a patch of grass was to be seen. He slowly lowered himself down onto the roof, allowing his legs to dangle over the side, then wiped sweat off his brow, cursing the heat and the fact that he'd been forced to wear a long-sleeved smock over his armor.

The roof creaked behind him again. Then, Elsie's gravelly voice above his head. "Big crowd." The stocky woman sat down next to him. She smelled faintly of spice. Probably had come straight from the warehouses.

"Bigger than I expected."

"The weavers and priests are coming now." Elsie pointed to the right.

The evening sun was low, piercing the corner of his eye, and he put a hand up to block it as he swung his head around. The procession had cleared the last of the shacks on the east side of the common and was now wending its way northward to the specially constructed stage. A sea of heads bobbed and shifted as people craned and strained to catch a glimpse of the arriving dignitaries. There were more of those than Ruadh had expected too. Not only Magister Thane and Arch-priest Nuria, but at least a half dozen or so other Lumins and another half dozen weavers, all in splendid robes—the Lumins in white and gold, the weavers in blues, reds, and greens. He was sure that was the Merchant's Consul and the Northland Consul with them, too. What was his name? Nate Ridger, that was it. And a full company of spikes around them in case the crowd got ugly. Which it soon would.

Ruadh scanned the crowd again as the procession continued to circle the edge of the crowd. "There's a lot of women and children, I don't like it," he muttered.

"Didn't know you were such a softie," Elsie returned. She rubbed a hand through her short, straw-like hair.

"Fighting's a man's job."

"Really?" Her sarcasm was heavy.

He shifted. "It's just not right. As you've said enough times, we men are savages. And we're bigger, stronger. Women and children aren't fair game."

"A woman's knife cuts as deep as a man's." Even before the words were out of her mouth, she had a blade at his throat.

He laughed, the edge of the knife pressing against his skin. "All right, woman, I get your point, but how many of them down there you think has a knife on them? And if the crowd starts pushing, you think those little ones will be able to keep on their feet?"

Elsie's knife disappeared as quickly as it had come out. "I don't disagree with you. But this is all Moth's plan, not mine. We just follow orders."

Ruadh grunted, his eyes back on the procession. Thane, the arch-priest, and the two consuls were getting onto the stage, while the other weavers and Lumins remained standing on either side of it, Lumins on the left and weavers on the right. The spikes fanned out around them. There were many more stationed around the outside of the crowd, easy to spot with their bronze cloaks and glittering spears. "This could turn into a right bloodbath," he said. "The spikes have never had much patience with New Arindelers, same the other way round."

"Don't I know it." Elsie too had shaded her eyes, and was squinting first at the procession, then at the crowd. "We'll wait 'til Magister Thane starts talking. He's going first, I heard."

"Aye." *Could he really be a bloody Ilk mage?* He remembered the summer five years ago when he'd first seen Ilk. Remembered the lad, Gidion, they'd tried to kill, along with the woman who controlled them. And then the lad disappeared without a trace, Moth's best people unable to find him. Thane had been interested in the boy. Could there be a link? There had been no sign of the Ilk again until now. He'd started to think it had all been a bad dream, that the Ilk he'd seen weren't really Ilk, just creatures that looked like them. *And now, I have to go fight stoning Ilk in some Eleusian town.*

He wiped the sweat out of his eyes again and blew air up on his face to try and cool it. *Bloody heat.* The Eleusian town was in the Deepwood, Moth had said. At least he'd be out of the damn sun for a while. Hottest summer he could remember, and he could feel his face burning even though it was late.

A horn rang out and the voices of the crowd gradually began to die as all eyes were fixed on the stage. Once there was complete silence, Danial Thane began to speak. "Today is a momentous day." His words rang out loud and clear, as if he were standing right next to him. More than a few people began to murmur in surprise. Weaver magic. "This is the first time that weavers and Lumins have worked together since the Ruin, and by that, of course, we mean, for the first time ever." He smiled, and even drew a few chuckles from the listeners. "What has brought us together is you." Now a pause, to let the words sink in.

Ruadh caught the look on some of the nearby women's faces. Starry-eyed was about right. The weaver was too pretty for his own good. Even so, he didn't look evil, and Ruadh knew that evil often showed. He'd met enough bad men in his time.

"We want to help you. We have seen the filth and squalor. We have heard you talk about the crime, about the lack of work and proper housing. We know you have been forgotten about, left behind. We know you go hungry, when inside the walls others have plenty to eat, and we want to change all that."

"Do you reckon they mean it?" Elsie said.

"No one cares about New Arindel. This is just some game they're playing." *A Lumin working with an Ilk mage. Does she know, or is she in on it too?* He'd love the answer to that question.

Thane kept talking, announcing plans for how they were going to replace the shanties with real buildings, dig sewers, and pave roads. He listened with increasing skepticism. Would the weaver families really stump up enough money for all this, as Thane promised? What was in it for them? More power, he supposed. The weavers weren't loved by New Arindelers. Most of them came from the poorer parts of Vycenia, where the Lumins were strongest. He looked at Nuria, standing close to Thane, nodding and smiling along to his words. She was attractive enough for a priest, with her black hair and eyes. She seemed genuine, but Ruadh had no doubt there was cold calculation lurking under the surface.

"That's the clock," Elsie said. "It's time."

Indeed, more than one clock was ringing out the seventh hour, bells echoing all around. Ruadh caught the eyes of a tall, blond Northlander standing at the back of the crowd, not too far from the shack on which Ruadh was sitting. He gave him a thumbs up and the man responded with the same. Moments later, he and some of the men around him began chanting in unison, "Weaver scum, get out of our slum!" Some nearby men turned on them. Telling them to be quiet, maybe. Then the pushing and shoving started. Women shrieked and tried to move away, holding their children close. Fists started to fly and then a counter chant was struck up. When Ruadh finally made out what it was, he snorted. "Lily face get out of this place!" Trust Southerners to come up with a stupid insult like that. Not all Northlanders even had fair skin. He looked for the spikes. They were on the move, using the shafts of their spears to prod and poke people out of the way. "Right, let's get on to the shop," he said to Elsie.

She answered by getting smoothly to her feet and making for the ladder. Ruadh followed her, the chants echoing in his ears. "Weaver scum get out of our slum! Lily face, get out of this place!"

The pawnshop was a half-minute's walk to the south through New Arindel's stinking streets. Three of Moth's men were standing across from the shop and stepped forward to join them as soon as they arrived.

"Remember, no killings, no edged weapons," Elsie said to them. "We go in there, drag the smug fucker out, rough him up a little, set fire to the shop. Then put the blaze out before the whole street goes up."

Ruadh marched up to the door, roared, "Let's show him what we do to misers here!" He raised his right knee and then smashed his foot into the flimsy wooden door, once, twice, leaving a large, splintered hole. Not satisfied, he rammed the door with his shoulder, and it fell to the ground with a crash.

The pawnbroker, a pot-bellied little man, stared at him white-faced from behind a rough counter as he marched in. He had two toughs with him, but they were in on it too, and didn't try to stop Ruadh from dragging him out onto the street.

"Hold him, lads!" Ruadh said. Two of Moth's men gripped the pawnbroker while Ruadh, Elsie,and the third man scooped some of the rank mixture of piss, shit, and mud that oozed between the shacks. "Let's see how you like the taste of your own medicine!" He hurled the stinking mud at the man, and it splattered all over his pudgy face, running in streams down his chin and onto his chest. More mud hit his round belly and skinny legs. Some passers-by stopped to join in, yelling fresh insults as they pelted the pawnbroker.

Ruadh wiped his hand with a rag and ducked back into the shop, taking it all in with a single look. There was nothing but the counter and a shabby, red curtain that covered a gap in the wall behind it. He vaulted over the counter and pushed the curtain aside to make sure no one was hiding there. Nothing except for markings in the earth that showed where containers had previously sat. Locked safes no doubt, removed in advance by the pawnbroker. Moth had given him that little mercy.

Returning to the front of the shop, Ruadh took out his fire kit and threw some oil onto the counter and curtain. Then he struck up a flame and put it to the oil before running back outside. The pawnbroker was now sniveling, begging to be let go as more gathered to sling mud and shit at him. Seconds later, the flames reached the walls of the shop, and the mudslingers fell back with cries and curses. As pre-arranged, Moth's men let the pawnbroker go, and he staggered off in the direction of the river.

Ruadh slipped into the workshop across the street, where barrels of water had been stashed earlier in the day. A pair of skinny youths were lounging against a workbench. "Right lads, fire's blazing, off you go."

The youths grabbed the nearest of the barrels between them and staggered outside. Ruadh followed them out and then shouted to the gathered crowd, who had suddenly found themselves with nothing to do but stare at the licking flames.

"The spikes have started attacking Northlanders at the commons. Let's show them we won't be bullied!" he roared. It worked exactly like expected. The crowd had had a taste of trouble, and now they were hungry for more. Pausing only to pluck sticks or stones out of the mud, they ran for the commons, calling on others to join them as they went.

Ruadh found Elsie by the pawnbroker's, directing the fire extinguishing efforts. "Time for me to go."

"Lucky you," she said.

If you knew I was off to fight stoning Ilk, you wouldn't think so. "Enjoy the fun." He struck out westward toward the stables housing his horse and the rest of his gear. But he'd barely gone ten paces when he saw thick, black smoke rising a couple of streets ahead of him. Then an explosion shattered the air. Ruadh stopped and stared in astonishment as wood, metal, and flames burst into the sky. Shouts and screams quickly followed. "Ruin and stoning ruination!" This hadn't been part of the plan. He broke into a run and was soon enveloped in billowing smoke that burned his eyes and throat. Flames in purple, blue, and orange were leaping high into the sky, spreading from building to building with unnatural speed. He stumbled over something, looked down, saw the body of a young man. His left arm had been blown off, his face frozen in open-mouthed shock.

Some people were already throwing water at the flames, but without much effect. Others were shouting at the burning remains of a collapsed shack, trying to move in and search, but beaten back by the flames.

Shit and fucking shit. This is going to go to the pits. But he couldn't stay, couldn't afford to let himself get caught by the spikes. He turned away, thinking to circle around.

"Please, mister. You look strong. It's my little one, she's in there, under that timber. She's alive, I know it. Please help, mister." The woman was thin and sharp-featured, still very young, hardly more than a girl herself. She was pointing to a heap of wet, splintered wood and smoldering canvas.

"I'm not sure anyone could—"

"Lara, Lara, there's a man come to help," called the woman.

A tiny trembling voice cried "mama" in reply.

The fire from the nearby buildings was so close that he could feel the burn of it against his face. But he couldn't just leave. "Wait here." He moved in and started to lift the first of the pieces of wood, moving slowly so as not to dislodge any more of the rubble and accidentally crush the child. The heat intensified as fresh flames leaped up close to him. More screams as another building collapsed. His hands were sore, his throat raw from smoke, but he could see the child now, a flash of bluish cloth and flesh underneath the canvas. He cleared the last of the obstructions and gently pulled her out. Other than some scratches and bruises, she seemed unharmed, blinking at him silently as he carried her to safety. Even as he was doing so, there was another explosion, followed by a fresh burst of heat and a noxious, bitter smell. Ruadh muttered some choice curses under his breath. Innocents were going to die. "Life isn't bloody fair, though, is it."

"Thank you so much, mister, may the Lady shine on you always. I'll light a candle for you in the temple," the woman was saying.

He waved away her thanks, turning his attention to a clump of people who were running toward the flames rather than away. The Watch, and a couple of weavers. Thank the Lady for that. It was going to take more than water to deal with these flames.

"Get far away from here," he said to the woman. "Things are going to get worse before they get better. Do you know anyone who lives inside the walls?"

"My cousin." She hugged her child close.

"Well go to your cousin, don't come back until you hear it's safe. I have to go now."

"Lady be with you, mister!" the woman said again as he began to run.

Chapter 42

Fay

A Lumin priest must not commit crimes against the laws of any state. They will be judged and sentenced according to the laws of the offended state. Those found guilty of murder will be expelled from the priesthood. Those guilty of lesser crimes must appear before archpriest of their region to receive an additional sentencing. At its most severe, the priest will be defrocked or expelled.

—The Lumin Priest's Handbook

Fay sat on her bed, trying to read the book on Eleusian history she'd stolen from the Archpriests' Library a couple of days earlier. She was still working through the first chapter, which talked about Eleusia's origins as a small kingdom in southern Teleriol. But she struggled to focus, her mind constantly working over the planned escape. What if Alexios was already taken away, murdered? She'd been to check on him in the early morning, going straight from Papa Julia's to avoid Lothar. He'd said the Ilk mage hadn't returned but that his food and water were low, which could mean another visit soon. Danial Thane would be busy with the rally today, though, and then the riot. It should be safe enough, shouldn't it?

The rally made her think of Nuria. She felt guilty that they were destroying the archpriest's carefully laid plans. She was probably in the slum already, preparing to speak. Fay should have gone with her but had pleaded sickness. *Unless, of course, she's in on it all with Thane.* The idea of a Lumin archpriest working with Ilk mages was somehow more frightening than that of the Ilk mages themselves.

The bell rang out for evening prayers, jolting her out of her thoughts. Setting the book aside, she got up to light her candle clock. In three hours, the kitchen and cellars would be empty, and she'd be able to move the ladder to the tunnel entrance. The rally was most certainly underway.

Lest she forget later, she removed the vial of sleepfast from her chest and put it in her pocket—a backup plan for getting Arianna out in case things went wrong with Alexios. On impulse, she also took out the bottle of apricot brandy. Only a few sips, to settle her nerves. But it did little to soothe her. The very thought of returning to Alexios's Gloom-filled prison was draining her strength. She dreaded facing the voices in the darkness again. What if they bumped into the Ilk mage? Yes, Zethir was coming with her, but if they came up against the likes of Danial Thane, he wouldn't stand a chance. Danial Thane was one of the most powerful weavers in the world, if not *the* most powerful.

Fay swallowed another gulp of brandy, then put it away determinedly. She couldn't let her mind fog up. She went back to her bed, picked up the book again, read the same lines over and over. Glanced at the candle clock, kept glancing, until finally, the wax had burned down to the right mark. A surge of energy borne by relief. Time, at last, to move, get it all done with.

A knock at the door. Who would come at this hour?

Icy fear leaped in her. *No, please not.* The handle turned. *Him, him, it must be him.* She stayed completely still. Let him think she wasn't there. The handle turned again. Then she heard something rattling in the keyhole. A key? *Shit, shit.* The lock tripped.

A creak as the door opened, revealing the gold-banded robes of an archpriest.

Lothar.

Fay rushed to the door, thinking to slam it shut. But by the time she reached it, he was already over the threshold. Her puny efforts were nothing against his weight and size, and she stumbled as he pushed the door back against her.

He stepped into the room, shutting the door with his back. His pale blue eyes gleamed with malice. "I've been waiting long enough."

"Get out," she said, her voice quavering. Panic was turning her limbs to liquid.

Lothar locked the door with her own key. Then he put the key into his pocket. "I'll have my report, but first, I'll have you, sweet whore," he said, lumbering toward her.

She stood frozen, mind and body refusing to react.

He grabbed her by the shoulders. Her nose filled with the reek of his sweat. "Get on the bed."

"Please, leave me alone," she whispered. *No, no, no, no, no.*

"Oh, come on, you're a whore. Enough of this false modesty." He tugged on her girdle with one hand, the other pushing her onto her bed. She felt the frame against the back of her knees, used it to try and resist him. It was no good. He shoved her hard, and she fell onto the mattress. But he also lost his balance, and as he grabbed the bedpost to steady himself, she wormed out of his reach and scrambled out of the bed. He grabbed the back of her robe and whirled her around so violently that she fell against him.

One meaty paw squeezed her breast, the other her behind, and the hard ridge of his prick pressed against her belly. Then, he shoved her back onto the bed again. She scrabbled back, looking around desperately for some weapon. There was only the book, and she flung it at his head. It crashed into his face, knocking him back, and he shouted in anger and pain. She rolled off the bed and onto her feet.

"You're becoming tiresome," he growled, trying to snatch at her robe and missing. His face had reddened, and his breathing was coming in little puffs.

She tried to think through the dizzying panic, but no ideas came to her. Then her eyes fell on her trunk. In there, a knife. Why in Lumia's holy name had she not kept that knife on her person? She backed over to the trunk, hands outstretched to ward Lothar off.

He came at her again as she reached the trunk and slammed her against the wall.

A stunned moment during which he grabbed her hair and yanked her face toward his. Smell of cloves. Wet tongue forcing itself through her lips. Then some survival instinct kicked in, and she smashed her knee up between his legs. He howled, bending over to clutch his injured parts.

Fay squeezed around him, dipped to unlock the trunk, then threw it open. She slid her hand down the side until she found the knife in its sheath. She drew the blade free and pressed it against the side of his neck. "Leave now."

He looked up at her, eyes watering with tears. "Just," he gasped. "Just ... a moment."

"Go," she said, trying to sound strong and in command. "Go now." She pressed the blade harder against his neck, nicking the skin. Tiny beads of blood welled out.

Lothar half straightened, fury mingling with pain in his pale blue eyes. "I'll punish you for this," he said. "Don't think I won't."

The tone of his voice sent new waves of terror through her, but she kept her voice firm and told him again to go. To the pits with Moth, she wasn't going to let this disgusting oaf touch her again.

He waddled toward the door. She watched him, trying to hold in a ferocious need to piss. All of a sudden, he turned and lunged, faster than she'd ever seen him move. He grabbed the wrist of her knife hand and twisted sharply, causing the blade to clatter to the ground. Then he flung a blow to her head that sent her reeling sideways. He crouched to pick up the knife, but she recovered in time to stamp on his fingers with a sandaled foot. He screeched in pain. She kicked at his face with her heel. He grabbed her foot and yanked it.

She tumbled to the ground, head cracking against the floor. Stars danced across her eyes. His foot smashed down between her ribs, and the breath exploded out of her. She doubled over, gasping for air. By the time she had begun to recover, he had untied his robes, revealing his swollen cock. Fat, like a pork sausage.

He knelt over her, clasping a large hand over her mouth, pressing her head down painfully against the floor and leaving her little room to breathe from her nose.

There was something hard against her back, digging into her spine. The knife. She slid a hand beneath her. If she moved slowly enough ...

He pushed her legs apart using his knees, one hand still maintaining its crushing weight on her face, the other working to pull her robes up. She didn't resist so he wouldn't try to pin her arms. Instead, she kept moving her hand up ever so slowly, seeking the hilt of the knife.

He worked his hips between her legs as her hand closed on the knife. As his hand reached down to his groin, she swept the blade out. The tip of his member brushed the inside of her leg, and he grunted as he adjusted himself. She stabbed the knife into his side, but it lodged in a rib. Even so, he shrieked, his hand crushing her lips against her teeth as he tried to get away from her. Metallic taste of blood. She stabbed him again, this time getting the meat of his thigh. He fell away screaming, landing on his behind.

She scrambled back to her feet. *What next, what next?* Her eyes lit on the water jug at the other end of the room. She ran over, grabbed it, and smashed it against the back of his head. He dropped to the ground, eyes rolling up blankly.

Take that, you prick. But no time for gloating. She needed to get out. She ran to the door, remembered he had her key. Was he still unconscious? Yes. She hunkered down, rifled through his robes, found the key, and leaped back up. Then she noticed the blood. All over her hand and arm, all over her clothing. *Shit, fuck.* She tore off her robe, used it to wipe the blood off her skin, then went to the wardrobe and snatched another one.

As she was changing, Lothar groaned and stirred. *Pits, don't wake up.* No time to get dressed properly. She half tied her girdle, then, with shaking hands, unlocked the door. But as she started down the hallway, she realized she needed to stop Lothar from getting out. When he woke, he was sure to sound the alarm. So she doubled back, locked the door, and then half-walked, half-ran, to the cellars.

But when she got to the kitchen, one of the kitchen maids was in there, clearing out the ashes of the fire. She looked around in surprise when Fay entered. *Pits.* With an effort, Fay smoothed her expression and drew herself to full height. "Good night."

The girl got to her feet and pressed her palms together, bowing her head. "Good night, Your Light."

Her instinct was to start spouting excuses for her presence, but Fay suppressed it. She had no need to explain herself to a kitchen maid. Instead, with head high, she strode on through the kitchen and into the top cellar. But she was unable to shake an uneasy feeling that she was being watched and followed, her every nerve jangling.

She saw no sign of the ladder in the first cellar and her anxiety increased a notch. It must surely be somewhere? Hardly daring to breathe, she went into the second cellar, and there it was, by the door. A small shot of relief. She dragged the ladder over to the wine racks in front of the tunnel entrance, wiped the sweat from her forehead, considered the wine bottles. *I should take one to cover myself.* She grabbed the nearest one and returned to the kitchen. The girl was still there, scraping away, but avoided Fay's gaze, which suited her fine. She made her way to the side exit of the temple, still clutching the wine, to meet Nim and Zethir out near the woods.

Outside, it was purpling into twilight. The sky to the west was still bright, with tinges of red and orange, but black smoke was billowing in the air beyond the city walls. Ruadh's fire. Fay prayed that no one would be badly hurt, but with that much smoke, it seemed unlikely. *No one ever cares about New Arindel.*

She set off toward Spire Gate, marching at full speed in the warm night. Her mind was all Lothar, his vile breath, his grasping hands, his fat, bouncing cock. Would he tell the truth about her in retaliation? Probably. Although that might depend on him getting out of her room unseen. If he called for help, he'd have to explain himself. Archpriests didn't visit the rooms of common priestesses, certainly not at this hour. But even if he said nothing, she couldn't go back to the temple. He'd get her eventually, and she couldn't let that happen.

I need to give Moth something else, something better. But she couldn't think of what might please him. She should get away, go to another city or town. Maybe she could send a message to Moth later, apologize, beg for his forgiveness.

Spire Gate rose ahead of her. It was closed, but there was a small door to the side, manned by a pair of guards. "I need to leave."

The guards, noting her Lumin robes, opened the door for her without question. She hurried through, heard it shut behind her. Soon, she reached the crossroads where she was to meet Nim and Zethir. No sign of them. *Pits, have they gone already? They can't have.*

But then they appeared out of the darkness. Zethir's face was blank, but Nim looked furious. "Where you been?" he demanded. "We been waiting ages. Thought you wasn't gonna come."

"I got held up," she said. "Come on, let's just go."

"I agree," Zethir said shortly, and she realized he was also annoyed, only showing it less.

They walked toward the woods and the small track that she and Zethir had followed after finding Alexios. Fay found herself constantly peering into the darkness for the Ilk mage, jumping at every creak of a branch or snapping of a twig. The trees also cast distorted shadows as they passed through them, making her think of Ilk.

The oak that marked the turnoff for the tunnel exit was closer than she remembered, and before long they had reached the boulder that guarded it. Zethir used his magic to move it aside, then crouched by the side of the entrance holding his glowglobe above it. "Go," he said, taking her and Nim in together with his gaze.

Nim hopped down first, then Fay. Zethir followed, rolling the boulder back into place after him. They made their way down the tunnel, and dread dug its claws more deeply into her. *This will be the last time.* But the thought did little to calm her.

They reached the entrance to the old temple, and Zethir put his glowglobe away to light a lamp. Then he pushed the door open, revealing the Gloom. He stepped through, his lamp fading to a flicker.

"I ain't goin' in there," Nim said, standing before the doorway.

"We have to," Fay said. She grabbed hold of his skinny arm and hauled him through, making him stumble.

Darkness enveloped them, and then began its whisperings. "*Murdering little whore, killed him, didn't you?*"

Fay tried to tell herself that Lothar wasn't dead, that he deserved what he'd got and more.

"*Not the first time you've killed, though,*" said the darkness.

Rotting flesh, sickly sweet smell of it. Pa, blubbering. "*Please, please stop. Stop! I gave you life. You owe me. You owe me, you little bitch whore.*" Worms crawling around his ribs and eye sockets.

"*Murderer. They'll hunt you down, squeeze the life out of you with the rope.*"

Nim tried to pull away from her, jolting her free of the voice's hypnotic words. "Let me go!" he shouted. "Let me go!"

Fay hung on to him. "It's the Gloom. The voice isn't real, ignore it."

Except *she* couldn't ignore it. The voice was mocking her relentlessly. "*Just a little, loveless whore, good for nothing more.*"

"I ain't stayin' here!" Nim yanked himself free. He took two steps toward the door before Zethir got hold of him, but he slipped out of the weaver's grasp and ran.

"Fuck!" Fay cursed as she and Zethir both chased after him.

Nim was only a few paces ahead of them in the tunnel, but Zethir raised his red focus stone. It flared briefly and Nim went sprawling to the ground.

Magic. Fay shivered.

The weaver marched over to Nim and hauled him to his feet using the back of his shirt. “Pull yourself together,” Zethir snapped. “Be a man.”

Nim stared at him with wide, terrified eyes. Blood seeped out from a cut on his pointed chin.

“Nim, we need you in there,” Fay said more gently. “The Eleusian has been locked in that prison for days. We need to free him.”

Nim shoved a hand into his pocket and then pulled out something brown and spongey. Raw skybark. He popped it into his mouth and began to chew. Fay winced. It was horribly acrid. But Nim hardly seemed to notice.

Disgust plain on his face, Zethir grabbed hold of Nim’s elbow. The boy didn’t try to resist, but Fay took hold of his other arm, just in case. She felt bad. He was little more than a child. Probably had as many bad memories as she did. The Gloom liked those.

They returned to the lightless temple, and this time, Nim didn’t try to escape. She could feel his trembling, though, and it mirrored her own. Up the stairs they went, and to her relief, the door was still bolted. No Ilk mage.

Zethir told her to open the door, while he kept a firm grip on Nim, holding his lamp in the other hand.

They got the door open, heard a clanking as Alexios shifted position.

“We’ve come to free you,” she said, following the sounds of the manacles to the far corner of the room.

“Demeia?” His voice was faint, much fainter than before.

The puny light of her lamp fell on his face. His eyes sunken. Dulled and distant, like he was seeing something else. He blinked at her, seemed to return to the present. “You came back.”

"Are you alright?" she asked him, then cursed herself for an idiot. Of course he wasn't alright.

Alexios didn't answer, his eyes instead going to Nim, standing next to her, Zethir behind him, a hand on his shoulder.

"Do what you have to do," she said to Nim.

"Shine a light on the lock," he said, opening his waist pouch. He removed his picks and then knelt to work on Alexios's manacles. His hands were shaking visibly, and it took him a few moments to get a pick into the keyhole. Meanwhile, Zethir went to the doorway and stood facing the outer room.

At last, Nim succeeded in tripping the lock, and Alexios was free.

Fay gave him novice robes to change into, turning away from him as he changed.

"I'm done," he said hoarsely.

She faced him again.

He was on his knees, trying to get up. Hand against the wall, one foot on the ground, then the second. But when he tried to transfer his weight he fell forward onto his hands and knees.

"Help me get him to his feet," Fay said to Zethir.

The weaver silently came over, and they each took hold of one of Alexios's arms to get him upright. He stood sagging between them, breathing heavily.

Nim scooped up the manacles. "Moth wants these," he said.

They exited the prison and went to the cellar entrance. Fay tripped the mechanism to open the hidden door and stuck her head out—no one there, and the ladder was still in place. Zethir sent his glowglobe floating through, and she clambered down. She stood at the bottom of the ladder as Alexios came after her.

He made his way slowly and unsteadily. Fay was sure he'd lose his grip and fall, and stood ready to catch him. A click as the door to the tunnel shut, hiding Zethir and Nim. Their part was done, and she wouldn't see them again.

Alexios's feet touched the ground. "I think I can walk," he said, his voice still faint. But he took only three steps before staggering and nearly falling again.

"Wait here. I'll put the ladder back and then help you," she said. She moved the ladder to where she'd found it and then took hold of his arm. "Lean on me."

He did, rather heavily, and the effort of climbing the steps into the kitchen caused his breathing to harshen further. "Are you going to be able to use your magic?" she said.

"I'm ... not sure ..." he said, squeezing his eyes closed a moment. "I'll ... try." He stopped and stared at his hand, and then suddenly reeled against her, sending them both crashing against the wall. "I can't, not yet," he said when they had righted themselves. "I'm too weak."

Pits! "Let's rest here a little. You can have something to eat and drink." She brought Alexios to a stool by the large kitchen table, then gathered up some bread and cheese. She also poured him water and a measure of cooking brandy. "It won't taste very good, but it should wake you up," she said of the brandy.

Looking at him eat with his shaking hands, Fay realized they would have to resort to the backup plan and put the guards to sleep. He was obviously in no condition to spin illusions, even if the food did help. She put her hand into her robe to get the vial of sleepfast and then froze. The vial of sleepfast was in her other robes. The one she had torn off herself after stabbing Lothar. *Pits, shit, fuck, fuck, fuck. What are we going to do now?*

Chapter 43

Ina

In the past, the greater good of one's tribe was paramount. No individual was above it, not even the elkiri who ruled the tribe. But this rationale was used to justify continual war—against other tribes, against the Eleusians. Since the Exile, we are but one tribe, one people. We are the people of Chel, and our every action must be to protect their world and the creatures within it.

—Teachings of Old Tsu

"Why didn't you at least try to deny it?" Mia said, sitting next to Ina in her prison.

The despair in her mother's face made her feel guilty. And she was realizing now that she'd gone about it all wrong. She'd pushed much too hard. Accusing the elders had been a bad move, it had only hardened them against her. But she'd been so angry. Fear and shame of what she was had blackened her whole life. And all because of a lie.

"Do you think the elders know the truth?" she said.

"About what?" Mia said. "You said yourself Lin'Elkir returned secretly. Takan'Ri may never have known it was put there by Lin."

"The curse, they lied about the curse," Ina said.

"Not lies, Ina. A perspective," Mia replied, sounding exasperated.

"A perspective that says murdering children is peace!"

"The powers of old are clearly dangerous. Even in your leviathan's version, magic-users caused Sīut's Price. Who's to say they weren't guided by Sīut?"

Ina felt as if she'd been slapped in the face. "So you think I should die too?" she said in little more than a whisper.

"Of course not!" Mia said, seizing both of Ina's arms. "You are my daughter, ever since you were born my whole life's task has been to protect you. But you don't listen!" Mia shook her hard, and then to Ina's complete surprise, burst into tears.

"But it can't be one way for me and another for everyone else," Ina said. "You can't save me and yet choose to abandon Tani." Where was Suni now, Ina wondered. Oh, to see her face, to hold her hand and hear her voice.

Mia released Ina and wiped her tears. "It was a great risk to try and help Tani," she said. "Look where it got us."

"It got us the truth," Ina said. "Even if they kill me, the Godstone is broken. It will betray no more children." *And who knows, maybe that was the whole of my task, to destroy the Godstone, so that other elkiri are born and survive. Maybe I'm the last sacrifice, along with poor Tani.* The thought of Tani, sweet, pure little Tani, being given poison to drink, was awful, the thought of Suni witnessing that even more awful. It would surely break her. *There must be a way to save Tani. Something I can do!*

"If you had kept quiet, they might have set you free. And then you would have been able to continue with whatever purpose it is you think Chel has for you."

Ina realized that now, and it made her sick to think how she'd thrown the chance to save Tani away with rashness and heated words. "Maybe I'll have convinced enough of them," she said, more for her mother's sake than her own. She thought of the Games, due to start in ten days. It was unlikely she'd take part in them, that she'd even be still alive by the time they began. How would Oyu feel about that? Horrified to learn she was cursed, glad she was gone?

"I doubt you convinced anyone of anything other than that you are mad as well as cursed," Mia said.

Ina agreed with her mother, but years of conflict kept her from showing it. She'd been foolish to think that the elders would change five centuries of tradition and belief simply because the Godstone was broken, because Ina had attacked them with the truth. She'd thought the elders had known about the Godstone somehow, that faced with their own lies, they'd back down. They were the elders, they were supposed to know everything. But her mother was right, if Lin'Elkir had returned in total secrecy, how would they have known her intentions? Still, it had been wrong to murder children all these years.

The door shutter rolled up again, and Jiu'Ri entered, bearing a cup, Mūak hovering behind. "You must drink this," he said, hunkering down and holding it out to her.

"More clawtongue?" Ina asked.

"You must drink," he repeated, firmly but not unkindly.

Ina considered refusing. What would he do to her if she did say no? Would he spear her immediately? Or send Mūak in to do it? Surely, he'd wait until the elders had spoken?

"I'll have to force you if you don't drink it willingly," Jiu'Ri said.

"She's already full of it," Mia said. "Can't you see how weak she is?"

"She must drink."

"I'll drink," Ina said, not wanting to stir up more anger against her.

Jiu'Ri tipped the cup so that the tepid liquid poured into her mouth. It had been sweetened, so she couldn't taste the clawtongue. The small kindness heartened her. Perhaps they'd listen after all.

When he and Mūak left, her mother surprised her with a question. "What did you see of ... of old Chelakan?"

"It was beautiful," Ina said, allowing her mind to fill again with great forests that had stretched from coast to coast, cut through by deep valleys and rushing streams. To the north lay the great mountain range that had separated Chelakan from Eleusia, its highest peaks covered in snow all year round. The Chelaki had only ever had one city, which they'd shared with the Eleusians during the time of Gala Peacemaker. It was built high in those same mountains, and its gleaming towers had caught the sunlight from dusk to dawn.

As Ina described Chelakan to her mother, she found that her mind began to clear a little and that some of her energy returned to her. Could the last dose of clawtongue have been a weak one? She tried opening her mind to the Cloth, but the fog barrier was still there, the Cloth muted and inaccessible. *Just my desperate imagination*.

The door shutter rolled up again, admitting Jiu'Ri and Mūak. The Elder appeared stiff and withdrawn, but Mūak was brimming with satisfaction. Ina guessed from that what the outcome of the deliberations had been.

Her suspicions were confirmed as soon as she re-entered the meeting room. The elders regarded her almost unanimously with the same, stony expression. Only two seemed uncomfortable. One of those was Jiu, the other a woman from Yon'il, with long, white hair and intense eyes, whose name she couldn't recall. Lana'Ri maybe. She carried no spear or other weapon but stood with her hands clasped in front of her.

"It has been deemed that through your own words, you have admitted to being cursed. You have broken the Godstone and are clearly a pawn of Sīut. In accordance with the laws of our people, you are to be sent back to Chel," said Naomi'Ri in a flat, toneless, voice. "You will be given the starweed potion now, as you should have drunk it fourteen years ago and are a danger to our people."

Mia's wail of despair cut across the room but left the elders unmoved.

But Ina's fear had melted away. Instead, she was angry—at their short-sightedness, their arrogance, their presumptions and lies.

"You may say some last words," Naomi said.

Ina decided she might as well continue on the attack and die proudly rather than in shame. "You're right about one thing," she said, thrusting her chin up. "I am Ina'Elkir, descended from the last skyrider, Lin'Elkir. I have her self-same powers, granted to me by Chel, who put me in this world."

Outrage among the elders, many of whom shouted at her, having lost all possession of themselves. But even as Ina finished speaking, she felt the last of the fog lift from her, and her unprepared mind was assaulted by a barrage of emotion and sensation, the Cloth coming glimmering into view. She glanced at Jiu, who was regarding her silently and intently. *There was no clawtongue in that last potion,* she realized exultantly. *That's at least one I've managed to convince.* But she needed to think quickly—how might she use her returned powers to save herself? Could she splice now, with Lin's memories to guide her? She needed to make more time for herself. The clamor was dying, and Alik'Ri had picked up a cup, which surely contained the starweed potion.

Ina spoke again loudly. "In that you are right, but in everything else, you are wrong. If you ignore the warning of the Godstone, our people will be finished, and the Cloth shredded by Sīut's true pawns. In sending me back to Chel, you send away our hope of survival and true peace."

"Don't let her speak anymore poison!" Niak'Ri spat.

Alik'Ri had been moving toward her in slow, ceremonial fashion, but now picked up the pace. Those elders who had been hunters followed behind him, holding spears. Her words had had the opposite effect to what she'd intended.

Breathing slowly to control her fear, she let herself be flooded with Lin's memories, parsing through them for instructions on how to splice, and there were many. No need for hand gestures to open onto the Sīut's Realm, she discovered. Those were only for show. And yes, she could see where she'd gone wrong before, too much force here, and not enough there, a need to access and channel more of her inner strength. She could do it. She could open a path back to the Godstone. With the storm raging outside, the elders wouldn't be able to follow her there for a time. She began to part the Cloth.

Alik'Ri halted before her, and the spear-wielding elders circled around. "Drink," he said, "Or you will be speared where you stand."

The tip of a spear pressed against her side, right over her liver.

"No." Ina finished her splice and stepped into Sīut's Realm.

The world vanished. In its place was a bone-crushing pressure, as if invisible fingers were squeezing tightly around her but at the same time pulling her out, tearing her apart. She could see nothing, smell nothing, touch nothing. There was no color, no sound, nothing to stand on, nothing to hold on to. Worse, there was no air. Her lungs began to heave, and panic seized her. Was this where it ended? In Sīut's Realm, like the elders had warned?

But even as she thought this, the blank ahead of her resolved itself into color and shape, to violet storm clouds and bare grey rock. She was ejected violently through the opening, landing on her face and smacking her chin against the ground. A blinding headache shot up through her left eye, and her stomach churned and heaved. She struggled to her hands and feet and vomited weakly onto the wet rock beneath her.

It was only once the heaving had stopped that she became conscious of the rain, pummeling her with all the fury of the storm. Still on all fours, she raised her head and peered from left to right. She was back on Uruk'il's peak. The Godstone was broken into large, jagged pieces that had fallen more or less where it had once stood. Lightning cut across the sky, immediately followed by a sharp crack of thunder. Then she remembered her chin and carefully touched it with her fingertips. They came away red with blood. She felt at the wound some more, trying to gauge how deep and how wide it was. Not too serious, but enough blood that she would probably have had Suni sew it in ordinary times.

She tried to get to her feet, but the wind was so strong that it threatened to topple her. Too weak to stand against it, she crawled across the slick, wet rock to the path that led down to the beach. The first part was very steep, so she turned herself to go down feet first. She continued like this until the path spiraled around to the leeward side, where she was finally free of the wind. Here, she staggered back to her feet and walked until she came to a rocky overhang two-thirds of the way down. There was just enough space beneath it for her to squeeze in if she lay flat. She went right up to the opening, then stretched herself out on her back and used her heels to slowly slide herself in, the rock scraping against her bare legs. The space was so narrow that her nose practically touched the rock, but at least she was out of the rain and wind. And now she needed to think.

She had three options, none of them appealing. She could try and live on the island, for a time at least. It wouldn't be too difficult to harvest food from the sea, the rocks, and the many bird's nests. And while there were no streams or permanent freshwater pools, the storms would provide her with enough rainwater to survive. But it was the storms that also presented the most danger—the island didn't have much shelter, and when the biggest storms came, the waves could reach up almost as high as she was now. Her people would eventually come, too, maybe as soon as the storm died if they'd guessed where she'd gone.

The second alternative was to try summoning the leviathan again, ask him to take her somewhere else. Perhaps there were other islands in the Endless Sea, more habitable ones. But she wasn't sure that he would want to carry her again, and did she really want to spend the rest of her life on some lonely island with no one to talk to but the birds?

The third option, of course, was to try and go to the barbarian lands and seek out those who had gone into exile there. Perhaps they hadn't shunned the elkiri and would welcome her. Maybe the drakiri were even there.

It didn't take long for her to realize this was by far the most logical option. After all, Lin had created a waystone so that she could do just that. Not that she'd ever heard of such a thing as a waystone before. And where had Lin put it? Despite what she'd said to her mother, she wasn't sure it was the Godstone itself. She had the impression Lin had used something else. The memories were no real help. Mostly, they were flashes and fragments of people and places she had never known. It wasn't like when she'd been asleep, when the memories had played like more or less coherent dreams. She called to mind the dream about the moment Lin had returned to Uruk'il, but she couldn't see the waystone in it. And if it was the Godstone, then the way was gone, because the Godstone was broken.

There was another consideration—Suni and Tani. Almost as clearly as if her beloved were standing before her, she saw Suni's hair dance when it was picked up by a sea breeze. She wore that shy but warm smile that stole over her whenever she and Ina met in their place in the woods. Ina knew that she couldn't leave without her. The very thought made her ill. And she had promised to help Tani. There had to be a way to take them both with her. Lin had sent entire units through Sīut's Realm. "*Only very experienced splicers can carry others through ol'Sīut.* The words weren't her own, but Ina pounced on them, tried to follow their thread to an instruction. "*Practice with one person first and hold them close to you.*" She was granted a brief image, no more than a flicker, of Lin holding the arm of an older, dark-haired man—her teacher, maybe—as she made a hole in the Cloth. And that was it. Ina kept digging, hoping to find something else that might be useful, but the few images that came to her were confused, gone almost as soon as she grasped them.

After a while, she gave up and decided instead to focus on the waystone. Where had Lin put it, and how was she to use it? But even as she started sifting through the memories again, her eyelids fluttered, then closed. She forced them open again. She had no time for sleep! She had to figure out how to get away before she went back for Tani and Suni. But her exhaustion was so complete it felt as if she hadn't slept for days, and her mind kept drifting to random thoughts that turned into the beginning of dreams, until at last, she succumbed.

Chapter 44

Fay

This world is not a safe one, and the only way to guarantee independence is to have an army of our own. It is for this reason that the Defenders of Light exist. We are the only entity permitted to have a private army in Vycenia, as it should be. The Council knows the Defenders would come to the country's aid if we were ever to suffer an attack.

—The Lumin Priest's Handbook

Fay sat for an anxious half hour with Alexios in the kitchen as they waited for the food and drink to reach his starved body. All the while, she cursed herself for a fool for having forgotten the sleepfast. The only other she could think of was to attack the guards, but she'd need to get Zethir for that, and he was long away.

"I feel stronger now," Alexios said, breaking the silence. "Let me see what I can do." He stood, and this time seemed steadier. Then he took in a deep breath, fixing his gaze on the fire.

Fay watched, astounded, as it gradually turned into a plain brick wall. His next target was the kitchen table. Bit by bit, it too disappeared, so that it seemed there was nothing but the grey kitchen tiles.

Abruptly, both the fire and table returned to view. "I think can do it, but it will be difficult," he said, his breathing harsh again. "It might be better if I go into the prison cell alone to get the Guardian. You stay outside."

But Fay had another idea. "I'll take a bottle of wine to the guards," she said, "and talk to them to keep them distracted in case your illusion fails."

"A good plan," he said.

Fay hurried back to the cellars to grab a bottle, picking up some glasses on the way out. Then they made their way to the prison, reaching it without incident.

Fay opened the door and went in. There were only two guards on duty—Jos and Smugface. Maybe because it was late. They were playing a game of cards with wooden chips instead of coins for stakes. Priests of Lumia were not allowed to gamble.

"Hello," she said with her most winning smile, letting her eyes linger on Jos in particular.

"Oh, Fay, here to see the prisoner again?" Jos said. "Bit late, isn't it?"

"Not this time. I thought you might like a drink. I wasn't able to sleep, and I could use some company," she said, fluttering her lashes at them both.

Even Smugface smiled in response.

"Sure, sit down," Jos said, indicating an empty chair next to him.

"Will you show me how to play that game?" she said as she poured the wine for them. *If only there were sleepfast in it!*

She took a seat, trying not to glance in the direction of the door or the keys, wondering if Alexios had already entered.

Jos took a sip of wine. "This is good," he said. "Better than the average fare."

"Of course," she replied. "You work so hard down here, and at all hours. You deserve something nice." Her eyes flicked toward the keys, and she thought she saw them move for a fraction of a second before they appeared still again. Had Alexios just taken them? She strained with her ears, terrified he'd make a sound, but there wasn't even a whisper.

Jos began to explain the game as he and Smugface continued playing. She barely paid any attention to what he was saying, her mind whirling with what-ifs. Then she heard noise from the direction of the cell, footsteps. *Pits!*

"Did you hear something from down the cells?" Jos said, looking at Smugface.

Fear locked every muscle in her body. If Alexios and Arianna were caught, she would surely be implicated. Between her note-writing and her presence here, they would soon put two and two together. She'd either hang or live as an outlaw for the rest of her life. And Moth would provide no protection. In fact, he might turn her over out of spite.

"Huh?"

"I'm sure I heard something from down the cells."

Oh dear Lumia, don't let them go down there. I want my jun shack.

"Rats. Or one of the prisoners. Who cares. You're just trying to dodge this." Smugface indicated the card he'd put down, which depicted a Vycenian consul.

"I'm not!"

"I didn't hear anything either," Fay said. "And anyway, what is there to hear? There's only the cells down there. Maybe it was a prisoner."

But Jos was getting to his feet, chair scraping on the floor, and walking toward the cells.

Fay began to mutter silent prayers to Lumia, trying to still her shaking before Smugface noticed.

Jos picked up a torch from a sconce in the wall and walked to the beginning of the passageway to the cells. He stopped and squinted, then took a couple of steps forward.

Again, Fay had a sudden, desperate need to piss. *Maybe I should make a run for it now, before they catch us all.*

Jos looked for a moment longer, then did a half shrug, and turned away.

"Told you it was rats," Smugface said as Jos was replacing the torch.

"I suppose," Jos said, returning to the table.

"So, you were telling me that this card beats all the others," Fay said, pointing to Jos's last card, which depicted a weaver. Her voice sounded far too high to her ears.

"No, no, the opposite," Smugface replied. "It's one of the weakest cards in the deck. That's why he's in trouble."

"Not as much trouble as you think," Jos said, putting down a card of an archpriest.

Smugface laughed ruefully. "Alright, alright, trick's yours."

Jos grinned and swept up the cards into a pile which he put next to him.

Whispering noises in the guardroom. Fay talked quickly to try and cover them. "Can we try playing a game together? I learn better when I play."

"When we're done with this one," Smugface said, slapping down a card of a city guardsman in his bronze cloak.

But Jos began to cast about, brow furrowing above his nose. "I can definitely hear something."

Fay swallowed back a fresh onslaught of nerves. *Please, please, please, dearest Lumia, don't let them be seen.*

"What's up with you, man?" said Smugface, slapping down a card. "You're as jumpy as a new novice."

"No, I ..." Jos frowned in puzzlement, then shook his head and peered down at the card Smugface had put down.

To her fright, Fay saw that Arianna and Alexios were flickering in and out of sight, right by the door. *Don't look, either of you,* she prayed.

But Smugface's eyes left the cards, idly wandering about the room and then flaring wide. "Hey, what the pits?" he cried, leaping to his feet. His chair went crashing to the ground.

Jos whirled around. "Magic!" He too jumped up, sending his chair flying.

Arianna, now fully visible, squared up to them. "You will let us leave and no harm will come to you."

Her voice was strong and authoritative, but the Defenders, to their credit, weren't cowed. Instead, they rushed for their spears. A second later, both stopped short and began to clutch at their throats, as if they couldn't breathe.

"Quickly, out, both of you," Arianna hissed. "I can't do this for long."

Alexios tossed the keys to the cell on the ground and opened the door. Fay didn't hesitate, leaping to her feet and running out, Alexios following. The door closed behind them. From the guardroom, a clatter of metal on stone. The Defenders, falling? *Please let them not be dead. They don't deserve that.*

Arianna came through the door, shut it, and pressed her hands against it for a few heartbeats. "That will keep it from being opened for a while."

"Did you kill them?" Fay asked. *Fuck, fuck, fuck. They don't deserve to die.*

"They're just unconscious. But we should hurry."

They'll know I was involved. I can never come back. Dear Lumia, help me.

"Can you walk?" Arianna asked Alexios.

He was as pale as a corpse and drenched in sweat.

"I ... may need help," he said, his voice little more than a whisper.

Trying to calm the mad rush of her thoughts, Fay took one of his arms, while Arianna took the other. They started to climb the stairs, Alexios's breathing coming ever harder.

Fay wished they could move faster. What if Lothar was already out of her room and looking for her? What if he'd raised an alarm? *I should have killed the prick. The Defenders must have seen me. I'll hang if they catch me.* She should tell Arianna about stabbing the archpriest, in case someone came looking for her, but she couldn't make the words come out.

They reached the stop of the stairs, went out into the corridor. Not long now before they reached the exit. Fay wondered what she was going to do. She would have to leave Arindel at the minimum. But go where? With Alexios and Arianna to fight Ilk? *No way, that's crazy. I can't use a sword and I have no magic.*

Someone walking up the passageway. Fay let go of Alexios, held her breath. A priest, no one she knew. He barely gave them a look. She let out the breath, took Alexios's arm again. They reached the side exit without coming across anyone else. No one was guarding it either, no one trying to stop traitorous priestesses from leaving. Fay unlocked the door, and they passed out into the street. A warm breeze brushed her face, a sharp contrast to the chill of the temple. Although they'd escaped, her anxiety still squeezed hard as they made their way to their next stop, an inn owned by Moth near Spire Gate. The smell of smoke was now heavy in the air and there was a brightness in the sky to the west, even though the sun had long set. With this much smoke, the fire had surely gotten out of control. How many slum dwellers had died in the flames so that two mages could escape their prisons? *Has it really been worth it?*

They reached the stable and were met by a scruffy boy maggot in the yard. He had four horses saddled and waiting for them. They mounted their steeds, and then they were on their way to the Spire Gate and another of Moth's safe houses on the outskirts of the city.

When they passed beyond the road lights, Fay lit an oil lamp that had been attached to her horse, holding it up on a pole. She peered out for the track that would take her to the safe house, marked by a dead elm.

It was easy to find, and a short while later, they reached their destination, a small farmhouse. Golden light flickered in its bottom two windows. On a different occasion, it would have seemed inviting. Instead, it seemed to taunt her, to remind her she had lost all safety and security. They dismounted outside the door, and Fay knocked on it.

Galinda opened it, breaking into a rare smile at the sight of her cousin. Fay stepped aside as the two women hugged briefly.

"This is Alexios, our Eleusian friend," Arianna said to her cousin, gesturing at him.

He was leaning against his horse, eyes half closed, looking like he might collapse at any moment. At the sound of his name, though, he roused himself, gave her a nod.

"Well met," Galinda said, inclining her head with more respect than she'd shown Fay. "I'm Galinda Velden, cousin to Arianna."

There was a flicker of recognition in Alexios's eyes at the sound of her name. But it was quickly muted.

"You go on inside," Fay said to them. "I'll see to the horses."

She brought the animals around into the stableyard, and saw there a pair of plain carriages, illuminated in torchlight. These would take the party as far as the town of Wren, keeping them out of sight of prying eyes. One of Moth's wasps, Hargan, was standing by a carriage, smoking a roll-up. "Any problems?" he said, exhaling a thin stream of smoke.

"No." *Except that I stabbed Lothar and the Defenders probably saw me so I can never go back to Arindel or the temple again and Moth is going to kill me.*

"Thin, help me with these 'orses," Hargan shouted into the darkness behind the carriages.

A muffled response and then a man appeared from the shadows, big and burly with a rolling walk. Another wasp, judging by the leathers and puckered scars that crossed his face and forearms. Fay left the horses with the men and went into the farmhouse.

Arianna and Galinda were standing in the middle of the sparse living room, talking to two strange men. The latter were dressed in leathers, but they looked too sleek to be Moth's people. Arianna's weaver friends, no doubt. She'd mentioned two of them were coming. Alexios sat slumped on a chair by a small table. On the table rested a large, rounded steel helm with a visor. Ruadh's? But there was no sign of him.

The weavers noticed Fay and stopped talking. "So, this is your savior, then," said one, a stocky man with sandy hair and a thick beard.

"Fay," Arianna said with a tight smile.

"I'm Griff," said the weaver who'd spoken. "Thank you for all you've done." He stepped forward and held out a hand.

Surprised to be treated on such an equal footing, Fay took his hand and shook it.

The other weaver, tall, lean, and dark, introduced himself as Bailin. His voice was smooth, accented like a highborn, and his movements were careful and contained.

The door opened, and Fay whirled around. But it was only Ruadh, glittering chainmail covering his enormous torso. Soot streaked his face, and patches of his beard were singed.

"Alright, Fay," he said with a grin. "Glad to see the Ilk mage didn't nab you."

"And you are?" Arianna said, arching an eyebrow.

"Ruadh Stormson," he replied. "I'm coming with you to the Deepwood." He began to stretch out a hand, then stopped and folded his arms across his chest instead.

"Ah, the siege expert," she said.

"Aye, sieges. But not Ilk. Going to be a right laugh, eh?" He chuckled, but no one joined him.

"You were at the riot? Tell me, man, what happened?" Galinda said.

He scowled. "Whole place was going up in flames when I left. I warned Moth."

"It will keep Thane busy, though," Galinda said with satisfaction. "He'll be working to put the fire out."

Ruadh just grunted, then, pointing to a pile in the corner of the room, "There's clothes, armor, and dye for your hair over there."

"I suppose it will be necessary." Arianna sighed, then, motioning for her cousin to follow, went to inspect the items.

"I'll sort out some food," Griff said.

Fay went to the table and sat next to Alexios. His eyes were half closed but opened fully when she approached.

"I can't thank you enough for what you've done," he murmured. "There's a chance now we can save them all."

That was all he ever seemed to think about, saving his people. Saving them but not himself. So curious. Could it be real? It seemed to be real. Suddenly, she wanted to go with him. *No, that's stupid. They're not my people. I can't help. I've done plenty.*

Ruadh got a wineskin and joined them, bringing with him a stink of smoke and leather, and sweat. He uncorked the skin with his teeth and took a swig, then held it out to Fay. "Rastian Red," he said. "Not the finest but easy enough on the tongue."

Fay took the skin from him and tipped the wine into her mouth. Only a couple of mouthfuls, then she offered it to Alexios. He hesitated, then took the skin and had a sip. His eyebrows rose. "It's good," he said. He had another sip, then returned the skin to Ruadh. "We don't have wine in Neopoli."

"What, no wine?" Ruadh cried. "What do you have? Beer? Jun?"

"What's jun?"

"It's made from moonberries," Fay said.

"Cheap poison," Ruadh added.

Alexios frowned in puzzlement. "Poison?"

"Not really poison," Fay said. "Unless you have too much of it. It's very strong, a glass or two will make you drunk. And you can buy a bottle for only a few vics." *All of New Arindel is drunk on jun, even the children.*

"We have nothing like that," Alexios said. "Only beer."

"No other spirits?" Ruadh said, bushy eyebrows rising.

Alexios shook his head.

Ruadh's eyebrows climbed almost to his hairline. "Ruination! Beer is fine, aye. Great for quenching a thirst, especially when the sun's hot. But a man needs fire in his guts from time to time."

Fay thought about her apricot brandy, still in her room with Lothar. Unless Lothar had escaped already and sounded the alarm. No returning to the temple. So, go to the Deepwood? To die fighting Ilk instead of at the end of a rope? No, she could flee to another city, start again somehow. But with what money? She'd have to turn flea, live her life in fear of capture. Groaning silently, she held out her hand for the wine, and Ruadh passed it to her. As she drank, Arianna's voice drifted to her from behind, and she strained to hear what she was saying.

"... did you say when you left?" Sound of water splashing into a basin.

"Heading to my estates to escape the heat," Bailin said. "Griff coming with me."

"Let me pour that water over your head." Galinda's voice.

A tiny cry from Arianna. "Ooh, that's cold." Water dribbling into water.

"I'm going to rub the dye in now. Don't move unless you want to end up looking like a Tunian."

"Hey, Fay? The wine?" Ruadh, poking at her arm.

She focused back on him, passed him the skin.

He took a swig. "When you going back to Arindel?"

Fay made a decision. "I'm coming with you." *At least as far as Wren, as far away as possible from this city.*

"Oh? Moth never said."

"Change of plan."

Ruadh's expression became teasing. "Could always use a pretty lass to lighten the journey." He was relatively harmless, so she just rolled her eyes at him, and he laughed and handed her the wine again. "You can finish it."

The skin was almost empty, and she drained it in a mouthful. She set it down, basking in the wine's first, soft, numbing effects. Then glanced at Alexios. He barely seemed to be aware of what was going on, his face pale and strained, as if it were all he could do to keep himself upright, even with the chair's help.

Griff returned to the table with plates laden with grainy bread, sliced mutton, apples, and red cheese. "Food's out!"

The sight of the food triggered her appetite, and she helped herself to some bread, piling meat on top of it.

Arianna and Galinda came to the table, their hair now a deep brown, still clinging wetly to their heads. Arianna had exchanged the novice robes for a well-cut dress, like Galinda. They were posing as well-off women, but not highborn. The women took their food over to the other side of the room and ate standing up, speaking to one another in low voices. Fay wondered what they were talking about, but they were too far away for her to make out any of the words.

As they were finishing their meal, Hargan came in. "Carriages is ready," he said.

They polished off the last of the food, then gathered their things and went out into the stableyard. Pairs of horses had been harnessed to each carriage. Thin was sitting at the front of one, holding the reins in his large hands.

Arianna, Galinda, and Alexios took one carriage together, with Hargan driving. Fay, nervous about sitting with the weavers, opted to ride on top of it with Ruadh. Bailin and Griff took the other carriage, and once all the provisions had been loaded, they rattled out into the night.

Chapter 45

Ina

The storms are a trial we must face every year. Sīut sends them to remind us of his presence. And so we make offerings to Chel and ask her to protect us.

—Teachings of Old Tsu

Ina woke to find that the storm had died somewhat, the rain falling more softly beyond the overhang. She was shivering and cold, still wet from her earlier exposure. She could tell that she had been asleep for a while—it was fully night. There was no time to lose, she'd have to figure out the waystone later, go for Suni and Tani first. She squirmed out of the shelter and started the walk back up to the peak. Instinct, or perhaps Lin's memories, told her that it would be easier to splice from where she had spliced previously. But she'd have to splice to a different location on Lun, maybe South Beach, since she knew it so well. Or the forest clearing where she and Suni had so often met. Yes, that seemed fitting.

Thankfully, the gale had reduced to a gusting wind, making it possible to stand on the peak safely when she reached it. She also felt stronger than she had before she'd slept, so maybe on balance it had been a good thing. Opening herself to the Cloth, she detected where she had made the splice before. The threads were pulled ever so slightly out of shape. Was that why they said it was wrong? Was she destroying the Cloth with her splicing? But what choice did she have?

She snagged the threads again, pulling them apart to make a hole large enough to pass through. This time she filled her lungs as deeply as she could before entering.

The passage was as uncomfortable as the first time, but she managed a better landing, falling on her knees rather than onto her face. She wasn't spared the headache and nausea, though, and her stomach heaved so hard it felt like it was trying to heave itself right out. All that came out was a thin stream of yellow bile. She wiped her mouth and struggled to her feet. Was it always going to be this bad?

When the pain in her head had lessened, she cast out with her lifesense to see if there were any people nearby. But the pain instantly redoubled in intensity, and she retreated into her own mind, pressing a hand against her left eye and gritting her teeth, willing the agony to leave her.

It reduced after a few heartbeats, and grimly she started toward the forest path, keeping her normal senses sharp but avoiding her other sense. She would need to use her powers again to leave the island and could only hope that time, however brief, would restore her strength.

The path was about thirty paces away, and after peering up and down it to check there was no one there, she followed it until just before she reached the main entrance to the village. Here, she sought once more the cover of the trees before circling around to Suni's home, a small, round hut in the family quadrant. She paused once she had it in sight—what if Mūak was in Suni's room? He usually liked staying at the fire late, but probably not on a night like this. Suni, she knew, usually went to bed early with Tani. Well, best find out whether he was there first. If he was, she'd think about what to do.

Bracing herself for the pain, she cast her lifesense toward the hut. One presence. Suni's. Ina would always know her easily. She closed her mind to the Cloth. It was still risky to go to the hut. Someone might see her, or Mūak might come home. Maybe she could try using her lifesense to wake Suni, encourage her to come out to her? Lin seemed to have been able to make the mind connection work both ways, not just emotions coming in, but also going out.

Ina opened her mind again, and wincing in pain, followed the threads to Suni's sleeping mind. But now she was at a loss. She knew how to read emotions, but she didn't really know how to manipulate them or speak mind to mind. In the memories she had accessed, Lin simply projected her thoughts through the threads, but when Ina tried to do that, they went nowhere. Or at least, Suni didn't respond. Frustrated, Ina pulled back, the headache making it too difficult for her to concentrate. She focused again on the memories, and finally, a man's voice came to her, Lin's teacher? *"To impress your thoughts on another's mind, you must intertwine your mind threads with theirs."*

"Doesn't this open you up to them?" Lin asked.

"Yes, if you don't know how to shield yourself. But that's a different stage, and difficult to master."

Ina wasn't so concerned about hiding her thoughts from Suni. She needed only to get to her, to tell her to come. Again, she reached out, doing as Lin's teacher had explained, taking the threads that connected her mind to the Cloth and spinning them around Suni's. The connection this time was very different, much stronger, and Ina was hit by a shock of terror and anguish from her lover's mind, from the dreams that consumed her. Fighting to control her own emotions, she whispered, "*Come outside to me. I can help Tani.*"

Suni stirred, half coming out of her dream.

Ina repeated her words twice until Suni was completely awake. To Ina's relief, she made a response, instinctively reaching along the connection Ina had created. "*Ina, is that you?*"

"*Come around the back of the hut and meet me under the trees,*" Ina said, retreating there for cover.

Suni rolled up the door shutter with barely a squeak and tiptoed around, following Ina's instructions. When they were finally face to face, Ina's heart burst at the sight of her, and she pulled Suni close for an embrace. The other woman returned the hug, kissed her face, then pushed her gently back. "Your escape. They haven't stopped talking about it. People are terrified of you."

"I'm the same as I ever was." But even as Ina spoke the words, she knew them for a lie.

"Mūak told me what you said to the elders. We're not allowed to speak of it to anyone else. Is it all true?"

"Yes."

"They won't take you back," Suni said. "It won't matter what you say. They've ordered the hunters to kill you on sight. They're out there, looking for you."

"Mūak?"

"Looking for you, too."

"Well, I'm leaving the islands. And I want to take you and Tani with me."

Suni crossed her arms. "Take us where?"

"I'm going to try and find the tribe that went into exile in the barbarian lands to the east."

She shook her head. "There's no way to get there. The Maelstrom—"

"The memories have shown me a way. Is Tani ... still with us?"

"At midday tomorrow, they'll send her back to Chel." Suni's voice thickened with grief and broke on the last word.

"I can take you both with me. I have the power," Ina said. Was that true? It had to be.

"Is it like of old, then? You can move through Sīut's Realm? But of course you can, you ..."

Ina was heartened by the flash of hope in Suni's face. "Where's Tani? We need to go quickly."

"Take Tani, but I can't leave."

The words were sharper to Ina than the jab of a spear. "I can't go without you."

"My place is here," Suni said. Seeing Ina's hurt, she put a hand to her cheek. "My love, I can't. What use would I be? But Tani can go with you. I don't think Chel wants her yet. Perhaps that is just a mother's love, but it was through Tani that ..."

"Would you really let us go and stay here alone?" Suni's eyes glistened with tears and Ina jumped on the weakness. "Come too. There's no need to lose us both."

The tears made slow tracks down Suni's cheeks. Ina put her arms around her and drew her close. Suni submitted to the embrace, her shoulders shaking silently. At last she calmed and broke free of Ina's arms to look at her. There was resolve in her eyes. "Fine, I'll come."

Ina hugged her once more with relief. "Where's Tani?"

"She's being kept in the House of the Elders," Suni said. "They wouldn't let me stay with her."

That was cruel. Usually, the children spent their last nights with their parents. No doubt because of Ina. "I'll fetch her. Gather some things for a journey, we'll need food and water. Then meet at our usual place in the woods. As soon as you can."

Suni gave her agreement. Ina planted a quick kiss on her cheek, and then made her way to the House of the Elders.

Chapter 46

Alexios

I saw a man in a dark cloak with the hood pulled up, stalking narrow streets at night. I believe it was the same city where I saw the king being crowned. He was following someone, a young man. When the man turned into an alleyway, the masked man followed him and hurled two daggers. Each struck the man in the back of the knees, and he stumbled and fell to the ground. A moment later, the hooded man had severed his target's windpipe.

—Visions of Keeper Alexios Arathraxis

Alexios opened his eyes. Fay was sitting in the carriage opposite him, staring out of the little window at the passing landscape, winding a dark curl around her finger. "Do you know where we are?" he asked.

She jumped, evidently startled, and turned her eyes on him. "Near Wren," she said. "There, we'll exchange the carriages for horses to go into the Deepwood."

Close, so close. Hope and anxiety knotted his stomach. Over two weeks since he'd passed through the first time. Too long. The food stores in Neopoli would be running low—they'd never stocked in preparation for a siege. And the Ilk might have already attacked, the Ilk mage—Inyaki—become bored of waiting. He might arrive to find nothing but corpses. *Or not even corpses,* he thought, remembering the cookfires and the farmers. And they only had four weavers. Four! He'd hoped for a hundred.

Fay looked out the window again, biting the inside of her lip. Then she shifted her gaze back to him. "Are the Ilk very terrible?"

Red eyes, a rotten stench, nauseating fear. "Yes."

She nodded, her eyes screwing up a little, as if she were contemplating something.

"You don't need to come with us. You've already done more than enough."

Again, her gaze switched between the window and him. "I want to see the Ilk for myself. If they win, they'll probably come for us sooner or later. There's already at least one Ilk mage in Arindel. If I stayed there, I'd only be putting off the inevitable. At least this way, I know what we're up against." A pause. "And we'll need witnesses to spread the word, warn everyone."

"She's right," Epiktet said. *"The world will need to be warned. It's not enough for us to simply defeat the Ilk at Neopoli."*

The other souls agreed.

"We can keep you away from the front lines and get you out if the worst happens." He felt relieved. Her, he would keep safe, like he hadn't Nixos and Demeia.

She smiled suddenly, a smile full of charm that dimpled her cheeks. "I'll admit I'm also very curious about seeing your town and your people. I was reading a book about your history."

"We're not what we once were. You'll find us almost uncivilized compared to Arindel."

She opened her mouth, hesitated, then said, "Is it true that you used to fly above the world using magical horses?"

Alexios laughed at that.

"What's so funny? That's what I read," she said, her forehead creasing in irritation.

"It's just the idea that the gliders looked like horses," he said. "They were disk-shaped, with a rail around the edge for support and to stop people from falling out. Watch." He spun an illusion of a flat steel disk bearing three people. It wasn't full size, there wasn't room for that. "We used these for getting around the city. There were other, bigger designs being attempted at the time of the Ilk War. Those would have enabled long-distance travel and would have been much like this carriage—covered, with seating. Flying would have been good deal more comfortable, though."

As if to punctuate his words, the carriage rolled over a stone in the road, sending them bouncing off their seats. His behind slammed back down with such force that his teeth clacked together.

"Can't you make gliders anymore?" Fay asked, pressing a slender hand to the side of the carriage to steady herself.

"No. We've tried. But we've produced nothing that flies for more than a second or two." His old frustration ignited, along with that gnawing sense of not being good enough.

"And the weavers, have they ever been able to make them?"

"You'll have to ask them. But Vycenians were never as skilled as our artefactors in these things. We taught them to make heatstones and glowglobes, but even then, there were only ever a handful who could do it successfully."

"I don't understand anything about magic or how it works," Fay said.

"I'm not sure that anyone does," Alexios said heavily. "Even those of us who use it." *So much I don't know still, even after two hundred years of trying.*

Fay shifted, leaned forward a little. "I mean, you talk about weaver magic and Eleusian magic and then also the magic of the Chelaki, the Ilk mages. But isn't it all the same magic? Doesn't it all come from the same place? Why can't you do the same things?"

"Good question. In a sense, yes, I suppose it's the same magic. Those with mage gifts can see the fabric of the world. We can manipulate that fabric in different ways to produce different effects. I'm not sure why different peoples have different strengths in this. Maybe the abilities developed over time, as people found certain types of effects more useful than others. We Eleusians, for example, have always been inclined toward peace, so we didn't develop the warlike magic of the Vycenian weavers. Instead, we learned how to spin illusions to create art and beauty—we can enhance sound to give more power to our music, for example. And, of course, we wished to make useful objects that would make our lives easier, like glowglobes or gliders."

"And what about the Ilk mages? What's their magic?"

"The magic of Antiphos is different. It comes from outside the Lace. That is how they make the Ilk and why the Ilk are so dangerous. They bend the Lace out of shape, make it unstable. If it becomes too unstable, you end up with tears in the fabric and, ultimately, cataclysmic destruction."

"Like the Ruin," she said, nodding. "So it's really *that* magic that's dangerous to the world. Not *your* magic."

"Yes and no. If we try to do too much spinning or weaving, we can also distort the Lace too much and cause it to tear. A balance must always be kept."

"I see." Her gaze turned inward, thoughtful.

Alexios realized the carriage was entering a town. He recognized it—Wren. They drove most of the way through and came to a stop outside a large building with a stable attached. Griff came to their carriage door and opened it. "These lands belong to Arianna and Galinda's family. They'll be known. Can you spin an illusion to change their appearance?"

"Of course."

"I really don't like that Galinda one," Doris said. *"She's got cruelty in her."*

"Not cruelty," Eliana said. *"More like indifference to those she thinks weak or unworthy."*

"She respects only power," Alexios said.

"And will use her power to keep those in the place she deems fit for them," Eliana said.

Alexios got out of the carriage and stretched to remove the stiffness from his limbs, breathing deeply of the air, which was tainted with the smell of sewage. Then he went to the other carriage. Bailin was standing outside it, looking around, but Galinda and Arianna were still inside.

He changed their appearance so that they looked like blond-haired sisters, and then they got out. The two carriage drivers went into the stable and shortly reappeared with several horses and a stableman who unhooked their own horses from the carriages. There was a bit of a fuss when Fay found there was no mount for her.

"There was only seven to be got," said the one called Har. "Thought you was coming back with us."

"No, Moth wants me going to the Deepwood too," Fay said. "Someone obviously didn't get the message right."

She's lying. But to me or them, or both?

"She's a skilled actress," Demeia said approvingly. *"It makes her a good spy."*

"We didn't get coin for eight," Hargan said.

"Just get her a horse," Ruadh said to him.

The man frowned, shook his head, went back into the stables, and returned with a bony animal. "That's as good as we can get you," he said, handing Fay the reigns.

They rode out, and Alexios found to his relief that his days of sleeping in the carriage were finally paying off. Most of his energy was back, and he was able to maintain the pace with the others. It was Fay who struggled most, admitting that she had no experience of riding when Ruadh told her that she was going to wear her backside off. He gave her a few tips, and Alexios listened in, still not confident about his own abilities.

All in all, they made good progress, and reached the edge of the Deepwood at twilight. They agreed to stop on the fringes rather than try the forest at night. Alexios was impatient to keep moving, but it would be hard going, and he told himself that dawn came early at that time of year.

As they were sitting around the fire, eating, Arianna asked him to explain what it meant to be a Keeper. Fay was nearby and drew closer to listen.

He answered with reluctance. *I'm no real Keeper.* "In Eleusia of old, there were twenty Keepers," he said. "One for each of the districts. It's a sacred duty, commanded by the Makers. We guard the memory of our civilization."

"So you're priests, then," Fay said.

"Of a kind, but we must also be mages."

"To do soulbindings," Arianna said probingly.

"What's a soulbinding?" Fay asked.

"Every twenty years or so, the soul of a person is bound to a Keeper's. Most usually, it will be the soul of a mage and someone who was related by blood to the Keeper. Soulbinding grants the Keeper extra years of life, slowing our aging." Alexios had done his first soulbinding at fifteen, too early. It had taken a decade for him to reach full manhood.

Fay reared back at his words, looking shocked, even repulsed. It hurt him for some reason.

But Arianna nodded coolly. "I'd wondered if the accounts were right. How do you do it? I've always been curious. It doesn't seem to be something that we weavers can do—not that we've tried in recent times. It would be forbidden."

Alexios hesitated. He wasn't used to talking about such things. Should he be sharing sacred knowledge with outsiders? What if the weavers could gain the ability but then used it wrongly, like the Ilk mage had? He settled for something vague, hoping he wouldn't be pressed on it. "A person must agree of their own free will to have their soul bound to a Keeper's. Soul bindings only take place when that person is close to death, although we control the exact moment of death so that the Keeper is prepared."

"But ... what happens to these souls?" Fay asked. "Don't they go to ..." She hesitated. "Wherever it is the souls of your people go after death?"

"The souls will eventually return to the Makers, when the Keeper gives up his or her burden." He realized he sounded defensive. He didn't like how Fay was looking at him.

But she smoothed the expression away, as if she'd decided it wasn't her place to judge. "And how does a Keeper 'give up the burden'?" she asked.

"Eventually, the Keeper starts to wear out. The soul bindings fail as often as not. When that happens, usually after about two thousand years, the Keeper must leave this world. A successor is chosen in advance—once they've passed a series of tests. When it's time for the successor to take over, the Keeper binds his soul to theirs. The other souls are released back to the Makers. Because the Keeper has lived for so many years with the souls, their memories are implanted in his or her mind. Thus, the chain of memory is preserved through time."

"Can you communicate with the souls?" Fay asked.

"Yes. Their consciousness lives in my mind."

"That sounds exhausting. Don't you ever want to be alone?" Fay said.

Often. "You get used to it. I don't have to listen to the voices all the time."

"Do you remember everything that happened to the souls attached to you?" Arianna asked.

"Do you remember every moment of every day you have lived?" he countered.

Arianna arched an eyebrow. "Of course not."

"It's much the same. Some moments stand out clearly. Some memories appear only when sparked by another memory, a situation, a thought. And I can never be sure that it is a true memory. We falsify even our own memories of the past."

"So what's the point of it all?" Fay asked.

What *was* the point? Nothing seemed clear anymore. "The Keeper provides wisdom. Only experience and long life grant true wisdom. But it is also our duty to transfer our memories through art—through poetry, through drama, through music. A Keeper is chosen not only because of their magical ability, but also because of their artistic skill and dedication to learning. All of those born with the ability to soul bind spend their first forty years of life in training. Then, they must pass a final test, and if they are found worthy, they are added to the pool of possible Keepers."

"What tests did you have to pass?" Fay asked.

"I ... did no tests." *Chosen from a pool of one, not a real Keeper.* "After the Ruin, there were only nineteen of us left. I was the only one with the soulbinding power. I had to teach myself everything I know."

Arianna raised an eyebrow. "You mean nineteen Eleusians?"

"We were all that remained."

Fay looked horrified. "And then what, you went to Neopoli?"

"Eventually. Some more joined us over the following weeks and months. Perhaps another thirty or forty. I can't really remember. I was only seven years old."

"I can't imagine what it must have been like," Fay said.

Mama, papa. When will I see them again? They're gone, dear heart. They're gone to the Makers. I'll look after you now. Epiktet. A good man, who had lost his children and his wife and his own father and mother, who had raised Alexios like a son.

"Oh, let's not go there again," Epiktet said. *"We'll meet them all again eventually."*

"I'm sorry, I didn't mean to bring up bad memories," Fay said.

He waved away the apology, but said nothing more, and neither Fay nor Arianna pressed him further.

They rose with the sun and entered the forest. It was as dark as ever, but they made good headway initially, following woodsmen's trails. Then at last they had to strike out through the undergrowth, forcing them to dismount and lead the horses. Ruadh and Arianna took the reins of Bailin and Griff's mounts so that they could go ahead and clear a path with the blades of their battlestaffs. The steady rise and fall was hypnotic to him, helping to ease the torment of his thoughts.

"Can't you use weaving?" Ruadh asked.

"We could set fire to the bushes, but with this dryness, it would quickly spread," Arianna said. "And we need to conserve our energy for the battle."

"Chopping wood takes energy too," Ruadh said.

"Not as much as weaving, warrior," Arianna replied.

He said nothing to that, and they continued in silence, stopping only twice to rest and eat before the day began to fade into evening. Indeed, so little was said that when Ruadh spoke, it startled Alexios. "Hear that?"

Alexios could hear nothing.

"Hear what?" Galinda asked, shooting Ruadh an irritated look.

"Exactly," the warrior said.

"What do you mean, man?" Galinda snapped. "Stop talking in riddles."

But Alexios caught on to what the warrior was saying. "There's no birdsong."

Everyone came to a halt, as if by unspoken agreement. They cocked their heads, listened.

"He's right," Arianna said. "I can't hear anything at all."

"Not even wind," Griff murmured.

"It's the Ilk," Alexios said. Was that why his anxiety had increased? Was the Gloom affecting him even from here? They were still at least an hour from Neopoli.

"The Gloom can reach far," Epiktet said. *"Even in the rearguard, we could feel it."*

"You think they might be wandering the woods?" Ruadh asked, hand straying to the hilt of the shortsword at his waist.

"Keep your eyes sharp and your weapons ready," Arianna said, taking hold of the threads.

The other weavers also summoned the threads to them. Fay looked around uneasily, fragile and near defenseless. Catching his eyes, she gave him a weak smile. Why had she come, he wondered again. She was so young, hardly older than Demeia had been.

"She's got a lot of courage," Demeia said. *"She'll fight if taught."*

"Best she uses that courage to spread word of the Ilk if all goes ill," he said.

"We'll succeed," Demeia said determinedly.

"Let's get a move on," Ruadh said. He raised his axe and brought it down through a thorn thicket.

Finally, in late afternoon, they reached the parts of the forest that Alexios knew well. They were perhaps one mile from the Ilk lines, or at least from where the Ilk lines had previously stood.

"I'll go ahead alone," he said. "We don't know what we'll find there, and I'm not sure if I'm strong enough to hide us all with my illusions."

"Shouldn't one of us go with you, at least?" Griff said.

"Better not. Give me a day. If no one returns here for you, you may assume the worst."

"Very well, we wait," Arianna said, in a tone that brooked no argument.

They all deferred to her, he'd noted, and did so again now. He wasn't sure if he liked her or not. She seemed haughty and proud, but it was obvious she had a keen mind, and she had asked him many penetrating questions about his people.

"She's not as bad as her cousin," Doris agreed. *"I'm still not sure I trust her, though. They accused her of murdering the First Weaver, maybe they were right to. Did we ever really question it?"*

Doris was right. He himself had just gone along with the plans laid by Fay and her master, desperate to be released. Perhaps Arianna was an enemy, waiting for her moment to strike. But there was nothing for it now. They'd come this far.

He bid his goodbyes and struck out for Neopoli, leaving his horse behind so that he would be unburdened. As before, he felt the presence of the Ilk long before he could actually see them. The sense of wrong in the Lace was palpable, and the Gloom tugged at him, trying to drag him down. But if there was Gloom, there were Ilk. And that meant his people were probably still alive, or at least alive and fighting.

He considered making himself invisible in case there were Ilk in the woods, but then decided to conserve his energy. It would be difficult to cross the lines again. So he kept out a sharp eye and ear until finally, he saw the trees thin ahead of him, afternoon light shining through. When he broke tree cover, shock stopped him in his tracks. What had once been open farmland was now a ruin of blackened stubs. The Ilk had razed everything. *Will they not starve themselves?*

But that wasn't the only thing that had changed. A deep trench ran around the town, the dug-up earth piled on the Ilk side to make a rampart. The sides of the trench were completely vertical. He would have to not only drop down into that trench and find a way back up but also climb over the rampart, all without a rope and under illusion. *Makers help me. How do I manage it?* But maybe the trench didn't go the whole way around. The northern side of the town, where the ravine was—that was his best hope. He went back into the forest and walked along the edge of the tree line, keeping his eyes on the trench and the Ilk.

They weren't manning the entire length of their rampart, he discovered. Instead, they were clustered by the southern entrance, probably by the eastern one too. A skreek still guarded the western exit. It wheeled overhead, sometimes loosing ear-splitting shrieks.

When he finally reached the northern end of the town, he discovered to his relief that he was right. The Ilk hadn't dug a trench, trusting the natural gorge, fifteen feet deep and running east–west, to do the job for them. Its sides were slanting enough to allow him climb down, and the water running along the stony bottom was reduced to a trickle due to the hot, rainless summer. The situation would have been vastly different after the winter storms, when it filled with raging white waters. *Small mercies.*

Before he began the descent, he watched and listened for signs that Ilk were guarding it. But there was nothing. He wasn't surprised. The ground around the gorge was uneven, not good for fighting or quick escape, and there was no northern exit from the town. Even so, he decided to spin invisibility in case the skreek changed its movements.

The way down into the gorge was treacherous, and he went slowly, feet carefully picking out rocks that would bear his weight. Despite his caution, though, he slipped on loose scree and fell onto his behind, sliding down a terrifying few inches before managing to stop himself by grabbing onto an outgrowth of gorse. A hundred pinpricks of pain flared in his hand, but he held on grimly as he tried to re-establish a foothold, his heart churning a violent rhythm.

At last, he made it to the bottom and hopped across the tiny stream before walking eastward to try and find a way back up to the walls of Neopoli, which loomed directly above. There were a couple of guards on the wall, looking out onto the ravine, but he didn't dare show himself or call out in case there *were* Ilk.

After he'd been walking along the bottom of the ravine for a few minutes, he found a way back up. It was even more dangerous, and he had to use his hands more than once to pull himself up past a particularly steep outcrop of rock. Doing it all under illusion made it five times harder, and by the time he reached the top, his chest was burning. He sat to catch his breath, legs dangling over the edge. But as soon as he felt able, he was clambering back to his feet to walk around to the western gate.

The skreek overhead made him feel exposed. Was it any better at seeing through illusions than the other Ilk? But it seemed not, for there was no change in its circling.

He was about to knock on the gate to gain entry, but then worried that the skreek might hear him. He had no idea how good its hearing was, and the wall would be no barrier if it decided to attack. But there was an entire army outside the southern gate, the Ilk mage maybe among them, able to break his invisibility. So he took a deep breath, then rapped out a set pattern of knocks on the gate.

A voice called faintly through it. "Knock again."

He glanced up. No sign from the skreek of having heard him. He banged out the rhythm again.

"It's him!"

The gate opened a fraction, and Alexios swiftly stepped through, letting his illusion fall so that the two waiting guards could see him. Their eyes lit with delight when they saw him.

"Keeper! You've returned!" exclaimed one, a fair-haired young man called Pallas. He grinned widely, but then his grin suddenly died. "Did you ...?"

"I've brought some help but came ahead alone," Alexios said, guessing at his meaning.

Palpable relief on both their faces.

Alexios's stomach knotted. He wouldn't tell them how tiny their force was. "I'll go directly to the Chamber. Send for the rulers and tell them to meet me there."

Pallas looked like he wanted to ask more questions but instead went to a boy of about twelve sitting on the ground by the gate. The boy shot to his feet, nodding vigorously as Pallas spoke to him before sprinting off into the heart of the town.

Alexios bid the men goodbye and made his way to the Chamber. Of course, he was recognized by all he passed. They saluted him but didn't try to stop him or ask questions. It wasn't their place. Still, many followed, and he was acutely conscious of their curiosity, their desperate hope. He could see their hunger too, the sleeplessness that showed itself in the shadows around their eyes. Even the children were quiet, playing outside their homes under the watchful gaze of their elders.

There were few young men about, but he discovered why when he reached the central square—they were all practicing with spears. The air was filled with the sound of scuffling feet, of wood clacking against wood, of grunts and curses and shouts of pain. He paused at a corner to watch them, realized there were women among the ranks.

Emotion—tenderness, sadness—eddied through him. *None of them warriors, but look how hard they train. How many will die so that the rest might live? No one should be called to make that sacrifice. Truly, the Chelaki were put in this world to test us.*

He was about to continue to the Hall when noticed something else. Walking among the trainees were others wearing white surcoats printed with a curved black blade. Looking longer, Alexios realized they were teaching, stopping to correct a hand position or demonstrate a strike. The Blades, now come into their own. Demeia. She should have been with them. "*But I'm with you,*" she reminded him. Alexios tore his eyes away and marched up the steps to the Hall. There were thousands more lives to be saved.

It was empty, as was the Chamber, but he hadn't been sitting long before Theophila and Castes came. Their faces were webbed with even more creases, their eyes puffed and bloodshot.

"Alexios, I'm so glad to see you returned," Theophila said.

"Have you been successful?" Castes asked without preamble, looking around as if expecting weavers to jump out from the walls.

Alexios wearily told them of his ordeals and of the weavers waiting in the woods. During the story, Periklis and Hereia arrived, but he didn't restart. Let someone else fill them in.

"We'll send illusionists to get the weavers now," Castes said. "Who do you suggest?" He glanced at Hereia as he spoke.

"I'll go," she said.

But Alexios shook his head. "With all respect, the gorge must be crossed."

"And my old knees will not bear up," Hereia said. "Ah, to be ever young like you, Keeper."

You wouldn't wish it if you knew what it was like.

"Thais and Epi," Hereia said. "And maybe one other, to be certain?"

"Youno," Alexios said, naming Hereia's own grandson.

Castes went to the door and sent a runner to fetch them.

"Tell me we've made progress in designing new weapons?" Alexios said. "With only five weavers ..."

Theophila, Periklis and Castes exchanged looks. Their expressions didn't fill him with hope.

Periklis answered. "We've been trying to make a weapon that can attack the Ilk from afar, but it still isn't ready. The design isn't quite working."

"The Vycenian weavers have experts on warcraft among them," Alexios said. "They may be able to help. There's a Vycenian soldier too, who has experience of sieges." Then he asked another question he feared the answer to. "And food? How much do we have left?"

"We can last another week if we ration carefully," Castes said. "We've sent some foragers out under illusion, but like you, they've had to cross the gorge, so it hasn't been easy. And there are Ilk hiding in the woods. They killed two on the first day. We've been a lot more careful since."

So he'd been right to worry about that. A wave of tiredness passed over him. How would they put an end to this?

Chapter 47

Fay

The Ilk were the most formidable army anyone had ever faced. Many battles in the Ilk War ended before they'd even begun, with defenders fleeing as soon as they caught sight of the monsters and experienced the full weight of the Gloom.

—The Ilk War: A History, Carolin Morgan

They sat huddled together under the trees as the day faded to evening, waiting for Alexios to return. They eventually lit a fire, more for comfort than anything else, but nobody talked very much, eyes and ears straining for any sight or sound of Ilk. Fay was very aware of the Gloom, dragging her down, but it didn't seem strong enough here to trigger the voice. She simply sat and brooded on her predicament. What had possessed her to come? Now that they were within spitting distance of the Ilk, it seemed the most reckless decision she'd ever made. She certainly hadn't planned it. They'd reached Wren, and suddenly she hadn't felt like striking out on her own. *It was a shithole of a town, I'd have been bored. And with no money, where would I have stayed? I'd have ended up a whore again or worse.*

She glanced over at Ruadh, sitting with his back to a mossy stump, sharpening his axe, which glinted in the firelight. Not for the first time, she wished she'd been born a man. Men had freedom and power. If she was as big as him and able to wield that axe, she'd be laughing. *But then men are assholes.* Except for Alexios. Fay kept waiting for some word or deed that would betray his true nature. But none came. He genuinely seemed to *care.* And that role he played as Keeper, having all those souls stuck to him for hundreds—thousands!—of years, just so his people could remember the past. *He's got no freedom at all. Even less than me. Bad enough being stuck with yourself half the time. Imagine being stuck with a load of dead people too?*

Movement, somewhere off in the trees. Fay's ears pricked—Alexios or Ilk?

"Something's coming!" Griff called, the orange gemstone in his staff flaring to life.

The stones of the other weavers also glowed as they leaped to their feet, peering in the direction of the noise. Ruadh put his helm on his head, his entire face disappearing behind the polished steel. Then he got up, surprisingly fast for a man weighed down with so much metal.

A deepening of the dread. Loud crashing and snapping, getting ever closer. It was too dark to see very much beyond the pool of light thrown by their fire, but Fay knew what was coming, and began to shake.

"Form a semi-circle in front of the fire!" Arianna cried.

"Stay behind me," Ruadh said to Fay as they scrambled into position, backs to one another.

She didn't need to be told twice. She was no warrior, all she had was her knife. The fire, close behind her, was scalding but comforting. Surely, Ilk couldn't pass through it?

A giant, wolf-like thing burst through the trees, its slavering jaws so wide they looked like they could fasten around a head and rip it right off. Alexios had described these, called them rippers, and it was easy to see why.

The monster came directly at Arianna, who pointed her staff at it. Sizzling blue light leaped out to strike the monster in the chest. It blackened the ripper's scaly hide, but the monster didn't slow. Another giant step forward, and it raised a clawed hand, preparing to slash her. Arianna shot more flame, this time at its face, burning its eyes, and it halted, claws swinging wildly. Fay expected shrieks of pain, but heard only snarls and grunts, as if it were inconvenienced rather than wounded. Another stream of flame, and its face began to melt away. Still no signs of pain, and the thing fell to the ground only when the flame had penetrated its skull.

More monsters surged from the trees, these ones smaller, wielding swords and spears. *They're the golls.* Screeching and jabbering, they moved quickly to surround the group. How many were there—nine, ten? Fay clutched her knife hard, praying they wouldn't break the circle.

A second ripper emerged from the trees, going for Ruadh. It was half again as big as the warrior, swiping out with its long claws, catching in the mail on his chest. It yanked its arm back, lifting Ruadh clean off his feet and slamming him to the ground. Fay screamed as it clamped its enormous jaws around Ruadh's head. But its teeth clanged against the metal of his helm. Ruadh stuck a knife into the monster's foot, but it didn't even seem to notice, reaching down again with its claws, trying to find the warrior's flesh. Then Griff struck its face with blue fire, and it snarled. Ruadh raised himself up on one knee and sliced the back of its leg with his knife. The monster fell, missing Ruadh, but taking down two of its smaller fellows, crushing them beneath its gigantic weight. Ruadh didn't hesitate, getting to his feet and swinging his axe down double handed to chop the ripper's neck off.

All around, blue flame was eating the Ilk, filling the air with the acrid stink of burning meat and hair. It seemed to be more effective against the smaller ones, who were covered in fur and leather armor rather than scale. Fay had never felt more of a liking for weavers than she did now.

Shouts and yells from the woods. Her heart quailed. More Ilk? No, a group of Eleusians, Alexios at their head. Fay sagged with relief. Some of the Ilk turned toward them. But as the monsters charged, the Eleusians disappeared. Ruadh used the Ilk's resulting confusion to run at them from behind, slicing one's head off before his axe got stuck in the body of the one next to it. Something invisible struck the thing in the eye, gouging it and giving Ruadh time to loosen his axe and meet the onslaught of another. A loud clash of metal as it parried his first swing with its sword, stronger than it looked. But Ruadh's second swing broke the sword in half, and the third landed deep inside the goll's skull. Ruadh yanked the axe out, kicking the dead goll away from him as he did so.

A goll charged toward her, taking advantage of the gap in the circle that Ruadh had left. But Griff swung his battlestaff around, and there was a clash of metal as the monster's sword met the blade of the staff. The impact jerked Griff off balance, and he stumbled. The goll lunged in with its sword, trying to bury it in Griff's belly, and he barely jumped out of reach.

Fay looked back at the fire, crouched, and yanked out a burning brand, then flung it at the Ilk. The creature didn't see it coming, too focused on its attack, and was hit squarely on the temple. It staggered, confused, and with a wild shout, Griff stepped in with his battlestaff, half severing its neck in a single sweep. The goll toppled to the ground, sword falling from its fingers.

And then it was over, a dozen monsters on the ground, smoking, oozing blackish blood.

Alexios and the other Eleusians reappeared from thin air, startling her. "Are any of you injured?" Alexios asked, taking them all in with his bright, blue eyes.

"Just a couple of scratches," Bailin said, nose wrinkling as he regarded the Ilk gore staining his leathers.

No one else had been seriously harmed either, although they all looked bloodied, their clothing torn. Fay felt useless. She'd done almost nothing but cower behind them all. Throwing a burning stick didn't really count for much. *Why in great Lumia's name did I come here?*

"Let's go quickly to Neopoli, before more of these things find us," Alexios said. He looked toward the horses, still all alive, but pulling at their leads, eyes rolling wildly. "We can't take them. There's a deep trench around the city, and the Ilk are patrolling it. There is a point where we can cross a little more easily, a ravine on the north side of the town. We'll have to get there through the woods and wait until the last moment to spin the invisibility illusions. They aren't reliable with the Gloom putting so much pressure on the Lace."

"In that case, we should set the animals loose. Those stinkheads will only take them and slaughter them," Ruadh said.

No one disagreed, and Fay together with Ruadh untied the beasts. Some went running immediately, others when they had been slapped on the rump.

Alexios was looking at the dead golls. "We should take their arms," he said. "Any metal we can get will be useful."

He said something in Eleusian to his compatriots, sparking some argument. But Alexios had the final say, and with obvious reluctance, they stripped the metal from the monsters' bodies.

Then they inched their way through the woods, using the light from the Eleusians' small glowglobes and the weavers' focus stones to see. For the sun had dipped low, and the little light left in the day was obscured by the canopy.

At last, Alexios stopped them. "We're nearly there. We'll cloak you now." He took out some lengths of rope. "Each of you will be tied to an illusionist. You won't be able to see anything, but the rope will guide you."

Fay was tied to a dark-haired young woman called Thais, who smiled at her as she knotted the rope around Fay's wrist.

Then everyone disappeared and they continued through the trees, soon reaching the ravine that Alexios had spoken about. Just beyond it rose the wooden wall of the town, guards standing on it, looking out.

Thais stopped her at this point, presumably because others were going down first. Fay squinted, trying to break the illusion. At times, she thought she saw a shifting blur, but she would never have noticed if she hadn't been looking. Then, Thais was pulling her forward, and they picked their way down and back up again. When they reached the wall, Thais untied the knot that bound them together and put Fay's hands on an invisible rope ladder. Feeling exposed and insecure, Fay climbed it, using only her sense of touch. At last, she was at the top, being helped over by some other invisible man, perhaps Alexios. When they were all up, the Eleusians dropped the invisibility, startling her again.

"I'll take you around to the eastern gate," Alexios said. "The rulers of our town are waiting for you there, and you'll get a view of the Ilk camp."

They circled around in the gathering twilight, Fay watching the blackened fields, looking for Ilk. As Alexios had promised, the rulers were by the eastern gate, and inclined their heads respectfully when the weavers were presented to them. Another man was also there. Periklis was his name, master of the city guard. He spoke no Vycenian at all, and the rulers only a little, so Alexios acted as translator.

When the introductions were finished, Bailin walked to the edge of the rampart and gazed at the fires of the Ilk, now springing up everywhere. "They won't be easy to defeat if that skirmish was anything to go by."

Fay realized how true that was. The numbers had been evenly matched, but all the combatants save Ruadh had been mages. And Ruadh seemed far deadlier than any of the puny-looking Eleusian defenders she'd seen. How would they fare against Ilk, with no magic, no steel helmets, no coats of mail?

"Aye, we'll need to cook up some clever strategy," Ruadh said, scowling as he first took in the Ilk and then the length of the wall.

I should have stayed in Wren. Even Moth is less frightening than these things.

"What thoughts do you have?" Castes asked him.

"Tell me about your defenses," Ruadh replied. "And let's take a walk around the wall."

They did a full circle together, Ruadh asking them all sorts of questions—about the weapons they had, the number of trained soldiers, the depth of the wall's foundations. Whenever he fell silent, Arianna or Bailin would find something else to quiz them on.

The warrior's final estimation was brutal. "Your defenses are shit. You have a wall, but it's low and easy to climb. Plus, there's no ditch, not on the outside, not on the inside. Didn't anyone think that might be useful?"

Fay saw Alexios turn red with embarrassment and noticed the same flush on the faces of Periklis and the Rulers.

"Have you been checking whether they're digging tunnels?" Ruadh asked.

"We've been digging our own tunnels," Castes said. "But we've seen no evidence that they have also tried to dig."

"Have you gone out there and checked?"

Castes shook his head.

"Well, you need to. They could use tunnels to undermine the walls, dig their way right into your town. I've seen it done. And what about sewers? I suppose you've got some as your town smells too clean."

"We do," Theophila replied.

"And springs that supply water?"

"That too."

"Well, you'll also want to check they don't come through the sewers and don't poison the water."

"We'll do as you suggest, warrior," Theophila said, maintaining her calm in the face of the warrior's blunt words. She nodded at Periklis, and he rattled off instructions to a nearby guardsman.

"You mentioned you're digging your own tunnels? To hide?" Ruadh said.

"To evacuate the women and children," Theophila said. "But we haven't been very successful. There are many underground streams."

"I'd evacuate only as a last resort," Ruadh said. "If the enemy get wind of it, they'll easily pick you off once you're in the open. The Ilk patrolling the forest are probably waiting for you to do something like that."

"We've come to the same conclusion," Castes said stiffly.

"But it's definitely worth having a tunnel so you can hide the women and children underground in case there's a breach," Ruadh said.

Castes looked out at the Ilk. "And them? How do we defeat them with the forces we have?"

"What have your scouts learned about the camp?" Ruadh said.

"We haven't sent scouts," Theophila said. "The Ilk mage spotted two of our best illusionists when we sent them to kill him. We haven't dared send more."

"Well, you'd better stoning send some. We need to know how they're organized, if they're building siege engines, how they get their supplies, if they're planning an assault."

"I can go, my illusions are strongest," Alexios said.

"No," Castes said. "We can't—"

"Lose me, yes, I know," Alexios said heavily. "But we need the information."

"No battle is won without risks," Ruadh said.

Castes hesitated, then gave a sharp nod of agreement.

"I suppose if we must," Theophila said.

How did Alexios stand it, Fay wondered. He'd survived that dreadful prison, and now here he was, volunteering to go among the Ilk again, even when he knew his illusions mightn't hold.

"You mentioned you've been designing new weapons?" Arianna said.

"Yes. The artefactors have taken over Tychon's forge in the northern outer circle," Castes replied. "It's not far."

"Let's go take a look, then," Ruadh said.

Their little group descended into the town to go to the forge. Fay looked around as they walked, finding herself a little disappointed by the normality of it all. The buildings were all of wood, with the occasional one of brick. They rose one or two stories, with slanting wooden roofs. The main streets were cobbled, but the smaller side streets were packed earth crossed with slats of wood. Not at all what she had imagined an Eleusian town to be like. The book she had stolen from the Archpriest's library had described their great cities, run almost entirely on magic. Everyone had hot water that came out of taps in their homes and heatstones to warm their homes, like in the Spire and pre-Ruin houses of the rich in Arindel. But, of course, Alexios had warned her of this.

She was more struck by the haunted, wasted appearance of those she saw. Whenever their eyes lit on the weavers, though, hope flickered in them. *Are we enough to save them from the Ilk? I'm not of any use, that's for sure.*

They were close enough to the forge to hear hammering when they were stalled by a fight. Two middle-aged women were screeching at each other. A man, maybe someone's husband, was trying to calm them down. Then another man appeared from a nearby house and threw a bucket of water over the two women. They fell into shocked silence, staring at each other and then at the two men as if they weren't quite sure what they were doing there. Then they realized who was watching them and let out a string of mortified apologies to Alexios and the Rulers.

Alexios said something to them in calm tones, raising his hands in what appeared to be a blessing.

Immediately, they bowed their heads and murmured a reply.

"These happens are often," Theophila said in halting Vycenian when Alexios returned to them. "Everyone always is anxious. And then happens a little thing and they lose themselves."

"The Gloom," Alexios said.

Yes, the Gloom makes us all mad. And they're living with it, day in day out.

They reached the forge, a low brick building that sat a little away from the nearest houses. Heat blasted them when they entered.

At their arrival, a hugely muscled man rose from one of the anvils and came over to them with a rolling gait. He wiped his hands down on his leather apron and then placed hands over chest and bowed.

"Tychon, our master blacksmith," Theophila said, and continued by introducing the Vycenians to him.

Then Castes said something, and Tychon nodded.

"I'll translate," Alexios said.

The blacksmith swept a hand out at the main forge, Alexios repeating his words in Vycnenian so they could understand. "As you can see, I've taken on extra apprentices. To make spearheads." He jerked his head to indicate two young men beating metal with huge hammers. "I've brought in new anvils for them."

Then the blacksmith walked them to a work bench on which a handful of spearheads and arrowheads were lined up. "These are cooling."

Ruadh and Bailin peered down at them. "Good work," Ruadh said, and Bailin concurred. Alexios translated for them, and Tychon grinned, showing a missing front tooth.

"How many in total so far?" Castes asked.

"Two hundred or so," Tychon said. "There isn't a lot of metal. We've been making them from stone too."

"And arrows? You people know how to use a bow?"

"Close to four hundred."

"Armor, helmets?" Ruadh asked, looking around. "Made somewhere else?"

"We don't have enough metal," Tychon said. "There are craftsmen making padded jackets."

"Boiled leather would be better," Bailin said. "Harder."

"You should talk to Yanis about that," Tychon said. "But we don't have much leather either."

Ruadh started muttering under his breath, but Fay wasn't able to catch any of it through the din.

Castes thanked Tychon for his time and then led the way to Eutrop's workshop, which was on the other side of the road. Eutrop was a carpenter, and Tychon's brother. They looked very alike, with deep chests and thick arms. Even their voices, low and buzzing, were similar.

Eutrop gave them a brief overview of the ongoing work. A man working a lathe to make spear shafts. Three half-grown boys polishing spearheads. A woman fastening the polished heads to shafts, finished spears stacked in a rack against the wall behind her. More women fletching arrows around a table.

And a tall, thin man fiddling with a peculiar-looking contraption. "Oxil, our High Artefactor," Alexios told them. Up close, the machine he was working on looked like a giant bow that had been bound horizontally to a wooden frame using twisted rope.

"Ballista," Ruadh said with an appraising look. "Bit smaller than I've seen."

"Yes, I believe that's what they were once called," Oxil said when Alexios had finished the translation. "We've finally solved the problem of attaching the bow securely to the frame, but the bolt still doesn't have enough power to reach the Ilk lines." He placed his hands on his narrow hips, his brow furrowed with frustration. "If it were made of metal or stone, we could use weaving to help, but with wood ..."

"No need for weaving," Bailin said, crouching to look closer. "Siege weaponry was one of my magister's specialisms. I can show you what you need to do." His brown eyes glimmered with excitement as he ran his hand over the frame.

Oxil's face cleared. "We'll be glad to have your help, weaver."

"Bailin." The weaver stood and thrust his hand out.

Oxil looked at the outstretched hand in confusion and Alexios said something to him.

Only a tiny twitch of the lips betrayed Oxil's awkwardness as he took the weaver's hand. Bailin gave it a brief, tight shake. Afterward, Oxil wiped his hand against his brown work smock.

"What else have you developed?" Alexios asked.

Now Oxil smiled, barely hiding his pride. Then he brought them over to a large wooden box on the ground that was full of round pebbles. "Flash bombs," he said. "We adapted the principles of heatstone making. Let's go outside."

He picked up some stones, and they followed him out into the walled yard at the back of the forge. "Stay back," he warned before flinging a stone at the ground about six feet in front of him. With a burst of light, it exploded into tiny fragments. "Not deadly," he said. "But they can be used to blind and disorientate. The weave in them needs to be activated by rubbing before they're thrown. They'll explode on relatively light impact." He handed them each a stone. "We're working on larger, more powerful ones which can kill or maim. We're also trying to design a way to launch them at a greater distance, maybe with the ballista."

"A mangonel would be better," Ruadh said. Oxil looked at him in confusion. "It's like a giant sling, you can use it to throw stones."

"I can help with that too," Bailin said with relish.

"If we had more metal, there's a lot more we could do." Oxil pursed his lips together, shook his head.

"These are good," Ruadh said, rolling a flash bomb in one huge hand. "A few mangonels, some of these big ones, we can kill quite a few of those stinkers before they get anywhere near the wall."

So maybe we aren't all going to be eaten alive after all.

"Right, let's go sit somewhere so we can plan," Ruadh said. "And I need some stoning wine." Alexios opened his mouth, but Ruadh continued, "Or beer. I'll take beer."

They walked to the center of the town, to a square flanked on two sides by long, rectangular buildings of red brick. The entrances to both buildings were accessed by a set of ten steps. Alexios indicated that one was the Temple of the Makers and the other was the Hall of Congress, where the political representatives of his people met. It was into this building they went, passing through a large hall full of benches and into a smaller one at the back, which Alexios told them was called the Ruling Chamber.

They took their seats around a large table, and food, beer and water were brought to them by a serving woman.

Ruadh began with a speech. "There's four keys to winning a siege, whichever side of the wall you're on." He took a swig of beer. "The first is to have more food and water than the attacking army—whoever runs out first will go down. I guess even the Ilk need to eat, I saw their fires. But *what* do they eat?"

"We believe they eat ..." Alexios began, and then trailed off, seemingly unable to continue.

"They eat meat," Castes said. "And not just that of animals and birds."

Even Ruadh looked sick at that.

"There's no wildlife left in the forest," Arianna reminded them. "So they must be getting food from somewhere else by now."

"Did they harvest the crops before burning the land?" Ruadh asked.

"No," said Castes. "They started the burning the day after Alexios left."

"So that's top of our list," Ruadh said. "We need to figure out how they're getting fed. If we can cut off their supply lines, we can force them to either storm the walls or retreat."

Theophila started writing on a large sheet of paper she had spread out in front of her.

"Disease is the next thing to worry about," Ruadh said. "Passes quickly through large groups, sometimes bad enough to force an army to pack up and go home—or wipe out the defenders. Usually comes into play when food and water are low."

"But the Ilk aren't people, so we don't know if they're even affected by disease," Griff said, stroking his beard.

"Aye, it's us I'd be more worried about. And that brings me to the next thing, because they're closely connected." Ruadh paused, downed half his beer while everyone watched him. Foam edged his beard, but he cleared it in a single swipe with the back of his hand. "Morale. That's a big one, the biggest one. Greens always underestimate how important it is."

Theophila stopped writing when Alexios had finished translating the sentence. "Greens?"

"People who haven't been at war before."

Alexios translated, and the puzzled expressions around the room cleared.

"Anyway, as I was saying, morale. People get hungry and thirsty, disease spreads, they've been waiting for weeks and months for the siege to end, maybe taking losses—and finally, they lose the stomach to fight. At best, they're less effective when you send them against the enemy, at worst, they'll mutiny or turn traitor."

"People have been going mad," Castes murmured.

Fay thought of the fight they'd seen in the street. The terror of Alexios's prison. The Gloom. That could kill them as well as the Ilk.

"How do we fight an enemy when it affects our very minds?" Theophila said.

They all looked at Ruadh.

He slugged down more beer. "Wits. Wits is what wins you sieges."

"Not manpower?" Galinda said coolly.

Ruadh bared his broken teeth in a savage grin. "That's important, aye, especially if you want to storm the walls or mount a blockade. But ideally you want to win a siege with as little bloodshed as possible. Numbers don't matter as much if you're smarter than the enemy. Really, it's about how cleverly you use what you've got—and how good you are at predicting what your enemy's going to do next."

"So we need to do something unexpected," Alexios said.

"Aye, but first we need more information on their camp. I want to know why they haven't attacked yet, what their plan might be and how they're getting supplies. There might be some weakness of the Ilk we don't know about—maybe their leader doesn't control them that well. You're lucky he isn't the impatient type. If they'd tried to storm the walls already, you'd probably all be dead."

Blushes among the Eleusians.

"I think he's playing a game," Alexios said. "He doesn't want it to end quickly—*they* don't."

"He might be afraid to lose his Ilk. We don't know how long it takes to spawn Ilk or how hard it is," Arianna said. "In the past, the Ilk lord had many humans in his armies along with monsters. Obviously, that isn't the case this time."

"Most sieges turn into a waiting game, truth be told. Why waste an army on a wall when you could just starve out those behind it?" Ruadh said.

"There's no way we can take the battle to them?" Castes asked hesitantly. "Finish it quickly ourselves?"

Ruadh shook his head vigorously. "Not a chance. Not with those ramparts they've built and not with your half-trained townsmen. You'll be slaughtered. No, we need to get them either to leave or storm the walls. We have a chance on the walls. Their army isn't that big. We can do a lot to improve your weapons and fortifications even in a few days if we get all hands on it. But we need to make sure they don't catch wind of what we're doing and decide to surprise us."

"You think we can win, then?" Castes said with hope.

"With a bit of luck and a lot of preparation," Ruadh said. "I've faced worse odds."

Was he just saying that to give them heart? Could you really compare an army of Ilk to an army of humans?

Ruadh finished the rest of his beer, holding the tankard above his mouth to shake out the last drops. A smack as he put it back down on the table. "Let's get started."

Chapter 48

Alexios

I saw the most wondrous city. Giant birds flew in the skies, and on their backs sat Chelaki riders. But Eleusians walked the streets, too. Chelaki and Eleusians at peace. This must have been the great city of Kirion, built in the mountains that divided our lands. The sight of it triggered great sorrow in me, for this was where the first blow was struck in the war that we now call the Cleansing. To think we once had that. But the Chelaki are vile, deceitful pawns of Antiphos. They proved that again with the Ilk War.

—Visions of Keeper Alexios Arathraxis

As he circled around to the Ilk camp, Alexios breathed deeply to stem the liquid terror sparked by the Gloom. He walked as lightly as possible, unwilling to try a muffling illusion until it was completely necessary—illusions of sound were hard to maintain, especially around the Ilk, where the Lace was so unstable, so difficult to shape.

He also kept his invisibility relatively loose. The Ilk mage would easily find him if he was looking, but the Ilk seemed less discerning, and it was dark.

The monsters were mostly sitting around the embers of their fires, not paying very much attention to the wall or those atop it. They stank—of rancid meat and unwashed bodies—causing his stomach to roil.

"Just how aware are they?" Alexios asked Cassander and Epiktet. *"I know they rely on the Ilk mages for guidance. But can they work independently at all? Will they attack if they see me?"*

But neither of them had an answer to that.

He drew level with their lines and felt a sharp spike in the dread he'd been feeling. It made him lightheaded and weak, and his mind filled with fresh visions of Nixos's and Demeia's deaths. He stumbled and almost lost hold of his illusions, then rolled his hands into fists and breathed deeply against the rising panic.

One of the smaller Ilk suddenly looked straight at him with its red eyes and cocked its head. He froze, but the monster turned away again, evidently unaware of his presence.

Then he was behind the lines, walking toward the eastern camp. The Ilk continued to ignore him, and there was no sign of Inyaki, the Ilk mage. But Alexios expected him to appear at any moment, to break into his maniacal laugh and tear his soul to shreds. He both dreaded it and yearned for it. An opportunity to exact revenge, to end this and save his people.

"Don't think to do it alone," Demeia said. *"He's very powerful. Much more powerful than you."*

"A weak Keeper, chosen from a pool of one," hissed the voice of the Gloom. *"You'd never have passed the tests."*

Alexios tried to block out the voice. He would have to be good enough, it was as simple as that. He couldn't fail. His people were relying on him.

"But you're no warrior," whispered the voice. *"You don't have it in you to kill."*

"I do," he said, making himself believe it. He put a hand to the hilt of the long knife in his belt. A blade for Inyaki if Alexios should see the opportunity. *I can kill if I have to. I can.*

The voice laughed mockingly.

Alexios tightened his grip on the knife, then released it and crept on, getting as close to the glowing fires as he dared, to see what weapons the enemy might have that he had not yet seen. But all he saw were swords and spears among the golls. It seemed they weren't trained to use a bow or other projectile weapon. The rippers relied only on their claws and teeth. But those were more terrifyingly effective than any blade wielded by a goll.

He came to the end of the southern camp without seeing any sign of siege engines or digging. It seemed Inyaki really did plan to wait the defenders out. As he approached the eastern camp, though, he noticed a line of figures marching out from the forest, faintly outlined by the rising half-moon. Drawing closer, he realized they were people—prisoners. Not Eleusians but men with dark skin and long, braided hair, wearing only loincloths. They walked with hands tied behind their backs, heads down and shoulders slumped. Alexios counted nine. Golls walked beside them, driving them on with jabs from the butts of their spears.

The line of men stopped at a large bonfire burning high, surrounded by Ilk who were grunting, shaking their fists, and stamping their feet. They were excited, looking at something by the fire. He inched forward, saw a man on a raised chair, facing the bonfire, wearing a bone mask. Inyaki. Alexios's heart beat faster, fear and rage swirling inside him. Frustratingly, though, there seemed no way to reach Inyaki to try to kill him, not sitting where he was, with all those Ilk around. If Inyaki broke his invisibility, he was dead.

But what were they all looking at? Alexios didn't dare get nearer in case the mage could sense him. Then some of the Ilk shifted aside, and he saw two rippers wrestling, slashing at each other with their claws, biting each other's necks, like dogs. Inyaki called something out in his language, and then laughed, slapping his hand on his thigh.

How can he laugh amidst the Gloom? How does he stand it? Are the Ilk mages immune to it? Are they even human themselves?

One of the rippers managed to get the other on its back. It straddled its fallen fellow, pressing a clawed hand down over its throat. The other bucked and squirmed but couldn't escape. Then its thrashing became weaker, died altogether. The victorious ripper got to its feet, cavorting and waving its arms in the air. Triumphant. So, they could feel emotions? Or was it Inyaki manipulating them?

Inyaki laughed and clapped, while the watching Ilk screeched and grunted. Alexios peered at the fallen ripper. They would kill their own? But then the downed monster stirred, began slowly to get to its feet. It lumbered out into the crowd and was replaced with another of equal size.

The watchers shifted again, and Alexios realized there was a second fight going on, this one between golls. They had dispensed with their armor and weapons and were pummeling each other with their hairy fists. Finally, one knocked its opponent out with a blow to the chin. Immediately, another stepped in to challenge, winning a swift victory.

The prisoners had been brought to a halt in front of Inyaki and were standing facing the bonfire. The Ilk mage pointed at the victorious goll and ripper and said something. The goll snorted and went to a man at the end of the line. It drew a knife and then plunged into the man's bare chest. A long, agonized scream as the goll carved a circle into his flesh and then reached in to pull out a dripping heart. The goll raised the heart in the air, grunting and cavorting, while the man's lifeless body fell to the ground. The ripper went to the second man in the line, reached out with its claws. This time Alexios couldn't look, pressing his hands against his ears to try to block out the screams.

When he dared cast his eyes on the prisoners again, the two Ilk were tossing the hearts onto glowing wood at the edge of the bonfire. A sizzling, and then the smell of roasting meat. Alexios's stomach churned. Other golls got busy with axes and cleavers, chopping the two corpses into pieces, which they carried to Ilk at nearby fires. Then another set of wrestling matches began while the terrified prisoners looked on.

Alexios crept away, wishing he could unsee what he'd just seen. *This must end. Inyaki is even more depraved than I thought.*

"It's not the first time I've heard of Ilk mages feeding human prisoners to the Ilk," Cassander said.

"They worship Antiphos, are we so surprised?" Demeia said. *"We need to destroy them."*

"Find out where the prisoners have come from," Epiktet urged. *"Perhaps there are more that we can free."*

"If we know how they're getting the prisoners here we might also learn how the Ilk have come," Cassander said.

Alexios agreed with them and began to make his way to the part of the forest from which he'd seen the prisoners emerge. He came upon a wide path that had been chopped into the trees, the ground beneath trampled by many feet. There appeared to be no one on it, but he walked along cautiously, muscles tense, ears pricked.

He had walked perhaps fifty paces when the trees fell away from him on either side. A clearing. It was too dark to see very much other than the outline of a structure ahead and to his left. But he heard sounds—of men talking, groaning, weeping. Red eyes appeared in the darkness. Ilk, patrolling.

"Those must be the prisoners you hear," Epiktet said. *"Get closer."*

Alexios was starting to feel the strain of maintaining his illusion. The distortion of the Lace made it so much harder than normal, and a headache was building. *Hold on just a bit longer.* Sweat damping his forehead and tunic, he stole around to the edge of the clearing, approaching the outlined structure from behind. Feeling with his hands, he encountered wooden bars, close-spaced, running vertically and horizontally. Two men muttering on the other side. A cage, he realized, and his disgust grew. *They treat them like animals for slaughter.*

He kept walking along the back of the cage to see how long it was, working hard to keep his illusion going. He came to the end after four paces, but then spied a second cage beyond. How many people were locked up here? Where were they coming from?

"We need to get them out," Doris said, almost hysterical. *"Get them out now."*

"No," Demeia replied. *"The Ilk will see and kill them. It will be impossible to hide them all. We need to come back with more illusionists."*

Demeia was right. Even now, he was forced to grit his teeth against the sharpening pain in his head. Soon, the illusion would fail. But he still hadn't discovered how the prisoners had been brought here. He kept walking, reaching the end of the clearing, where he saw another path leading off into the trees. Little black spots started dancing across his vision. Then he reeled in the grip of sudden dizziness, lost some of the threads. It was too much. He abandoned the muffling illusion.

"Get away, Alexios!" Epiktet cried. *"Hide!"*

"I need to know where they've come from," he said. But as he made for the new path, a pair of Ilk walked toward it from the clearing.

"You can come back," Cassander said.

But Alexios needed to know. Where did the path go? He took a few steps, following the Ilk. More threads slipped out of his grasp, and his mouth twisted with the effort of holding the others in their unnatural position.

"Get out of sight!" Epiktet said again. *"There's nothing to be gained by being caught, and everything to lose."*

It was no use, if he didn't get away now, he was done for. Frustrated, he made for the cover of the trees, and with a relieved sigh, let the threads go.

"We can come back tomorrow," Demeia said.

"Yes, in daylight," Cassander said. *"It will be easier to see, and Ilk seem to prefer the dark."*

Alexios wearily agreed. Tomorrow would have to do, and at the least they would free these poor prisoners.

Chapter 49

Mūak

Anger is a dangerous emotion and should be curbed. It leads to violence and to breaking the Oath. Rather than let your anger simmer, talk to the one who has caused you anger. Find agreement between you, and if you cannot, go to the elders, who will help you find peace.

—Teachings of Old Tsu

A gust of wind shook the branches of the tree in which Mūak was perched. He clung tightly to the trunk until it passed, feeling every hour that he hadn't slept. Warm rain dripped all around him and slithered down his face, but he wouldn't give up until he had her. She'd destroyed everything, taken everything from him. Sīut's pawn indeed. He knew the other hunters wouldn't give up either. They'd always had a double duty—supply their people with food, but also keep them safe from aggression, from within and without. If Ina returned, it would be to see Suni, he was certain.

He thought back to the moment on Uruk'il when he'd noticed Ina was gone, realized that she was going to do something terrible. He'd left Tani and run all the way up to try to stop her. But it had been too late, the Godstone already in pieces around her.

And she'd escaped justice! He ground his teeth. She wouldn't escape again. He would impale her with his own spear.

Movement among the trees. He squinted through the misty rain. It was her! It must be. He resisted the temptation to spring down and take her. She'd hear him coming, have time to vanish into Sīut's Realm like she'd done during the trial. He needed to time it carefully.

She continued to creep through the trees until she was out of sight. He was contemplating getting down when he heard other movement. Suni, coming out of their hut, going to her. What poison was Ina whispering to her? He had to go now, stop her before something even more terrible happened. But then he mastered his panic. No, he couldn't afford to be rash.

He was still considering what to do when Suni reappeared, going back into the hut. There was no sign of Ina. He had to talk to Suni. He slithered down the tree so quickly that he scraped his shins and arms. But the pain was nothing compared to his fear. He found her attaching her healer's pouch around her waist. She was fully dressed in skirt and short tunic.

"What are you doing?" he asked.

Suni spun around to face him, her expression all guilt and fear. "Someone needs my help."

"Don't lie to me," he said, grabbing her arm.

"You're hurting me," she said, trying to pull free.

He relaxed his grip, but kept it strong enough to hold her in place. "Where are you going?"

Suni looked at him wordlessly.

"You're going to help her, aren't you?" He had to get her to admit it. He couldn't stand that she lied to him.

"She plans to leave," she whispered. "Just let her go, Mūak. She'll take Tani. They'll be no threat to us but at least they'll live. Our daughter will live."

"She's twisting your mind with her powers," he said. "You know we can't let her go—or Tani."

"She's our daughter," Suni said, and burst into tears.

"I don't want to lose her any less than you do, but you know it must be done. Sīut has her now." His voice choked, grief almost making him waver. But even worse than thinking of Tani gone was thinking of her fully grown as Sīut's pawn, wreaking chaos and destruction.

"Please, Mūak, let them go," Suni said again.

His heart tore in two. She would be broken from this. He was already broken. "What did she tell you?" he asked roughly.

"She's going to get Tani and then leave the islands to find the drakiri and our ancestors who went east."

"Did you arrange to meet her again?"

Suni nodded, tears leaking down her cheeks. "To say goodbye to Tani."

"Where?"

"The forest, our usual place," Suni said. "Please, Mūak." She clung to his arm. "Please let them go."

To Sīut with Ina! To see how thoroughly Suni was under her spell, it made him sick. But he forced himself to show none of this. Instead, he sighed, as if giving in to her. "Fine, go, see Tani off. But keep me out of it, and be sure no one sees you. The elders have been lenient to you once, they may not be so kind again."

Suni put a hand to his arm. "Thank you," she said quietly.

Something frightened him about the way she was looking at him. Looking at him like she might never see him again. Did she intend to leave too? Was she still lying to him?

She grabbed a yaka-leaf cape and then kissed him goodbye and went out into the rainy night.

He watched her from the doorway, but as soon as she was out of sight, he hurried into the next hut, where Han resided with Ria. They were both awake and dressed, spears next to them. Seeing him, they leaped to their feet.

"She's come back," he said. "Suni is meeting her in the forest, off the path to South Beach. I know the place. If she somehow slips past the guards in the House of the Elders we'll get her there."

They nodded and followed him out. As they passed through the village, they went into other huts to gather other watchers. They took winding routes, keeping to the shadows, but all inexorably moving in the same direction to catch Ina in their trap.

At last, they reached the forest and began to spread out, some climbing into the trees, others hiding behind trunks and bushes. Suni stood in the clearing, clutching her cape around her. She hadn't heard them, for they were hunters, and were used to hiding from creatures with sharper ears than hers.

Mūak took position close to his bondmate. He held his spear thrower above his shoulder, ready to launch at the first sign of Ina. What a pleasure it would be to see her lifeblood bubbling out of her. To finally banish her baleful influence over Suni. He'd lose Tani, but at least he'd regain his bondmate.

Chapter 50

Fay

Nobody knows how the Ilk were made. And if anyone did find out, they're dead now.

—The Ilk War: A History, Carolin Morgan

"I need a bloody drink after all that," Ruadh said. "There's a tavern down this road."

Fay was in full agreement, her mind still reeling with what Alexios had said. Human prisoners, being fed to the Ilk? Hearts ripped out while they still lived? *Even whoring is better than that fate.*

They came to the tavern, which looked much like the other buildings around. The only difference was the door, which was painted with the image of a barrel. Inside, only a handful of older men, talking quietly at rectangular tables. It was clean, the wooden floor well swept. Ruadh went to the bar and mimed drinks. The bartender poured them from a barrel behind the bar, but when Ruadh tried to give him money, he shook his head and said something in Eleusian. Ruadh grinned at the man and thanked him in Vycenian, then they sat down in a corner.

"Is this like other sieges you've been in?" Fay asked.

Ruadh barked a humorless laugh. "Are you joking?"

"The Ilk," she said, sipping from her beer to cover her embarrassment. It was on the sour side, but a drink was a drink. "Have we got a hope?"

"Always have hope," Ruadh said. "Or you might as well lie down and let them have you."

"How many sieges have you been in?"

Ruadh screwed up his eyes, looked at the ceiling a second, then shrugged. "Maybe ten, twelve. Mostly on the other side."

"All in Tarsis?"

"Aye. Lawless, nasty place. Never a shortage of work for a fighting man." He drank deeply from his beer.

"Why did you come to Arindel, then?"

"Got to the point where pickings were slim no matter who you were fighting for. The country's bled dry from war."

Bled dry by the mercenaries, Fay thought. But she didn't want to annoy him by saying it. "You never thought to go back to where you came from?"

"Northland?" Ruadh snorted. "Makes Tarsis seem wealthy. There's nothing but rocks up there. Rocks, and mines for digging up the rocks. My pa broke his back clawing out silver from the ground, and he could barely put food in our mouths."

"So you decided to become a sellsword."

"I'd rather die with an axe in my hands, not breaking my back in a stinking hole." Ruadh looked down at his axe, lying on the ground next to him.

"Even if it means facing Ilk?"

Ruadh bared his teeth. "Especially if it means facing Ilk. The Eleusians are right about one thing. They're bloody abominations. Need to be wiped out, every last one of them, and especially the stoning mages who went about spawning them."

Fay drank, remembering what Alexios had told her, that the Ilk mage had stolen his son's very *soul*. She shuddered, her resolve melting away. She should never have come—at least with a common hanging she'd have kept her soul. To stop herself from thinking, she chanced another question with Ruadh. "When's the last time you saw your family?"

Ruadh's expression darkened, and she regretted the question, expecting him not to answer. But he did. "Pa's long under the ground. Blood cough got him when he was in prison. And before you ask, it wasn't his fault he was in there. He did nothing wrong, only asked for a mite more coin so we could stoning eat."

Fay decided she didn't want to ask him about his mother. She knew all about the wretchedness of the poor.

Ruadh wasn't done, though, surprising her again. "Ma married his brother. Uncle Ger. But they'd been screwing since long before pa died. Not sure which of my sisters are his and which are my pa's." He barked a laugh. Then he looked at her. "You want to tell me about your people?"

Fay shook her head. That was a story she'd rather forget. And putting it into words wasn't going to help with that.

Ruadh shrugged. "Don't blame you."

"The plan sounds like it will work, right?" Fay said to change the subject. Part of her felt disappointed that she couldn't join in. But she'd be no use, she wasn't a warrior. *Just a whore, a priestess of a religion that everyone here treats as heresy.*

"The prisoners, you mean?"

She nodded.

"There's a fair chance," Ruadh said. "But nothing's certain in war."

"I feel useless here," she said. "I wish I had something to do."

Ruadh raised an eyebrow. "Didn't Moth have some task for you?"

"Moth doesn't know I'm here," she said. Then cursed herself. The beer had got to her. She shouldn't have let that slip.

"Aye, thought as much," Ruadh said. "But what made you come? It's going to turn into a right shitstorm once the fighting starts. I'm only here on orders. I'd be miles away, otherwise."

Fay sighed. "Lothar." She told him about the archpriest's attempted rape, and Ruadh glowered.

"I'll never get why some men think it's more exciting to take a woman against her will. It's weak," he said. "I'd rather conquer her heart than her body. That's the real challenge,"

"And yet you have no wife," Fay said, teasing, glad to change the subject again.

Ruadh snorted. "I didn't say I'd let a woman conquer me. I'm not a man made for digging potatoes and dandling children on his knee."

It was rather hard to imagine him doing either. Ruadh was a beast of a man, with biceps bigger than her thighs. He was covered in a network of scars, some white and near invisible, others red and puckered. And yet despite the aura of violence, she'd always sensed a gentleness in him.

"There's no whores here, did you know that?" Ruadh said. "It's against the law." He shook his head. "Don't know how the men handle it."

"Maybe they have more respect for women here," Fay said. "Maybe men here have learned to enjoy their pleasure with their wives and sweethearts instead of paying for it." But she found it as hard to believe as Ruadh. Men always thought they were entitled to a fuck, whether they could find a woman willing or not. Was that why Alexios was so unusually caring? Were all Eleusians the same?

"I have full respect for whores," Ruadh said. "They provide a willing service, and I provide them with good coin."

Fay remembered Madame Sisi's, the men her pa had forced her to lie with. Ruadh might be respectful, but many weren't, and it wasn't a choice if the only other option was to starve.

Ruadh cocked his head. "I don't suppose you're planning to go back to that are you?" He grinned, insinuating.

"No, and don't even let the thought cross your mind," she snapped.

He raised his hands. "I wouldn't."

"Good." She drained her drink, tense and angry. "I'm going to go and find something to do with myself." She got to her feet so abruptly that her chair almost tipped over. Barely pausing to right it, she stamped toward the exit.

"I didn't mean to offend you!" Ruadh called.

She ignored him, yanking open the door and letting it slam shut behind her. But once on the street, she found herself at a loss, looking left and right, not even knowing in which direction to turn.

The door opened behind her. Ruadh, looking apologetic.

She glared at him and strode off down the street, heedless of where she was going. To her relief, he didn't try to follow, but it was only once she'd reached the central square that she came back to herself. The defenders were doing weapons drills, as they had done the day before. With little else to do, she sat on the steps in front of the Hall and watched, trying to master her fury, trying not to hate herself for snapping at Ruadh when he was about to risk his skin to save men from being eaten alive.

Her eyes lit on a young woman of no more than twenty. She was slight, with cropped fair hair and the bright, feline eyes typical of all Eleusians. Her opponent was a much taller man. But despite his advantage in weight and height, she was making quick work of him, dodging and ducking, dummy spear flashing to strike him on the legs, the torso, the face.

Fay counted how many more women there were. Twenty out of a cohort of a hundred. What would it be like to hold a spear? To feel the weight of a real weapon in her hands? But she was no warrior. *Although I did stab Lothar, the prick. And Pa. No, let's not think about that.* She looked at the other women. None were as good as the fair-haired one. But some were still quick and nimble enough to stand their own against the men.

Then the trainer shouted something, and they all fell smartly into line, snapping their spears to their sides. He said something else, and in unison, they stamped the spear butts on the ground. Another shout and they began to disperse.

Before she realized what she was doing, Fay was walking toward the trainer. His eyes widened when he saw her, and he said something in Eleusian, pressing his hands against his chest and bowing. *He thinks I can weave.* Fay mimed raising a staff in the air and shook her head. "I'm not a weaver."

He frowned in confusion.

She mimed explosions and shook her head again, stabbing a finger at herself. "No magic."

He said something else in Eleusian.

She pointed at his spear. "Teach me to use that." But he remained confused, so she gestured for him to pass her the spear. He did so, looking reluctant. She began to wave the spear about with deliberate incompetence. "I can't use it. Teach me," she said again.

But if anything, the man appeared even more bewildered than before.

Fay heaved a sigh. It had been a stupid idea, anyway. *Wasn't even an idea. I don't know why I'm here.* She returned the spear to the trainer and was about to go and find something to eat herself when she saw Alexios come out of the Hall. Acting again on impulse, she gestured at the trainer to wait and then ran over to the illusionist, shouting his name. He looked over at her, evidently discomfited, and she remembered that Eleusians didn't shout in public, or run, or do other unseemly things. She forced herself to slow to a walk. "I want to join the training," she said when she reached him. "But I can't make him understand." She pointed at the trainer.

Alexios frowned. "You—what?"

"I want to learn how to use a spear. I want to stand on the wall with everyone else when the time comes." *I* am *mad. I've gone mad. The Ilk have made me mad.*

Alexios seemed to think the same thing, his hands coming up in a gesture of denial. "No, no, no, you don't need to do that. You've already done so much."

"I hate feeling so useless. I've been wandering around here doing nothing. And, who knows, maybe I'll have to fight anyway if ..." If the Ilk breached the walls, but she couldn't say it.

Alexios opened his mouth, paused, then suddenly smiled. "I have a better idea," he said. "We need people on the wall who can help with the wounded, distribute water, bring fresh spears and arrows. Someone who can help others deal with the Gloom. You've already experienced it, you know what it's like."

"I could barely stand it," she said.

"But at least you're prepared. You can help others prepare."

Fay glanced back at the dispersing trainees. She was no warrior. But as a priestess she had trained to bandage cuts and wounds and treat common diseases. She hated tending to the sick, but no one else would help the poor of New Arindel. "I suppose you're right," she said. "I'm better suited to that."

Alexios looked relieved. "I'll take you to Hymne at the Panaceon. She's one of our chirurgeons and is responsible for organizing the assistants."

So Fay followed him to a long, single-storied wooden building that lay behind the Hall of the Rulers. The first room was small enough, with a wooden bench running along three sides and a door in the fourth. There was also a desk in the far-right corner. Alexios went to the person sitting behind it, a young man in a plain blue tunic. They exchanged some words and then Alexios took her through the door into a short corridor. "Her room is at the end he said," he said, pointing. "Let's hope she's there."

She *was* there, greeting them with a warm smile that immediately made Fay feel at ease. Maybe it was also due to the air of matronly competence that hung around her. She looked like she would brook no nonsense, but at the same time like she'd be quick to rustle up a warming soup if you so much as sneezed. Of course, the woman didn't speak a word of Vycenian, but Fay had picked up enough Eleusian to introduce herself.

Then she and Alexios launched into rapid Eleusian, Fay unable to catch a word. When they were done, he explained. "She's going to bring you into a training room where you'll meet the other physic's assistants. She'll pair you with one of them, who'll show you all the basics."

"Tell her I'm ready to start," Fay said.

Alexios spoke to Hymne, and the woman nodded and smiled at Fay.

"I have to go now, but—thank you," Alexios said.

"Don't thank me, it's my pleasure." The words surprised her. Pleasure? She hated tending to the sick. She didn't want to bandage wounds. She didn't want to stand on the wall when the Ilk came for them. *But here I am, and I might as well make myself useful somehow.*

Alexios said some final words to Hymne, then left her. The woman gestured for Fay to follow her into one of the rooms off the corridor. There were a dozen or so young people inside, all engaged in different chores—some preparing ointments, others cutting bandages into strips or preparing healer's kits.

The girl she was paired with was tall, with large blue-green eyes and golden hair that tumbled halfway down her back. Her name was Daphne, and she started by taking Fay all around the room, pointing at things and people and saying Eleusian words for Fay to remember, words like bandage, stretcher, arm, leg, water, blood.

Fay's tongue folded clumsily around the words, and she noticed Daphne repress a laugh more than once as she corrected her poor pronunciation. But despite her embarrassment, Fay discovered a pleasure in adding Eleusian vocabulary to her own. She felt like she was being initiated into a secret society with its rules and codes, and listened intently whenever Daphne spoke to others. Of course, it was all a meaningless babble, but by the end of the day, she had started to pick out the odd word from Daphne, who spoke more slowly and clearly for her sake.

In the evening, she joined the healers with drills on the wall. They practiced pulling "wounded" people away from the wall and down to makeshift infirmaries in nearby homes. She also learned the various horn calls and what they would mean: attack, withdraw, skreeks coming, wall breached.

If the wall was breached, they were to go underground, taking what wounded they could with them. If they were lucky, they would be able to escape through the tunnel that was being dug in the crypt of the temple to connect with the sewers. But Fay prayed to Lumia that it wouldn't come to that, that somehow Alexios, Ruadh and the weavers would deliver a miracle and save not only the prisoners but also the rest of them.

Chapter 51

Alexios

I saw dead bodies rise from the red dirt in a land riven by deep fissures. What a horror to behold! They were under the control of a sorcerer, a necromancer of some sort, who wore a bone mask on his face.

—Visions of Keeper Alexios Arathraxis

Alexios went out over the northern wall in the late afternoon sun. The four weavers came next, and he and Epi spun illusions to keep them hidden from the Ilk. Ruadh, Youno, and Miro followed, and then they crossed the gorge, using rope to get down more quickly.

They began the tough walk through the forest around to the eastern side of the town and the clearing with the prisoners. Upon earlier agreement, they didn't speak and kept their footsteps as quiet as possible. They wanted to avoid spinning illusions until they got closer to the clearing.

The problem with walking in silence, though, was that it gave you too much time to think. Everyone was white-faced, shoulders knotted and tense. Except for Bailin, who always managed to appear cool and self-possessed.

Alexios tried not to worry, tried not to think of what he'd done wrong and what he might fail to do yet. But the closer they got to the Ilk, the more his failures ate at him. *It's the Gloom,* he told himself. But then, *my failures are real. I let Nixos and Demeia die. I should never have let them go. I should have rescued at least one of them. What if I fail again now?*

"You are the strongest person I know," Eliana told him. "*You will prevail."*

"I never realized you doubted so much," Demeia said. "*I think I preferred knowing you from the outside."*

She was joking, but there was a bite to the words. Of course, he'd always projected an air of being in command, of pretending he knew what he was doing, even when he didn't. He was the Keeper, and his people needed to see him strong and wise and unbowed, especially now, when the Gloom was eating away at their courage and sanity. He couldn't allow anyone to see the cracks, the doubts that haunted him.

When they finally neared the clearing, Alexios waved for the group to hang back while he got closer to scout. He came up behind the cages, and in daylight could see there were only the two that he'd discovered the night before. Many men were crowded inside—gaunt, dirty, wearing loincloths, their skin a deep brown, their hair woven into many small braids. All had their hands bound behind their backs with rope. He slipped between the two cages to get a better view of the clearing, counting eight golls standing there. It should be easy enough to take them down. Then he crept around to the front of the cage to see how the door was locked. A simple wooden bolt in front of a panel so that the prisoners couldn't reach it from the inside. He returned to the others and told them what he'd seen.

"We weavers can take one or two each," Arianna said. "The golls are weak to our magefire."

"Let's go in from two sides, catch them in a pincer," Ruadh said. "While we attack the golls, one of you should release the prisoners."

"Miro, you do it," Alexios said.

He nodded.

"Galinda and I will go from the left," Arianna said. "Griff and Bailin, you go the other way."

"I'm with you," Ruadh said to Arianna, and she nodded.

"Remember, we lead the prisoners into the forest and then to Neopoli. If Ilk follow us, you weavers hang back to fight them while Miro takes the prisoners to safety. Epi and I will cover you with invisibility to protect you."

"Right, let's do this," Ruadh said, hefting his axe.

The illusionists did their work, and they made their stealthy way to the clearing. They divided into two when they reached the cages, circling around to launch their assault on the golls. Alexios hung back from the fight, working to cloak them, while Arianna and Griff shot blue light at the creatures. It was impossible to fully hide the magefire. The best he could do was a kind of blurring, but the golls never saw it coming. Ruadh's axe he *could* hide, and it sliced the head clean off one of the monsters before it even realized it was being attacked.

Behind him, he heard Miro opening the cage doors, telling the prisoners to get out. Men stirring, stumbling, running. Out of the corner of his eye, he saw brown limbs and torsos. Triumph swelled in him. Success already, with no harm done to anyone.

But his joy was trampled by the sound of many feet coming from the path into the forest. Rippers, lumbering into the clearing—two, three, four of them. And more behind. "Ilk coming!" he shouted—then reeled as his illusions were attacked by an impossibly strong force. The same force that had destroyed his forest illusions when the Ilk had first come. Inyaki.

Ruadh, Galinda, and Arianna flickered into view. He tried to respin the Lace, but the wrongness of the Ilk, coupled with this other power, was making the threads burn and whip away from him. Bailin and Griff also reappeared, Epi and Youno obviously under attack too.

The golls were dead, but now they were facing ten or more rippers, with more Ilk coming down the pathway, an apparently endless stream. A fresh army? He couldn't see Inyaki, though.

"Retreat!" Arianna shouted. "Griff, Galinda—three-round break. Griff left, Galinda right. Bailin, keep them off us!" Bailin shot blue fire at the eyes of the nearest rippers, slowing them momentarily. At the same time, the air quality changed, and then the ground started to shake and vibrate. Moments later, a long crack opened beneath the front line of the rippers. Some went tumbling in, others tried to go around it. But even as they did, two more cracks broke open perpendicular to the first, taking more down and hemming the rest in.

Then the weavers ran, Alexios, Epi, and Youno with them, Miro and the prisoners ahead. Some rippers managed to get around the cracks and followed, their long limbs eating ground fast, taking them through thickets as if they were no more than grass. Alexios called out a warning, and the weavers turned to fire blue bolts at the closest two, pushing them back.

He tried again to spin the threads and, to his relief, found them more amenable. Immediately, he worked to hide the weavers, calling for the other illusionists to do the same for those around them. The rippers paused, confused as their prey disappeared.

They started running again, Alexios aching and sweating from the strain of the illusions. Along the way, they came upon straggling prisoners evidently too weak to move far at speed. With the rippers lost behind them, Alexios made himself visible and called out to the men. They regarded him with relief, following his lead back toward the town.

At the ravine, they found prisoners already scaling the northern wall with a rope ladder. Miro had them loosely hidden from sight, but Alexios could easily see the shifting movement.

He motioned for the prisoners to use the rope tied to a nearby bush to lower themselves down into the ravine. A second rope had been hammered into a stake in the ground in front of the wall for them to use to climb up. They did so slowly, evidently weakened by their captivity, and one man lost his grip and fell. He was lucky, acquiring only fresh cuts and bruises. In the end, they made him tie the rope under his armpits and Ruadh heaved him up, muscles bulging and straining.

Finally, he was himself crossing the ravine and climbing over the wall to join the prisoners, who were waiting at the bottom of the steps to the wall. They looked around uneasily, talking to each other in a strange language. Alexios noted that many had black stripes inked around their biceps and forearms, some of them only one or two, others at least ten.

"Where did you come from?" he asked one of the men in Vycenian.

The other looked at him blankly, then said something again in his own language.

"They look like they come from Federation lands," Ruadh said, coming to stand next to Alexios.

"What is the Federation?" Alexios asked.

"Empire to the south of Vycenia. They call themselves a Federation, but the emperor didn't exactly give the states much choice in whether to join or not," Ruadh replied. "Lots of dark-skinned folk down there, though. These are obviously warriors, defeated in some other war. Likely they're Rifters. There's been word that the Federation is finally beating them into submission."

"Does that mean the Federation is also employing Ilk?" Alexios asked.

Ruadh rubbed his beard. "If it was, we'd probably have heard of it by now. But there's obviously some connection. Let's see if I can get any sense out of them. I have a few words of Zenian, the Federation's common tongue."

"Let's take them to the Panaceon first and get them food and water," Alexios said, realizing it was cruel to keep them out in the sun in their state. "Then we can try to get more information out of them." He sent a defender to tell the rulers to meet them there, then led the way there himself, flanked by Ruadh and the mages.

At the Panaceon, they put the men into one of the larger wards, and assistants hurried to bring them sustenance, Fay among them. She seemed relieved to see them and paused to speak to Ruadh. Two physics also came to examine the prisoners for injuries or other maladies.

Theophila and Castes soon arrived, and they went to one of the healthier-looking men to interrogate him.

Ruadh spoke to him in a language filled with soft sounds and vowels. The man answered haltingly, making gestures. Ruadh nodded, said something else, and again the man answered. Ruadh turned to Alexios. "I was right. These are Rifters. He says he can describe what happened if he has something to draw on."

Alexios signaled and someone brought the prisoner slate and chalk. He began to scrawl on it. A large plain, men sitting high up on the backs of strange, two-legged beasts with large jaws and long teeth. These were his people, he said. Then he drew men on horses and on foot wielding long spears, attacking the Rifters. Federation soldiers, Ruadh explained.

Next, he showed his people being defeated, using large Xs to strike them out of his drawing.

Ruadh asked more questions, and the man spoke animatedly.

"He says he didn't see anyone in bone masks. And he saw no Ilk until he was taken to those cages we found."

"But how did they get to the cages?" Alexios asked.

Ruadh spoke to the man again. Another crude image followed, this time of prisoners being bound then taken into a hut. The man spoke some words, pressed his hands hard against his temples, and then mimed like he was choking, his hand against his throat.

Ruadh's brows drew together as he tried to make sense of what the man was saying. "They went into the hut and from there into a place with no air, which tried to crush them."

The man drew another image showing the prisoners emerging from the hut into the woods and then the cages.

What did it all mean?

When the prisoners had been seen to, Alexios sought out Theophila.

"Even so, it's obvious the war has already spread wide," Theophila said. "How long have they been planning this?"

It was a rhetorical question, but Alexios had an answer. "Perhaps centuries," he said. "The Ilk mages eat souls to keep themselves alive. This may be a continuation of the war we thought finished two hundred years ago."

"Our greatest mistake, perhaps, was to think we'd won the war the last time," Cassander said.

"The Unraveler will ever seek to destroy us," Epiktet said.

"But in losing so much the last time, we fooled ourselves in thinking it would be enough," Cassander said.

"We must warn the other nations somehow," Theophila said.

How quickly things have changed, Alexios thought. *Weeks ago we thought only to hide, now we seek to connect to the entire world.*

"If it's not already too late," said Bailin, who'd just arrived and obviously overheard. "If the Ilk mages have infiltrated the Federation as well as the Spire, the war would seem nearly over already."

"We'll need to raise a great army," Arianna said. "And we're locked out of Arindel." She clenched her fist. "They've been clever, moving against us before we even knew a game was being played."

"First, we need to defeat the Ilk here," Ruadh said. "That looked a lot like reinforcements coming down that path earlier."

"Which means they're probably getting ready to storm the walls," Bailin said grimly.

"Let's get to the Chamber," Arianna said. "We need full reports on the state of the defenses and to put everyone on battle alert."

"Aye," Ruadh said. "Could be they know Alexios got help and have decided it's a bad idea to keep waiting." He turned to Theophila. "Put every man—or woman—who can wield a saw or a hammer onto finishing the mangonels. If they work through the night, we'll have enough ready by morning."

She nodded, and then they made their way to the Chamber.

That night, Alexios found himself unable to sleep. Whenever he closed his eyes, he saw rippers tearing the hearts of men from their chests. He smelt the reek of the Ilk and heard the mad, mocking laughter of Inyaki. And the voice of Gloom whispered in his ear always, reminding him of his failures. Finally, it drove him out of his bed and back to the wall. He needed to think, find some way to save his people.

When he'd climbed up to the eastern side of the wall, he heard a shout farther along. Hurrying in the direction of the noise, he saw a man in midair, arms and legs flailing as he fell to the ground beyond the wall. A defender was leaning out, hands outstretched, crying a long "no." Alexios stopped next to him and looked down. The man was lying on the ground, neck twisted at an unnatural angle. He didn't move.

"I tried," the defender said in a broken voice. "That's the second this week."

"The second?"

"And one last week," the defender said, eyes glistening with tears. "I tried. I keep an eye out for them. I tried."

The Gloom, they had to find a way to fight its poison. "What's your name?"

"Patos."

"Don't blame yourself, Patos. This is the work of Antiphos, but the Makers are still with us. Come, let's bring him in."

The man nodded, wiping at his eyes. They went down to the gate and asked for it to be opened, then hurried around to get the body. Alexios took the man's legs and the defender his arms.

"Do you know who he is?" Alexios asked.

"I know his sister," Patos replied.

"I'll go with you to talk to her. But first, let's put him somewhere dignified." Several buildings had been designated as mortuaries for when the battle came, but Alexios was loathe to use one of these now, so they carried him into one of the smaller temples near the wall. Then Alexios went with Patos to deliver the sad news, his steps heavy, his heart heavier still.

But as he walked with the man, he started to think, *we won't be able to withstand this. The Gloom will eat our courage. The Ilk will destroy us.* He needed to do something unexpected, as Ruadh had said before. But what? A daring plan came to him. He'd go out and look for Inyaki himself, finish him, do what he ought to have done in the first place. Then his people might be spared.

"No," Demeia said. *"You've already felt his power, how easily he's able to tear apart illusions. You'll just be killed. You'll be doing exactly what he wants."*

"I have to do something," Alexios said. *"Do you really think our defenders will be able to hold firm? The Ilk numbers are only increasing. And the Gloom with them."*

"Demeia's right," Epiktet said. *"Don't sacrifice yourself foolishly."*

"No, the attempt should be made," Cassander said, surprising him. *"Inyaki will think us too afraid to come after him directly. He may be overconfident and therefore careless."*

The other souls chimed in, most disagreeing with Cassander, saying Alexios shouldn't risk himself. But Alexios's mind was made up by the time they were at the dead man's house, giving the news to his wailing sister.

Once the grim task was done, he bade Patos goodbye and went to the northern side of the wall under invisibility. He tossed out one of the rope ladders that were curled up on the ramparts and climbed down, then shook it loose and stowed it under a bush. Crossing the gorge in the darkness wasn't easy. He could mostly feel out his footing, but even so, he slipped and slid more than once. There were no major mishaps, though, and he snuck around to the Ilk camp sporting only a few new bruises.

As he approached, he realized there was something strange about the darkness ahead of him. It was thick, choking. The light of the moon didn't penetrate it. He summoned the Lace, looked intently to see if anything was amiss. The sheer number of threads made it difficult to spot when another illusionist was at work, and at first, Alexios thought all was in order. But to be sure, he began to pull gently on the threads near the camp. They felt tight, too tight. He pulled harder, felt an answering pull, a resistance. Someone had respun them. So Inyaki also had the ability to create illusions? It was almost unheard of, a mage with the power of all three peoples—Vycenian, Chelaki, and Eleusian. Perhaps he had others with him, traitors as Ruadh had warned of? But Alexios couldn't imagine how one of his people would go over to the Chelaki side, to Antiphos.

He needed to get right into the camp to find Inyaki, so he kept moving toward the heavy darkness. He reached the edges of it, was suddenly slammed with paralyzing fear. *Dear Makers, watch over me, give me your strength.* He braced himself, stepped into the darkness, expecting to lose his sight. But instead, the darkness vanished, and he saw something altogether different.

The Ilk were no longer sleeping or lazing. They were moving, massing together into columns, weapons in their hands. They were preparing to attack!

What was he to do? He wanted to keep looking for Inyaki, but the Ilk mage might be in the other camp. He needed to warn his people. With the illusion of darkness, the guards on the wall probably wouldn't see the Ilk until they were almost on top of them.

Seething with frustration, he turned and stepped back through the darkness. At first, he went at a slow jog, then launched into a full run once he was away from the camp and could be looser with his illusion. He dropped his invisibility entirely when he was far enough away, already feeling the strain and mindful that he would soon need all his strength.

He went up to the wall before he reached the gorge and squinted up, seeking. A man was silhouetted nearby, and between heaving breaths, he called out to attract his attention.

"Keeper!" came the surprised reply.

"The Ilk are preparing to attack!" he shouted. "Sound the alarm!"

Moments later, the first horn was blowing, long and loud, three times. It was soon followed by more horn blasts, ringing out all over the town.

The defender he had alerted found a rope ladder and tossed it down for him. He scrambled up, then half-walked and half-ran around to the eastern gate, dodging the men and women who were already gathering for the defense.

Finally, he reached his own assigned position, near the gate. The Ilk were on the move, their red eyes shining through the fog of night. The battle had started at last.

Chapter 52

Ina

Since the Exile, there have been very few murders. The Oath has proved effective, as have the lessons of the past.

—Teachings of Old Tsu

Ina was very close to the House of the Elders when she heard footsteps about to cross her path. Heart thumping, she pressed against the side of a hut as the person went past. The near miss made her doubly alert, but she met no one else.

When she reached the House of the Elders, she stole around to the back of it, then prepared to spread out her lifesense to find Tani and see who else was inside and where.

"*Think of a fishing net. You cast it out and then pull it back in. The little fish you don't want will slip back out again.*" The words that floated into her mind had been spoken by a man—Lin's mentor again?

She tried doing as he said, pulling her net around the House of the Elders, letting all the small pulses of insects and rodents fall out of it, focusing on the stronger, steadier beacons of the Chelaki inside. It *was* easier, thinking in these terms, and her headache seemed a little less.

Inside, she found twelve people. One was Tani, her open mind calling clearly to Ina's. There seemed to be four others close to the child. Guards? Perhaps some were even in the room with her. Five other people were dispersed throughout the house and by the entrance. More guards, no doubt, as the elders didn't sleep there. They really must be afraid of her and Tani.

She'd have to splice straight into Tani's prison and immediately silence those with her or they'd raise the alarm. But how to do that when she hadn't even managed to land on her feet yet? What would Lin have done?

She thought about one of the dreams she'd had in the House of the Elders, of a scouting mission in which Lin had used her power to make people unconscious. A stun strike. Calling the dream to mind, she concentrated on what Lin had done. It seemed to be something like shouting, but silently, through her connection to the Cloth, spreading it out to other minds along the threads. A bit like screaming into someone's ear. Well, maybe that would work. If not, hopefully she could keep the hole open and grab Tani and run.

More quickly than before, she made a hole in the Cloth, using her lifesense and knowledge of the Elders' House to form the passageway into the building. Then, filling her lungs with as much air as she could, she stepped into ol'Sīut.

The journey was quick as a flash, but she landed outside Tani's door instead of inside, stumbling against the two male guards who were standing there, stomach roiling and heaving. They cried out in surprise when they saw her, raising their spears. Panicking, Ina summoned the force for the stun strike and sent it out with everything she had. Again, the shrieking pain in her own head, but the hunters crumpled to the ground without a word. Ina peered down at them through the lights flashing and dancing in her vision. Nisith and Taki. Those two had never liked her and had taunted her when she was a child because she was always too sick to join their games. Their minds appeared to her now as a scrambled and fragmented mess. The meanest part of her felt a spark of satisfaction, the best part hoped the damage wasn't permanent.

She opened the door to Tani's room and saw two more hunters, both female, slumped in their chairs. Mika and Gisi, two who had always been kind to her. She stared at them, paralyzed by the realization of what she had done and what she was about to do. She had raised a hand against her own people, she had broken the Oath of Peace. She was what the elders had said her to be. Cursed, a creature of Sīut. *No, I follow Chel, no matter what they say.*

Then she remembered Tani and shifted her gaze to the child. She was completely motionless. Ina shook her gently, but she didn't stir. "Tani, it's Ina," she said in a low voice, shaking her again. The child didn't move. She must have been stunned too. She hadn't been badly hurt, had she? Reaching out with her lifesense, she could tell that the child was still alive, but her mind was different than it had been before—drifting, fuzzy. She was about to scoop Tani in her arms when she realized she might need weapons. Returning to the two unconscious hunters, she took Mika's rope belt and fastened it around her waist. Then she took both their belt knives and stuck them inside the belt. She would have liked a spear too, but she needed to keep her hands free. After a moment's hesitation, she also took their water skins and fixed them to the belt. When she was ready, she opened a path to the forest clearing through ol'Sīut. Then she took Tani and stepped in.

It was different going through with someone else. The pressure was stronger, it seemed to take all her energy to keep it from crushing her like an insect beneath a stone. But it was over almost before it began, and she emerged on her knees, Tani flopping out beneath her. The answering headache was so bad she cried out, her vision spinning and blurring.

And because of it, she was slow in realizing what was going on around her.

"There she is!"

She peered into the gloom, left eye shut tightly against the pain. Hunters, five of them running from behind the trees and swarming around them, spear-throwers over their shoulders. Mūak right in front of her, glowering with anger. Next to him, Suni. Her eyes begged forgiveness. Had she betrayed Ina, or had Mūak overheard them? Had the others been waiting here all along, foreseeing what she would do? They must have, to come so quickly.

She staggered to her feet, still half blind. Elder Alik appeared next to Suni. And—great Chel—there was Oyu, spear-thrower ready. She tried to signal to him, but he turned his eyes away from her, his mouth set. She looked for her mother but didn't see her. Desperately, she called to them. "I don't wish anyone any harm. I only want to leave with Tani."

"We swore an oath, Ina'Elkir. You can't be allowed to remain in this world," Alik'Ri said, his voice low, calmly determined.

Even though she had adopted it for herself, it was strange to hear this new name from him. Elkir, not Yakir. Skyrider, not skyhunter. Cursed, not pure.

"Don't let her speak!" said Elder Kumi. "She'll bend your mind with Sīut's powers. Hunters, ready!"

"No!" Suni's shriek followed her as she ran to cover Tani's prone form. "Don't kill her, please, not like this!"

"Move away, Suni'Ish," Alik'Ri said. Two hunters surged toward her, dragged her back.

"Send the Cursed One to Chel!"

A hum as the light spears flew at her. Instinctively, Ina spliced up into the air, a trick Lin had often used. Shouts of surprise and pain as spears passed through empty air, hitting hunters standing on the opposite side. Ina landed back on the balls of her feet.

"Take her away, Ina!" Suni screamed, struggling between the two hunters who'd grabbed her.

More spears flew at Ina, and again she spliced out of the way. But this time, there was a nouk spear waiting for her when she dropped back to the ground. She twisted, just enough so that it sliced across her ribs rather than penetrating them. The male hunter pulled the spear back to strike again.

"Hold on to her! She can't go anywhere if you hold on to her!"

Her legs were pulled from behind, and she fell heavily to the ground, the pain from her wound flaring in response. She scrambled into a guard position on her back and saw her assailant. Oyu. "Let me go," she gasped. "I only want to go and take Tani with me."

"Don't speak, Cursed One," Oyu snarled, as if she were no one, as if they had never been friends.

He managed to pass one arm through her guard and press down on her shoulder to keep her arm from moving. It was the wounded side and Ina couldn't repress a scream. "Oyu, please, aren't we friends still?" Black spots danced across her eyes.

"It's you who ended our friendship, Cursed One."

He moved, but she shifted her hips in time to stop him from pinning her down completely. "I didn't want to hurt you." Her breathing came hoarse and ragged between the words.

Oyu didn't respond, but she knew from his momentary stiffness that he was affected. Then he suddenly changed position and she wasn't quick enough to stop him from wrapping her up more tightly. He was one of the few in all the island who could best her in a grappling match. And she was greatly disadvantaged now, weakened by the wound and days of too little sleep and too much magic.

"Oyu, please, if you ever did love me, let me go."

He didn't answer, scrambling into the next position. She tried to fight him off, but he was too fast, and she was too tired. He got a lock on her neck. All he had to do was squeeze a little harder and she was done for.

Over his shoulder, she saw one of the hunters standing above Tani, spear raised over the child's body. The woman's eyes and mouth were screwed up in horror. The hunters were never called upon to kill people, let alone children. Then her eyes hardened, and her mouth straightened. The spear came up and then down in a deadly arc.

A shriek. Suni, throwing herself down between Tani and the spear. Too late for the hunter to stop. The spearhead drove into Suni's back, below the shoulder, and planted itself deep inside her flesh. She screamed as blood began to seep out around the spear shaft, but almost instantly she seemed to run out of breath, her body flopping down on top of her child. As the hunter pulled the spear out, she gave a low moan but barely stirred. Blood drenched her dress.

"I'm sorry, Oyu," Ina said silently before sending a stun strike through the threads. He went limp, and she dragged herself free of him. They were pulling Suni off Tani. Blood was gushing out from the wound at her side, too fast. Ina could tell that she was still alive,

but only just. Ina smashed the hunters around her with another stun strike. They crumpled and fell, dropping Suni. Ina sprang toward her beloved.

"Take Tani." Suni's voice was a pained rasp.

"I'll take you too." Ina began to make a hole. How was she going to take both of them, when neither was able to move?

"Please ... Tani," Suni said again. "I'm ..." She began to cough blood.

"No!" Ina said. "Stay alive! I'll fix it, just stay alive." Two of the hunters were already stirring. She didn't have much time. She stretched the hole wider.

A whisper. "I love you."

"No, no, wait! No! Stay with me!"

But Suni's eyes had closed, Ina could see the threads of her soul start to detach from the Cloth. A low moan of despair escaped her.

"My time's done," Suni said, barely audible. "Please ... be ... mother to Tani."

Tears pooled in Ina's eyes. "No, stay, I need you, we both need you. I love you."

Suni smiled faintly. "Take my pouch." Then she let out a long, rattling breath.

Ina wanted to shake her, to press the life back into her, but her soul was drifting away, finding its way to Chel's Haven. And the hunters were getting back to their feet, searching for their spears. Tani was still lying senseless, looking soft and vulnerable and so like Suni.

Blinded by tears, she sliced Suni's pouch free of her belt, and then widened the hole, making it larger enough to step through. Something sharp thudded into her shoulder, rocking her and nearly making her lose the passageway. Mūak raised his spear directly above her, his expression knotted with rage and despair. Ina wrapped her arms under Tani's armpits and dragged her into Sīut's Realm.

Chapter 53

Fay

The most effective way to kill Ilk is with fire, or even better, magefire. They don't bleed and they don't feel pain, so ordinary wounds won't even slow them. You need to hack right through their limbs to disable them and sever their heads to kill them. Some witnesses report Ilk continuing to fight even without their heads, but this is anecdotal.

—The Ilk War: A History, Carolin Morgan

As the warning horns blasted around the wall, Fay peered down into the darkness. The Ilk were little more than black shapes, shambling toward them at a half-run. They used no light, as if they didn't need it. Fear pulsed through her, set her heart to racing.

"Stand back," Ruadh said. "Stay away from the line."

She tore her eyes away from the monsters to glance up at him. He was dressed in full mail, only his eyes and mouth visible beneath his steel helm. The sight made Fay wonder why she had ever thought she could pick up a spear and join the fighting. His arms were five times the size of hers, and he could probably slice the head off an Ilk in a single blow of his axe. Although, in all honesty, he was the only one who looked like he would survive the battle. The Eleusian defenders, in their padded jerkins, seemed like children playing war games next to him. They stared down at the Ilk in rapt terror, faces white in the dim light of the glowglobes.

She squinted back down at the Ilk. There weren't so many of them, she tried to tell herself. Plenty would die on the wall. But as the monsters got closer, her dread grew. The rippers were huge.

"Stand strong, lads. Lassies," Ruadh shouted. "We'll take these boneheads down. We'll carve a pretty smile on their ugly faces!"

The Eleusians couldn't understand him, but those nearest him seemed to take heart from his tone, standing a little firmer.

Where was Ruadh's interpreter? She looked around, then saw him running up the stairs, carrying no spear. He came to a panting halt next to Ruadh.

"We'll take 'em," Ruadh shouted. "They look scary, they feel scary, but they're just stupid boneheads. Be smarter than them."

The interpreter relayed the words in a shaky, breathless voice.

"Pull yourself together, man, or get out of here," Ruadh growled at him. "We need stones up here, not lily livers."

"I'm sorry," the interpreter said, quailing. He took a deep breath. "I ... can do better."

"Hold strong!" Ruadh roared again.

The interpreter repeated the words in Eleusian, this time with more gusto.

The ballistae and mangonels roared into action, exploding stones tearing up the Ilk lines, sometimes the very bodies of the monsters. But the creatures were unfazed and continued their shambling advance, only their glowing red eyes visible through the cloak of night.

She heard Alexios call out a little farther down the wall. A moment later, flaming arrows rained down onto the massed ranks of monsters. Most found their mark, but the Ilk pulled them back out or snapped them off, showing no pain. Yet some of the creatures burned, fell to the ground, rolling to put the flames out. Their fellows trampled over and around them, barely slowed.

Meanwhile, men arrived with pots of boiling water, prepared in haste nearby and distributed along the line.

Fay told herself that the number of Ilk looked small. The arrows and mangonels were working. The fire was working. She kept trying to tell herself this—until the Ilk reached the foot of the wall, and then the full effect of the Gloom crashed over her. The voices in the old temple returned, no longer a whispering but a roaring cacophony. "*Murdering whore. Filthy. Unclean. You'll die here, and you'll deserve it. Jump off the wall. Die, die, die.*" It was as if the Ilk themselves were speaking to her, shouting at her. She began to say her mantra. *Light burns away the darkness, conquers all our pain. Light burns away the darkness, conquers all our pain.* She sent prayers to Lumia, and then, after a moment's hesitation, to the Makers. This was their territory after all. But despite her prayers, her legs were turning to water. She couldn't think, could barely breathe. Only see the red eyes of the Ilk in the darkness and hear the voices of the Gloom. On either side of her, people began to flee.

"Come back here and fight!" Ruadh shouted at them. "Fight for your wives and children!" A breath. "Fight for your husbands!"

But they didn't even look back. They ran, jumped down the ramparts into the town, and disappeared among its streets.

"Bloody cowards," Ruadh spat. "We can take these boneheads. Stand firm! Show them they don't scare us!"

His interpreter transmitted his words, but his voice had turned shaky again. Fay wondered if he'd added the bit about cowards.

Someone began to vomit over the walls. And then, as if it were a cue, others began to heave the contents of their stomachs out onto the heads of the Ilk.

If only puke was deadly acid, Fay thought, and a hysterical laugh exploded from her. *I'm losing it.*

The rippers began to scale the walls, digging their claws into the wooden ramparts to pull themselves up at insane speed. The defenders stared down at them, some utterly immobile, others shaking so much their spears rattled.

"Flash bombs!" Ruadh shouted.

No one moved. Then a stir as someone else fled.

"Get back here, coward!" Ruadh shouted furiously. Then, down at the Ilk, "Come on, shitstinkers, my axe is hungry, and it feeds on monster blood."

His defiance rallied a few of the defenders, and they began to fling flash bombs down onto the heads of the creatures. That spurred more into action, and all along the wall came popping sounds as the stones exploded. Some of the rippers were dislodged and fell back to the ground. But others treated the flash bombs as little more than annoying flies. They showed no signs of pain or fear, and only climbed the faster.

"Water!" roared Ruadh, and the pots were tipped over the edge.

Some of the rippers were taken by surprise and lost their grip. But most, even though plainly scalded, continued as if nothing had happened.

They don't feel pain.

"I need more bombs!" shouted someone.

Fay jolted herself, pulled back from the edge of the parapet and dug stones out of her sack. She hurried along the line, distributing them, but then the first wave of rippers was on the wall, and she fell back.

The man nearest Fay stabbed out with a spear, aiming for a red eye, but the monster simply reached out with one clawed hand and ripped it out of his grasp. He nearly went flying over the wall with it, only Ruadh managed to yank him back by his jerkin. A second later the ripper fell away as Ruadh's axe smashed through one wrist and then the other. The man backed away from the edge, calling for another spear. Fay snatched one up from a stack and thrust it into his hands. He returned to the front of the wall. This time, his spear went through the neck of a ripper. But this didn't stop it from taking him with its claws, tearing his cheek open. Screaming, his blood flowing freely, he yanked the spear out, and another defender beside him stuck his spear into the thing's eye. It fell, taking two of its fellows down with it.

Dear Lumia, watch us and save us. Every instinct told her to flee, to escape the stench and the terror. A hand grabbed hers, tightly, squeezing so hard her fingers might break. Daphne. She smiled bravely at Fay. Said something, but Fay never heard it because a man fell screaming back, crashing into them. He was clutching at his stomach, and Fay caught sight of his intestines glistening rope-like between his fingers. She gagged. Daphne, though, moved. Fell to her knees, started to wrap bandage around his middle. But he was surely dead, not now, but soon. Gut wounds always killed, Ruadh had said.

A prickling in the air and a sharp smell. Then a sheet of blue light swept across the front of the wall, and Ilk tumbled to the ground screeching. When the magefire had passed, the section of wall was entirely clear of monsters. Below, rippers struggled to free themselves from the bodies of their smoking fellows. Fay grinned. *Ha, take that stinkheads.*

"Help me get him down," said Daphne beside her. She pointed to the defender she had bandaged, now only half conscious. They grabbed a stretcher and put the man on it, then put the stretcher into a pulley system to lower him down into the town, where other assistants were waiting. All along the wall, Fay saw other downed men and women being moved in the same way. How many had they lost? Fewer than the Ilk, she hoped.

"My arm," gasped a man behind her.

She turned. His arm was half severed above the wrist, and he was holding the two parts together. Blood was fountaining out. How could there be so much blood? *Stay calm, stay calm.* She got out a bandage from her healer's satchel, wrapped a tourniquet around his arm, and then sent him down to the nearest wounded shelter.

There were others with more minor injuries, but there was little time to treat them as a fresh wave of Ilk mounted the wall. Again, blue fire swept them away, and Fay began to think they were going to win. There hardly seemed to be any Ilk left.

Ruadh dashed this hope a moment later. "Something's wrong," he said. "There's not enough of them. Doesn't ring right. Unless their leader is really stupid, they're not going to win the wall."

"Have they underestimated us?"

"I don't know. But I don't like it." Ruadh shouted at his interpreter, "Send a runner. Find out how many are attacking elsewhere."

The man nodded and ran.

Fay peered down over the edge of the wall. The golls had reached the bottom and were beginning to hurl up climbing spikes and ladders. The defenders tried to remove them but were soon occupied with swiftly clambering rippers. Fay fell back again, watched horrified as the huge, wolf-like rippers picked men and women up and flung them down, seemingly uncaring where they landed. The falling defenders slowed the advance of the Ilk, but it was scant comfort, their death screams chilling.

"All right you stinking boneheads, come get a taste of my axe!" Ruadh roared as he smashed his blade down through the nearest ripper's head. The axe punched a hole clean through its skull, and the monster fell.

More bolts of blue light fizzed around her, sending Ilk flying back down to the ground.

The golls gained the top of the wall. They used swords and spears, jabbering as they thrust and cut. But they attacked with little finesse. They weren't even as well trained as the street toughs in Moth's pay, which was the only thing saving the defenders. The Gloom had intensified now that the monsters were among them, and some froze, not even raising a spear or shield in defense when the monsters attacked them.

A goll found its way through the defenders in front of her. Its red eyes met hers. It snarled. Its spear thrust in. She tried to move, but it was like she was stuck in mud. There was no Ruadh to save her. No bolt of magefire.

The goll's spear pierced her arm. Hot pain. She staggered back. It came at her again, and again she fell back. She lost her footing and found herself tumbling down the stairs, coming to a stop against someone's legs. Daphne. She reached out with a bloodied hand, helped Fay to her feet.

"You're hurt."

Fay looked at her arm. A large gash, blood welling from it. Strangely, she could feel no pain.

"Go, get it bandaged," Daphne said, pushing her to one of the wounded shelters.

Fay went stumbling down, seeing only red, red eyes.

Chapter 54

Alexios

I saw a dark-haired weaver walking through the grounds of the Spire. I thought I would see him do something of interest. But I was pulled away as he walked into one of the towers. I didn't recognize him.

—Visions of Alexios Arathraxis

"Shoot at will!" Alexios shouted to his bowmen as the Ilk came into range. Over and again, they launched arrows at the advancing horde, but while the volleys burned and killed Ilk, they neither deterred nor slowed the others. The Gloom gathered force, and it ground out his failings through the din of battle. "*A failed Keeper who doesn't deserve the name. Might as well give up now. Run away. You're not up to this.*"

He wasn't the only one affected. All around him, men and women quailed, some entirely immobilized by fear, others suddenly turning and running, heedless of those who called for them to return.

"Ignore the voices in your head!" Alexios said. "The voices aren't real. Pray to the Makers." He began to pray aloud, using the threads to amplify his voice so that he could be heard over the din of battle. "Makers watch us and ward us, strengthen our hands and our hearts." Around him, men and women joined in. Their voices cracked and quiet at first, then firmer. All along the wall ran the prayer, rallying, bolstering.

The first of the rippers started to climb. He spun illusions to make it seem like the wall was higher, and rippers reached out with claws that met nothing but air. Sometimes they fell and dislodged those climbing below. But others managed to catch themselves, and then it was up to the spearmen to push them back with panicked jabs. When too many monsters started to gain the wall, the bowmen exchanged their bows for spears.

Many were torn to pieces. Alexios saw insides yanked out with long, curving claws, saw women with bitten-off noses and bloody eye sockets, saw throats torn to crimson shreds. Smelled sweat and urine and blood and feces—and always, the rancid stench of the Ilk. He hadn't expected battle to smell so much, nor to be so loud. The screams and snarls, the shouts of bravado. The clanging of metal on metal, the crunch of breaking bone and breaking spears.

When the weavers managed to clear the wall twice with their mage-fire, he felt hope. But Arianna said they couldn't do another attack like that soon. "That last one stretched the Tapestry a lot," she said. "With the wrongness of the Ilk putting pressure on it as well, I'm worried we'll end up with a bad rebound effect."

"They're dying, though," Alexios said.

Arianna pressed her mouth into a grim smile. "At least we know that they die."

The smaller creatures, the golls, began to throw up scaling ladders. Again, Alexios spun illusions to confuse them about where the wall ended, but they weren't as effective. Even if the hooks overshot, they tended to land on the parapet more often than not. With the rippers scaling the wall at the same time, the beleaguered defenders were unable to dislodge the hooks with speed. Soon, golls were swarming up to join their larger brethren.

Alexios kept himself invisible and spun illusions to make extra defenders, sending the Ilk after targets that didn't exist. He felt a coward, hiding himself, but they had agreed this was the most effective way for the illusionists to fight. They were too valuable to be killed early.

Boom. Boom. Boom.

The sound was coming from his left, from the gate. The rippers had brought a ram, a great tree trunk chopped down from the forest, and were striking the gates with steady force. They had no protection, though, and arrows and flash bombs rained down on them. But although they accumulated injuries, the monsters were unfazed by the missiles, continuing to pound against the gate, which bulged with each attack. It was being bolstered by carts and barrels laden with oil, but such was the might of the rippers that Alexios wasn't sure those would keep them out for long.

Then came the familiar prickling feeling that signaled magic was about to be wrought. What were the weavers up to this time? A moment later, a huge explosion of power burst against the gate, blinding white. When Alexios could see again, the gate was in twisted ruins, and the Ilk were swarming over the blockade. Inyaki? Where was he? Infuriatingly out of sight as always.

As planned, bowmen shot flaming arrows at the obstacles behind the gate. Vivid orange flames leaped up as the oil-drenched wood took light, consuming those Ilk who had already broken through and slowing the influx of those massed on the other side.

Horns blew long and loud, summoning defenders to reinforce the gate, while bowmen rained more arrows down onto the heads of the Ilk. Blades, easy to spot in their white surcoats, charged at the monsters from left and right. They'd been waiting for this, their time to shine. But Alexios saw some of them freeze under the effect of the Gloom and be slaughtered. Even so, their skill showed, their ability to work together, warrior and illusionist, to confuse and kill the enemy. It had been Ruadh's idea to put them here, and not for the first time, Alexios sent silent thanks to the man for his wisdom.

A long, piercing shriek rent the air, then another. Skreeks shot down from the sky, three of them. Men and women who tried to block their ears, were skewered by swords and claws. The mutant birds landed on the heads of defenders, picking out eyes with sharp beaks, grabbing men and bringing them high into the sky to release them, screaming, onto those below.

Bailin, who was among those standing on the wall by the gate, aimed a bolt of blue light at a skreek, but missed. He tried again, and missed again, then a third time, and caught its tail. It dipped toward the ground, flapping its wings to try and regain altitude. But Bailin's fourth shot got it square in the head, and it fell in a dead drop. A roar of triumph from the weaver, and around him, defenders cheered. Alexios even allowed himself a smile. Arrows eventually drove away the other two skreeks, but Alexios was sure they'd gone to find easier targets. Those defenders who didn't die here would die elsewhere.

The flames lessened, and then it was time for Arianna and Bailin to do their next task. The ground in front of the gate began to shudder and shake, the air filling with the tang of magic. Then it split open, taking golls into the depths of the earth, making it impossible to access the gate. At the same time, though, Alexios felt his control of the Lace ripped away from him, the threads vibrating too fast, lashing him when he tried to take hold of them again. Too much magic was being used here, the Ilk adding too much pressure.

Those Ilk caught on the inside of the gate were dispatched by the defenders, but the toll was high. Alexios saw too many of his people go down, torn to pieces, skewered on the end of blades, their blood soaking the ground.

"We can't do any more weaving here," Arianna said. "The Tapestry is very unstable."

"I've lost control of it too," he replied. *What to do now?*

"I'm going farther down the wall," she said. "I should still be able to help elsewhere."

He nodded, and she called out to Bailin, both then running along the ramparts, which were crawling with Ilk.

Alexios stayed where he was, shouting orders and encouragement, but holding himself back from the fight. Again, he felt like a coward, but he was equipped only with a knife.

"You're of better use when you can spin illusions," Cassander said.

"Yes, I know," Alexios replied. *"But see how they sacrifice themselves while I do nothing."*

"That's not true, the defenders take heart from your presence," Cassander replied.

"It would be a terrible blow if they saw you go down," Epiktet added. *"Be patient, and your time will come."*

But time was not a luxury they had.

Chapter 55

Fay

The Ilk Lord was reputed to have powers that no weavers ever possessed. One was the ability to move across great distances in an instant. I find these reports hard to credit, though.

—The Ilk War: A History, Carolin Morgan

Fay tried to quell her horror at the sight that greeted her in the wounded shelter. It was already filled with men and women, moaning, screaming, their bodies torn, their faces mangled. Some, like her, were still able to walk and were being treated so they could return to the wall. But too many looked like they were on the verge of death, lying in pools of their own blood while the assistants and physics did their best to patch them up.

Now that the initial shock of the wound had died down, Fay was feeling the burning pain of it. Although she'd pressed a bandage against her arm, blood was leaking out too fast, and it was already soaked through. But she had to wait her turn.

Finally, an elderly female assistant came to clean the wound, shortly followed by a young male physic who examined it carefully and then told her he'd need to sew it back together. She clenched her teeth as the needle bit in, her head swimming. Somehow, she managed not to faint, and when he'd wrapped a fresh bandage around her arm, she thanked him for his work. But now she was dreading the return to the wall, fearful of what she would see out there. *Why, why, why didn't I stay in Wren?*

But as she was on her way out, Hymne came to her and stopped her. "We need more bandages from the Panaceon," she said in slow Eleusian. "Will you go?"

Glad for an excuse not to return immediately to the front line, Fay accepted the task. When she got outside, she took a look at the wall, saw that the defenders still seemed to be holding the Ilk atop it. The former were much fewer than before, but the number of Ilk didn't seem to have increased measurably.

Feeling a little heartened, she went to the Panaceon at a fast walk, the sounds of battle echoing all around her. The streets of the town were near empty, non-combatants having been sent down into whatever underground shelter they had been assigned to.

She reached the central square and there stopped short. A clawed hand had appeared in mid-air, detached from any body that she could see. A failing illusion? A second claw, a scaly foot, another scaly foot, the gaping wolf-like jaws of a ripper. Then it was lumbering forward, looking for prey.

Fay hid around the corner, watching with mounting terror as more and more rippers appeared seemingly out of nowhere. *What magic is this? Have I gone mad?* And then, *Shit! This is what Ruadh was worried about. I need to warn them.*

Golls came pouring out of the invisible gateway, holding flaming torches. They scattered to nearby buildings, tossing their torches through doors and windows that they broke open.

Oh dear Lumia, save us. Fay turned and sprinted toward the eastern gate to warn Alexios and Ruadh. *This is it. This was their final plan. They've got us. We're fucked, we're totally fucked.* Already her breath was burning in her chest, her legs starting to fail. She summoned every last bit of her strength, trying to ignore the screaming of her body.

At last, she was at the wall by the eastern gate, where she'd last seen Alexios. He was still there, visible, shouting commands. She scrambled up onto the wall, dodging defenders and Ilk alike to reach him.

"What's happened?" he asked.

"Ilk, in the city," she gasped. "They're torching the buildings."

Alexios's eyes widened, and when they both turned to look at the town, they could see flames and black smoke coiling in the air.

"Go, get Ruadh and then get out," Alexios said. "You'll need to take word to the outside world about what's happened here."

"What will you do?" she said.

"I'll see to it that as many escape the wall as possible," he said.

Fay nodded, suddenly filled with grief. She wouldn't see him again. He was probably going to die here, trying to save his people. "I'm sorry," she said.

"Don't, you've done much already." He clasped her shoulder briefly, then turned away to start shouting orders.

Fay ran down the steps and then along the bottom of the wall and back up again to reach Ruadh. His mail was spattered in blood and gore. Monsters died left and right as he brought his axe down upon them. Fay waited until he'd finished a goll, then shouted out what had happened.

"Ruin and bloody ruination! We should have guessed, if they could move prisoners from another continent, they could move Ilk into a town." Ruadh slammed his axe down on the fingers of a ripper that was trying to gain the wall, and it went tumbling back down. He took a quick look along the wall. Then, through his interpreter, began to call men and women to him. "We go to the main temple to guard the tunnel! Sound the horn!"

Together, they went running down into the town, in the direction of the flames.

Chapter 56

Alexios

The Keeper is a guardian. A guardian of memory, but also of the people. We are not trained in the arts of war. We guard in other ways. In my case, my illusions guard our people from the dangers of the outside world. No one can attack us if they don't know we're there.

—The Role of the Keeper, Alexios Arathraxis

As soon as Fay was gone, Alexios went to the nearest horn blower. "We're being attacked from within. Sound the call to evacuate."

The man paled. "How?"

"That doesn't matter, sound the call!"

He put the horn to his mouth and four long blows rang out. Moments later, these were echoed farther along the walls and then in the center of the town. It was a signal for all combatants under thirty to either beat a retreat out the western gate, through the tunnel, or over the northern wall. The illusionists would go to the shelters they'd been assigned to in order to hide the people inside from the invaders.

But many would die, perhaps most. Unless he could find Inyaki. It was the only hope. He must be inside the city. He grabbed Miro, "You're in charge here. I'm going to find the Ilk mage."

Then he ran into the town under a shabby invisibility. The air was thick with the smell of burning wood. The Gloom pressed in all around. Ahead of him, flames reached high into the sky, vivid orange, surrounded by rolling black smoke. Inyaki had to be here somewhere, it was his magic that brought the Ilk into the town.

Golls came running down the street ahead of him. They were carrying torches or burning pieces of wood, kicking open doors and tossing the fire inside buildings. But at least they didn't seem bothered to search the homes. Those hiding underground might still have a chance.

He considered trying to kill some of the golls, but quickly dismissed the idea. It was Inyaki he needed to kill. So he dodged around them, making for the central square. If Inyaki was anywhere, it would be there.

As he went, he saw people running toward the tunnel entrances, protected by defenders assigned to the task. Whenever the Ilk spotted them, they went charging to attack. Alexios didn't wait to see what happened, only prayed again to the Makers to deliver them.

The closer he got to the central square, the more intense the flames. Soon he was entirely surrounded by burning buildings, the heat scalding him. Ash floated down, and along with it pieces of fiery wood that made holes in his tunic and blisters on his skin. His ears filled with the sounds of crackling wood and distant screams. *All is lost, Neopoli is lost.* The souls clamored their mourning but also urged him on. *"Kill Inyaki, kill Inyaki,"* they all said.

He reached the central square. There didn't seem to be any more Ilk arriving in mid-air like Fay had described. Maybe they'd all come through. He looked around. The Hall and temple weren't alight, being made of brick, but everything else was aflame.

And then he saw Inyaki, on the roof of the temple, in his bone mask. He was holding a weaver's battlestaff in one hand, the green focus stone livid. However, he wasn't shooting any magefire or doing anything else that Alexios could discern. He was laughing.

Fury welled in him. *I'll kill him if it's the last thing I do.*

"Yes, kill him," Demeia said fiercely. *"Take revenge for Nixos, for all of us."*

"Revenge!" cried Doris and Eliana together.

"Revenge, revenge!" echoed Auxentius.

"Take him, kill him!" roared Lycurgus, normally so calm.

Fueled by their rage, Alexios ran to the temple, taking the steps two at a time to get inside. The double doors were open but there were no Ilk inside. However, he did see the charred bodies of two defenders in anteroom—murdered with magic.

He didn't allow himself to be distracted by them. Instead, he pushed through a door on the right, which took him to a stairwell and the long passageway that ran along the perimeter of the building. He ran up the stairs, to the viewing gallery on the second floor. The stairs to the roof was at the other end of the gallery, and again he ran, pushing himself to greater speed. Magic use had made him weak, though, and he reached the next stairwell wheezing.

He took a moment to recover then started the stealthy climb to the roof. There was a trapdoor at the top of the stairs, and he pushed it open a fingerswidth, then two, then three. When the crack was wide enough, he peered through it to see Inyaki still standing at the other end of the flat roof, looking out toward the south. Alexios hated as he'd never hated in his life. Rage boiled through him, hot enough to burn away the dread of the Gloom. *He destroyed Nixos's soul. He's taken everything from us.*

He pushed the trapdoor open further and crawled out onto the roof. Inyaki didn't seem to notice. Alexios got to his feet and drew his only weapon, a dagger. This would be the end of it. *This* must *be the end.* But even as he crept forward, doubts ate him. Could his illusions hold out longer than those of Demeia and Nixos? Could he get close enough to kill?

He moved forward slowly, respinning the threads with every movement, taking extreme care. His heart beat violently. He couldn't let himself fail again. This was the only way to save his people from extermination.

Slowly.

Slowly.

But as he approached, he realized Inyaki was enveloped in a magical shield again, the Lace around him twisted and knotted. He was holding onto the threads, the green focus stone in his battlestaff flaring brightly. An arrow came at him and simply bounced off.

Alexios ground his teeth in frustration. He would have to find some way to destroy the shield to get the knife through. But how? If one of the weavers were here, they could probably attack him with their magic. He'd seen them use similar shields. But he had no idea how to do it himself. It hadn't been something he'd needed to teach himself. *Instead, I learned to spin illusions that kept us weak and isolated.*

He turned his thoughts inwards, tried to meditate on the visions he had previously been granted. Nothing. He called to Demeia. "*Any ideas?*"

"*This was what happened when we tried to kill him,*" she said. "*We got close, but my knife met the same resistance. He caught us then.*"

Abruptly, Inyaki swung around to face Alexios, as if he knew exactly where he was.

Without thinking, Alexios sprinted forward with the knife, but was met by a wall of weaving that threw him to the ground. He lost control of his invisibility illusion, and the knife flew out of his grasp.

Inyaki tutted through his bone mask. "Did you *really* think to sneak up on me like that? Didn't you learn *anything* from the death of your children?"

Violent rage swirled through Alexios. He scrambled to his feet and ran forward wildly, only to be hurled to the ground once more.

Inyaki started laughing. "You're like a puppet. It's too easy."

Fresh anger surged through him, blinding in its intensity. He got back to hands and knees. He would kill Inyaki if it was the last thing he did. An invisible force whipped his backside, forcing out a yelp. But it also cleared his head, and shame replaced the anger. *You're no child, to lose control of yourself like that.* He clambered to his feet, found himself shaking and unsteady. "You might as well tell me your name," he said, to make time. How had Inyaki been able to sense him when he'd reached the roof? He was sure he'd spun a good illusion. He hadn't even felt Inyaki try to attack it.

Inyaki cocked his head. "Didn't Thane tell you?"

"Is that the one who imprisoned me?" He could see no way to destroy the shield. But Inyaki's power had to give out at some point. Eventually, the shield would surely fail, and then Alexios would have his chance. First, though, he needed to get the knife—and he needed to hide from Inyaki's senses.

"I suppose you thought you were clever with your escape from Arindel," Inyaki said. "I mean, it wasn't a *bad* plan. After all, I made it up for you."

Those last words gave Alexios pause. What did Inyaki mean? That he'd allowed Alexios to escape? But then he shook the thought loose. Inyaki was trying to distract him.

An idea came to him. He should try spinning multiple illusions in addition to the invisibility. That might hide him better. It would use all his remaining strength, but he couldn't see any alternative.

"Good idea," Demeia said.

"I'm glad we're getting to play a little longer," Inyaki said.

Alexios made himself invisible again and took a few steps back, toward the fallen knife. Then he spun two copies of himself, placing one where he had been standing and another behind Inyaki. They were full illusions that would trick all the senses—smell, hearing, and touch as well as sight—and they took nearly all his might to maintain.

Inyaki regarded the illusion in front of him, then glanced back at the other.

Was it working? Had Alexios managed to fool whatever sense it was Inyaki had used to find him?

But Inyaki started laughing. "Target practice!" He raised his staff, and two bolts of blue light leaped out to strike both illusions. They immediately dissolved.

Sweating, Alexios spun three more illusions of himself, then moved closer to the knife. The three illusions stood in a loose semi-circle formation around the Ilk mage.

"I'll admit, you're doing a bit better than you were. Better than your children. You should have taught them this trick."

Alexios reached the knife, swooped down, got his fingers around the hilt. At the same time, three simultaneous bolts of magefire tore down his illusions. Just how powerful *was* Inyaki? He straightened, painfully respun his illusions. Then he crept closer to the Ilk mage.

He still hadn't worked out how to get through the shield. But maybe he could get close enough to push Inyaki off the roof.

Inyaki paused his attacks. What was he doing? He seemed to be concentrating on something. Trying to discover where Alexios was?

He moved closer, now only three paces away from Inyaki's back. He only had to reach out and push. His hands came up, but then froze. The shield. Suddenly, he was certain that if he touched it, it would destroy him. He didn't know how that came to him. Perhaps some old memory, some fragment of a vision. Was that Inyaki's plan? Was he allowing Alexios to get closer, playing a deliberate game? Maybe his illusions hadn't been working so well after all.

Frantic thinking, then a new idea. He spun another illusion, one that very slightly lengthened the roof behind him and Inyaki, as well as the section to Inyaki's left. Then he backed away and dug his hand into his pouch to take out some of Oxil's flash bombs. He rubbed them between his fingers, still backing away.

Inyaki turned around to face him. "Have you thought of a better way to kill me, Keeper?"

So Inyaki *was* able to tell where he was. He created a new illusion of himself, standing to his right, and at the same time dropped his invisibility. Then he threw the flash bombs at Inyaki, making the illusion do the same. Alexios had hoped the onslaught would confuse his enemy, cause him to step onto the illusory piece of roof and lose his footing. But he didn't move, evidently confident in his shield. The stones exploded with little flashes of light and smoke. When it cleared, Inyaki was laughing so hard his shoulders shook.

A piercing pain was working itself up in Alexios's head. It was getting harder to hang onto the threads, to spin them as he wished. He needed to succeed quickly. He became invisible, then spoke, making his voice sound like it came from everywhere and nowhere. "How did you bring the monsters into the city?"

Inyaki seemed unfazed by the disembodied voice. "The same way we reached your charming little town in the first place. You hardly thought I marched a thousand Ilk through the Vycenian countryside, did you? Think of the stir it would have caused!"

"Some foul magic of Antiphos, I take it."

"We call it ol'Sīut," Inyaki said. He seemed to be having trouble sensing Alexios, was no longer looking at him directly. Or was it another pretense?

Alexios threw more flash bombs at him, and this time Inyaki shot up into the air. Or rather, he disappeared from the roof and reappeared in the air, about three feet above Alexios's head.

Then he was on the roof again, laughing. "There's a little demonstration for you. Did you like it?"

Alexios threw more stones, and again, Inyaki jumped clear using his magic. But this time, Alexios noticed that for a heartbeat after he reappeared his shield was gone. Was he weakening at last?

Alexios's heart drummed faster. He needed to keep forcing Inyaki to use magic, wear himself down more. But even as the thought struck him, his headache seemed to double in intensity. He reeled with dizziness and almost lost control of his illusions.

A bolt of blue light streaked across vision, coming from behind. So close he could feel the crackling energy on his face. But it had no effect on Inyaki, just melted when it hit his shield.

Alexios looked back. Griff, mouth set in a hard line, face and clothes blackened with soot and streaked with red. He strode toward Inyaki, attacked him again with magefire, orange focus stone burning.

Alexios made himself invisible and ducked out of Griff's path. Hopefully, distracted by Griff's attacks, Inyaki wouldn't be able to sense him as he had before. Even so, Alexios went right to the edge of the roof, intending to circle around behind the Ilk mage. More black spots floated in front of his eyes, and his stomach heaved. He couldn't keep this up much longer. *If I die and take him with me, it will have been worth it.* The souls agreed. Alexios gripped the dagger hard. Either he'd get the blade in, or he'd push Inyaki off the roof and they could die together.

The ground began to shake. Alexios's legs gave way and he fell to his knees, almost sliding off the roof. Everything was suddenly blinding, too white. Then he realized, blurrily, that Inyaki was also on the ground. Griff shot another magebolt at him, but his shield held. Inyaki got back to his knees, giggling.

The ground shook again, and this time it was Griff who fell. A large crack opened in the roof of the temple. A part of Alexios's brain screamed, no, we are desecrating the shrine to the gods.

The next of Griff's attacks dissipated around Inyaki's shield, so close it prickled Alexios's skin. He crawled along the roof. One good strike. That was all he needed.

Then Inyaki sent a weave against Griff that threw him violently to the ground. The weaver's head hit the roof so hard it bounced. Afterward, he didn't move.

Alexios staggered to his feet and lunged at Inyaki. But the Ilk mage whirled around, looked straight at him despite his invisibility. "Still going, Keeper. I'm almost impressed." He pointed his staff.

Alexios expected blue light to come out and fry him. Instead, he found himself caught, paralyzed in an invisible web.

Inyaki walked right up to him, standing so close that Alexios could feel the heat from his body. "Mother wants you alive," he whispered, his breath caressing Alexios's face. "So I won't kill you. But you'll watch your town burn to ashes and your people die." He glanced back at Griff, who was starting to stir. "That one, though. His soul will taste good, and I need a refreshment." He went to Griff, taking his time, like a stroller in the woods.

Alexios tried to break the bonds of weaving that held him in place. But he couldn't see the threads that Inyaki had used. This wasn't his magic.

Screams echoed from the streets below and around him. His nose filled with the smell of burning wood, of burning flesh. Of Ilk. And he could do nothing. He was a fly caught in a spider's web. And that spider would consume him, but it would not let him die, because it knew his weakness. *You've failed, again. The worst Keeper in the history of our people. You have no right to be alive, no right to the souls you've bound to you.* A fresh realization struck him. *He'll steal all the souls. That's what he wants. That's what he does. That's what they all do, him and his kind. They'll shred the souls, and we'll wander this world for eternity.* He deserved that, for his failures. But the others didn't. Not Nixos, not Eliana, not Epiktet and the others. Not Demeia.

Inyaki stopped a few paces from Griff, who was now on his knees. He looked dazed, but his staff was still in his hand. He used it to push himself back to his feet.

"You don't die easily. I admire that," Inyaki said. "But it's over now."

Chapter 57

Fay

We tend to speak only of the Ilk Lord when we think of the Ilk War. But he was not the only sorcerer who controlled the Ilk. He had several generals, although their names are lost to us. For all we know, some of them even escaped the Ruin.

—The Ilk War: A History, Carolin Morgan

Fay stood behind Ruadh on the street as he took on another goll. Her legs were starting to buckle under the weight of the woman she was carrying. She had little more strength left in her. The woman was slight, but Fay had picked her up not far from the wall and wasn't used to such physical work. Daphne had been there too, and was walking next to her, supporting a wounded man of her own.

Fay's defender said something in Eleusian, tried to stand a bit straighter, but then slumped against Fay again. There was blood all over her, but her only serious wound was the long gouge in her thigh, now covered with a bandage. Fay had also tied a tourniquet above the wound. The bandage was blood-soaked, but the stain wasn't spreading rapidly. She hoped the woman would live. She'd seen her take down the goll even as it had sliced her leg open. More guts than most.

Ruadh finished the goll with a swing of his axe, and they continued their trek down the flaming street.

"There," Daphne said, pointing. "Just ahead." Her voice was breathless, and she also staggered under the weight of the half-conscious man she was supporting.

Fay saw the temple, their way out, rising above the flames that were consuming the buildings around them. No Ilk ahead. The temple only fifty paces away. Could they reach it before more Ilk found them?

Forty. Thirty. Twenty.

There were people on the roof. Fay squinted through teary eyes. Alexios and the Ilk mage. They seemed to be looking at each other, maybe talking. Then Alexios suddenly vanished out of sight. *Dear Lumia, watch over him.*

"He's the Keeper, he'll prevail," Daphne said, also watching.

Really? Against all this? He's weakened. He's not a warrior. But she said nothing. She didn't want to crush Daphne's hope.

Three golls ran onto the street, caught sight of them and charged, jabbering the sounds that gave them their names. "I'll take these little stinkers," Ruadh said, stepping forward to meet them. "You go on in. I'll follow."

As Ruadh engaged the Ilk, they staggered around and up the steps to the temple, reached the door. It was one of the only buildings not yet on fire. Daphne led them through a door at the far end of the worship chamber, to where there should be stairs leading down into the crypt. When they entered, there was no sign of any stairs, only some dead Ilk. But suddenly the stairwell appeared, along with an illusionist and a handful of defenders.

Daphne said something to them, and then they made their stumbling way down the stairs into the crypt. More guards down there, so many that they blocked her view of the room. The tunnel had been dug into the ground right next to the stairs, a ladder leading down into the depths. A rope dangled next to the ladder, fastened to the ground with a metal ring.

One of the guards shimmied down the rope ahead of them. Then Daphne spoke to her soldier, helped him sit. He opted for the ladder, wincing with every movement. She hurried down after him. Fay's defender pointed at the rope, said something Fay couldn't understand. Fay helped her get to it, peered down into the smooth-sided, magically dug tunnel, lit with glowglobes. No sign of Daphne or her wounded man, but the guard was there, waiting to catch her if needed. The wounded woman slowly lowered herself into the tunnel, face screwed up with the strain. Fay didn't hesitate in choosing the ladder. Her tired arms wouldn't hold her weight for long.

She reached the bottom, remembered the tunnel that had led out of the Spinners' temple, the one dug by the Ilk mage who had imprisoned Alexios.

Alexios. He was up there, alone, fighting. *I couldn't have done anything to help. I'm just a whore and a bad priestess.* She put her arm around her wounded defender, faced the tunnel. Somewhere along it, a glowglobe had been planted, providing just enough light to see by. Daphne was a little ahead, moving slowly. Fay and her defender began walking. But she was still thinking about Alexios. *I shouldn't have left him to face the Ilk mage alone.* She kept walking. *What use would I be? If anyone can deal with the Ilk mage, it's Alexios. Or one of the weavers. This isn't my fight. I've done enough. And I need to get this woman to safety.*

And yet Fay felt that she was abandoning him. He was up there, dying on a roof, still thinking about everyone else before himself. What kind of a man did that? *He can win. He might not die.*

They caught up with Daphne, who was breathing hard, moving slowly now that the immediate danger had passed.

A male physic whom Fay vaguely recognized came running up the tunnel from ahead. "Are there more we can save?" he said. Blood spatters on his face. Streaks of blood on his blue tunic. His arms bathed in blood, glistening red, crusted brown.

Daphne replied, and Fay gathered she was telling them that Ilk had now overrun the town.

How many more would survive long enough to get here? And Alexios, would he survive against Inyaki, who had eaten his son's soul?

Fay came to a sudden decision. "Take this woman," she said to the physic. "I need to go back for Alexios."

He looked at her in confusion.

Fay didn't bother trying to explain further, instead pushed her wounded defender onto the physic. "I have to go back." Without giving either the physic or Daphne time to react, she turned and ran. *What am I doing? I should go, save myself. Alexios is doomed.* But then, *you think you can hide from the Ilk everywhere you go? It's like Arianna Velden said, there won't be a normal soon.* But she could hide, there were surely plenty of places to hide. Up north, for example, in the Icelands. Even the Ilk wouldn't want to conquer the Icelands. She'd be cold but she'd be alive—and free. Yet Fay kept running, reached the tunnel entrance. The guards didn't try to stop her. Up the ladder and into the crypt, up the stairs into the perimeter passage. Here, she paused and looked around, saw more stairs going up. This one brought her to the upper viewing galleries. But there was no way onto the roof from where she was standing. *Shit.* She began to jog along the viewing gallery, which stretched the entire length of the temple, reaching a door at the end of it. Pushing through, she found herself in a stairwell going up, this one narrow and winding. *This must be it.* Up she went, chest and legs burning, finally coming to a trapdoor.

She stopped. *I* could *go. Alexios might be dead already. The Ilk mage could be coming over right now.* She closed her eyes, breathed in. *Fuck it.* Put her fingers to the trapdoor, pushed it open a crack. There was Inyaki, walking over to a figure on the ground. Alexios? Was he dead? No, the hair was the wrong color. That looked like Griff. Where was Alexios?

She pushed the trapdoor open a fraction more, scanned the roof, hoping desperately to find him somewhere, still fighting, still alive. She was about to give up when he suddenly appeared at the other end of the roof. He seemed immobile, his expression transfixed in pure horror. Why wasn't he moving? Had Inyaki done something to him?

There's nothing you can do here. They're dead or as good as. You don't have any magic. You're just a whore. Look out for yourself.

But Inyaki hadn't noticed her. He was saying something to Griff, who had got to his knees. The weaver threw himself at Inyaki, aiming for his legs, as if he planned to wrestle him to the ground.

Inyaki disappeared. Reappeared right in front of Fay's nose, but with his back to her. *Stab him in the back!*

Fay thrust with the knife but met hard resistance a fingerswidth away from Inyaki's robe. Ruination! Some kind of invisible shield. The one blessing was that Inyaki didn't notice. Instead, he sauntered back over to Griff, laughing. Griff shot blue flame at him, and it just fizzled away. Inyaki was definitely being protected. She squinted, trying to see the magic he was using. There did seem to be a faint blurriness in the air around him. Like a painting that had been smudged, its outlines no longer clearly visible.

I should go. I should get another weaver. There's nothing I can do. But there wouldn't be time. Alexios and Griff would be dead before she reached the street. She glanced at Alexios. He was staring at her. Their eyes met, and he began to mouth something. He was telling her to go. *No, I'm not getting told what to do again.* She'd defied her father. She'd defied Lothar. She'd defied Moth. Well to the pits with it all, she'd defy Alexios and this Ilk mage too. She wasn't running.

Griff shot another mage bolt at Inyaki. This time some of it seemed to get through, singeing Inyaki's robes. Fay's spirits lifted. Maybe Griff *could* defeat him.

"I really *do* need a refill," Inyaki said—and blasted Griff with a torrent of crackling blue light.

The weaver screamed as the magefire consumed him, but the sound was quickly choked off. The smell of burning flesh reached her, acrid and vile. Inyaki stood over the smoking body, unmoving.

Was that blurriness gone? Yes, maybe. Hard to tell for sure. But Griff's last bolt had almost got through. The shield could be gone. Inyaki was clearly distracted. *Run. Griff's dead. You'll be dead too. He'll hear you coming. He'll burn you with his magefire or eat your soul.* She glanced at Alexios, still shaking his head at her, looking anguished. *Fuck it.*

She charged at Inyaki. She was lucky. He didn't hear her until she was a pace away, only had time to half turn before she sank the blade into his side. He took a step back. She followed, stabbed again, blade slipping easily into flesh. Stab, stab, stab. Fast as possible, often as possible. He fell to his knees, dropped his staff. She heard screaming. Realized it was her screaming. She slashed the blade across his throat. Dug in hard, hit bone. Dark red blood spurted out, drenching her hand. The sharp smell of blood in her nose. Blood all over her. Gaping wound in Inyaki's throat, just like her pa's. Inyaki collapsed onto the ground. Shit stink. She vomited the little left in her stomach.

His mask had fallen loose. Face of a youngish man, maybe in his thirties. Fine black hair, smooth cheeked, copper skinned. He was grinning, as if death were amusing to him. Fay shuddered. Who could find death funny?

Then she noticed that his left hand was half in and out of his pocket, the fingers locked around something. A stone rod. Crystalline white, shaped like a prism. What was that? He must have grasped it even as he'd died. She leaned in.

An ear-splitting screech from the sky. A skreek, flying down at her. Talons out, ready to pluck her into the air or tear her to shreds. Its eyes glowed like burning coals. Another shriek, a hideous pain in her ears. Talons inches away from her nose. She flung a hand up. Uselessly, hopelessly.

Blue light shot at the skreek, hitting its torso. It was knocked off course, away from Fay. Another bolt of blue light struck it, this time in the wing. The creature went spinning down to the street, still shrieking. Arianna entered her field of vision, running to the edge of the roof, looking down. She shot more magefire, watched for a second, turned to Fay. Gleam of triumph. Turned to Griff, smoking and dead. Ran to him, eyes wide, mouth open in a wail.

Fay looked back at Inyaki, but he was gone. All that was left of him was a spreading pool of blood, dark wine and bright ruby mingled together. What in ...? Where had he gone? She scanned the roof. No sign of him. But he was dead. Had to be. She had cut right through the artery, slashed his windpipe. Smelled his death shit. No one could survive that wound. Pa hadn't. But where was he? How had his body disappeared?

Then she realized that Inyaki wasn't the only one missing. Alexios. Had he made himself invisible? She called out his name, but couldn't hear her own voice, only a high-pitched whining. *I'm deaf? Have I gone deaf? Where is he? Where is he?*

Arianna was still there, gazing at Griff, leaning heavily on her staff. Her expression was agonized fury, a startling contrast to her usual cool reserve. She hunkered down, closed his eyes, and picked up his staff, which had fallen out of his hand. Then standing up, she channeled blue fire into his body until it turned to ashes. She pulled out a pouch and emptied its contents carelessly onto the ground before scooping as much of the ash pile as she could into it.

Fay called Alexios's name again and ran to the edge of the roof, looking down, hoping to see him. But she saw only burning buildings. The fire had spread across most of the town. Ilk had completely overrun the walls, attacking the few remaining defenders from two sides. There was no one alive in the streets. She ran along the roof, still seeking him, but saw only the same dismal sight.

A tap on her shoulder. Arianna, mouth moving, but Fay could hear no words. She pointed at her ears and raised her hands in the air in a helpless shrug.

Shock and pity. But Arianna quickly mastered herself and pointed toward the trapdoor. Fay nodded and followed the weaver off the roof.

The flames had finally reached the inside of the temple. The door to the worship room was open, the wooden pews inside it all alight. Smoke filled the air, searing her lungs with every breath. She coughed, eyes stinging and watering until she could barely see.

They went to where the stairwell should be, saw more dead Ilk and dead guards. As they approached, it became visible to them. Arianna said something to the defenders waiting there, and they blanched and nodded. Down the stairs and into the tunnel they hurried.

Then she realized that Arianna had stopped, wasn't coming with her. She looked back. The guards were all pouring down into the tunnel, Arianna by the entrance. Once all the guards were in, she raised her hands, still holding her staff and Griff's. Her focus stone brightened, and then brick and earth came tumbling down, blocking the entrance. No one else would escape through here. Fay thought of Ruadh, hoped he'd gone through already. He didn't deserve to die in a foreign town.

Chapter 58

Ina

Those who remain true to Chel will return to her haven once they leave this world. There, they will be free of Sīut and dwell in eternal peace and joy.

—Teachings of Old Tsu

Ina exited ol'Sīut on her face and instantly blacked out. Sometime later, she opened her eyes to find that the rain had lightened to a drizzle and the sky was brightening to the east. Her torso was a shredding mass of pain. She struggled to her knees, grunting from the pain, looked for Tani. The child was lying next to her, senseless. She leaned over and pressed her fingers against a tiny wrist. There was a faint pulse. She, at least, was not dead.

And then it hit her. *Oh, Suni!* Her mouth formed into a silent wail, and for several heartbeats, she felt only the pure, intense agony of loss, her muscles seizing, her fingers scraping bare rock. She clenched her teeth, trying to contain the pain. It seemed too big for her, too vast and impossible. A sob shuddered through her, and it brought a different kind of pain. A very physical one that told her she was badly injured.

Wiping tears from her eyes, she peered down at herself. A cut on her ribs, not deep, although blood still oozed out of it. Much worse was her back. A throwing spear was lodged in her shoulder blade. Not a deadly blow, but she'd still need to get the spear out before the wound infected. If she pulled it out herself, though, she risked opening more blood vessels and losing too much blood before she could clean and staunch it. If there was ever a time she needed Suni, it was now. The memory of her beloved's red-drenched form flashed into her mind. A part of Ina was dead already. She slumped. Why go on? But no, she wasn't giving them the satisfaction. And Suni had given her life to save Tani. Some of her was still alive in her child.

She turned back to Tani and the amount of blood on the child nearly made her choke. Had she been hurt too? She looked more carefully, but there were no obvious injuries. The blood belonged to Ina or Suni, or both. She gently shook Tani's shoulder, then called out her name in a weak voice, dreading the moment when the child did awake, with her mother dead. At that thought, Ina again gagged with another pain. Wiping tears and rain from her face with the back of her hand, she called Tani again.

The child's eyes fluttered open, then widened with shock when she saw Ina.

"Tani," Ina said again. She realized she didn't even know how to speak to the child, not really. Children had always left her feeling uncomfortable.

"Where are we?" Tani asked, blinking at her with Suni's eyes.

"I ..." Where to start?

The child's gaze fell on Ina's shoulder and she gave a little shriek. "You're poked like a nouk!"

Yes, that's it. Speared like a beast. I would have scored a kill, though. "I need your help to get it out."

Tani blinked and looked around. "Where are we?"

"On Uruk'il, by the Godstone."

The child scrabbled onto her knees, and then frowned. "The Godstone's not there."

"It's broken."

Tani peered through the rain, "Oh yes, you're right." She fixed her gaze back on Ina. Why did she have to look so much like Suni? "Why are we here?"

"You know they were going to send you back to Chel tomorrow?"

Tani's eyebrows drew together. "Yes."

"Well, I didn't think they were right to do that, so I took you away."

"But if I'm cursed isn't it bad if I don't go back to Chel? You're cursed too, aren't you? Mami told me. That's why you ran away when we were on the island, and then they found you and put you in the House of the Elders, too."

"That's right. But the elders are wrong." Aren't they? "The Godstone—now I know this is going to sound strange—the Godstone had the memories of my great-great-great-great grandmother inside it." She didn't know how many generations there were between her and Lin. But it sounded about right. "It was some kind of magic that she was able to do with Chel's help. So when I went back and touched it, I got her memories and I learned that Chel has a purpose for us."

Again Tani frowned. "Us?"

"Yes, you and me. We have to go find the drakiri. Imagine finding them again!" *I don't care about the drakiri, I only want everything to be as it was. Why didn't I listen and stay away from the Godstone?*

"Where's Mami?"

"She had to stay behind." *Don't ask more, please, I can't say it.*

"Couldn't she come with us?" Tani said in a small voice.

Ina rubbed at her forehead. "No." *She's dead, she's dead. How can I go on without her?*

"And Papi?" *That piece of goat dung. He betrayed us.*

"We'll see them again when we find the drakiri. When we find them, everyone will realize that our magic isn't a curse and we'll be able to go home." I *don't even believe that.*

Tani considered her words, but then said, "I still want them to come with us. Let's go ask them."

Ina closed her eyes briefly. "They can't come with us. We need to use our magic."

"But I want them. I want Mami." Tani's voice took on a plaintive edge.

"I know, but she can't come." *She's dead. Great Chel, how do I tell her?* She closed her eyes again as dizziness swept over her.

"You don't look well. Mami could help you."

Ina opened her eyes and fixed them on Tani. "Well, she's not here so I need you to help me instead. You've watched her fix people, haven't you?"

"Yes, but I'm only little. She'd do it better."

"You have her blood in you. And I'll tell you what to do."

"I suppose I can try." There was something between tearfulness and stoicism about Tani, as if she couldn't decide which she needed to be.

Ina remembered that she had taken Suni's healer's pouch and looked around to find it on the ground next to her. Inside were bandages, a few small pots which she knew to contain ointments and dried herbs and, crucially, needle and thread. The wounds would need to be cleaned first. She unscrewed a few of the pots until she found what she thought was the cleaning solution, made from honey and crushed featherleaf. Next, she unhooked one of the water bottles and handed it to Tani.

"First, put some water onto a bandage and then clean this cut on my ribs. Then some of this ointment."

Tani did as she said, pursing her lips as she worked carefully. When she had finished, Ina told her to get a long bandage and wrap it around her torso. Once that task was done, she unsheathed one of the belt knives and poured some water on it to remove any dirt. Ideally, she would have used a fire to sterilize the knife and needle, but she'd have to make do with the cleaning solution, which she rubbed on, using the same bandage that Tani had used for the first wound. Afterwards, she handed the knife to Tani. "You'll need to use this to get the spear out."

Tani frowned at the knife in her hands. "Why?"

"You'll have to cut around the spearhead to make the wound a bit bigger so that we can pull it out safely."

"But I'll hurt you!"

"This is what healers do, like your Mami. You want to be like her, don't you?" This knowledge hadn't come to her from Suni, though. It had come from Lin.

Tani bit her lip and nodded.

"When the wound is big enough you can take the spear out. Then you'll have to pour some water on the wound to clean it. After that you'll have to sew it. You've learned how to sew, right?"

"I've sewn cloth, not people!"

"It's the same thing." *Isn't it?*

"I'm afraid," Tani said.

"I really need your help. I could die if we don't get it out and clean the wound."

"I don't want you to die."

"Good, I'm glad." Ina attempted a smile, but it turned to a pained grimace. "Start with the top of the wound, just over the shaft of the spear. I'm going to lie down first." Ina carefully laid herself out on her belly.

"Now?" Tani asked once she was done.

"Yes, now." Ina braced herself for the fresh onslaught of pain, determined not to show any of it to Tani. But these intentions vanished as soon as the knife sliced into her flesh. Her scream was muffled only by the rock.

Tani stopped, whimpering apologies.

"You're doing well," Ina said, breathing shallowly. "Cut a little more to the left." Again, the knife scythed through her flesh and Ina hurled out her agony. "And to the right." Another fresh agony. When she could breathe again, she continued her instructions. "Take the shaft of the spear and pull on it to see if it moves."

"Are you sure, Ina'Yakir'Suk?"

"Do it."

Tani said nothing but grasped hold of the shaft and tugged at it gently. "It's not moving."

"Put your foot against me if you need to—but try to take it out straight."

Tani did as she said, pulling harder. Ina felt the head come loose. "Keep pulling, slowly, through the hole you've made. If you feel it catching against something, stop."

"I will." The child continued to draw the spear out, swathing fire running along its path. Ina lost consciousness, then came to again as the last of the missile left her body. "There's a lot of blood!" Tani exclaimed.

"Put some water on the wound and then press a bandage down on it for a bit to soak up the blood."

Tani did as she said and then, under Ina's instruction, began to sew the wound together. Each pierce of the needle brought a new agony. She clenched her teeth and drummed her feet against the sand, trying to stop herself from screaming. At some point, she lost consciousness again.

"I've finished."

Tani's words penetrated the fog of pain and brought her back to wakefulness. She sat up woozily. The child was still holding the needle and thread, and there was fresh blood on her hands.

"You're the bravest person I know," Ina said. "And you've saved my life."

"Then we're even, I suppose," Tani said gravely.

"We are." Ina took the needle and thread from her and pointed to the cleaning ointment. "Pour some of that on a bandage and then wrap it around my chest to cover the wound."

"My hands are dirty."

"We need to save the drinking water. Let the rain clean your hands."

Tani stuck her hands out in front of her obediently, allowing the fine rain to fall onto them.

Meanwhile, Ina put away the needle and thread and sheathed her knife.

When Tani had managed to get most of the blood off her hands, she began to prepare the bandage. Ina raised her arms with difficulty so that Tani could wrap it around her chest and then her shoulder, tying it off with a knot. "Are you sure we can't go get Mami?" she asked when she was finished.

"I wish we could, believe me," Ina said. "But this is our adventure."

"But I don't want to go without her!" The child's forehead wrinkled, and her lower lip started to tremble.

"Well, we have to. If we go back to the island, they'll kill us," Ina said. "Do you understand that?"

"I suppose so." She still looked like she was on the verge of tears.

"We need to find a special stone," Ina said. "A waystone, it's called. We can use it to go find the drakiri."

Tani sniffed and rubbed at her eyes. "Where do we find it?"

Good question. "I think it's around here somewhere. I'm not sure what it looks like. Put your hand on any stone that you find, see if you can sense anything strange about it."

Tani set off and Ina watched her, marveling at her resilience. How many children would have been able to do what she'd done? Truly, she was Suni's child. Her eyes fell on the broken shards of the Godstone. She went over to the place where it had stood, hoping to trigger a useful memory. The earth beneath it had been stirred up and flung away, leaving a hollow depression. Pushing up through the base of it was a vaguely spherical object, yellowed but still crusted with earth. Ina got down to her knees and began to remove the wet earth from the object with her fingers. Tani joined her to help, and very soon it showed itself to be what she had expected—a grimacing yellow skull, black eye sockets long shorn of life. Other pieces of bone poked up through the earth, and Ina began to clear it away, gently teasing the last handfuls away from the bones until the entire skeleton was revealed, the legs drawn up over the ribcage.

Ina sat back on her haunches. Stark memories inundated her—Lin digging her own grave with a pick formed from a spearhead. Using her hands to scoop out the stony soil, the skin under her nails sore and inflamed, small scratches multiplying on her hands like the spots of a rash. Digging until her fingers cramped, digging on anyway, digging until the grave was finished. It wasn't very deep, had only needed to be large enough for her to lie with her knees drawn toward her chest.

"No more!" Ina cried aloud. She didn't want to share this moment.

"What's wrong?" Tani asked, eyes wide with fright.

Lin had knelt in the grave first—to roll the stone most of the way over the opening. Had lain on her back then, used her feet to push it the rest of the way, drowning herself in darkness. Lying there, she'd thought about those who had gone before her. The list of sorrow was long and full of blood, at its head not her son or bondmate, nor even her last lover, a crafter called Jai, but her drakir. Her memories of Moondancer were many and joyful, and Lin had spent her last moments among them. When the air had become too thin to breathe, she had pressed her fingers against the base of the stone and called on Chel to deliver her memories to it.

"There's a stone under the bones," Tani said.

Ina shook herself out of the memory and looked where Tani was pointing. Sure enough, there was a rectangular, flat, grey stone underneath the skeleton's spine. Whispering an apology to Lin for disturbing her grave, Ina removed the bones and laid them carefully next to the hole they had dug. Then she reached down and put her hands against the stone. She could feel the connecting line instantly. It thrummed powerfully through her, a permanent passageway that led to the other side of the world. With it came a memory of what to do. She could open the passageway through a trigger thread. She'd still need to use her own power, but the passageway would be stable.

"Is it the waystone?" Tani asked.

"I believe so."

"Are you sure we can't go and get Mami and Papi?"

Ina shook her head.

Tani rubbed one thumb against the back of the other, staring into the grave. Then she said, "Mami's gone back to Chel, hasn't she?"

Tears flooded into her eyes. She couldn't answer. Tani put her arms around her waist and Ina hugged her, burying her face in Tani's wet hair. They both began to cry.

After a while, Ina realized that she could feel warmth on her head and back. She looked up and saw that the clouds were clearing and that the sun had broken through. It didn't seem right. Suni was gone, she was light, she was sunshine. A world without her ought to be grey forever.

"I need to pee," Tani said, shrugging free of Ina's embrace. Her eyes were swollen and red. Ina supposed she looked much the same.

As the child went to find a private spot, Ina lay on the ground, looking at the blue sky and thinking about Suni.

"The big canoe, I can see it!"

She was so lost in memories that the words didn't make sense to her at first. "What was that?"

"The canoe, it's coming."

Already? They hadn't wasted any time. "Are you sure?"

"Yes. It's halfway here."

"We'd better go, then." She didn't feel at all ready to use the magic again. All she wanted to do was sleep and forget about where she was and what had happened. "Go get the spear. We'll need it again for hunting."

While Tani went to do as she said, Ina stood up and looked out toward Lun'il. Sure enough, she could see a large canoe making its slow way toward them. They must have set off while the rain was still falling for them to be so close. There was little time to lose.

She knelt by the grave and placed her hand against the waystone to trigger the passageway. It opened above the grave, a man-sized gateway of swirling nothingness. Tani joined her again, spear in hand. She looked at the gateway fearfully.

"Take a few deep breaths and then when I say, hold the last one, like when you dive underwater. I'm not sure how long we'll be in here, and there'll be no air."

"I'm afraid," Tani said, taking hold of Ina's hand with her free one.

"It will be fine. You passed through ol'Sīut to get here."

"I don't remember that, though."

"One day, you'll be able to make these gateways yourself. Now, are you ready? Take a deep breath."

To her relief, Tani obeyed. Ina did the same, each inhalation a mini torture. When she felt she had filled her body with as much air as possible, she told Tani to take the last big one. Then, with the child gripping onto her arm, she stepped through the gateway and into another world.

Chapter 59

Fay

The skreeks are perhaps the deadliest of the Ilk. They didn't appear until toward the end of the Ilk War, however. Just five or six of them were enough to fell an army of several hundred. It's because of the dreadful sound they make, a screech so high-pitched it can rupture eardrums.

—The Ilk War: A History, Carolin Morgan

The night after they fled Neopoli, they camped under the trees. Bailin, Arianna, and Galinda, despite their evident exhaustion, cleared enough of the undergrowth for them to be able to stretch themselves out side by side. Their band numbered some two hundred people, but there were other survivors. It had been agreed before the battle that refugees would travel in separate groups to increase their chances of survival. There had been no sign of Ilk since they'd left, though, not even of the skreeks. Maybe it was because Alexios had killed the Ilk mage. Or maybe they considered their work done or didn't realize that some townspeople had escaped.

They lit no fires and ate rations prepared for the evacuation—flatbread and honey. There was little conversation that she could see. She was still unable to hear anything but a whining sound in her ears. It was driving her mad. *Is this going to last forever?*

As she ate her flatbread, her back pressed against a tree, she wondered again what had happened to Alexios. It seemed no one had seen him. He'd disappeared along with Inyaki's body. The enemy had him, that was the only conclusion. They'd used the same magic to take Alexios that they'd use to get the Ilk in. What would they do to him? She tormented herself with thoughts of his torture, of him being locked in some horrific Gloom-filled prison again.

Ruadh had also disappeared. She was told that he'd escaped, however, so she imagined he was on his way back to Arindel to deliver his report to Moth. Fay, for her part, had no idea what to do except to remain with the Eleusians. Arindel was most certainly out of the question, and there was at least one Ilk mage in the Spire. The weavers seemed determined to stay with the Eleusians, for now at least.

She glanced sideways at Arianna. Galinda was wiping some of the blood from her face. Galinda herself looked relatively whole and unharmed. Bailin was also still in one piece, staring at Griff's staff, which was lying across his knees. *Handy to have magic. Gives you a much higher chance of survival. Although poor Griff. He wasn't a bad one.* She didn't know all the illusionists, but she recognized a few in their group—Epi, Miro, Thais—along with Oxil the High Artefactor. She had no idea what had happened to the rulers or Periklis. Either dead or with another group. As for the Rifters, she supposed they were all dead. They had all insisted on fighting on the wall, or so Ruadh had told her. *Rescued only to die anyway, but I suppose it's better to die fighting than have your heart ripped out and eaten.*

Her mind's eye filled with visions of flames and slaughtering red-eyed Ilk. How many of the townspeople died? Hundreds upon hundreds, she reckoned. Most of those who had escaped had already been hiding in the sewer. Children, the old and infirm, who might not survive their long trek north to mountains. Young women hadn't been spared as they might have in other conflicts. Many had joined the defenders, or like Fay, had gone to the wall to help with the wounded. They too would have been caught by the rampaging Ilk.

She thought of what lay ahead. Their destination was another Eleusian enclave in the mountains. But even if that hadn't also been besieged or destroyed, they couldn't stay there forever. This was only the beginning of a larger war. One that Fay wasn't sure they could win, even with all the weavers fighting. The Ruin had been the consequence of the last big conflict. Would anything be left standing this time?

I've been unlucky. If I'd been born fifty years ago, I'd have missed all this. But she'd been born at this time, and she was right at the heart of it all.

She looked around at the Eleusians, huddled together, some crying, some merely staring blankly. They had lost everything but their lives. What must that feel like? *I never had much to begin with.* Maybe that was better, in a way. To have nothing so you could lose nothing.

Suddenly, she felt exhausted, her eyes drifting closed. She let sleep take her. Tomorrow was another day. Tomorrow, she would worry more.

Chapter 60

Malai

Those blessed with the gifts of the elkiri were made to rule. Those who seek to strike us down are afraid, for they know they are lesser.

—Words of Ilis'Elkir

Malai looked down at the body of her son, blood soaked, his throat a wound, his eyes glassy with death. Her throat closed. *Storms take you, Inyaki, for your foolishness.*

"Don't worry, he'll return to us," said Ilis, standing next to her. In his hands was a crystal rod, prized loose from Inyaki's dead hand.

"Are you sure it will work?" she said. *Storms take you too, Ilis, for convincing him of this. And for not telling me.* She heard Inyaki's voice: "*You wouldn't have let me, mother.*" He was right. Grief and fear threatened momentarily to overpower her. She could not lose her son.

Next to her, Ilis was smiling, golden eyes gleaming. "It worked for me, didn't it?"

"But you're different, special," she said. "It was your destiny."

Ilis took her hand and squeezed it. "I was with him when he transferred his soul into the stone. He did exactly what he was supposed to. Come. Let me show you the body I've prepared for him."

He began to pull her away from Inyaki, through the lava-warmed tunnel into an adjoining room. Inyaki's new body was lying in the center, encased in a translucent membrane, a faint stream of prime force-feeding it. This version of it looked much larger than the one he'd been born in. The one *she* had made for him, in her belly, so many decades ago.

"Are you sure it can be done this way?" she said, looking at the form.

"I've practiced many times. It will work."

Seen from up close, the body was more than big, it was huge. Standing, it would reach as high as one of the wolf-Ilk. The chest was deep, the shoulders broad. A giant. "It doesn't look much like him." Except the face, that was still him, especially the nose, thin and straight—like hers—and the jaw, square like his father's.

"He wanted to be bigger and stronger when he returned."

That was Inyaki, always wanting more. "Can you restore him now?"

"Yes. The sooner we return his soul, the more intact his mind will be. Or so I believe."

It had taken Ilis most of a year to fully regain himself when she'd restored him from his soul stone. Even now, five years later, there were things he still hadn't remembered, that she needed to remind him about. "He always planned to die in that town?" *Foolish men.*

"It wasn't planned as such. We knew it was a possibility, and we prepared for it."

"But what was the point of your attack? I thought we'd agreed to starve the Eleusians out, save the Ilk for other battles. We've lost at least a third of them." *And you didn't tell me. Everything I've done for you,*

Ilis. And now you don't trust me with your plans. Little pinpricks of rage, but she dampened them.

Ilis waved an impatient hand. "We needed to see how the Ilk would perform in combat, and Inyaki needed practice in managing them. With the extra four hundred we sent against the town, it wasn't too difficult to take. It's now completely destroyed. And as a result, our spy is firmly embedded and will not be suspected. It was all worth it."

At least they've taken the Keeper, and I will get what I want from him. "And the refugees? You've let them go." Another point he hadn't conferred with her on.

"They'll starve and suffer and eventually die. Now, shall we begin?"

She stifled her anger. "Yes. I want my son back."

Ilis smiled again, picked up the hand of the inert body, closed its fingers around the soul stone, and wrapped his own hand around both. A surge of elemental power, passing through Ilis, into Inyaki's new body. Ilis's face twisted with pain. He was so brave, to endure that pain, over and over, so that their armies could be created, so that Inyaki might live again. How could she stay angry with him when he was so magnificent?

The membrane around the body dissolved. The eyes sparked to life, blinked, lit on her. The mouth curved into a smile. "Hello, Mother."

THE END

Fellow adventurers,

I hope you enjoyed reading this book! If so, I'd really appreciate it if you took the time to leave a short review. It helps readers like you to find it.

To get "Deathstalker," a free short story set in the world of The Unraveling, sign up for my newsletter on www.elmcinerney.com. Signing up also gives you discount codes for direct purchases from my website. Plus, you'll be first to hear when new stories are published and to learn about any prizes and giveaways.

Overlord, the prequel to The Unraveling, is out on 4 February 2025. It tells how the Ilk Lord returned to life after 200 years, and features some characters from Soulstealer. There are also new characters who become important in Book 2.

To pre-order, go here: www.elmcinerney.com/pages/overlord

Scan the code for my website:

This code will take you to my Amazon author page:

Yours, El

Acknowledgements

Only one person's name goes on the front of this book, but it was in reality a team effort, and I would never have been able to produce it without the help of a long list of people.

First and foremost, I would like to thank my late father, Micheál, whose love, inspiration, and support throughout my life has been fundamental. He introduced me to the wonder of Tolkien as a nine year old when he gifted me a beautiful, illustrated edition of *The Hobbit*. I was initially unimpressed by a story about a small man who lived in a hole, but he cleverly offered to read it aloud to my sister. Of course, I wasn't to be left out, and thus started a nightly ritual whereby he read not only that enchanting tale but also that great progenitor of modern epic fantasy, *The Lord of the Rings*. I was so taken that I began to pen my own stories of adventure, drafting the very first version of this novel at the tender age of 12 in a series of hardback notebooks.

On the professional front, my thanks go out to my editors Adam Jackson, Jonathan Oliver, and Dannielle Kimpel, who helped me forge, hone, and polish this work to make it fit for public display.

I am equally indebted to my alpha and beta readers, particularly Brigid, Rosie, Michael, Laura, and Harrison. You each provided a unique perspective that challenged me to look at the story in different ways. It wouldn't be the book it is without you.

I'd also like to extend my thanks to those who provided comments on individual chapters, especially those who mentored me on the Creative Writing Programme with New Writing South and my fellow writers on the course. You all helped me to improve different aspects of my writing craft.

My deep and heartfelt thanks also to friends and family who provided other types of support—moral, financial, and creative. Again, the names are many, but I'd like to mention in particular my friend Brian, who has shared my writing journey from the earliest days, and my partner Mim, who stops me from going insane.

Thanks also to Fred at Stardust Book Services for designing the map you see at the front of this book, and to 100 Covers for the beautiful cover they created.

And finally, my thanks to you, the readers. I hope you've enjoyed reading this book as much as I enjoyed writing it.

About the Author

I live in London, but I'm half Irish and half Belgian, a fact I blame for my wine-drinking penchant and compulsive need to tell stories.

My love of fantasy began at age nine when my father bought me *The Hobbit* as a Christmas present. At first, I thought a story about a man who lived in a hole was supremely ridiculous, but he insisted on reading it to me and my sister every night—soon winning over two eager young fans. He followed this feat with *The Lord of the Rings*, and thus my doom was written.

I graduated to books from the Dragonlance and Forgotten Realms worlds, and then on to David Eddings, Robert Jordan, and Raymond E. Feist, along with many other great fantasy writers of the 1980s and 1990s. Later, I found my way to the darker worlds and deep character work of Robin Hobb and George R.R. Martin.

My whole life, I dreamed of writing an epic fantasy series that combined my favorite elements of all these stories The Unraveling series is the product of a lifetime spent dreaming, writing, and developing my craft.

I've got a PhD in Spanish Literature and Cultural Studies from Trinity College Dublin, and a background as a martial artist, political activist, and musician. Now, my attention is fully devoted to words – those of others, which I edit, and of course, my own.

9781738430512

RE - #0004 - 190325 - C0 - 203/127/36 - PB - 9781738430512 - Matt Lamination